The Restless Crucible

Printed in the United States of America

Published by Mt. Nittany Press,
an imprint of Eifrig Publishing,
PO Box 66, Lemont, PA 16851.
Knobelsdorffstr. 44, 14059 Berlin, Germany

For information regarding permission, write to:
Rights and Permissions Department,
Eifrig Publishing,
PO Box 66, Lemont, PA 16851, USA.
permissions@eifrigpublishing.com, 814.954.9445.

Library of Congress Cataloging-in-Publication Data

Agawu-Kakraba, Yaw
   The Restless Crucible. A Novel, by Yaw Agawu-Kakraba

   p.   cm.

Paperback: ISBN 978-1-63233-328-5
Hardcover: ISBN 978-1-63233-329-2
Ebook: ISBN 978-1-63233-330-8

   1. Fiction: History 2. Fiction: Africa, Brazil
   I. Agawu-Kakraba, Yaw, II. Title.

26 25 24 23 2022

5 4 3 2 1

Printed on acid-free paper. ∞

The Restless Crucible

A Novel

Yaw Agawu-Kakraba

Mt. Nittany Press

Lemont | Berlin

PRAISE FOR
The Restless Crucible

"When the world is so flawed, and there are no heroes, the storyteller must invent/reinvent a new way to narrate such a tragic story of the past of a world that still haunts us today. Yaw Agawu-Kakraba's spellbinding, and heart wrenching novel portrays the horrors of the transatlantic slave trade and slavery. *The Restless Crucible*'s compelling telling of the other story of the transatlantic slave trade in the Portuguese world and the plight of African peoples taken from their homelands is haunting. You will be intrigued by the author's narrative skill and voice that are both African and American, excavating a story of the other worlds we could not have imagined. Here is a great storyteller, reinventing tradition, bringing together two worlds: the Africa of his original homeland, and America, his new homeland, two conversations about a world we thought we already knew. This book will keep you turning the page as you discover how our past has come to meet the present. This is an urgently necessary book."

~*Patricia Jabbeh Wesley*, author of **Praise Song for My Children: New and Selected Poems**

"Yaw Agawu-Kakraba's *The Restless Crucible* is a dazzling feast for the senses, a story from centuries past that manages, through the author's deft skills of perception, to comment upon our own vexing times. With penetrating insight, Agawu-Kakraba reminds us that the politics of slavery, of human beings' need to control each other via subjugation, never truly ebbs, leaving a scar as long and harrowing as time itself."

~*Kenneth Womack*, author of **The Time Diaries**

"Agawu-Kakraba's novel is ambitious in scope and rich in detail. *The Restless Crucible* is full of the stuff that makes compelling stories: characters behaving badly, and occasionally redeeming themselves, in a well-rendered setting and world. Go on this word journey. Ready yourself for some surprises."

~*Steven Sherrill*, author of **The Minotaur Takes a Cigarette Break, Joy PA**, and much more.

"The trickster Pedro de Barbosa will haunt the reader's imagination. Ultimately, this is a tragic tale of a man who chooses to use the weapons of the strong, with hopes of emancipating himself, even if it means sacrificing others with whom he has shared a common fate."

~*Joan B. Landes*, Walter L. and Helen Ferree Professor of Early Modern History and Women's Studies Emerita, Pennsylvania State University.

"In *The Restless Crucible*, Yaw Agawu-Kakraba succeeds in creating a fast-moving, can't put down, palimpsest that drills deep into the minds and souls of the characters who created and those who suffered one of colonialism's darkest horrors: slavery. Traveling to three continents we viscerally experience some characters' fight to survive, bring down slavery, and to thrive; others who violently fight to maintain systems that still haunt and divide us today."

~*Roselyn Costantino*, Spanish, Women's, Gender and Sexuality Studies & Latin American Studies Professor Emerita, Pennsylvania State University

"Breathtaking in its depiction of a different era and mores, Yaw Agawu-Kakraba's *The Restless Crucible* weaves a fascinating tapestry of intriguing and vivid landscapes while presenting an insightful understanding of the protagonists' personal and individual motives for overcoming the pernicious status quo. A magnificent read!"

–*Arthur J Hughes*, Professor of Spanish and Director of Latin American Studies, Ohio University

"This is African storytelling at its best! This captivating novel offers a new understanding and appreciation of the Afro-Brazilian experience as it interweaves first-person renderings with historical facts. An enjoyable read of the African Diaspora experience in Brazil!"

~*Henry Codjoe,* Director of Institutional Research and Assessment, Dalton State College

For Sena Afi, Delali Aku, and Anne Elise

CAST OF CHARACTERS

Adibo, Kalesea: Prince Akonde's counselor
Afiriwa: Ouidah queen
Agossou: Dahomey prince
Aholuvi, Kosi: Pedro de Barbosa's aide
Ajohan: Ouidah kingmaker
Akonde: Ouidah prince
Akoli: Allada royal treasurer
Almeida, Rosalinda: Archbishop Eusebio Thrillo's housekeeper
Álvares de Andrade, Paulo: Salvador police chief
Amamu: Ouidah kingmaker
Andreia: Felipe de Barbosa's housekeeper
Atakora: Ouidah kingmaker
Azonton: Ena Sunu's cousin
Bagulho, Manoel: slave boy on *Fazenda* Barbosa
Barbosa de, Agostinho: Felipe de Barbosa's son
Barbosa de, Fidelia, Felipe de Barbosa's wife
Barbosa de, Felipe: slave owner, Pedro de Barbosa's master
Barbosa de, Joan: Felipe de Barbosa's daughter
Batista Braga, Pedro: slave master of Lucinda, Eduardo, Constância, and Affonso
Bekou: King Daguenon's counselor
Belarmino, Gregorio: retired judge, father of Ladislao Belarmino
Belarmino, Ladislao: Portuguese governor to Dahomey
Belarmino, Matilde: Ladislao Belarmino's wife
Belarmino, Terezinha: Ladislao Belarmino's daughter
Bernheim, Jean-Marie: French slave merchant
Brute: member of Cabula gang of homeless boys
Cabral, Paulino: ex Portuguese soldier
Caetano, Evaristo: first mate on slave ship
Cantarelli, Zé: member of Raposa gang of homeless boys

Cardoso, Jacinto: freed slave, Pedro de Barbosa's housemate
Carragoso, Jorginho: supervisor on *Fazenda* Barbosa
Carvalho, Galtero: circus owner
Coelho, Cristiano Ronaldhino: King John VI's special envoy
Constância: *Pedro Batista Braga's* slave
Cunha, Virgilio da: Portuguese merchant
Cutpurse: member of Cabula gang of homeless boys
D'Almeida, Jorginho: *Casa da Silva* cook
Dreamer: member of Cabula gang of homeless boys
Eduardo: *Pedro Batista Braga's* slave
Erasmo: member of Cabula gang of homeless boys
Fansinnou, Sintana: commander of *N'Nonmiton*, Dahomey's all-female warriors
Faustino the Chimney: member of Cabula gang of homeless boys
Ferreira, Josefina: Pedro de Barbosa's adoptive mother
Ferreira, Ronaldhino: messman on *Cisne Vermelho* ship
Fovi: Queen Ena Sunu's twin son, Dahomey prince
Fuseina: Ouidah queen
Gahnwa: Allada historian
Guimarães, Antonio: *capoeira instructor*
Hanto Tona: Dahomey spy
Hounsa: eunuch, servant in King Gesa's palace
Ikurisiare: Ouidah voodoo chief priest,
King Daguenon: king of Allada
King Dozan: prince and later Ouidah king
King Gesa: Dahomey king, Queen Ena Sunu's husband
King Haffon: first Ouidah ruler to contact the Portuguese
King John VI: king of the United Kingdom of Portugal, Brazil and the Algarves from 1816 to 1825
King Tezifon: Ouidah king, Prince Dozan's father
Langanfin: voodoo high priest
Lighthouse: member of Cabula gang of homeless boys
Lord Castlereagh: British Foreign Secretary
Lucinda: Pedro de Barbosa's wife
Mácula: Pedro de Barbosa's name after joining Cabula gang
Martins, Gaspar: Brazilian slave ship captain

Migan Hounsa: King Gesa's royal treasurer
Migan Nagoba: King Gesa's principal counselor
Migan Mizéhoun: Dahomey's minister of war and defense
Montcho: Dahomey royal legal master
Novi Sia: Dahomey army general, recruiter of *N'Nonmiton warriors*
Nuno da Silva Mendes, José: Jesuit priest
Quadros, Emilio: member of Cabula gang of homeless boys
Queen Kin-Ha: Dahomey queen, King Gesa's first wife
Queen Lawani: Allada queen, Ena Sunu's mother
Queen Noanti: Dahomey queen, King Gesa's second wife
Queen Yiram: Ouidah queen, King Dozan's first wife
Resendes, Marcelo: *Fazenda* Barbosa overseer, Pedro de Barbosa's instructor
Ribeiro, Santiago: policeman
Runner: member of Cabula gang of homeless boys
Salgado, Romero: Portuguese slave ship captain
Sinha Olinda: mãe-de-santo—mother of the saints—Candomblé priestess
Soares de Souza, Federico: Portuguese governor in Dahomey
Sossa: Queen Ena Sunu's twin son, Dahomey prince
Souza, Mácula de: Pedro de Barbosa's invented name
Spinner, Aleixo: member of Cabula gang of homeless boys
Texeira, Rafael: leader of Raposa gang of homeless boys
Thinker: member of Cabula gang of homeless boys
Thrilho, Eusebio: Salvador da Bahia archbishop
Togbega Ahialu, Ouidah royal accountant
Togodo: Ouidah war and defense minister
Trunk: Cabula gang of homeless boys leader
Silva da, Silvio: *Casa da Silva* proprietor
Sunu, Ena: Dahomey queen
Van den Berg, Jon: Dutch slaver
Viegas, Salvador: ex-seminarian, circus boxer
Vila Nova de, Salvadore: Salvador police chief after Paulo Álvares de Andrade
Yessu: Allada courtier
Yovogan Abalo Bajani: Ouidah minister of slave trade
Yovogan Nondichao: Dahomey minister of the slave trade

Part I

Salvador da Bahia
1793-1815

Chapter 1

My life changed when an errant wind made me its accomplice. Among my many chores as *Senhor* Felipe de Barbosa's slave, I delivered a large basket full of breakfast and lunch items to Archbishop Eusebio Thrilho. The routine included observing the morning Mass that the priest celebrated for the faithful at the *Catedral Basílica de Salvador* in Salvador da Bahia. At the end of the Mass, I carried the crate to the cleric's vast living quarters in *Igreja de São Pedro de Clérigos* on the *Terreiro de Jesus* plaza. Rosalinda Almeida, the middle-aged woman who cleaned the premises, swapped the basket with the empty one from the preceding day.

It was during one such delivery that a forceful gust from the Bay of All Saints lifted the napkin covering the basket. The wind thrust a letter addressed to the archbishop into the air. As though desiring to play a game, the wind levitated the note when I undertook to rescue the purloined item. The envelope's contents were empty when I recovered it. At the spot where I had left the basket, a purple paper flaunted its bright color in the air. A quick trot and I plucked the letter with its exquisite penmanship. Three words caught my eye before I could stash the letter into the envelope: your son, Agostinho. "What the hell!" I said to myself, curiosity getting the better part of me, I unfolded the note and read it. That singular decision, and the ones I made after, set the course of my life forever. But I'm getting ahead of myself. A proper introduction is imperative.

My name is Pedro de Barbosa. I'm an ex-slave, a con artist, a slave trader, a warmonger, and a lover. This is a memoir about how I became one of the most powerful and wealthy slave merchants in

Dahomey until . . . I'll leave that part for later. Having cultivated no scruples, I'm not interested in pandering to the fragile emotions of those partial to ascribing to higher moral ground. I couldn't give a rat's ass if, after reading this first impartial reflection of me, your dull and delicate sensibilities have been so marred that you decide to cease reading this memoir. Should you continue, you should know that my narrative is honest, regardless of what you may read elsewhere about me. My many enemies wouldn't hesitate to distort with glee my life story. But as you proceed, I pray you suspend or, better still, bookmark the earlier descriptors I used in presenting myself.

I was born in 1793 in *Fazenda* Barbosa, a sugarcane plantation that belonged to *Senhor* Felipe de Barbosa in Santo Amaro da Purificação, a God-forsaken village twenty miles north of Salvador da Bahia. Had I been born in Salvador, a city whose streets are replete with slave children, my life story would have been different. So would have been my fortuitous status as a literate slave. Two things of considerable importance marked Santo Amaro da Purificação: *Empório Baltazar*, a medium-sized retail and wholesale goods store, run by Antonio Vargas and his wife, Poala, and *Cabaré Fortuna Fullass*, a nightclub that doubled as a bordello. Although in the backcountry, Santo Amaro da Purificação boasted of numerous brothels and cabarets, thanks to the astronomical rise in the price of sugar and rumors that several fat plantation owners squandered thousands of *réis* gambling and fraternizing with whores.

Cabaré Fortuna Fullass was in a class of its own. It was the only place in these backwoods that musicians from Salvador came to play *forró*, *xote*, *lundum*, waltzes, polkas, and mazurkas. The brothel was the port of call for the numerous plantation owners, foremen, and overseers who descended on the village from the surrounding sugar plantations at the end of their day's work and over the weekends. When the plantation owners' dignified wives visited the cabaret to avail themselves of prevailing musical trends and fashion from the big cities, their husbands pretended they hadn't paid homage to the establishment earlier in the week. They also feigned knowledge of the illustrious workers in the house.

One couldn't say the same thing about Jorginho Carragoso

and the ten unmarried supervisors who worked on *Fazenda Barbosa*. It was common knowledge among the slaves on the *fazenda* that the frequency with which the whip came down was commensurate with the length of time the foremen had spent at *Cabaré Fortuna Fullass*. I didn't have the fortune or misfortune to have my parents confirm or deny that the intensity and regularity of the whip on their black skins lessened because Jorginho Carragoso and his cohort had come back satiated from sprees with the women of easy virtue. My mother, an African slave from Dahomey whom I never knew and whose name was foreign territory to me, died in childbirth. *Senhor* de Barbosa sold my father to another slave owner when he found out that not only did my parents have an unapproved relationship, but also that my mother was pregnant. Before selling him, *Senhor* de Barbosa tied my father to a tree and flogged him several times a day for one week as a deterrent and a warning to the other slaves. Before I could take my first breath and utter my first cry beside a mother whom I couldn't cuddle, I had already become a victim and prisoner to a system that guaranteed my ruination. That disaster took a dramatic turn when *Senhor* de Barbosa announced he would bring me to Salvador as his two children's servant.

Fazenda Barbosa was an *engenho*, a latifundium, an extensive sugarcane plantation that included my master's *casa-grande*, a large two-story-high structure with blue stucco walls and latticed windows that stood on a hill overlooking the farm. A large wrap-around porch circled the first floor, filled with wicker tables and lounge chairs. Several hammocks dangled from the crossbeams that held an exposed verandah on the second floor, accessible by stairs in front of the house. Birdcages, teeming with colorful saffron finches, competed for space with the hammocks. On any particular day, the inescapable scents of violets, dahlias, daisies, roses, carnations, and sunflowers from the expansive flower gardens would drift through the *casa-grande*'s open windows and doors. A smaller house for Marcelo Resendes, the plantation overseer, sat next to the *casa-grande*.

The *fazenda* also boasted a *senzala*—fifty huts and rectangular buildings that sheltered the plantation's two-hundred slaves—, a large construction for the sugar processing equipment, and several stables for the horses and donkeys that carried the harvested sugarcane to the mill. In the middle of all these buildings stood a small chapel where the slaves gathered every other week with Father Fernando Santos Candido. The Jesuit priest came to celebrate mass or to baptize the black babies that were born to legally married couples on the plantation. Legally meant marriages that *Senhor* Felipe de Barbosa had authorized with the clear understanding that the bride would spend her wedding night in the *casa-grande* with *Senhor* Felipe de Barbosa. Therefore, it wasn't unusual to see many creamy-skinned children with hazel eyes on the plantation who were supposedly fathered by black-skinned slaves like me.

My earliest memories of *Fazenda Barbosa* were sounds of the rhythmic *whoosh, whack, thwack, thud,* and *thump* of slaves cutting sugarcane, accompanied by a song that would remain etched in my memory.

Leader: What's that thing in the red shirt?
All: Ain't nothing there, silly brother
Leader: Don't you have any eyes, brothers, sisters?
All: How can we when the sweat comes a-pouring into our eyes?
Leader: Ah! Let me wipe your faces, brothers, sisters
All: 'Bout time
Leader: Can you see now? Can you see that figure now, brothers, sisters?
All: Oh! Yes! Oh! Yes! We can!
Leader: Who then, may I ask that you see, brothers, sisters?
All: Ah! we see him now
Leader: Who then, may I ask that you see, brothers, sisters?
All: It's him, the devil himself. He's the one who gave us these blunt machetes
Leader: Oh yeah?
All: Yeah, and now our hands are calloused
Leader: And, what're going to do about that?
All: One day, they'll no longer be
Leader: Oh yeah?
All: One day, the machete will be sharp
Leader: What the hell will you do then?
All: That day, we'll all slay the devil in the red shirt

I wondered whether it was the song's beautiful notes or the passion with which the slaves rendered it that captivated me. The song's real significance would become clearer much later in life. I remembered watching the slaves loading the cut sugarcane onto the backs of donkeys, horses, and onto their own backs as they trudged through a sugarcane field with sharp and hostile leaves that didn't discriminate between man's tender skin and the tough hide of beasts. When I got older, the whole process became familiar: freshly cut cane, processed quickly to avoid fermentation, feeding the mill through wooden rollers to crush the cane and to extract the juice, boil, purify, and filter it, the resulting crystals pressed and formed into blocks, the liquid turned into pure molasses, boiled, and refined to make *cachaça*, a distilled spirit made from sugarcane.

How could I forget the unrelenting and pervading smells? The bagasse drying, the smoke rising from the smokestacks as it burned to heat the cane juice, the wafting into the air of distilling alcohol, the smell of the shit left beside the mill by the horses and mules that worked the wooden rollers to press the sugarcane. The heat, the flies, the smoke, the sweat, and the smell of the slaves who worked around the clock to ensure that the long trays that cooled the sugar crystals and enabled the syrup to drain into the barrels didn't spill. The earth's rich smell, especially after the torrential tropical rain that brought about humidity so dense one could cut through it with a machete. How couldn't I know that these smells, though offensive to the visitor, were the fragrance of a unique universe reserved only for the native-born? How couldn't I remember? How couldn't I remember the voices? The foremen and supervisors, all white men, who worked under Marcelo Resendes and cursed the slaves and were quick with their long whips? *Crack*! *Crack*! *Crack*! Followed by the expletives, the insults "*Escravos preguiçosos!*"—Fucking lazy slaves! How could I forget Aloisio and Lourenco, two teenagers who lost their arms below their elbows on the same day when the wooden rollers crushed their hands along with the sugarcane?

What about the children, old men, and women with bent backs, and the maimed like Aloisio and Lourenco, who could no longer work on the sugarcane plantation but couldn't be discarded like the bagasse because they still needed to earn their keep? What about them? What about the long hours they spent working on the *Fazenda*'s gardens and orchards that produced vegetables and fruits, including cassava, cashew, yams, capuassu, papaya, pineapple, hog plum, and plantains? And the chickens, goats, ducks, pigs, milk cows, guinea fowls they raised? And the nights with dogs barking and cows bellowing plaintively? What about the poorly thatched-roof shacks that housed legally married couples and their children, many of whom bore little resemblance to their fathers? And the long rectangular buildings that were home to the unwedded slaves? What about the nights when there were singing and the celebration of rituals, despite concerted efforts to catholicize these slaves who still preferred their own ways? *Oludumaré* and his *orixas*, the lesser gods who served him?

These were memories that I couldn't simply purge from my mind, even if I wanted to. But perhaps, the most important one that set the course of my life was the conversation that I overheard between *Senhor* Felipe de Barbosa and Josefina Ferreira, the biracial woman who raised me. Tall and regal, Josefina Ferreira possessed one of those faces that one couldn't contemplate just once and look away. It was a face that had a magnetic pull, the sort of face that forced one to accept in all humility that, despite one's best efforts, one could never match one's plebeian looks with such immense, unattainable beauty. Her keen warm eyes, luscious lips, along with a luxuriant head of black wavy hair, often lodged in an immaculate white turban that accentuated her unusual height of six feet, three inches, were among some of her flawlessly sculptured features. Such external attributes offered Josefina Ferreira a presence that made it impossible to contemplate her without being struck by her haughtiness and self-assuredness.

It may not have been the essence of the conversation between her and *Senhor* Felipe de Barbosa, which was significant, that struck me. Rather, it was the force with which Josefina Ferreira stated her feelings that was noteworthy. It was much later that I understood why a slave would have the nerve to talk to her master in this manner: Josefina had on a perpetual leash not only her master's constantly throbbing heart but also the tool dangling between his legs.

"Over my dead body," she told her master.

"Over your what?" *Senhor* Felipe de Barbosa asked in dismay.

"You heard me. I'm not letting Pedro leave the *casa grande* to live in the *senzala* with any of the married slave couples in one of the shacks on this plantation," Josefina Ferreira said as she walked towards *Senhor* Felipe de Barbosa, a full six inches shorter.

Senhor Felipe de Barbosa responded after weighing Josefina Ferreira's defiant response.

"Who the hell are you to tell me what to do with Pedro? Have you forgotten that, like you, he's my slave? No one decides where he'd live and what work he'd do on my plantation. Do I make myself clear?"

I hadn't heard what *Senhor* Felipe de Barbosa had told Josefina Ferreira to elicit her audacious response and our master's subsequent rejoinder. But I clearly understood that not only was I the subject of their conversation but also that my future was at stake. Josefina Ferreira had adopted me shortly after my mother died. Earlier on, she had had a stillbirth after 28 weeks of pregnancy. I would learn later that three things led her to adopt me: the grief for her loss, her inability to bear any more children, and the fact that, somehow, I carried a striking similarity to her stillborn son. Like her dead baby, I had a mole just beneath the left side of my eye. It didn't matter to Josefina Ferreira that her dead son and I had quite different skin tones. For her, what mattered was that God had given her another son with the same mole to replace her dead child, and she adored me with sincere and uncomplicated love. The other enslaved women, some of whom successfully birthed, besides those fathered by none other than his *senhoria*—lordship—but couldn't nurture them, scorned Josefina Ferreira for her position. Unlike them, she was the master's mistress on the *fazenda*, lived in the *casa grande*, and didn't work on the plantation but in the *casa grande*'s kitchen along with two other younger slave girls. And it was in the *casa grande* that Josefina Ferreira wanted me to stay, as I had done all along since I was born.

I held my breath and sharpened my ear, daring not to move a muscle behind the door from where I had been eavesdropping. All was quiet except for the caged saffron finches on the porch that deployed gleefully their extraordinarily extensive syllable repertoire as they combined and recombined those syllables to produce remarkably variable songs, rarely repeating a song before switching to a new one. Despite the urge to remain quiet, I couldn't help myself from peeking through the crack between the door and its hinges. Josefina Ferreira stood a few inches from *Senhor* Felipe de Barbosa.

"Yes. We're all your slaves. We all play different roles on the plantation," Josefina Ferreira finally responded and paused for a minute or two. "Pedro can work in the vegetable gardens and the orchards like any other seven-year-old. But I'm begging you to have him stay in the *casa grande*. He'll take off your boots when you come back from the fields and when you arrive from Salvador. He'll fetch your pipe, your tobacco, and whatever you need. But please don't take him away from me," Josefina Ferreira said as she put her long arms around her master's shoulders and pulled him towards her. No one knew more about her master's most singular flaw than Josefina Ferreira, and she determined to exploit it to the full. The plantation owner buried his head in Josefina Ferreira's big taut bosoms, breathing in her sweet smell, producing the desired effect on the inveterate libertine. It forced *Senhor* Felipe de Barbosa to succumb at the altar of Josefina Ferreira's scintillating body, a body that many a man on the *Fazenda* lusted after and which she deployed as a weapon with spectacular results. Otherwise, how else could she have gotten Marcelo Resendes to become my tutor behind *Senhor* Felipe de Barbosa's back?

With bulbous green eyes that danced and beamed fervently, Marcelo Resendes had coveted his boss' mistress with unrelenting passion. He had been laying siege unsuccessfully to Josefina Ferreira until she acquiesced on her terms. Before that, the overseer knew which boundaries one could never cross. Like everyone on *Fazenda Barbosa*, Marcelo Resendes was too aware of the heresy of appropriating *Senhor* Felipe de Barbosa's property, irrespective of its nature. Educated at the famous Diamantina Seminary in Minas Gerais but forced to pursue a different career as an overseer on *Fazenda Barbosa*, Marcelo Resendes had an encyclopedic mind. Josefina Ferreira's proposition overwhelmed him with delight and desire, and he accepted the plan without a second thought. For his reward, Marcelo Resendes would spend the nights in the big plantation bedroom with Josefina Ferreira when *Senhor* Felipe de Barbosa was away in Salvador, where he lived with his family. By insisting that I become educated, Josefina Ferreira gave me, perhaps, the best and most significant gift that I would ever receive.

"I cannot read or write," she said to me the day I would become Marcelo Resendes' pupil. "But I know what education means. Knowledge is a powerful tool, and it might one day help you to be free," she added.

But Josefina Ferreira's status on the *Fazenda Barbosa* didn't mean that I didn›t work on the plantation like the other slave children. Like the other kids, my tender back started tasting the whip of Jorginho Carragoso, the foreman in charge of the vegetable farms and orchards when I was barely seven. He was a surly, uncommunicative man who made no pretense of hiding the fact that he despised humanity. It appeared as though it was worse if you were a black and a slave. Like all the slave children on the plantation, I endured the pain without telling Josefina Ferreira. We learned very quickly at that young age that complaints led to more abuse. It was better to absorb pain and violation without protest. I had a visceral hatred for Jorginho Carragoso.

"Why don't you want to take off your shirt for your bath?" Josefina Ferreira asked me one evening after I had returned from the orchard where I had spent the whole day. I shrugged and tried to move away from her. But she knew me more than I knew myself. Lifelong bondage and violence offered her a glimpse into a space that many couldn't fathom.

"What happened, *meu amor?*" she asked as she knelt and pulled me gently towards her. I was silent. She removed my shirt carefully. The lines were fresh. She lifted me gently into the bathroom and bathed me, making sure not to hurt any further my bruised back. Josefina Ferreira applied a soothing salve to my back without uttering a single word. Underneath that calm, however, was raging fury. In no time, Jorginho Carragoso left the plantation. But the new supervisor was no different. *Crack! Crack! Crack!* The whip continued to dance on youthful skin. There were only so many times that one could use one's goodwill and influence on a slave plantation, where hierarchies were clear-cut and etched into an entrenched racist belief system. Josefina Ferreira had exhausted all.

As though the physical horror wasn't enough, terror and violence at the hand of some of the older children with whom I worked would become the norm. My offense? I lived in the *casa grande,* and mine was the only name that *Senhor* Felipe de Barbosa seemed to remember. These children found this tiny detail important, even though I wouldn't say the master's treatment of me, with whatever modicum of humanity he still possessed as a slave owner, amounted to very much. For them, this was enough of a legitimate mandate to loathe and to resent me.

"Oh, look who's here? The master's little pet slave," said Manoel Bagulho one morning. He was a sinewy twelve-year-old who had learned very early on to fake coughs and all kinds of ailments that kept him with us when, given his age, he should have already become a veteran in the sugarcane fields.

"Yeah, and I hear he not only pulls off his master's boots when he comes from the fields. He also licks them like a dog," said Santiago d'Almeida, a much older boy than me. Laughter rang through the twenty-odd kids.

"Does it mean he licks the shit that the cows and horses drop on the plantation as well?" asked Laura Abreu, a girl my age with a distended stomach. She had been so famished that she fetched the lowest bid on the slave market the day *Senhor* Felipe de Barbosa went looking for more slave children in Salvador. Despite being at the *fazenda* for almost a year, she still bore her signature look. I rushed Laura Abreu, intending to pummel her, but Manoel Bagulho intervened. Before I knew it, he bent my arm behind my back, pushed my face into the dirt, pulled out a piece of rock wrapped in a rag, and pushed its sharp and pointy end to my throat.

"I'll kill you if you touch anyone here. And you can tell your whore of a mother at the *casa grande* that I said so," said Manoel Bagulho.

"What's going on here?" bellowed one of the supervisors, who emerged as if from thin air.

"It's Pedro de Barbosa," said Laura Abreu. "He punched me in the face. Manoel Bagulho simply wanted him to stop," she added.

"How come he's on the ground?" Macario Almeida, the foreman, asked.

"He wanted to stab me with this stone, and I had to wrestle him to the ground," said Manoel Bagulho, handing over his improvised weapon.

"*Puta merda*,"—Holy shit—, said Macario Almeida. "Where the fuck did you get this?" he asked.

Before I could respond, his long whip was on its way. I was still on the ground, and all that I could do was coil into a fetal position, covering my head with my hands.

These were the experiences, the memories of *Fazenda Barbosa* that were gradually archived in my mind when, without notice, *Senhor* Felipe de Barbosa decided that I should leave the plantation and come along with him to Salvador. Josefina Ferreira fell apart.

"I will miss you, my little *principe*," Josefina Ferreira wept as she held me tight in her arms. Her voluptuous breasts almost smothered me as *Senhor* Felipe de Barbosa and I got ready to ride the horse wagon that would take us to Salvador.

"You'll have a better life in the city. You'll not be working on a plantation. You'll escape the ungodly labor that has always been a scandal to the muscles and a curse to the joints of all who work here," Josefina Ferreira said between tears.

Chapter 2

Andreia, the Portuguese housekeeper, screamed when she opened the front door and saw me standing with *Senhor* Felipe de Barbosa. I wasn't sure what the fuss was. She had certainly seen a young black slave before, and it wasn't as though I had arrived at the door yanking *Senhor* Felipe de Barbosa like a dog by a leash. She was a short, stocky woman with an olive complexion. Her breasts were full and large. Her blue eyes radiated mistrust of almost everyone and everything that fell upon their gaze. Her chunky, powerful body did not take well to the dress she was wearing. She must have been in her late thirties.

"Senhor Barbosa, que diabinho negro você tem!"—*Senhor* Barbosa, what a little black devil you have!—Andreia said in a high-pitched voice. I knew in that instant what her insalubrious and unwelcoming outburst meant. The *inho* diminutive that she attached to the "devil" did not carry a sense of affection that would have been the case with such diminutives: it implied contempt. In the spate of just a few seconds, Andreia had dispatched with efficacy a simple warning shot: she loathed me, and since I was going to work under her, I was entering her hell. She had drawn the battle lines between us even before I had the chance to set up my defenses. I already missed Josefina Ferreira.

The first city person I was meeting, Andreia, had crushed my excitement at going to Salvador, which I had considered as an adventure. It didn't matter that she was a housekeeper. What was of consequence was that she didn't live on a plantation. Besides, even though a domestic, she was white and free, which was significant in the city. I had heard Josefina Ferreira and the other slaves talk about Salvador. The big city, especially its allure of churches, plazas, and rich white men and their elegantly dressed wives and children, along with their slaves who carried them so that they didn't get their clothes soiled. Yet the women on the *fazenda* were apprehensive about the ways of the city people. Somehow, that inquietude and anxiety that they had so eloquently expressed engulfed and stifled me. It didn't make the situation any better when *Senhor* Felipe de Barbosa led me into the large living room.

The chandelier hanging from the ceiling in the middle of the room caught my eye. With sunlight penetrating windows with drawn blinds, the chandelier's reflective and refractive dangling crystal pendants captured and distorted the room's contents simultaneously: the well-polished chairs, along with several wooden armoires laden with drawers, sat comfortably on a carpet with decorations of pastoral fields in Portugal. Although the living room's opulence overwhelmed me, the stares of the four people did more. They stopped me in my tracks. Eusebio Thrilho, Archbishop of Bahia's Archdiocese, *Senhora* Fidelia de Barbosa, and her two well-dressed children, Joan, nine, and Agostinho, eight, sat in their designated places. I had never seen a clergy in his informal vestment. The priest's appearance struck me. On Archbishop Eusebio Thrilho's round head sat a *cappello romano*, a hat with a large circular brim and a rounded rim that reminded one of a jabuticaba fruit cut in half. He wore a purple cassock girded with a white cincture as a belt. A large chain with a crucified Jesus on a cross hung from his neck. His thin, long hands were home to a pair of soft, black gloves. Poking from the front of Archbishop Eusebio Thrilho's long cassock were the tips of two shiny black shoes that the candelabra miraculously reflected as well. His refined and dignified look stood in striking contrast with Father Fernando Santos Candido, the Jesuit priest who visited us on the plantation.

Senhor Felipe de Barbosa hesitated a little upon seeing Archbishop Eusebio Thrilho in his living room. Nevertheless, he went directly to the prelate, sitting on a chair next to *Senhora* Fidelia de Barbosa. An outstretched hand was out before he got to the man of God, who offered his episcopally ringed finger to my master. With the Archbishop's studied gesture and the deliberately executed extension of his delicate hand that dictated kissing, it appeared as though the priest was threading some spiritual force piously through his body to *Senhor* Felipe de Barbosa's. The archbishop's symbolic act was significant given the meaning of both his first and last names: Eusebio— pious, Thrilho—thread; The Pious Thread. I would learn later that the archbishop wove his piety thread deep into *Senhora* Fidelia de Barbosa's loins.

Senhor Felipe de Barbosa, who hardly spoke to me on our way from the plantation to Salvador except to tell me I was to be a servant in his house, said in a deep voice by introduction.

"This is Pedro de Barbosa. He will work in the house and in the garden for us. He'll live in the slaves' quarters with the other servants."

"Why's he called de Barbosa?" asked Agostinho, who was in a sailor suit and wearing shoes tied with a ribbon. They were the most elegant shoes I had ever seen on a boy his age.

"Silly, don't you see he is father's slave?" Joan asked her brother. She had freckles and large brown eyes.

"Do slaves have their father's names? Agostinho asked.

"Agostinho, don't you have eyes? How could a *menino negro—*black boy—be your brother?" *Senhora* Fidelia de Barbosa spoke in an icy voice for the first time. Her look was frantic. Under her large, brown, withering, and unkind eyes, a scowl played about her mouth as she spoke.

"Pedro is going to be your servant, and you can tell him to do whatever you want," *Senhora* Fidelia de Barbosa added.

"Does that mean that Pedro is my slave?" Agostinho asked.

"*Meu amor*, whatever belongs to your father is yours as well," said his mother.

Senhora Fidelia de Barbosa's use of the determiner "whatever" instead of "whoever" wasn't lost to me. I wasn't sure if Agostinho understood his mother's not-so-subtle message that he owned me. But by that tender age of ten, I had already resolved that I would not be anyone's property. It would take me several years to realize that it was not as easy as I had thought. Of the two siblings, Agostinho seemed more curious about me.

"Do you go to school?" he asked.

"What's school?" I asked, feigning ignorance.

Josefina Ferreira had advised me before leaving the plantation not to reveal anything about myself to anyone in *Senhor* Felipe de Barbosa's house in Salvador. She said information was a powerful asset that one should not divulge with ease. For her, that included the fact that I was already a proficient reader and writer, thanks to the extensive informal education that I had received from Marcelo Resendes.

"You don't know what a school is?" Joan asked with a gapped mouth stare.

"It's a place where you go to learn how to read and to write. I'll take you there if you'd like," Agostinho said.

"No, Agostinho," *Senhora* Fidelia de Barbosa said. "School's not for slaves, blacks, and servants," she said firmly.

"But why?" Agostinho asked.

"Because they're not intelligent enough," *Senhora* Fidelia de Barbosa said.

"But why? Agostinho pressed.

"Because God made them so," the young boy's mother stated. I waited a minute or so to hear from the archbishop, the man of God, to give his definitive endorsement of *Senhora* Fidelia de Barbosa's pronouncement or to refute it. I would have waited till kingdom come if my life had depended on it. He was as mute as a maggot. *Senhora* Fidelia de Barbosa's statement made no sense to me at all. If Marcelo Resendes had been here, he would have told her that despite my age, I had a firm grasp of the scriptures. He would also have informed her, as he did Josefina, that I was one of the most intelligent children he had ever encountered. I couldn't help recalling Marcelo Resendes' exasperation when I argued with him on end about the Holy Trinity.

"If the sum of two plus two is four, and it takes a man and woman, a cow and a bull, to produce offspring, why are you saying the Holy Trinity makes one?" I asked Marcelo Resendes during one of our lessons.

"Pedro," he said, "God the Father, God the Son, and God the Holy Spirit mean the same thing: God. This mystery is divine, and it's beyond our understanding," he added.

"Like the Virgin Mary having a baby without a husband?" I asked.

"Exactly," Marcelo Resendes responded.

"But wasn't she married to Joseph?" I asked.

"Ah, yes," he said.

"So, she was married," I stated matter-of-factly.

"Yes," Marcelo Resendes responded.

"And her husband helped her have Jesus, just like some of the married men and women do on the *fazenda*. Isn't that so?" I asked.

"No, it's different," my teacher said.

"Why?" I asked.

Marcelo Resendes sighed and said, "Mary had Jesus by immaculate conception."

"What's that?" I asked.

Marcelo Resendes was silent.

"There are so many things about the Bible that I just don't understand," I said.

"Like what?" Marcelo Resendes asked, relieved to put the Holy Trinity to rest. But it was to be a short repose.

"So, when Jesus died on the cross, there was no God for three days and three nights. Am I right?" I asked.

"No," he said

"Why?" I asked.

"Because the Holy Spirit cannot die," Marcelo Resendes replied.

"But God the Son died," didn't he?

"Let's move on to something else for today," Marcelo Resendes said.

We had similar exchanges in other areas of study that included Latin, the natural sciences, history, and literature. I liked José de Santa Rita Durão's poetry and his *Caramuru: poema épico do descobrimento da Bahia*. His treatment of the "noble savages" intrigued me a lot.

"So, are the Pataxó noble savages?" I asked Marcelo Resendes after he had explained what the term meant.

"Yes. According to José de Santa Rita Durão, they were before the white man came," said Marcelo Resendes.

"And when the white man came, they stopped being noble?" I asked.

"Yes," said Marcelo Resendes.

"So, the white man destroys good things and good people wherever he goes?" I asked.

"Well, yes and no," Marcelo Resendes replied.

"How so?" I asked.

"When two people from two different places meet, they exchange ideas. Sometimes those ideas are good, and sometimes they are bad. They can change people," said Marcelo Resendes.

"So according to José de Santa Rita Durão, the Pataxó have become bad because the white man brought bad ideas and changed them. Is that right?" I asked.

"Sort of," Marcelo Resendes replied.

I had unending curiosity, and I had a teacher with a fertile mind who fed my thirst for knowledge. What I enjoyed the most, however, was the art of penmanship. Marcelo Resendes made me copy over and over hundreds of passages from different texts just as they appeared to the extent that I could reproduce any document like the original. Born left-handed, Marcelo Resendes insisted I learn how to write with my right hand as well, making me ambidextrous, a trait that would become invaluable later in my life. Marcelo Resendes was sad to see me go. Despite his position as a general overseer and mine as a slave, we shared a bond that mutual interest in learning sustained. But my relationship with him went beyond that. He was going to be the first and, perhaps, the only male figure who would affect my life substantially.

I reflected on *Senhora* Fidelia de Barbosa's statement and smiled. I hadn't recalled reading anywhere in the scriptures that God, in His infinite wisdom, or perhaps in error, had made different grey matter that he stuck into the heads of white and black people. But I would not contradict the lady of the house. After all, I had learned at *Fazenda Barbosa* and the other surrounding plantations that some of the white men overseers, supervisors, and landowners were the most stupid in giving simple instructions for tasks to be completed by their black slaves. Often, it was the most idiotic of the laborers that came up with more effective means to perform such tasks.

"Am I intelligent?" Agostinho asked.

"You're a little dull, *pequehno sapo*—little toady— but you're still bright enough," responded Joan.

"Mother, she's calling me toady again," Agostinho whined.

"Joan, how many times have I ordered you not to call your brother, little toady? You realize he dislikes that. Now, can you take Pedro to the slaves' quarters and have Andreia show him around the house and the gardens?" *Senhora* Fidelia de Barbosa asked.

"I'll show him the gardens," Agostinho said eagerly, grabbing my hand and drawing me away from the living room.

"No, you won't. I will," Joan did as she snatched my other hand. Soon, we left behind the intelligent white adults in the living room.

*****

It didn't take me long to understand that Josefina Ferreira was utterly mistaken. If she assumed I was escaping what she called ungodly labor on *Fazenda Barbosa* for a better life in *Senhor* Felipe de Barbosa's house in Salvador, what I encountered was sanctified drudgery, recompense for moving from the plantation to the city of the civilized. It meant that I had to wake up at four o'clock in the morning, mop the floors, await *Senhor* Felipe de Barbosa and his wife, who slept in separate rooms, to wake up and empty their chamber pots. Ordinarily, emptying chamber pots wasn't such an unpleasant chore as one would have imagined. Provided what was left lingering in the chamber pots was nothing but urine. It was an entirely different matter when other substances found their way into that open space. Of the couple, the most frequent culprit was the lady of the house.

For some reason, unlike most Brazilians of Portuguese descent who had taken to eating *moqueca* with no harmful side effects, *Senhora* Fidelia de Barbosa had a complicated and unhealthy relationship with this particular dish of African provenance. I must confess that, of all the food that Josefina Ferreira made in the *casa grande*'s kitchen, *moqueca* was my favorite. Having spent most of my early years hitched to her skirt in her kitchen, I learned how to make several dishes, but I paid more attention to those I liked the most. Having lost my taste buds' virginity to *moqueca*, it was only logical that it topped the list. Even though the twain weren't supposed to have met, *Senhora* Fidelia de Barbosa's palate and mine did so at the altar of *moqueca*'s unusual capacity to bridge the gap between two diverse cultural landscapes. Despite what might appear to be a long list of ingredients, *moqueca*'s charm lies in the simplicity of its preparation. Its hidden danger, however, is in the amount of *malagueta* pepper that is added.

Although *moqueca* was my preferred dish at the *casa grande*, I stayed away from it in *Senhor* Felipe de Barbosa's home. The overpowering *malagueta* flavor warned me of its danger. Yet *Senhora* Fidelia de Barbosa craved the dish, and her reward for paying tribute to it was her stomach howling with disapproval, followed by cramps and diarrhea. A particular chamber-pot-emptying-episode has remained with me forever. In my later years, I would ban that vile object from wherever I lived. On the day in question, my dear madam had consumed an immoderate amount of *moqueca* the previous evening. She was not a glutton or a big eater. But with this dish, all bets were off. Not only did she eat more than everybody, but she also drank everyone, including her husband, under the table. It appeared as though the lady had overdone it this time. I had already become familiar with the distinct stench that enveloped her boudoir following a post-*moqueca* indulgence. As usual, I waited until *Senhora* Fidelia de Barbosa was in the bathing chamber before I entered her bedroom to perform my chore. I pulled the chamber pot from under the bed and stopped at the sight of the overflowing substances that also contained traces of blood. As though an agitated creature, the contents of the chamber pot came to life and spilled. In no time, the carpet by the bedside had become a flooded plain of shit, urine, and blood.

"*Puta merda*—" Holy shit!—I said to myself, attempting to hold my breath and not throw up. There was no way in hell, I told myself, that I was going to clean up that deadly spill. It wasn't part of the contract of being a slave, I said to myself. I carried the chamber pot at arm's length, held my breath sporadically, disposed of the contents as I usually did, washed the chamber pot, returned it to *Senhora* Fidelia's bedroom, and sneaked out.

"Pedro!" the unmistakable voice called out. I had moved on to my next chore of waking up Joan and Agostinho, helping them wash, and getting dressed.

"Are you deaf or something? Can't you hear mother calling you?" Joan, who hated waking up, asked after I had purposefully refused to respond to her mother's call. It didn't take a genius to know why *Senhora* Fidelia summoned me. She barged into the children's bedroom, giving me no time to respond to her or her daughter. She grabbed me by one ear and pulled me towards her bedroom.

"Didn't you hear me calling? You dumb black slave," she said as we crossed the threshold to her still stench-infected room.

"When were you going to clean up this mess that you made?" *Senhora* Fidelia asked, pointing to the pool that, by now, had journeyed across the carpet.

I had wanted to remind her I wasn't the architect of the thick liquid and that had she been measured in her consumption from the previous night, we wouldn't have been dealing with a breached dam. But I wasn't offered any time to gather the courage to put my thoughts into words. The next thing I knew, my face had become a mop as *Senhora* Fidelia rolled me in her waste. In no time, my whole body had become splattered all over with blood, urine, and shit.

As one might expect, I couldn't finish the rest of my morning chores of assisting the de Barbosa children in getting ready for breakfast that Andreia and I had prepared earlier on. Neither could I deliver the archbishop's basket. How could I have had time to wash? I couldn't have entered the church, trailing in my wake the scent of shit instead of the tempting smell of the pastries. Besides, one also had one's dignity to protect. And for these reasons, my master whipped me for not finishing that day's morning chores.

I resolved not to do anything the following day that would incur the wrath of *Senhor* de Barbosa and his wife. Evidence of the previous day's flogging still lingered on my sore back. I missed the preceding day's mass and looked forward to that morning's service. It was on this fateful day that the errant wind struck.

"Holy Mother of God!" I whispered. My hands quivered as though I was having a convulsion when I finished reading the letter. I reread it to make sure that my eyes weren't deceiving me:

My Dear E,   *March 21, 1805*

How could God and nature be so cruel to us? How could we be so condemned to such perpetual secrecy when my only wish is your warm embrace and to honor our prohibited love? Why must I fall in love with someone who has pledged his life to God? Have I become a Bathsheba and you a David? No, our baby didn't die in infancy. Your son, Agostinho, is alive, strong. To see him is to see you. There's another one on the way. Oh! I cannot withstand this imprisonment in our cells! He leaves for the plantations again in a week. I cannot wait to be in your arms. Be patient, my love. Our bodies will find their paradise in each other soon.

Your love,

F

It was much later that I understood why the archbishop came to the mansion only when *Senhor* Felipe de Barbosa was away at the plantation. His presence, we had been told, was to provide *Senhora* Fidelia de Barbosa her needed spiritual guidance and to keep her company and comfort her during her husband's long absences. That was some comfort, all right. But what was I to do with this volatile information? As I contemplated my dilemma, Josefina's counsel about knowledge and information crept slowly into my mind. I read the letter for the third time. There was no sign that *Senhora* Fidelia de Barbosa expected a reply from the cleric. None of the empty baskets that I had retrieved during the past year contained any missive. It would have been risky for the priest to communicate with my madam via the same medium. The chance of exposure was too high. If that was the case, I surmised the priest wouldn't have known about this letter. Given the letter's shape and form, I decided not to give it to the archbishop. After all, would he have believed my story that the wind singularly chose to play mischief and crumpled it? I decided to reproduce the letter, keep the original, and deliver the forged copy the following morning to the archbishop.

I knew where to look for the stationery when I cleaned *Senhora* Fidelia de Barbosa's bedchamber later that day. Dark paneling that seemed to encase the room surrounded the walls. Brass gilt frames, hanging from brown ribbons, imprisoned *Senhora* Fidelia de Barbosa's parents' portraits. From afar, they looked suspended in the air. Curtains with exotic patterns of tropical flowers, birds, and plants enclosed half of the room. Besides a large window overlooking one of the side gardens stood an elegant table with straight legs and a flat surface that arched down and locked when needed. It had many cubbyholes, one of which contained my *Senhora's* stationery, to which I helped myself. Late that night, I produced a new copy of her letter. It surprised me to notice that I hadn't lost my knack for text reproduction. Neither had my penmanship suffered for lack of practice. Marcelo had etched the art into my soul, brain, and hands. I enjoyed the process so much that I made two more copies, keeping the two and the original one and putting one copy in the envelope that I painstakingly addressed to the Pious Thread.

Chapter 3

For reasons that should be clear to any reader by now, it would be understandable if I stated that during the several months since my arrival in Salvador, I failed to notice that there were boys who slept in the drab alleyways, off streets such as *Rua do Obispo, Rua da Oração, Rua do Tabuão* that were not too far from the *Catedral Basilica* and other buildings surrounding *Largo de Terreiro de Jesus* and *Praça da Sé* in the middle of the upper city. I became aware of a group of such boys on one of my deliveries to the archbishop's residence. Apparently, they had been monitoring my morning routine and had reckoned that I transported food worthy of the recipient's station in the community. My demeanor and clothing told them that not only was I a newcomer to the city, but also that I was a servant in the home of one of the richest people in the city.

"Hey, *babaca*—asshole—what's your name?"

I turned around to face a tall, husky, brown-skinned boy. He had materialized out of nowhere as I left the *Catedral Basilica de Salvador* and was heading towards the archbishop's residence. Six other boys of varying ages and sizes followed him.

"What does my name matter to you?" I asked.

"It matters because I've asked you, *babaca*," the homeless street brat said as he inched towards me. The others gathered around.

"Pedro de Barbosa," I replied.

"What're you carrying?" the gang leader asked me.

"Food for the archbishop," I answered.

"Well, Pedro de Barbosa, today, I'm the archbishop," he said, as he reached for the basket.

I took a step back. The other boys laughed. One of them pushed me from behind. Just then, four altar boys came out of one of the Basilica's doors towards the plaza where they had me corralled. From the prelate's kitchen, Rosalinda Almeida, who had seen what was transpiring, came out running towards us. She had a broomstick in her hands like a musket raised to strike.

"Get out of here before I call the Civil Police, you worthless hoodlums," Rosalinda yelled.

The altar boys, who were bigger and taller than the street boys, ran towards us. But perhaps it was the mention of the Civil Police that made the street urchins disappear within a few seconds. With unsteady steps, I delivered, as usual, the basket. Why hadn't I noticed these boys earlier? I asked myself. Could their condition be worse than mine? Despite the indignities that came along with bondage, it occurred to me I had a somewhat better life as *Senhor* Felipe de Barbosa's slave than the street boys. But at what price? Weren't these young boys who went hungry better off than someone like me who had a roof over my head, enough food to eat, and yet trapped in the clutches of slavery? Something about the boys provoked a feeling with which I hadn't reckoned. I realized that in my eleven years, I hadn't a set of friends. Not in *Fazenda Barbosa,* and not in the São Bento neighborhood of Salvador where my master and his family lived. How could I have built any friendships on the plantation when I had to fend off the other young slaves who spurned me because they thought I curried favor with *Senhor* Felipe de Barbosa? And in Salvador? My daily routine and chores weren't sympathetic to any forays into companionships with boys my age. I found something extraordinarily alluring about how the street boys interacted with one another and with me during our brief encounter, even though it was under the most auspicious of circumstances. An instinctual necessity nibbled at me.

After delivering the basket the following morning, I ventured towards the alleyway of *Caminho Novo de Tabuão,* off *Rua do Tabuão,* to which I had hitherto been oblivious.

"Hey, Pedro, *babaca*! What're you doing here? Have you brought the archbishop of the alleyway his breakfast?" I heard the unmistakable voice of my heckler from the previous morning.

A howl of laughter broke behind the voice. As from the previous morning, the tall, husky, brown-skinned boy walked imperiously towards me. The others stood behind him. If these boys thought they could intimidate and push me around, they were gravely mistaken. Although I hadn't come looking for a fight or an apology for their previous day's attempted stunt, I had prepared myself for any eventuality. I may not have been a street boy. But I was no milksop, as Manoel Bagulho learned at the *Fazenda Barbosa* the hard way. A week after my encounter with him and Macario Almeida, I applied the same move he had used on me. It happened quickly. Before Manoel Bagulho knew it, he found himself on the ground. I shoved dirt into his mouth. Macario Almeida wasn't there to intervene as he had done the day before. That singular action liberated me from Manoel Bagulho and the other bullies on the plantation.

As the street boys inched towards me, I calculated my options. I could either retreat or confront them. The first option didn't seem workable, given their sheer numbers. Neither was the second, which I opted for, believing that in doing so, I was paying homage to that implacable urge that had led me there.

"I've brought the *babaca* of the alleyway some shit," I finally replied.

"Ooooh! He's got some *colhões*"—balls— said the lackeys, who latched on and rode on their honcho's coattails.

"Say that again, *compatriota*," the boss said as he moved in closer to me like a predator stalking its target.

"*Compatriota*, I said I've brought a shitload of shit for you and your shitload of underlings," I stated. I opened a bag full of *broa*, a type of cornbread seasoned with fennel and *salgado*, which comprised different finger foods made of dough wrapped around chopped meat, chicken, ham, or cheese that I had stolen from the kitchen earlier that morning. The sight of the bulging bag and the fragrance that its contents emitted prompted the gang's leader to make a rash decision; he quickly closed the gap between us in a heartbeat and reached for the bag. Quicker, I pulled the bag back and said, "Not so fast. First, I want to know your name and those of your clueless *compatriotas*. Second, I want you to thank me for bringing you the first thing you're going to be putting into your rotten mouths this morning."

My response may have been too much of an insult for the husky boy to suffer. He rushed me, holding out his hand to grab the coveted items. That was his mistake. I spun him around, as I had learned from Manoel Bagulho, and pulled with all my might his hand behind his back. He shrieked. I looked at his comrades. It dumbfounded them.

"I will break his bloody arm if you don't stand back, you little shits," I said to his underlings.

The scream continued as I kept the pressure on the husky boy's hand. After a while, I let go.

"Don't you assholes have any manners? I've taken the trouble to bring you *babacas* food, and this is how you treat me?" I asked.

There was silence. After a while, I turned to the leader of the group and said,

"I still want to know your name and those of your friends. Oh, and by the way, I still want you to say thank you."

"My name is Trunk, and that's all you need to know," said the gang leader, who, it appeared, was still nursing his bruised arm as well as his ego.

"Trunk? As in a tree trunk?" I asked. "What kind of name is that? Don't you have a first name? What about the last name?" I continued.

"Nobody asks me stupid questions," said the tree trunk.

"What then is your *parentesco*—parentage?" I asked.

"Fuck off. That's none of your goddamned business. Now, you either give me the shit you're holding in your hand, or you'll regret you ever set foot on our property," Trunk said.

"Property?" I asked.

"Yes, property, you damned *babaca*, didn't you hear me?" Trunk asked, drawing near me and putting his face very close to mine. I was right about their rotten teeth: his breath stunk. He was more than a foot and a half taller than me. I would be no match for him in any physical contest. He was a hardened street hustler, and his body language suggested that no one messed with him. I had already messed with him. He knew I had the upper hand in the transaction unfolding before all of us. Yet somehow, I questioned the wisdom of venturing and trespassing on their property, as Trunk had called their alley. His threat seemed palpable, and it triggered memories of *Fazenda de Barbosa.* Was this the norm with young boys? I pondered. If that was the case, I had already announced that I wouldn't tolerate whatever prompted boys that age to carry out their bullying tendencies. And yet, here I was, attempting to build a set of friends on detested street boys whose only crime was the cruelty that society had systematically unleashed upon them.

"Look, Trunk," I said. "I haven't come here to fuck with you, and neither did I come here for you to fuck with me. If you don't want the food I've brought you, I'll take it back."

There was silence. The contents of the stuffed bag continued to flaunt their aroma. A forced détente was inevitable. One of the young boys sped up that process.

"My grandmother, who they brought here from Dahomey, always said that when two elephants fight, it is the grass that suffers most."

"Cutpurse, I didn't know you ever had a grandmother," another boy chimed in.

"Never believe what Cutpurse says," said a boy with blond hair and blue eyes. "He's good at emptying pockets and even better when he's hungry. He'll invent stories when his stomach grumbles."

Everyone burst into laughter. The tense mood changed.

"So, your name is Trunk, and his name is Cutpurse. What are the names of the others?' I asked.

"Ha! don't waste your breath. Some of these jokers don't even know their names," Trunk said, looking at the faces of several boys who set their sights on the bag in my hand than the fact that their leader had referred to them as dunces.

"Fair enough," I said, handing over the bag to Trunk.

"Thank you," he said, as though someone was pulling one of his rotten teeth.

I thought there was going to be a ruckus. Instead, a symphonic orderliness followed that astounded me. Everyone sat down as Trunk opened the bag, pulled out a dirty handkerchief from his back pocket, spread all the items on it, and counted them. He then asked each boy to pick one piece after he had chosen the biggest and best pastry. I reckoned that there was a reason top dogs existed. After this second encounter with the street boys, I decided that *Senhor* Felipe de Barbosa's pantry would become a supply conduit for their partial nourishment. I wasn't sure whether it was pity or the need for camaraderie that dictated that impulse. What was clear to me, however, was the colossal nature of the undertaking to which I was committing myself. The risks involved were real, and the punishment severe if I got caught. But my fertile mind had already designed full-proof plans: I would exploit Andreia's habits. She got drunk on *cachaça* before going to bed; she kept dutifully her daily ritual of praying for ten minutes every morning before the de Barbosa family gathered for breakfast and trudged along to the *Catedral Basílica de Salvador* for morning Mass. I reckoned these habits would provide the opportunity to stuff food into a bag at night and in the morning. I would add it to the Pious Thread's already prepared basket. With this solemn resolution, a daily morning ritual was established. So was a relationship and a bond between me and Trunk's motley disciples. Hardly did I know that I would soon become an integral member of this fraternity.

*****

I had spent a year and a half at the mansion, but the relationship with Andreia hadn't improved. That intemperate woman hated me for being a black, a *preto*, a nigger, as she often called me. She spewed all the unimaginative racial epithets that came to her mind and hurled them at me like a Roman general commanding his army to catapult cannonballs at the enemy. It wasn't as if I had advertently or inadvertently breached some invisible wall of hers. Even if I did, no white flag that I hoisted irrespective of its size would have appeased her. All I could do was obey her orders. That still angered Andreia. Somehow, I had aroused her hapless indignation by my un-whiteness. I endured her abuse, especially when we were preparing for *Senhor* Felipe de Barbosa's social dinners. Andreia was at her worst during those preparations.

Before I arrived in Salvador, I did not know that *Senhor* Felipe de Barbosa was one of the wealthiest and most influential slave traders and plantation owners. His wealth, which he shared generously with the Catholic Church and the political establishment, gained him immeasurable power and influence. Like most of the elite, *Senhor* Felipe de Barbosa and his family lived in the upper city of Salvador. His lavish dinner parties, held every other month, were legendary throughout the city. Close to two hundred guests would flood his mansion and extensive gardens. Business deals and political decisions took place at these parties. To be invited to the de Barbosas' parties was a sign that one had finally ascended into Salvador's upper crust.

Preparations for these dinners took days, and they were a nightmare for me, Andreia, the other ten servants in the house, and the twenty hired extra hands. We prepared appetizers such as *acarajé*, made from peeled black-eyed peas formed into a ball and then deep-fried in palm oil, *abarás*, a grilled kidney bean casserole cooked in a water bath wrapped in banana leaf, *broa*, and *salgado*. Main courses included *feijoada*, made with beans, beef, and pork, and *Bobó de camarão*, a chowder-like dish cooked with shrimp in a purée of cassava meal. Also featured was *caruru* made from okra, onion, shrimp, palm oil, and toasted nuts.

The governor, the archbishop, presiding judge of the Superior Court, aldermen, bankers, sugar and cacao barons, and slave traders made the guest list. Paulo Álvares de Andrade, head of Salvador's Civil Police, with whom I would interact several times a few years later, was a regular.

Senhora Fidelia de Barbosa lived for these dinners. As the hostess, she was the toast of the guests for sumptuous meals and her warm reception. Impeccably dressed, *she* floated among her guests and exchanged pleasantries. Musicians entertained with Brazilian classical music by composers such as José Maurício Nunes Garcia, Francisco Manuel da Silva, and Gabriel Fernandes da Trinidade.

Pre-dinner cocktails ranged from imported Portuguese wine, *aluá*, prepared with maize, rice, and sugar, *cachaça*, *cauim*, an alcoholic drink made from fermented manioc or maize and flavored with juice, and an assortment of other drinks. An hour or so into cocktails, tongues became loose, language became course, secrets became public, and the attentive observer captured how the upper class controlled all the levers of power in the city and its surroundings.

"So, what's the news from Reconcavo?" *Senhor* Arsenio Velez, presiding judge of the Superior Court, asked Emiliano Nascimento, a zealous judge in the town of Maragogipe, at one of those memorable dinner parties. News had spread that on market days, slaves from different plantations who met each other and interacted with free people not only wandered the streets and taverns of Maragogipe at ungodly hours of the night but also took part in African singing and dancing. These activities took place in houses where these slaves had formed alliances and lived scandalously. They supposedly cohabitated brazenly in these homes in a direct affront to religion and the state.

"I will tell you what. If we don't get our act together to rein in these animals, the next thing you know, the previous revolt will seem like a cakewalk," said Emiliano Nascimento, the veins in his corpulent neck threatening to burst through the collar of his shirt.

"Oh, come off it," said the judge of the Superior Court. "After all, didn't we capture the slaves who took part in the revolt?" he asked.

"Yes, we did. But you know what? Our Bahian slaves are gradually becoming militant. I say, like the rotten molar, you remove it before the others get infected," Emiliano Nascimento said.

"I didn't know I had invited a dentist to this party. The last time I checked, the only decent one in Salvador died pulling his tooth," *Senhor* Felipe de Barbosa said, eliciting laughter from both judges.

"What is today's burning issue?" The host raised his glass in the air and toasted his eminent guests, who responded in kind.

"Ah, you know Emiliano. He's concerned that, somehow, our

dimwitted, clueless Hausa, Ewe, and Yoruba Bahian slaves are becoming bellicose and that we should do something about them," said Arsenio Velez.

"Have you forgotten what our very own distinguished historian, Luis dos Santos Vilhema, said?" *Senhor* Felipe de Barbosa asked.

"Something about not worrying about the sky falling because our slaves are restless?" Arsenio Velez ventured.

"Yes. And let me see if I can quote him '. . . if African slaves are treacherous, creoles and mulattoes are even more so; and if not for the rivalry between the former and the latter, all political power and social order would crumble before a servile revolt. . .' *Dom* Emiliano, there's no need to worry. The rivalry between these two groups is alive and well," said *Senhor* Felipe de Barbosa.

Other conversations among Salvador's elite dealt with the production and exportation of sugar, cacao, and tobacco to Portugal. Over time, one thing became patently clear to me. These men who congregated here were rich, and with their wealth came power and influence. Put these forces together, and they controlled the destiny of their fellow men. As I reflected on the vow I had made not to be anyone's property, it suddenly occurred to me that the only way to accomplish that goal was to become a *senhor*. And who, you ask, is a *senhor*? Based on what I had experienced in my short life, a *senhor* was someone, especially black or biracial, who had become wealthy and was conscious that his success in business and his accumulation of wealth and power would guarantee his freedom from the racist social determinism that condemns him to poverty, discrimination, abuse, and humiliation simply because he was dark skinned. I came to this realization because several biracial men were among the guests. One of them, in particular, intrigued me. He carried himself with purpose and poise, and the white folk that interacted with him treated him with the same decorum they offered their own. I would find out later that he was Danilo Pereira Devoto, the legitimate son of a Portuguese tailor and a biracial ex-slave. He owned slaves, and they had named him as acting president of the neighboring province of Sergipe. I had no clue at that time about how I was going to achieve my aim of becoming a *senhor*. I reckoned, however, that the most important thing was not only to have identified my life's goal but also that, to achieve that purpose, I needed to deploy whatever means necessary, notwithstanding the consequences of my actions on others. You may call me a callous son of a bitch, but I will tell you one thing. It's far better to be the one using the whip than the one receiving it. Trust me. I know.

While these conversations went on at these parties, *Senhora* Felicia de Barbosa occupied her favorite place at the head of the table alongside her husband, the governor, and Archbishop Eusebio Thrilho. During the rest of the dinner, the prelate became *Senhora* Fidelia de Barbosa's sole focus. No one considered this unusual. For most of the guests, the archbishop was a man of God and an significant representative of the Holy See in Brazil. *Senhor* Felipe de Barbosa took pride because he and his wife were in the church's good graces. A conversation that *Senhor* Felipe de Barbosa had with Paulo Álvares de Andrade at one of the dinner parties, however, changed things. This was a year and a half after I had taken possession of the cleric's letter and *Senhora* Fidelia de Barbosa had given birth to a girl, Adelina.

"As usual, your wife has outdone herself, hasn't she?" Paulo Álvares de Andrade said, walking up to *Senhor* Felipe de Barbosa, who was standing beside a fragrant rosebush in the mansion's front garden.

"Oh, yes. Behold her radiance. Isn't she beautiful?" *Senhor* Felipe de Barbosa said, directing his gaze towards his wife, who was engaged in an animated conversation with Archbishop Eusebio Thrilho.

"Yes, especially beside the archbishop," the Police Chief said with a knowing smile that *Senhor* Felipe de Barbosa failed to detect.

"Indeed," said *Senhor* Felipe de Barbosa.

"How is the young slave boy you brought from your plantation almost a year ago?" Paulo Álvares de Andrade asked.

"His name is Pedro de Barbosa," the host said, pointing in my direction.

"And how are Josefina Ferreira and your endless supply of *escravas negras*—black women slaves—on your plantation? Such a life you must have," Paulo Álvares de Andrade said with a wink and a note of envy.

"Oh, you know how these things work. I need some entertainment while on the plantation, especially since my wife refuses to set foot there. Women! They like all the jewelry, but they don't want to know how it's made," *Senhor* Felipe de Barbosa said.

"I guess all of us have a way to entertain ourselves, with or without our wives. Thankfully, they don't have the need or urge to do likewise. She's safe in the hands of the archbishop, though," Paulo Álvares de Andrade said.

"I would have been worried and jealous if she had such a close relationship with a fellow like you. Celibacy is insurance for men who don't want to be cuckolded," said *Senhor* Felipe de Barbosa.

"Especially if the celibate ones are as effeminate and delicate as our archbishop. Who knows? He might even be a faggot after all, which would make *Senhora* Felicia de Barbosa even safer," Paulo Álvares de Andrade said with a tinge of sarcasm.

Chapter 4

Senhor Felipe de Barbosa was no fool. They say the most prolific philanderers are the most jealous of their wives. This is so in a society that demands women's chastity yet is apathetic to men's debauchery. Paulo Álvares de Andrade's conversation with *Senhor* Felipe de Barbosa that evening rattled him. He knew the prelate visited his wife during his absence, but it was for serving her spiritual needs. At least, that was what she said. He had suspected nothing between *Senhora* Felicia de Barbosa and the priest. She had always been her sweet self, especially after his return from the plantation. She had commended him often for enduring the long trip and for living those extended weeks in a place that lacked all the comfort and luxury of the Salvador mansion. The Pious Thread had been, as usual, cordial, and thankful for his support of the diocese. The more he tried to put the conversation with Paulo Álvares de Andrade behind him, however, the more unsettled he became. Did Paulo Álvares de Andrade know something he was unwilling to tell him? As head of the Civil Police force, part of his job was to acquaint himself with whatever was going on in the city. He knew the merchants, the slavers, the whores, the schizophrenic, the crazy, the blacks. He knew almost everything about everyone in the city's top echelon. Their lust, hypocrisy, vulnerability.

Senhor Felipe de Barbosa played back his chat with him and remembered part of the conversation and Paulo Álvares de Andrade's tone: "She's safe in the hands of the archbishop, though." He'd known the police chief for many years, but none of their conversations had ever traversed that territory. *Senhor* Felipe de Barbosa realized that the only way to find out was to himself investigate the pious clergy's relationship with his wife. The thought of confronting Paulo Álvares de Andrade was out of the question. What if he provided him with incontrovertible proof? How would he handle that?

*****

Senhor Felipe de Barbosa summoned me to his bedroom, which was unusual. His and the *Senhora's* rooms were on the mansion's second floor but were far apart. The room's chief attraction was an ornate hardwood bed that stood in the middle of the room. Four luxurious armchairs stood by two expansive windows and beside the bed. An enormous desk and a chair with thin legs pushed under it occupied another part of the room. One wall had two walk-in wardrobes that housed his clothes and shoes. The carpet on the wooden floor was the same color as the walls in the bedroom: red.

"Sit down, Pedro," he said when I walked in.

We had all attended Mass that morning, and for the first time, I noticed that *Senhor* Felipe de Barbosa did not take the holy sacrament. For a devout Catholic like my master, sitting in the pew while others went past him to receive communion was akin to a rabbi who mistook a church for a synagogue, and it embarrassed him to acknowledge his faux pas and didn't want to draw attention to himself. Abstention from communion typically meant a person was conscious of grave sin and may decide not to receive the Body and Blood of the Lord without prior sacramental confession. *Senhor* Felipe de Barbosa did not confess at the confessional before the Mass, even though he could have done so. His resolute appendage to the pew, therefore, baffled his wife and, especially, the Pious Thread. Because I did not walk along with the family back to the mansion, I wasn't privy to any conversation between the couple. I sat on the chair to which *Senhor* Felipe de Barbosa pointed.

"Who comes to visit the house when I'm at the plantation?" he asked, fixing me with eyes radiating an intensity foreshadowing a brewing storm. The grooves in his weather-beaten face and forehead deepened. I knew there was trouble in my rearguard. I did not lose the magnitude of his question, and my central nervous system activated the warning flags of every one of the survival instincts and tactics my brief life had cultivated. The day of reckoning had arrived to decide what to do with my incriminating information and the evidence which laid hidden in one crevice between my bed's headboard and its wooden frame. I learned strategies of silence and obfuscation to protect my hide, but their deployment was suddenly doubtful, sitting face to face with a man who would use whatever means to find out that the man of God whom he trusted had been having an affair with his wife, fathering two of the children he thought were his.

"Sir, several of the *Senhora*'s friends drop by to keep her company. Sometimes, she also goes out to visit these friends," I said.

"*Babaca*, I asked who comes here and not where she goes," *Senhor* Felipe de Barbosa bellowed. "Did some of these visitors include men?" he asked, his nostrils flaring as though he needed more air in his lungs as he waited for my response.

"Except for the Archbishop, no other men come to visit the *Senhora*," I said. "But you already know that," I added, realizing that if one needed to lie, one had to begin with the obvious truth. Holder of the hidden truth, an inconvenient one, I became its sole Cerberus. It also occurred to me that providing brief, unvarnished responses trumped anything else.

"How often did he come during my absence?"

"Every day."

"What did he and *Senhora* Fidelia de Barbosa do?" *Senhor* Felipe de Barbosa asked calmly.

"I don't know. The *Senhora* asked not to be disturbed after I had served them," I said.

"Did he come when the children were at home?"

"No. At school, he stayed till they came back."

I should have stopped there but, unfortunately, I couldn't help running my big mouth.

"He treated them nicely, especially his son, Agostinho. Joan and Adelina as well," I added. Too late, I tried to cover up my blunder, averting *Senhor* Felipe de Barbosa's eyes. He was shrewd.

"What did you say about Agostinho?" he asked in a cold, calculated voice.

"He called Agostinho his son," I said, without making eye contact. *Senhor* Felipe de Barbosa stood up, sauntered to one wardrobe, and pulled out a long whip.

"What are you not telling me, Pedro?" he asked, standing in front of me. This wouldn't be the first time the whip would commune with my skin. The contours of the groove marks on my back from past whippings were enough testimony. Today's flogging, I reckoned, would be different, a notch higher than in the past. I shuddered.

"Sir, Archbishop Thrilho is a priest. He's a Father. He calls everyone his son," I replied.

The whip came before I finished my sentence.

"Do you think I'm a dumbass?" *Senhor* Felipe de Barbosa hissed. After several more lashes, he stopped and sat. His image from my tear-filled eyes was blurry, devilish. This would continue until he extracted the information he suspected I had.

"Listen, Pedro, you will tell me everything about what goes on between *Senhora* Fidelia de Barbosa and the archbishop. I promise not to punish you if you do. If you don't, I will whip you until you become unconscious. After that, I'll take you to the slave dock and sell you to another master. You're young and strong. You'll fetch me a good amount of money," he announced.

Both options were bleak. I opted for the first, unsure of its outcome, but I could expect the questions. Where did I get the letter? Why did I keep it? Why didn't I tell? Who else was privy to the damning material? Still sobbing, I responded, "I've *Senhora*'s letter to Archbishop Eugenio Thrilho."

Senhor Felipe de Barbosa stiffened. "Where's it?" he asked.

"In the servants' bedroom," I announced.

He hoisted me up by my shirt's collar and led me out of his bedroom towards the slaves' quarters. *Senhora* Fidelia de Barbosa, who was in the living room, was oblivious to the storm brewing under her nose. She had seen me held by the scruff of the neck. It wasn't a novelty for her. She paid little attention to us. Andreia, who was in the kitchen as *Senhor* Felipe de Barbosa dragged me towards my room, couldn't resist hurling one of her favorite insults at me.

"Fucking son of a bitch."

Senhor Felipe de Barbosa knocked down the door to the room I shared with other slaves and servants.

"Where's it?" he growled.

I bent on my knees, lifted the straw mattress on the bed frame, pulled the bed from the wall and freeing it from the headboard, I removed from a crevice the envelope that contained the original message without the two duplicates and handed it to *Senhor* Felipe de Barbosa. Hands shaking, he tore open the pouch and began reading the memo to himself, but with his lips moving. His knees buckled, and he sank to the floor when he finished. After a while, he pulled himself together, and looking at me, he asked, "Did you read the note?"

I nodded.

"Did you tell anyone about it?"

I shook my head. That was all he needed to know. He cared less about the fact that underneath my bed were several books that I had taken out of his library to read at night before going to sleep. Neither was he interested in finding out how and where I learned to read and why I had the audacity to help myself to books from his study. Erudition, it appeared, was not a celebration, as Josefina Ferreira hoped.

Chapter 5

Terreiro de Jesus, *Tomé de Sousa*, and *Castro de Alves*, three plazas, not too far from one another in the center of Salvador, bore landmarks no slave ever forgot. In each of them stood whipping posts where they flogged African slaves for various infractions and disciplinary purposes. The whipping of slaves, which took place every fortnight in these three plazas, known as *Pelourinho*—The Whipping Post—was a spectacle that brought out audiences. It was a fertile ground for Salvador's homeless kids to pick the pockets of both the rich and the poor. Tied to over twenty posts at any of these plazas, the frenzied crowd shouted, "*Chicoteá-los! Chicoteá-los! Chicoteá-los!*"—Whip them! Whip them! Whip them! The slaves writhed in pain as each of the long canes ripped through their bodies and opened flesh, oozing dark red blood. The spectacle was new to me, but *Pelourinho* was a well-known destination in Salvador. It was a veritable marketplace of violence and pain, a journey's end for those who experience unthinkable horror that would haunt them forever. *Pelourinho*, that unforgettable agora, remained implanted in the minds of those whose tortured bodies served as a diversion for many a Salvadoran.

This was the place, *Praça Tomé de Sousa*, where *Senhor* Felipe de Barbosa took me. My guilt? Lying about my ability to read and to write. In short, I lied about my pedantry. Of course, if they had caught me reading anything else besides the damned letter, the punishment for such a violation wouldn't have risen to the level calling for a visit to *Pelourinho*. The real offense, which *Senhor* Felipe de Barbosa failed to articulate, was that I knew the letter's contents and was privy to pernicious information. Josefina's panegyric of education and information came full circle; only in this case, it didn't come to emancipate but to castigate.

It was a splendid Saturday morning when *Senhor* Felipe de Barbosa, along with Andreia and all the servants, arrived at the *Praça Tomé de Sousa*. Ostensibly, my whipping was to serve as a warning to them. The bright blue cloudless sky, along with a brilliant sun, left pleasant shadows in its wake and offered the perfect backdrop to the whipping plaza. It rained the previous night, and muck and sludge covered the ground. Shops on *Praça Tomé de Sousa, Terreiro de Jesus, Castro de Alve*s *Rua do Saldanha, Rua do Obispo, Rua Guedes de Brito* and *Rua da Oração* did brisk business. Chaise-carts brimming with live chickens, pigs, and carcasses of butchered cows lined the way to *Praça da Sé*, three hundred yards from *Praça Tomé de Sousa*, our destination. Other merchants carted wares from the Lower City.

I shuddered at the sheer number of people whose feet thundered *Rua de São Francisco* and *Rua do Tijolo*. They shoved and screamed as we gradually made our way through *Rua da Misericordia*, a misnomer for a street that would have been best described as my *via dolorosa*, my desolate *via crucis*. The smells befuddled my senses: boiling *dênde* oil from *acarajé* stands, freshly caught fish on sale, animal carcasses, squalid bodies colonizing limited space. As we made our way to the center, Andreia put her arm on my shoulder. I looked at her, surprised at her gesture. She had tears in her eyes. She had become human, I thought.

"I'm so sorry. You don't deserve this," she said.

I didn't respond. I wasn't in the mood to help my tormentor atone for lapses committed by omission or design. The growing fear, tearing at my insides didn't allow me to be charitable, let alone to play the role of an expiator. How could one expect armistice when only one warring party declares hostilities?

Salvador's Civil Police were in full force to control people who whetted their appetites and feasted their eyes on a public flogging that offered them the illusion of settling scores that may have had nothing to do with their Pharisaic sensibilities. Paulo Alvarez de Andrade approached us as we got closer to the twenty posts. *Sen-*

hor Felipe de Barbosa took him aside and shared a few words with him. I wondered if he was part of the scheme to make me one of the day's major events for the crowd's entertainment. I doubted it. Led to a post like a dejected Christ, ready to shout, *Eloi, Eloi, lama sabachthani,*– "My God, My God, Why Hast Thou Forsaken Me?"–I heard a familiar voice. It was Trunk.

"I'm so sorry, Pedro de Barbosa. We're all very sorry," he said.

Sorry for what? I wondered. It occurred to me that Trunk may have thought they had caught me bringing them their daily bread and were being punished. How could he have known of my fool-proof methods, which had sustained our daily routine and arrangements? Bounded by a mob seeking unqualified vengeance for no infraction brought upon them, Trunk's voice served as a balm, a metaphorical Veronica wiping my face and soothing me on the way to my Calvary of *Pelourinho.*

The crowd was boisterous and cheerful. Several people whistled, hissed, whispered, or booed. Some took swigs of *cachaça* from flasks while others jostled for prime spots from which they could behold the spectacle yet to unfold before their eyes. By the time they tied me, along with the other slaves to our respective posts, the crowd's cheers, urging they flog us, had reached fever pitch, *Chicoteá-los! Chicoteá-los! Chicoteá-los!* they cried out. I reckoned cruelty and physical torture came readily to those who called for it if they didn't bear the pain. In my moment of panic, distress, and utter fear, I noticed two of the slaves, slated to be whipped, making hand signals to one another. Multiple slaves who had come to *Pelourinho* in a spirit of solidarity made similar signals: they lifted their fists in the air in defiance. I learned later this act meant more than resistance. Several of the slaves in the crowd lifted their fists. I didn't know wwhy, but I raised my fist in the air. In a split second, I felt solidarity and kinship with the oppressed and the downtrodden.

They unleashed the lashes in a fury. With indescribable searing pain coursing through my body, I lost count of the fifty lashes allowed. Although oblivious to its end, drifting in and out of unconsciousness, I remembered Golgotha and commended my spirit into the hands of that Father, if he even existed, who had forsaken me.

*****

"Welcome home, Mácula, welcome to the *Palácio*," said a soft voice. Unable to move, I lay on what passed for a bed made of wooden planks tied together with twine. My future home was underneath a large building recess, an incomplete warehouse twenty feet deep and ten feet wide on *Caminho Novo de Tabuão*. My nostrils trembled with the stench of a musty space that stunk of urine competing with other aromas exuding from the food that nearby vendors were preparing. The smells were persistent, pungent and in their combination, unfamiliar. The loud chorus that I had heard before everything went dark had melted away. I opened my eyes and saw blurry faces peering at me. Someone knelt beside me and attempted to lift my head to give me water.

"Don't touch me!" I shrieked, flailed my hands, and kicked as hard as I could. That didn't stop whoever tried to help me quench my thirst.

"You're safe now. Take a sip," said a voice.

The welcome effects of the water were soothing. *Pelourinho* slowly loomed large in my memory. Although my vision was still blurry, I remembered events of the morning, shuddering, and recollecting the first few lashes. I recalled being stripped from the waist up before the whipping. Still shirtless, I had on my blood-stained grey trousers. My shoes! A sigh of relief overcame me. Hidden in one of them was my insurance policy. I tried to stand up but couldn't.

"Slow, take it easy, Mácula," the voice said again. "You're hurt," it added.

"What happened? Where am I? Who are you, and why are you calling me Mácula?" I asked.

"A slave riot and rebellion began as soon as the whipping started," the voice began.

"Trunk?" I spoke.

"Yes, it's me. Before you could receive the fifty lashes, many slaves carrying torches appeared from nowhere. They came from both the Lower and Upper Cities, from *Rua Marcel Baixo*, *Rua de Laranjeiras*, and *Rua de São Francisco*, from *Ladeira do Farrao*, *Ladeira da*

Ordem 3a de São Francisco, and *Ladeira da Praça.* They threw the burning torches into the crowd. Everyone, including the Civil Police, ran. There was a lot of confusion. That was when we acted."

"What did you do?"

"We untied you from the whipping post and brought you here."

"So, that's why you said, Welcome home, Mácula."

"Yes," said Trunk.

"You know my name is Pedro de Barbosa. Right?"

"Yes."

"So, why call me Mácula?"

"Because, for us, you're no longer Pedro de Barbosa. You're now Mácula," Trunk said.

"Why?" I asked.

"You'll find out soon enough," said Trunk.

"A most stupid name," I said.

They burst into laughter.

"But it suits you," said Trunk.

Trunk was right. The name fitted me. Although the *mácula*—mole—beneath the left side of my eye grew with me, I hadn't paid it much attention. Now, it became my companion, a stamp making me stand out. Mácula became my nomenclature in the brotherhood, and it signified my baptism and investiture into the band. With a name, I shed my former identity and assumed a new one, enabling me to navigate the world of homelessness in which anonymity and subterfuge were vital ingredients not only for one's survival but to interact with the notorious Salvador Civil police and the city authorities. Mácula became one of the multiple tools in the toolbox of an imminent con man. As my vision cleared, I scanned the periphery. *Senhor* Felipe de Barbosa, the architect of the battered body which couldn't stand on legs, was nowhere in sight. There was no going back to São Bento, to *Senhor* Felipe de Barbosa's prison. With the many rootless kids populating Salvador's streets, parks, and alleyways, there was no way in hell he could ferret out his property and sell it to the highest bidder even if he tried. I was a freed slave. Or so I thought.

*****

In the weeks it took me to recover from my wounds, streets, alleyways, churches, and plazas in Salvador's Upper and Lower Cities became a canvass of sorts on which, like a painter, I could insert and extract myself at will, contemplating from within and from without, a world from which I had hitherto been exiled. With my freedom, a whole different space opened up before me, and I set to understand the difference between Salvador's Upper City and Lower City. I had spent most of the time trapped in *Senhor* Felipe de Barbosa's home in São de Bento, an area reserved for wealthy slave merchants and owners, landowners, white merchants, and government officials. Parts of the city were new to me: the Lower City, *Piedade* where the blacks lived, *Ladeira de Taboão*, Reconcavo, the waterfront, a place for the stevedores, freed slaves, tailors, bricklayers, petty traffickers, whores, and those who had little idea how the levers of power which controlled their lives worked. And so, I learned the internal dynamics of the Cabula gang.

As is typical of all gangs, they carved Salvador's inner center into turfs, each territory led by a leader. With fourteen boys whose ages ranged from eight to sixteen, the Cabula gang possessed an unwritten set of rules and code of conduct. No one snitched on another under any circumstances, regardless of the pain and torture by the Civil Police. Community members couldn't commit crimes against each other. Neither could they consume alcohol, especially the potent *cachaça*. They allowed smoking, and many crew members were prolific smokers who could inhale and keep the vapor in for a while before exhaling. *Senhor* Felipe de Barbosa and the men in his social class smoked, but no one of them did so with such finesse as ten-year-old Faustino the Chimney. With each puff, smoke rings swirled around his face. Eyes closed; the smoke patterns looked like strings of blue floating orbs that dangled from an invisible dowel. It was easy for the Cabula members to live under the laws of the clan. With no one having any family, the band provided an identity and a sense of belonging. In return, we offered it our loyalty. Bonding came to boys never nurtured by their parents, assuming they even remembered them. Trust among us was as crucial as were our suspicions of everybody else's intentions. That included *Sóror*

Magarida Pinheiro and *Sóror* Luana Sarmento, the two nuns from the *Igreja e Convento da Lapa* who brought us pastries, fruits, and other delectables every Friday morning.

The gang welcomed the food that the nuns delivered, but no one was ready to cozy with them and to listen to their gospel or whatever message they had for us. Ours was a business transaction. We needed food; they wanted to satisfy their call to serve the needy. Despite our reluctance, they always had us say the Lord's prayer before eating. Afterwards, they subjected us to a few scriptures. Most of the time, we sat, pretending to pay attention while suffering the innocuous claptrap of a homily.

But it was a different story when *Sóror* Mariana Campos, a twenty-year-old nun who accompanied the two older nuns, led the discussions. She was slim, with a sharp and well-made nose. Despite the veil and the coif over her hair, one could easily discern the immaculate crown of blonde hair that framed her thin face. Despite her loose-fitting habit, the attentive eyes, and imaginative minds of young boys on course to cavort with whatever that makes them tick at this age, could still detect or imagine, perhaps, her delicate breasts, flat stomach, well-sculpted hips, and legs. It was a sound, ripened, and complete body, and we limited our interest in whatever she had to say only to that body.

"Today, we'll talk about the Eight Beatitudes," *Sóror* Mariana Campos said during one visit. "Who's heard the Eight Beatitudes?" she asked.

"Isn't it what that street hustler told those homeless urchins such as us on an anthill?" I spoke. *Sóror* Mariana Campos laughed out loud, revealing a set of perfect white teeth in a well-defined mouth. *Sóror* Magarida Pinheiro and *Sóror* Luana Sarmento had a stern look on their faces. The younger nun stopped laughing when she noticed her superiors' sterile gazes. She cleared her throat and said, "Eh, yes. But Jesus wasn't a street hustler. And the anthill was a mount."

"What's different from what Pedro said and what you just mentioned? It was a man talking to children as though they were imbeciles," said Brute, not reputed for subtlety.

"Well, whatever the case, it doesn't matter. Let's discuss one of the Eight Beatitudes," *Sóror* Mariana Campos said.

"Why don't we discuss the third?" I asked.

"Oh? You know the Beatitudes?" The nun asked, cocking her head.

I rolled my eyes.

"Blessed are the meek, for they shall inherit the earth," I said, remembering exactly the order of the other seven.

"Bravo!" shouted *Sóror* Mariana Campos and the other nuns. I was unimpressed with the applause.

"Show off," mumbled Aleixo Spinner, a fourteen-year-old lanky boy who talked about wanting to do with *Sóror* Mariana Campos what his stepfather used to do with a neighbor when his mother went to the market. Aleixo Spinner was a spinner of tall tales, and no one believed him. It was common knowledge that he had no father or stepfather.

"You think she will show you her twat because you're smart?" Aleixo Spinner whispered into my ear.

I ignored him.

"So, what did Jesus mean by that?" *Sóror* Mariana Campos asked, her enthusiasm overcoming her. She mistook our rapt attention as our contemplation of the Beatitude when, in reality, it was the individual private fantasies of a different beatitude, a rapture, the bliss of being alone with her and doing with her what Aleixo Spinner's stepfather used to do with his neighbor when his wife went to the market. Brute punctured our secret fancies.

"This is the weirdest thing that your street hustler ever declared," said Brute.

"Because?" *Sóror* Mariana Campos asked, ignoring the pernicious label.

"Why haven't we succeeded on the earth? Why don't we have any place to go? Why must we beg, steal, and lie to survive? If you ask me, it is the strong who've taken over the good things in Salvador da Bahía, the earth," said Brute.

"Well," *Sóror* Mariana Campos began with uncertainty. "You're looking at it too literally," she said.

"Oh? How so?" A boy demanded.

There was silence.

"Brute, the Bible says one thing, but the priests and nuns say something completely different altogether. That way, they can pretend they're saving us." I stated.

The older *Sóror* Magarida Pinheiro intervened. "That's not true. It's a question of interpretation. In the third Beatitude, for instance, the word 'meek' does not mean weak, but gentle, docile, and submissive. So, even though the rich may get the good things in Salvador da Bahía, it is the gentle that will win Christ," *Sóror* Magarida Pinheiro said, with a faint beatific smile on her face.

"Best horseshit I've heard in a while," Trunk announced. "So, *Sóror*, are you saying that we should be submissive while the rich and powerful fuck us from behind, hoping we'll see your bloody street hustler after we die?" Trunk asked.

The three sisters made the sign of the cross, got up, and headed out of our *Palácio's* open gates from where we, the very experienced meek of the earth, were staunch cynics of an allegorical future earth designed by the roadway hustler for the docile. It was the last time that we saw the sisters. We missed their food. Some missed *Sóror* Mariana Campos more. But that came with the territory. Out of necessity, the Cabula boys had no choice but to be a tough bunch. The tacit set of rules and code of conduct defined a tribe that circumstances had forced to coalesce around the most basic human need: survival. Under these factors, the clan wasn't about to embrace even the most honest overtures from those who didn't belong.

Chapter 6

Each member of the group carved out a place in the *Palácio* where he slept and kept whatever he had. I must acknowledge that the Cabula gang had chosen their location well. *Caminho Novo de Tabuão* led one to the *Igreja Nossa Senhora dos Rosário dos Pretos* and *Largo Pelourinho*. From the *Palácio*, one could navigate the Upper and Lower Cities without having to contend with the steep gradient that separated both places from *Praça da Sé* and the waterfront. From their abode, the urchins could scale the hill above their dwelling and arrive at *Rua Ribeiro Dos Santos* or slide to the *Rua de Julião* and its many alleyways, an excruciating effort for the Civil Police or anyone else not used to living under the constant threat of being accosted.

In the *Palácio*, Trunk occupied the middle of the top platform deep in the recess. Brute and Runner, his deputies, shared this place of honor with him. From the raised platform, the triumvirate contemplated the masses. I learned later that the plain harmony among the troika hadn't always been the case. The gang's leader had been Brute until Trunk appeared on the scene. Brute used to have the last word on gang membership. Born in Salvador, Trunk knew the city as the back of his hand—the tenements, the streets, the churches, the waterfront—and had been in the Raposa gang led by Rafael Texeira. The clan leader had kicked out Trunk, although he had a knack for identifying unoccupied homes during the day for pillage. During a dispute with Rafael Texeira, Trunk had called the gang leader's mother a fat whore. To add insult to injury, Trunk said, although a whore, Rafael Texeira's mother wasn't very good at it because, when he, Trunk, had slept with her, it felt as though he was making love to a lifeless *peixe-boi*—a manatee.

Trunk felt as though the only way to prevent a reoccurrence of his experience with the Raposa gang was to become the leader of Brute's gang. Runner had introduced him to the group after he had met him in *Praça da Piedade* when both of them went tailing a few black street boys who were peddling for a candy maker, *pamonha,* a corn and milk paste wrapped in a corn husk and boiled and *pé-de-moleque,* coconut milk square-shaped sweet made with peanuts and sugar caramel. Trunk and Runner picked the same victim, stealing the sweets and dashing away in the same direction. Brute was disinterested in the newcomer, but Runner persuaded him to give Trunk a chance. The latecomer's prodigious knowledge of the Bahian city landscape and his propensity to choose freely where the band could strike soon earned Trunk friends and a place in the clan. Brute didn't take too kindly to it when Trunk suggested no single person should be in charge of deciding who joined the band.

"Who the fuck do you think you're to change the rules?" Brute asked Trunk with clenched jaws.

"Who set up the regulations?" Trunk demanded.

"*Vá se foder, filho de uma puta*—Go screw yourself, you son of a bitch—. I set up the rules and, if you don't like it, *vai tomar no cu*—you can kiss my ass," replied Brute.

"Well, I don't kiss nobody's ass, not of a *bicha*—faggot," declared Trunk.

"Ooooooh," the street imps replied in unison.

Now, there was a reason they called him Brute. The only way he settled any score, even minor, was through downright force. Anyone in his shoes would have considered his chances against the fifteen-year-old Trunk, who had a massive chest and muscular arms which protested whatever tattered shirt he wore, not to mention those thick husky thighs resting on robust legs. Perhaps Brute would have been circumspect under other conditions, but, in his world, calling someone a faggot in front of other people was not only the worst of insults but a challenge to his manhood, his dignity, and his leadership. He had no other choice than to jump on Trunk. It was violent, fast, and abrupt. By the time it ended, battered, bruised, and sore combatants lay on the ground. Brute compensated for his lack of build with a tenacity which surprised Trunk, which gained his respect. Runner announced the fight a draw. Instead of one leader, he proposed two: Trunk and Brute. The group applauded in agreement.

"No," said Brute. "We need a leader who's got the nose of a bloodhound to sniff out fortunes to be looted. Trunk is the person," replied Brute.

"And you and Runner will be my assistants. Agreed?" asked Trunk.

This was how Trunk became the head of the group, which he named Cabula, after his birthplace. And this was why he, Brute, and Runner occupied the place of honor, the most prominent place in my new palace: the raised platform.

*****

It appeared as though every tribe member had a particular gift that they brought to the fraternity of urchins. Trunk and Brute were Cabula's brawn for using pure force to rob. Runner was the fastest fourteen-year-old I had ever encountered. His role was to run with whatever the band stole from stores, markets, and any establishment that provided us with food. Lighthouse, a short, fat, and boisterous biracial born in the backcountry, found his way to Salvador by hiding in a sloop carrying fruits and vegetables from Cachoeira on the Paraguaçu River to Salvador. He had the natural gift of seeing before anybody else when the Civil Police came raiding or when the owner of a home or a business being robbed approached his property. Ten-year-old Cutpurse did magic with his hands. He could pick the pocket of the clueless visitor and the savvy city-dweller. No sacred cows existed in his world of pilferage after he swiped the badge of a Civil Police officer who had arrived at a scene to break up a fight between two drunk Portuguese sailors. Behind his back, they called him Six Fingers because of the small, stunted growth of a finger on each side of his pinkies. He could take on anyone, irrespective of his age and size, who referred to him by that nickname. It didn't matter that he got pummeled several times. Perhaps he hated that identity because his dad abandoned him and his mom after he was born with the tiny sixth finger. A firm believer in Yoruba tradition, his dad thought a child with those fingers was nothing but a curse. It was him or his infant child; he told his wife. Cutpurse's mom called her husband an aged fool who believed in primitive superstitions. She was a strong Candomblé practitioner who reckoned that her son's tutelary *orixa* guided and protected him. With one parent gone and his mom dead when he was seven, Cutpurse became a street waif. Aside from his thieving endowments, his smooth dexterity played well. He talked himself and his band members out of trouble with the police several times. In other instances, his tongue landed him and others in tight corners.

With these individual talents, I learned the requisite strategies for survival in an environment where everything and every moment were fluid and unpredictable. In stealing food from street food dealers, for instance, we used a very simple tactic. A young crew member approached one of the many road food vendors who sold foods such as *acarajé, cocada*—coconut candy, tapioca, *coxinha*, a fried breaded pie, presented in the shape of a teardrop and filled with chicken and cheese or just chicken, *esfiha*, a breaded pie stuffed with cheese, chicken, or peas. Having ordered and accepted what he wanted, the hawker watched in dismay as the youth runs elsewhere. The uninitiated merchant and we had several of them with whom to negotiate, gave chase, leaving his stall, the rearguard, open to assault. Other team members wasted no time to feast and escape with as much food as possible. It wasn't as if the other vendors and merchants in the neighborhood where our band carved out its territory were silent in the face of our transgressions. It was the sheer novelty, the scrupulous nature, and the precision with which we committed these petty breaches that left them too dumbfounded and unhinged to offer a collective response or resistance.

We fell back on a more reliable source of income when pilfering food from vendors in both the Upper and Lower Cities did not produce enough to keep us fed. It was from articles we stole from houses and traded to Antonio Allegretto. He was an Argentinian gigolo and con man who had a network through which he peddled stolen jewelry and rare properties to wealthy clients. We supplied the valuables he needed with efficiency. It started first with Trunk identifying a house capable of producing a good yield. It did not matter if maids were in these homes. We had an effective way of dealing with them. Dreamer knocked on the front door. When the maids opened it, they usually encountered the street boy at their doorstep wailing and writhing in pain. The sight was heartrending for maids cloistered in these privileged homes. Unsure of what to do, these conned damsels knelt beside the dying Dreamer, who only ratcheted up his wails. At that point, Trunk and Brute, with Runner in tow, either scaled the walls or the opened windows. Lighthouse acted his part, standing away from the house, his eyes flashing as though they were navigational beacons, performing the most crucial task of warning his comrades of any impending danger. Selective in their taste, Trunk and Brute chose the best homes and escaped with jewels and fashionable clothing, including women's underthings that the older boys kept under their pillows.

As I became an integral part of the gang, I wondered what I could bring to the group. It appeared everyone contributed something noteworthy except for me and *Pensador*—Thinker, a tall white boy with matted, tangled hair and brown eyes who wore spectacles. They named him Thinker because they thought he could read and write, although nobody had ever seen him do so. He had in his possession a book with tattered covers. That was enough to earn him his moniker. He was a loner who muttered to himself during the day and in his sleep. Nobody bothered him because it was an accepted fact that even the youngest clan member could beat him up in a fight. Thinker provided me with a way to contribute to Cabula.

It was midnight. The sky was clear, and it was a full moon. The church bells that announced vespers were silent now, and the troop members were in the house, except for Thinker who sauntered in and made for his place between Cutpurse and Lighthouse, who had just finished his duty of standing guard in front of the alleyway looking out for any potential police swoops or the trespassing of our property by other gangs in the neighborhood.

"So, Thinker, where have you been?" Cutpurse asked as Thinker sat in his spot.

"I've been admiring from *Praça Tomé de Sousa* the moon's reflection on the Bay of All Saints and the shadows in the Lower City. I saw the ship dock, the ships, and stevedores working late at night. The sight is spectacular," said Thinker.

"Yes. But you can see everything from here. Can't you?" asked Cutpurse.

"Sure. But the place is more splendid from *Praça Tomé de Sousa,*" said Thinker.

"You must love the City of the Saints very much. Don't you?" Cutpurse asked.

"Who wouldn't? It's the most marvelous city in Brazil," he said.

"And you've visited a lot of cities in Brazil. Right?" Cutpurse asked, giggling.

"No. But I know," said Thinker.

"Is that what your book says?" asked Cutpurse.

"What do you mean?" asked Thinker.

"Did your book say Salvador is Brazil's most beautiful city?" asked Cutpurse.

"I don't know," said Thinker.

"What do you mean by you don't know? Aren't you Thinker? Nobody here knows how to read and write except you. Right?" asked Cutpurse.

Thinker shrugged.

"Man, I'm sleepy. I need to get some sleep," he declared, kneeling beside his wooden planks, and removing his eyeglasses.

"I think he is a faggot. He's too effeminate not to be one. I shouldn't probably sleep close to him." Cutpurse whispered to Lighthouse. Or at least that was what he thought.

"Oh, don't bother Thinker. He says he's tired," I said.

"Maybe he is. Maybe he's not," said Cutpurse.

"Thinker, can I borrow your book?" I asked.

He hesitated.

"C'mon, Thinker, I'll give it back after I've read a few pages," I said.

"OK," he said haltingly.

With the light from a nearby oil lamp, I opened the book. It was a volume of poetry titled *Marília de Dirceu* by Tomás Antônio Gonzaga. I opened a page and read aloud a stanza from *Lira XIII*:

Who knows what destiny holds?
Yet, my beautiful one, today it imprisons me.
But how can I defend myself from its dangers in this and in others?
It might still be a bright day
But whether I adore you or not, I know I adore Heaven
And I kiss the holy hand that guides me to it.

There was silence. I read aloud a few more stanzas. The more poems I read, the more it became clear they were amorous verses Tomás Antônio Gonzaga wrote as a romantic tribute to Marília, his muse. As I read the sonnets, their warmth and gracefulness evoked feelings ranging from a sensual want to a longing for affection that, in its raw form, was an unadulterated yearning for love. The group soon established an evening ritual. I would ask Thinker for the book, which he reluctantly handed over. I read aloud poems I thought exciting. But one evening, Thinker didn't produce his intimate object, which had become our source of diversion and individual reflection for members.

"Where's the book, Thinker?" I asked.

"I don't know," he replied.

"What the fuck do you mean by you don't know?" asked Trunk, who had considered Marília his own and private object of desire.

"I've lost it," Thinker said.

"You've lost it? How can you just lose it?" Cutpurse demanded.

"I don't know," he said.

"The fucking *hijo de uma puta* says he doesn't know," Trunk said. "Can you believe that?"

"Man, I ain't going to sleep without hearing something read to me," stated Brute.

"Here," replied Cutpurse as he removed a newspaper from under what passed for his pillow of crumpled sheet and fabric stuffed into the body of a shirt. He had stolen it from the corner bookstore on *Rua Agostinho*. He threw it at Thinker. "Read us anything from the newspaper. I don't care what it is," he said.

There was silence.

"That thing about knowing how to read? I think Thinker has been lying all along. He wants to appear intellectual, so he doesn't have to go out with the gang to steal food," Lighthouse said. "And he ain't a good beggar either. Wonder what the fuck Brute saw in him," he added.

"Thinker," Cutpurse called.

"What?" Thinker replied.

"Lighthouse here suggests you're a liar. He maintains you couldn't read even if your life depended on it because you're blind in one eye," added Cutpurse.

"I didn't say that." Lighthouse protested.

"Of course, I can," declared Thinker.

"Oh yeah? Then read the damn newspaper," said Trunk.

We all gathered around Thinker. I sat behind him. Thinker had no other choice than to open the *Correio da Bahia*, Salvador's most prominent daily. His hands shook as he held up the paper to the yellow light from the nearest candle. He was perspiring. There was a long pause. Thinker couldn't read! As the entire group waited, I saw a section of the paper's column for stories.

"Rafael Vieyra," I shouted with excitement. I had read his works from a book I stole from *Senhor* Felipe Barbosa's library.

"What, who?" asked a confused Lighthouse.

"He's the best short story writer in Salvador. Here's one," I announced, snatching the paper from Thinker.

The day's drama discussed love's illusiveness and the futility of its attainment despite imminent failure. The story and those I read to the group every evening from purloined newspapers transported us to a fantasy world where we didn't have to grapple with the here and now. These were worlds where we could imagine ourselves as heroes who fought evil and injustice. We found archetypes we could root for, even if the author was sadistic enough to kill off our sweet and innocent beloved characters. But as readers of good literature know, at the end of the literary voyage, one comes back to shore, to a landscape where reality trumps the imaginary.

For the tribe, that real world was the news and rumors we had heard regarding what the city authorities had planned to do with its many street urchins. We had discounted those rumors even when we learned that the police had arrested four of the Raposa team members weeks ago. If the story series in *Correio da Bahia* hadn't absorbed us, we would have seen letters citizens wrote to the editor complaining about problems afflicting the capital. A reprinted news item wouldn't have escaped us.

"*Puta merda*," I blurted after I read it.

"What?" many voices demanded.

"*Livrando-se dos ouriços da cidade de Salvador*"—Ridding Salvador City of its Urchins" I read the caption.

"How? Why? Where are we to go?" cried Dreamer, the youngest boy in the gang who dreamed of becoming a ship captain one day. He burst into tears. "Where shall we go? How can we abandon the *Palácio*?" he asked.

"Oh! stop it," shouted Brute. "Let Mácula continue reading," he said.

I read.

> *At Salvador City Council's monthly meeting, the governor, the law enforcement chief, and aldermen concluded street urchins have infested the capital and are now a nuisance. The Council approved a new ordinance to deal with what the force chief has described as a pandemic. "We will lock up any homeless boy caught stealing or harassing Salvador's good citizens."*

Silence fell on the group. Our survival was at stake. Under siege were those effective methods which gave us daily bread. *Correio da Bahia*'s news couldn't have come at a worse time. We had noticed a gradual decline in our fortunes. Gone were the days when honest work like carrying luggage for travelers, begging, pickpocketing, stealing from drunken sailors, and holding up clueless visitors from the backcountry offered enough resources to feed ourselves. Empty stomachs often accompanied sleepless nights. Worse so, the Salvadoran police had picked up Antonio Allegretto a month earlier. The police claimed to have released him unharmed. Yet when his dead body turned up at the docks, it was full of bruises and broken bones. We learned later that they had caught him in bed with the wife of an unnamed prominent alderman who bought stolen items from the Argentinian playboy. It appeared as though Antonio Allegretto sold more than his refined merchandise. He traded love to married women whose husbands' tools no longer stood erect, despite all the cajoling in the world that their wives could muster to entice that limp member that was once active and recalcitrant during its heydays. The alderman didn't take to the fact that someone else was digging deep into a crotch that he could only contemplate because he lacked the strength and capacity to harvest that beckoning ripe pink fruit.

The news in *Correio da Bahia* had thrown a crimp into our very existence. As if that wasn't bad enough, Cutpurse and I had the misfortune of running into Rafael Texeira and four of his crew members on our way to visit Sinha Olinda, *mãe-de-santo*—mother of the saint—Candomblé priestess, and her altar in the Liberdade neighborhood. It was a meeting that distressed further the Cabula clan. Cutpurse often went to see the priestess, who he said reminded him of his mom, a believer in the Candomblé religion and its rituals. I accompanied him once out of curiosity and because no one in the gang wanted to go with him.

"Welcome, my dear son," Sinha Olinda announced the first time Cutpurse, and I entered her home. Her *filha-de-santo* who performed the ritual events and incarnate the *orixas* when in trance surrounded the *mãe-de-santo*.

"I see you've grown a bit since I last saw you. How're you, my son?" Sinha Olinda asked. She was medium height, thin, and had an air about her that demanded subservience in her presence. She wore her traditional Bahian dress with unparalleled finesse, and beneath her jovial face was a kindness.

"I'm fine, Sinha Olinda," Cutpurse replied. "This is my friend, Mácula. He joined us recently."

"Welcome, my son. I'm sorry you've had to endure so many hardships in your brief life," the *mãe-de-santo* said, extending her thin fingers out and touching me gently on the face. "But your *orixá* will never abandon you," she added.

How did she learn that my story of condemnation and ruination began the very day I was born into slavery? I wondered and discarded that question. Wasn't it our lot as blacks, whether or not enslaved? She must have been referring to life as a street urchin, I thought. Who in Salvador hadn't seen the many homeless boys who populated the alleyways, the markets, the waterfront in *Cidade Baixa*, the *plaças* in *Cidade Alta*, the very limits and delimits of that City of Saints which the wealthy had inherited with glee and aplomb?

Cutpurse withdrew a small pendant of colorful stone from his pocket, put it around his collar, and knelt before Sinha Olinda. I didn't realize he carried such an object with him and why. In a serene voice, the *mãe-de-santo* broke into a song accompanied by her *filha-de-santo*. As they did so, Sinha Olinda took the pendant from Cutpurse's neck and bathed it with sacred herbs. She had consecrated it, and, by that act, the jewelry and stone had shared in the *axé*, the force of nature adept at transmuting reality and ordering human existence as it integrates the practitioner into a cyclical world system. Somehow, whenever Cutpurse visited Sinha Olinda and returned to the *Palácio*, his dexterity at pilferage took a nosedive, which meant that we couldn't count on the artist whose fine job brought resources with which we could feed ourselves. Was that why nobody went with him? On this our second visit, I had wished to ask Sinha Olinda a few questions about Candomblé and how it related to the Catholic religion in which they steeped me, thanks to Marcelo Resendes and Father Fernando Santos Candido. But that was not to be because Rafael Texeira stopped us from making our way to *Ladeira da Soledade*, Sinha Olinda's neighborhood.

"Well, well, well. See who we've got here. None other than the legendary Cutpurse," Rafael Texeira said as his four followers surrounded us. "Where are you going? To snitch another police badge?" he asked.

Cutpurse looked confused. How did Rafael Texeira learn of the badge? How did he discover he had pinched it from a police officer? That the Salvador law enforcement hadn't come knocking meant Rafael Texeira had kept the tacit code among the gangs in the city not to share knowledge about one another with the force.

"Ah! I see you're rattled. Eh?" Rafael Texeira said. "Why don't you leave your band of hoodlums and join my group? We could use your unique gifts better," he added.

"Working with honest thugs often takes away my appetite. I'm still a growing lad, you realize," said Cutpurse.

"You're a are fucking smart-ass. I'll let this insult slide. But tell that son-of-a-bitch leader of yours that we'll soon exact our pound-of-flesh. It will be on our own terms, time, and place of our choosing, and when he least expects it," said Rafael Texeira.

"How can you exact a pound of flesh from someone who's not as fat and as lifeless as a *peixe-boi*? Cutpurse asked.

"*Puta merda*," Cutpurse will get us killed, I told myself. The sharp-tongued boy didn't even bother to find out what injury Trunk and, by extension, the Cabula gang had caused Rafael Texeira and his group and why they were seeking retribution. Armed with that knowledge, we could prepare our defenses. No, Cutpurse was more interested in flaunting his sarcasm and wit.

"Oh! Cutpurse, you incorrigible know-it-all!" I repeated to myself.

From his rejoinder, Rafael Texeira knew that the tale about Trunk and his mom was in the public domain. It didn't matter whether it was true. It was obvious individuals had consumed and regurgitated the story, giving birth to a new anecdote about his whoring parent that no self-respecting boy would tolerate. Rafael Texeira was smart enough to know that Trunk had provided us with the details of his expulsion from the Raposa gang. But to have gone into the niceties of his mother's size and her profession? It was altogether another story, and the irascible Rafael Texeira, king of the shiv, would not let this slide.

"Come again, Cutpurse. What did you say about my mom, *bundão*—punk?" Rafael Texeira asked, his eyes blazing.

"I don't reckon referring to your mom. Did I? Although I've never met her, I can state with certainty that by your handsome looks, you must've come from a splendid stock that bears no resemblance to a *peixe-boi*," Cutpurse said.

It appeared as though the mere mention of the word *peixe-boi* triggered in Rafael Texeira repressed fury because, in no time, he lunged at Cutpurse. He got to him before Zé Cantarelli, his right-hand man, stopped him.

"Leave him to me," said Zé Cantarelli. Tall, thin, light-skinned, and freckled, the fourteen-year-old Zé Cantarelli felt no pain, irrespective of its source. With a penchant to hunt stray dogs and cats and to skin them alive while being bitten, but with no clear malaise, Zé Cantarelli was someone to avoid at all costs. If he couldn't feel pain, he could dispense it with reckless abandonment.

"No, Zé. This one is mine. This is personal," Rafael Texeira said, pulling a sharp knife out of his back pocket.

Events unfolded at a lightning pace. We needed intervention to prevent a predictable outcome: Cutpurse filleted, and I? Who knew what?

"And that pound of flesh? The one you said you'd be getting on your own terms, date, and place of your choosing? Isn't that more important than this emaciated, scraggly, and scrawny thing in front of you?" I suggested, attempting to buy time to stave off what I thought was inevitable.

"You must think of someone else. I don't fit that description," replied Cutpurse, who, despite his protestations, matched that portrait to the letter.

"Yeah," Rafael Texeira declared, smiling. "I'll cut two pounds of flesh. First, this foul-mouthed asshole's and, second, your gang leader's for snitching on four of our members who've been in law enforcement custody," he continued.

"Ah," I told myself. That was what this pound of flesh thing was all about. I burst into laughter, contemplating how ridiculous was the proposition.

"What the hell's so funny?" asked Rafael Texeira.

Before I could respond, Zé Cantarelli was all over me. Punches came from everywhere, landing on my face, my rib cage, and on my stomach.

"This is to teach you how and when to laugh," he responded.

"Hey, what's that in your hand, and why did you do that to this *parceiro*—buddy?"

We all turned around to look at Antonio Guimarães and froze. For the Salvador Civil Police, he was a freed slave, a rabble-rouser who bought slaves from white slavers and set them free, a man who almost all of Salvador's *mães-de-santo* and *filhas-de-santo* respected because he would do anything to protect their *terreiros*—temples. Young black men in *Cidade Baixa* who practiced *capoeira*, revered Antonio Guimarães. Not only was he one of the best *capoeira* fighters, but he also had a place where slaves could learn this unique martial art form after they had put in several hours working either for their slave masters or for themselves to pay their owners any money that they made.

"You'll get nowhere with that stupid blade of yours," Antonio Guimarães said, looking at Rafael Texeira, who still had the weapon in his raised hand, as if suspended in time.

"Real men do not pick on kids younger than them, and especially if they are street boys like you," Antonio Guimarães stated.

"I know who you're, and I don't give a fuck. Don't put your nose in other people's business," Rafael Texeira said.

"Son, you might be biting off more than you can chew. I'll ask you again. Put away that knife of yours and scuttle," Antonio Guimarães spoke calmly.

Rafael Texeira made for Antonio Guimarães, but Zé Cantarelli stopped him.

"Let's make a run for it. Tomorrow will be another day," Zé Cantarelli whispered.

"Cutpurse, we're not done with you and your band of wimps," Rafael Texeira said as he and his followers walked away.

*****

Rafael Texeira fulfilled his promise one week after we met him and his crew. I was bent over from the blows I had sustained from Zé Cantarelli when Cutpurse and I returned to our alleyway. A few gang members reacted as they repeatedly did if someone went out alone and got pummeled.

"Hey, Mácula, did your girlfriend do that to you? I bet you wanted a piece of her, and she didn't because you stank," asked the eleven-year-old urchin, el Dobradinha. He earned his nickname for unrestrained love of quintessential Brazilian stew made with the intestines of cows, sheep, or pigs.

Several boys laughed.

"Oh, shut up, Dobradinha," said Cutpurse. "We run into Rafael Texeira and Zé Cantarelli on our way to visit Sinha Olinda. Mácula couldn't help calling Rafael Texeira's mother a *peixe-boi*," Cutpurse said, winking at me.

Laughter filled the space.

"Fuck you, Cutpurse!" I cried out.

"Well, Mácula didn't. I did. Indirectly," said Cutpurse.

"If Mácula's girlfriend didn't attack his *colhões*, how come the hunch?" Brute inquired.

Yet again, laughter rang through the Palácio.

"Zé Cantarelli wanted to find out if Mácula could join the club of the pain resistors," said Cutpurse.

"Can you cut the fuck out and tell us what the hell happened?" Trunk asked. His mood always soured when Rafael Texeira's name came up in a conversation.

I told the group what Rafael Texeira had said about wanting to avenge our snitching on his four gang members. Everyone laughed at the thought.

"*Bicha* lost his marbles the very day I left that lousy gang," said Trunk.

"And his dick," Brute added, eliciting more laughter.

I didn't laugh. Our meeting with Rafael Texeira and his four deputies unsettled me. Yet I couldn't find words to express it. I became restless, as though I expected something ominous to transpire. The calm before the storm? Then it happened. We settled for the night on one of those hot Saturday evenings. I had read a short story from *Correio da Bahia* to the group. As usual, Dreamer wanted me to invent stories, as I often did, after finishing those from the newspaper. The world of fantasy suited him just fine. He relished it more than any other person.

"No, Dreamer. It's late, and I'm tired," I said at the end of a story recounting misplaced revenge. Similar retribution fell on us a few hours later: our home became an inferno. Our assailants threw several burning torches into the *Palácio*. In no time, fire and smoke filled the space. Pandemonium became the logical call to action as everyone made for the entrance. But several obstacles blocked the recess. Trunk and Brute got out first. They did their best to remove the barricade. That singular effort saved all of us except for Thinker. We wondered whether, instead of rushing out, he had been looking for his glasses and his book.

Thinker's death shook me to the core more than anybody else. I had developed a special relationship with him after I discovered he couldn't read or write. I could have announced to the entire group that he did not differ from them: an illiterate. The repercussions wouldn't have been too dire. But no one in his right mind would have wanted to be the butt of jokes and mockery, especially at the hands of Cutpurse and his small band of followers who tormented gang members with pranks and caustic jokes.

"Thanks for not telling on me," Thinker had said to me the following morning as I was setting out for the Lower City.

"What do I get?" I asked him. The question opened a door, a threshold I was crossing with no hope of return. I entered a world where charity would become a foreign concept. Everything would have a price. I was on course to exact the greatest advantage from everyone and from every situation. It was a door to a world where conning was second nature, including other virtues heading to the realm of *senhorhood*.

"I don't know," Thinker responded.

"What's the most valuable thing you cannot afford to lose?" I urged.

"I don't have any idea. Nothing comes to mind," Thinker said.

"You're going to give me every *réis* you get, beginning today. I don't care how much, how, or where you got it. You'll regret it if you don't," I said.

"Okay, but how long will this take?" Thinker asked.

"Until I'm satisfied," I said, setting the course towards the bondage of the other.

The hapless Thinker, who wasn't a good thinker, agreed. But he did so under one condition: that I taught him how to read and to write without the others in the group knowing. Thus, was a short-lived relationship between the boy who passed for the group's intellectual and I, an emergent con artist, who cut his teeth into a field in which guile and other attributes were indispensable.

Fury, disconsolation, and revenge consumed the Cabula gang. There was no point or wherewithal to mourn Thinker's death. In this landscape, no one had space to process emotions. After they had removed his body, we did what we could to bring the *Palácio* back to its original grandeur. It was our home. Besides, there was nowhere else to go. In this, our abode, we never thought about the heat, humidity, and the smell of bodies that hadn't communed with soap or water in weeks, if not in months. Any point in the Upper City, such as *Terreiro de Jesus* or *Tomé de Sousa*, was sufficient. The exhilarating breeze, from the evening to midnight, served as a balsam that metaphorically cleansed us of our sweat, smell, and grime and cooled our bodies as we returned to our *Palácio*. A location cloistered underneath a building that trapped heat during the day and unleashed it at night.

Dreamer refused to sleep where he used to sleep, next to Thinker. Cutpurse visited Sinha Olinda, who gave him purified rosewater, along with several herbs he spread around the *Palácio*. It kept Thinker's spirit away and sanctified the space, he said. The triumvirate kept to themselves, often whispering. All of us knew who attacked us. Rafael Texeira had warned us, but we hadn't paid heed. How could the gang have believed his preposterous accusations? None of the many Salvador street gangs dreamed of collaborating with the police. Why did the Raposa tribe think we were architects of what had befallen their comrades? I wondered about plans Trunk, Brute, and Runner hatched. I felt whatever schemes they contrived would be rash, not well thought through. Trunk and his brothers weren't the strategic types. As the intermediary reader of authors, narrators, and texts that the Cabula street boys consumed, I understood that although they were street smart, the leaders and most of the group members lacked any sense of reflection, foresight, and planning. I wanted to usurp the Cabula leadership and dictate the wellbeing of the gang members as I saw fit. Attaining power like the fellows I observed in *Senhor* Felipe de Barbosa's home and determining the fate of others were jelling. I felt an opportunity that I couldn't let go.

"When someone messes with you, make sure you pay him back twice the injury that he inflicted on you," I said as I approached our three leaders who had separated themselves from the group and been sitting on a bench in *Praça da Piedade*. A Candomblé procession was going on, and we couldn't miss the opportunity to rob even the most devoted. Sacrilege was an alien idea for us. Heck, a week earlier, we had broken into a few churches to steal small religious reliquaries that unscrupulous antique dealers and collectors of such art form bought at a handsome price.

"What do you mean, Mácula?" Trunk asked.

"*Correio da Bahia* published accounts of the fire and Thinker's death. The article's writer concluded that Thinker's death meant there was one less street scamp in Salvador, which he thought was good for the city. Can you imagine that?" I asked. The newspaper had reported no such thing. Why would it? More important things had to be covered. Thinker's death, and the inferno that nearly sent us to the other side as Thinker, weren't among them.

"So? I don't get it. Does reporting the incident have anything to do with payback?" Runner asked.

Either he was too dumb to connect the dots between what I said and the newspaper article, or Runner played the idiot to get me off their game. I weighed both possibilities and concluded the former was the case.

"I don't know what you three are planning. You're itching to do something, and it's what happened to us. Right? I asked.

"Yes, and no. If it's yes, it will be big," said Brute.

"What's it?" I asked.

"You'll know when it happens," said Trunk.

"Don't you think you should share your plan? After all, whatever happens, will affect us all. No?" I shot back.

"We don't have to. There's a reason we are leaders," declared Trunk.

"I mean no disrespect, but I have been thinking about an action to hit Rafael Texeira and his Raposa band. They will learn never to mess with us again," I responded.

"What do you have in mind?" Brute demanded.

"I'll save my designs. You hold yours to yourselves," I responded, walking away.

"Mácula!" Trunk hollered. "You ain't got no shit. Just bluffing, aren't you? You want in on what we're planning. Ain't I correct? Well, pal, it ain't gonna happen."

I stopped and walked back to them.

"When the newspaper reports what I have done to Rafael Texeira and his group, you'll know I'm not fibbing."

"How're you going to do that, you son-of-a-bitch? Tell us before I smother you," spoke Brute.

I pointed to my head and replied, "It's all up here, and it's perfect. It will not come out even if you kill me."

There was silence. They knew I could read and write. In their world, that meant I was intelligent. If I claimed I had something to do with the Raposa gang that would appear in *Correio da Bahia*, it must be excellent, they rationalized.

"Okay, I'm sorry I claimed you were bluffing," announced Trunk. "We'll explain our plans, and you express yours. I hope it is better than ours because, if it isn't, you'd be sorry for fucking around and tricking us," he added.

I listened to their scheme, and as I had imagined, it was lousy. As I revealed my ideas, they nodded in agreement, and soon, an unrestrained enthusiasm swamped them. They understood they wouldn't do anything until the designated moment and under my direction. With this arrangement, the group's chiefs were now under my thumb. As is often the case, however, that capricious thing called time always has a measure to botch up things.

Chapter 7

As the weeks went by, the capital's decision to rid itself of street boys became a reality. Outright incarceration in *Refugio Pacífico*, the force barracks, replaced beatings and intimidations. Law enforcement hauled street urchins from several rival gangs. The City Council justified its actions. It was restoring public order by controlling vagrancy and crimes. For once, elated vendors credited the law for doing its job. *Correio da Bahia* reported on the progress. Governor Zé de Figueiredo and Civil Police Chief, Paulo Álvares de Andrade, trumpeted the campaign's success. When Spinner ran afoul of the law, we understood the extent to which Paulo Álvares de Andrade was implementing the governor's recent social control plans.

We had gone for a few days without food. Spinner threw caution to the wind and decided, against our advice, to rob Virgilio da Cunha, a notorious Portuguese merchant with a penchant to whip his slaves in front of his store for his amusement. We couldn't talk Spinner out of his scheme. We reminded him of the city's current drastic law against us. Spinner didn't listen.

"I've often thought you were stupid. Now, you're proving me right," said Cutpurse.

"Any bright idea, *Senhor* Cutpurse? Spinner asked.

"Yeah, steal from someone as dumb as you," replied Cutpurse.

"I have copped individuals and places more important than Virgilio da Cunha. You're too fucked up devising ways to plunder wallets to notice that others also have talents," Spinner replied.

"Yes, and we all know about your stepfather," Cutpurse countered.

Everybody burst into laughter. Spinner jumped on Cutpurse and trounced him. Trapped in the crossfire of flying punches and beautifully constructed vulgarity that both fighters spouted with ease and finesse, we separated the combatants.

"Well, if Spinner wants to rob that son of a bitch, so be it. Let's do what we often do," Trunk announced, ending whatever dissention that might have been brewing.

A general deposit, Virgilio da Cunha's, *Armazém Geral Da Cunha*, was in *Rua Agostinho Gomés* in the heart of the business district, where black porters trekked from place to place, burdened with furniture, barrels, and chests. Here, freed slaves easily plied their trade as chicken vendors, lace makers, bricklayers, and barbers. The area, off *Largo do Pelourinho*, took on a frenzied hubbub at mid-day. Shelves layered with an assortment of stock, consisting of garden tools and household commodities, lined *Armazém Geral da Cunha*'s entrance. None of these things interested our prospector. Neither did the items on the long counter in the middle of the store. It served as a display for an array of merchandise, such as locks, fabric, threads, plates, cups, jewelry, laces, and numerous knickknacks. The extensive rack to the left of the store's front that hosted cured meats, including *carne-de-sol, charqui,* and *quiejo-de-minas curado* was Spinner's preferred destination. Like an armada that left its port of the *Caminho Novo de Tabuão* and alleyways below it, we quickly dispersed into smaller regiments with specific duties designed to be carried out at high noon, the store's busiest hour. A small group served as lookouts for the Civil Police. Another distracted a hunt, bumping intentionally into pursuers if needed. The remaining clan members formed a relay team that passed the pilfered goods from one to another until we stored them away.

Quadros and Erasmo were in *Armazém Geral Da Cunha* when Spinner arrived. Buoyed by confidence from tried and tested diversionary tactics, the two ring members created a shouting match that rapidly degenerated into a staged fistfight.

"Get these hoodlums out of my store," Virgilio da Cunha yelled. Attention focused on Quadros and Erasmo, Spinner began filling his satchel with an assortment of the coveted products. A strong clutch landed on his shoulder as he was about to step out with a full bag. The grip was unmistakable. It belonged to someone trained to inflict maximum pain and to prevent escape. Anybody else would have succumbed to the agony. But not Spinner or anyone in our tribe. Surrender meant paying ultimate homage to the gang's betrayal, offering oneself on a silver platter to the authorities. Spinner swung the loaded knapsack over his head and hit his assailant in the face. The impact forced Santiago Ribeiro, Paulo Álvares de Andrade's deputy, to loosen his grasp. Spinner shot out of *Armazém Geral da Cunha*. But he wasn't alone. Virgilio da Cunha, who had seen what was going on, ordered his slaves to give chase. For someone who hadn't eaten in a few days, Spinner's speed was impressive. So were Virgilio da Cunha's slaves, who knew the repercussions of failing to catch the pilferer. Santiago Ribeiro, in pursuit, followed at a distance. He was tall and thin with an unkind protruding belly that made him look like a reed festooned purposefully with a foreign substance in its middle to prevent it from swaying in the wind. He appeared more peculiar with the small bag around his neck as he ran.

"Thief! Thief! Thief!" Virgilio da Cunha's slaves shouted, steadily gaining on Spinner. He sensed their closeness. The bulky backpack impeded his progress. He removed chunks of cured meats and threw them aside. A few stray dogs, witnessing the hunt from afar, suddenly became interested in the generous offerings an unexpected benefactor had dispatched. They joined the pursuit.

"What the fuck," declared Trunk. He stood with Brute, Runner, and me on the *Ladeira de Carmo* side of the street, two hundred yards from the store.

"Why doesn't he throw aside the damned fucking pouch?" I asked.

Trunk stared at me as though I were out of my mind.

"Because the sole theme of our existence is persistence. I expected you'd have known by now that it's how we survive on the streets, Mácula," Trunk declared.

Just when Virgilio da Cunha's peons readied to snatch Spinner, the second legion of our band moved in with rehearsed precision.

The pursuers found themselves on the ground, having bumped into a few of the gang members who offered their apologies for the accidental collisions. If we assumed that was the end of it, we were mistaken. When he realized the failed attempts of his pathetic chase, Santiago Ribeiro blew his whistle, summoning other Civil Police in the neighborhood. From afar, he saw what happened to Virgilio da Cunha's henchmen sprawled on the ground and nursing their injuries. To our consternation, several Civil Police agents materialized, as though ants emerging from dark holes to bask in sunlight after a torrential rainfall. The terms of engagement had changed. It wasn't only Spinner they sought. They wanted the entire clan. We learned that the best way to avoid inviting unwanted visitors into our lair in the *Caminho Novo de Tabuão* alleyway was to cross over to the adjacent turf that belonged to the Raposa gang: *Largo de Santo Antônio Além do Carmo.* The repercussions for our actions were obvious, but we still took our chances. Our escape drew us through *Ladeira do Carmo, Rua do Carmo,* and *Rua Direita de Santo Antônio.*

We roused the Raposa gang members from whatever they were doing when they heard the barking of dogs, the raucous whistles of the Civil Police, and the scurrying of legs through their turf. With the pursuit on our heels, they knew they weren't secure either. We left everyone to find his own escape route. After a point, we all reconvened in the alleyway. We accounted for all our members, including Spinner, who had run more than any other person. His satchel still hung around his shoulders, although its contents were far less impressive. But his knapsack had grown into the identifier, the signifier of the pilferer. Members of the Raposa group had seen him with it. Thus, when the police wrongfully hauled one of them, tagging him as the perpetrator of the theft, Rafael Texeira wasted no time to inform Virgilio da Cunha and Paulo Álvares de Andrade of the thief's identity. Rafael Texeira had committed another unspeakable offense against the Cabula clan.

*****

Lights emitting from handheld oil lamps jolted us out of our hunger-induced restless slumber when the law enforcement entered our semi-dark *Palácio*. It was in the early hours, a day after our abortive attempt to rob *Armazém Geral da Cunha*. We had counted our losses earlier and looked forward to another day. We hoped our luck would change. I thought I was dreaming when I heard a cadence that triggered in my subconscious an indelible sound. It was a sound I had picked up at another time and in another place. It exuded confidence and authority. It was the voice of the law.

"Get up! On your feet! Backs to the wall," Paulo Álvares de Andrade bellowed. His expression showed disdain and irritation at having to be up so early.

Fifteen bodies in several stages of stupor and panic obeyed. The Civil Police don't always visit one's home, let alone with the police chief in tow.

"Spinner," Paulo Álvares de Andrade called out.

Silence.

"Step forward, Spinner," Paulo Álvares de Andrade ordered. His voice a notch higher.

No one moved. One couldn't bridge so easily the barrier that sustained our honor code. Although we were up against a terrifying force, cowardice wouldn't come. We were all Spinner. We knew there was no demilitarized zone between the Civil Police and us. One couldn't draw a line on a battlefield where the opposing force could make mincemeat of the other. As the two combatting forces faced off against each other, contemplating what strategy to deploy next, we heard the clip-clop noise of footsteps on the cobblestones. It was easy to locate its provenance. As the noise drew nearer, an unmistakable silhouette emerged from the shadows. It adhered to a limp compensated for by a corrective wooden shoe on a right foot.

"Have you found him?" Virgilio da Cunha's voice broke through the momentary impasse between Paulo Álvares de Andrade's order and resolute defiance.

"No," Paulo Álvares de Andrade said. "The hens are playing tough," he replied.

"I didn't pay you to babysit hens. I must find who stole from me and make an example of him. All the merchants and street vendors in the neighborhood are behind me."

"We've got our own ways to sort these things out," said Paulo Álvares de Andrade.

"And I'm sure it's working well. The culprit is groveling at my feet with remorse."

The police chief ignored Virgilio da Cunha.

"For the last time, I'm asking Spinner to step forward," the policeman ordered.

Deafening silence accompanied his command.

"You assholes have offered me no alternative than to haul your pitiful smelly asses to *Refugio Pacífico*," Paulo Álvares de Andrade declared.

"Hold your horses, chief," cried Virgilio da Cunha. "None of these brigands leaves this place until I've exacted my pound of flesh," he added.

Another pound of flesh, I thought. It appeared as though the one already wrested from us a few weeks ago that led to death wasn't enough. Before Paulo Álvares de Andrade could respond, the crippled merchant unleashed the long lash that he had brought along with him. It accosted us from everywhere, like a starved, carnivorous predator. With nature's forces conspiring against me, I was one of the unlucky recipients of Virgilio da Cunha's strokes. The first contact with the lash sent me tumbling back to *Pelourinho*. A visceral rage and hatred possessed me. Yet I couldn't unleash these virulent emotions. At least for now.

*****

Refugio Pacífico barracks of the local police were in Bomfim, a narrow peninsula jutting out into the bay. Twenty separate units housed the men and their respective families spread across well-maintained acres. From afar, it looked idyllic, a location worthy of its name. It was a different story in the central building that contained the cells. Those on the ground floor resembled small internal garrisons designed to accommodate untamed beasts with unpredictable temperaments. The windowless ones, built below the ground, had thick walls. Like dungeons, it was impossible to hear screams in these cells. A few candles, positioned in specified angles, produced menacing shadows. These subterranean cells had an architectural ingenuity conceptualized by a man who may have had a full-time job designing torture chambers during the inquisition in another lifetime. They spared recently arrived inmates from these underground cells. The police reserved these chambers for the most recalcitrant inmates. It was also a space for forced sexual activities. They placed us on the upstairs floor.

Under normal circumstances, they shouldn't have brought us to *Refugio Pacífico*. Protocol demanded authorities provide thieves, criminals, and other felons a hearing before locking them. They didn't offer us that etiquette. The law officers had guaranteed our prosecution and conviction well in advance. *Refugio Pacífico* was a temporary holding place. Once sentenced, the law sent convicts to prisons spread across Brazil. Here, we encountered men who had committed far worse crimes than ours. Our new neighbors were murderers, destined for the gallows, debtors, drunks, and enemies of the state. They put us into five groups and twenty-foot cells with no beds or mattresses. Wooden pallets with thin layers of threadbare fabric passed for beds and bedsheets. I, along with Trunk, Brute, Runner, Cutpurse, Quadros, and Erasmo, got into a cell already occupied by four men. Hot air, must, the smell of human sweat that had marinated in armpits and crotches needing scrubbing filled the space. It wasn't as if we smelled like gardenias and frangipani when we arrived. Free rent in the *Palácio* didn't include showers. But unlike these inmates, we could enjoy the fresh air and breathe in the fragrances coming from the gardens surrounding the homes of the real inheritors of the earth in Salvador da Bahia.

Three of the inmates' facial expressions and demeanor were as congenial as cobras in a snake charmer's basket. We hadn't settled in before a venerable neighbor got up and walked over to Trunk.

"What brings you assholes to this resort?" the man asked, licking his lips and reaching out for Trunk's genitals. Our leader stepped back against the wall. He refused to respond to the man's question.

"I'm talking to you, *babaca*. Or are you deaf?" he shouted at Trunk. He moved closer.

"Leave the boy alone," came the voice of an inmate crouched in a corner. "I'm sure none of them have killed a fellow in cold blood like you," he continued.

"Oh yeah? *Viado*. The last time I checked, nobody made you protector and spokesperson for these pathetic thugs. Ain't I right, Salvador Viegas? Mother-fucker-ex-seminarian," Trunk's assailant declared. He walked toward the former seminarian. We breathed a sigh of relief. The abortive showdown between the man and Trunk moved elsewhere.

Ex-seminarian? My mind hurtled to *Fazenda Barbosa* and Marcelo Resendes, and I took a liking to this fellow who looked to be in his early thirties. Handsome, with brown hair and a few lighter hints, he had sharp cheekbones and a well-defined chin. Even still squatted, he looked imposing. On his feet, he might have a lightness of movement, I thought. What followed next confirmed my suspicions.

"Don't crouch there like a fucking hunchback. I asked you a question, and I expect an answer," said Trunk's aggressor.

The man in the corner was quiet. He shut his eyes as though meditating. The loud-mouthed felon lunged at him. The ex-seminarian's speed astounded us. Tall and muscular, he looked like someone who conditioned his body. He pushed his attacker back, took a step, and stood sideways. Elbows tucked, he planted his left leg and waited with both hands up. His opponent stepped in, firing an overhand that curled over his head. The ex-seminarian spun his head sideway, bent his knee, and averted the approaching punch. His opposition had made a fatal error in delivering an overhand and dropping his head too low. The once-seminarian came in with an uppercut at his opponent's chin. He jarred the assailant's head. The fellow tumbled and fell, hitting a surface as filthy as was uneven.

Although stupefied, we cheered. Two wardens entered our cell. They found Tiago Soares, for that was his name, prostrate. He stirred after they doused him with water.

"What the fuck happened here?" a warden asked.

"He refused to parley with his shoelaces, took a stumble, slipped, and fell," answered Cutpurse, our eminent verbal architect, and master fibber.

"Yes, I see. And the cockroaches hidden in the corners of your cells and in your beds' creases contributed to the shoelaces," the superintendent responded.

"What's there to say about those flying-sons-of-bitches?" Cutpurse asked.

The warden sauntered over to Cutpurse, and seizing him by the collar of his shirt, he lifted him up and threw him across the floor.

"Who the fuck are you? A wisecracker?" demanded the warden.

"Oh, no. A small man who's learned to pick on someone his own size," Cutpurse suggested, despite the obvious pain in which he was.

Just then, Paulo Álvares de Andrade arrived. The expression on Salvador Viegas' face hardened when he saw the Civil Police chief. The muscles in his jawline tightened as the look in his eyes drew on a fiery hue. We thought Paulo Álvares de Andrade had come because of the ruckus. He had other plans. He beckoned Trunk.

"Follow me," he said.

Salvador Viegas made for the door, but the two wardens stopped him.

"Where the hell are you going, fag?" one of them demanded.

"After that excrement of human species," the once-seminarian responded.

The wardens removed the batons tucked on their sides and clobbered Salvador Viegas. He did his best to ward off the blows. They left him in a heap. In less than an hour since our arrival at *Refugio Pacífico*, unprecedented events had shaken us. But Trunk's welfare concerned us more than anything. The limited taste of what had transpired within the hour revealed this wasn't a place for children. We understood the future ahead would not be a bed of princess flowers.

The veins on Salvador Viegas' forehead looked as though they would explode. His breath was shallow as he paced the cage back and forth. Everyone made room for him. After a while, he sat in his corner, tense and wound up as a string on a *berimbau*.

"He's upset because of what's happening to your friend," said one of the veteran occupants of the cell.

"What is that?" I inquired.

"You'll promptly find out when it's your turn," he said.

"Are you the seer who speaks in parables or someone who takes pleasure in scaring the shit out of unseasoned criminals? Quadros asked.

"All the aforementioned," the man said.

For a few minutes, the cell was quiet, each person lost in his own thoughts and wondering what the self-proclaimed prophet had just said. Before long, we heard voices and laughter. Paulo Álvares de Andrade, his two wardens, and Santiago Ribeiro emerged from the dungeons.

"He is a neophyte, but he'll quickly learn," Paulo Álvares de Andrade said.

"For his age, he is well-proportioned and endowed, said one of the police Chief's deputies. He and another officer had pulled Trunk out of our cell.

We had never heard Trunk cry. Tears pouring out of his yet startled eyes told something terribly wrong had occurred. We couldn't tell what it was. Our perfectly innocent form of life was still intact at this point. By the end of the second day, however, they had pulled and drawn us down to the Inquisitional cells. In seventy-two hours, our lives changed. We had reckoned with the gruesome, unutterable, and heinous crimes that Paulo Álvares de Andrade and his wardens unleashed. We said nothing about what had transpired, but silently, we conveyed the profundity and ferocity of our feelings. Together, the tears, rage, and desolation that had suddenly coalesced in our hearts, minds, and souls would eventually manifest themselves in unpredictable forms for all.

Chapter 8

"Fucking son of a bitch! Fucking son of a bitch!" Salvador Viegas kept saying throughout the third night of our detention in *Refúgio Pacífico*. We hadn't slept a wink, and it wasn't because of Salvador Viegas' cursing. We simply couldn't. How could we, given what had fallen repeatedly to us during our short stay? At six in the morning, Salvador Viegas got up and assumed the same posture he had held when he knocked out Tiago Soares. The wardens had moved the brazen-mouthed murderer to the infirmary. Salvador Viegas shadowboxed, using different boxing styles such as counterpuncher, boxer-puncher, and slugger. Each of these methods accompanied specific boxing techniques, including stance, attack, and defense. He mesmerized us. We had seen boxing matches when traveling circuses came through Salvador da Bahia, but we had never seen in close quarters the art that bolstered it. Salvador Viegas went through these motions for about an hour. We would have needed more than one towel to dab the sweat that coated his entire body. Under our spartan conditions, the thought of a wash meant contemplating infeasible supreme comfort. Salvador Viegas went back to his favorite corner and remained as though he had just come back from a leisurely walk in the park. He had a serene look on his face, and a gentle disposition appeared to have enveloped him. I reached over and sat by him. I took his hand and said, "Thanks for trying to protect Trunk and the rest of us."

He was silent.

"Would you teach me how to box? You're a good boxer, and you'll make an excellent teacher."

He turned and studied me. There was kindness blended with sorrow in his blue eyes. He said nothing.

"An ex-seminarian taught me how to read and write. You remind me terribly of him. Why did you leave the seminary?"

"It's a lengthy story, my boy," Salvador Viegas said with a slight smile. As he did so, dimples appeared in both cheeks.

"Well, from where I'm sitting, it doesn't appear I'm lacking for time."

Our conversation aroused the interest of others in the cell.

"Which version do you want? The long or the abbreviated?"

"Your choice, maestro," I said.

"I don't recall agreeing to be your maestro. Did I miss something?" the ex-seminarian asked as he playfully punched my cheek.

"You just did." And with that, Salvador Viegas began his story.

*****

Father Tomas Veloso, priest of *Igreja Santo Domingo*, a stone's throw from *Convento da Anunciada*, a Dominican convent in Belo Horizonte in Minas Gerais, celebrated mass with the convent nuns every Friday morning. On one of such Friday, he came across a bundle in front of the convent's gates. It wasn't uncommon for such packages to appear. Desperate mothers often left behind their children at *Convento da Anunciada*, counting on the nuns' goodwill that they would find suitable homes for their newly born babies. I was one of such babies. A few months earlier, Father Tomas Veloso's sister, Amelia, sought refuge with her infant son, Simão, at the convent. The Mother Superior protested when the priest appeared with me and appealed to her to take me in under his sister's care. One infant in the convent was enough, the Mother Superior argued. The other sisters pleaded my case when they learned of Father Veloso's request. Despite the impenetrable norms that regimented their covenant, that instinctual code of motherhood softened the nuns. They had given their wombs to God and to the church, but the reality of mother nature's gift, inscribed in that private sanctuary of the female body, superseded the vows that the fifteen nuns had made to the Almighty. The Mother Superior relented.

A few months older than me, Simão became more like a twin brother. Although the sisters doted on us, their disciplined lives became ours. By the time we turned seven, we were already proficient in cleaning, cooking, baking, milking the goats they kept at the convent, working in the flower gardens, and making the famous *quiejo-de-minas curado* for which the state of Minas Gerais was known. Father Tomas Veloso was our teacher and spiritual guide. From him, we learned how to read and write. We studied Latin, the natural sciences, and Catholic doctrine. As his altar boys, we memorized passages from the Bible and learned the rituals of daily and Sunday Masses. Once in a while, we left the convent with Amelia and some nuns to go to the market to sell eggs, cheese, and flowers from the convent's beautiful gardens. But we couldn't wait to return to our home, to the convent.

On my tenth birthday, the sisters organized a birthday party for me and asked who I wanted to be my guest of honor. The choice was obvious: Father Tomas Veloso. They prepared a sumptuous dinner, and the priest arrived in his best outfit. In the middle of the celebration, however, Father Tomas Veloso collapsed. The sisters called Dr. Abelardo Nunes, a devout Catholic physician and a friend of the priest. After examining him, he suggested they take Father Tomas Veloso to the Santa Lucas Hospital in Rio de Janeiro for treatment. Two weeks after his absence, Archbishop Geraldo Pereira of the Diamantina Archdiocese, under whose jurisdiction was the *Igreja Santo Domingo* parish, sent a young substitute priest. Father Eugenio Thrilho possessed a refined, dignified look, an almost aristocratic air about him. He had thin, long hands he kept in a pair of soft black gloves. All his gestures seemed to be deliberated and consciously executed. The first thing he did a few days after he showed up was to request Simão and I make a joint confession with him. This was quite unusual since we understood confessionals to be singular and private. It was stranger still when he asked us whether we ever lied? Who could assert to have never lied? Of course, we told little fibs, notably not revealing that we took bites of pastries in the kitchen before dinner and picked up little chunks of cheese without permission for our nightly snacks. Stranger yet was the priest's request that we understand how to hold secrets. This new priest perplexed Simão and me. Father Tomas Veloso mentioned no such thing.

As part of our chores, we cleaned Father Tomas Veloso's living quarters every Saturday morning. When we got to the lodging that Father Thrilho now occupied, he claimed we needn't bother to do the cleaning. He declared that there was a chore that required one person. He asked Simão to leave us alone. Not thinking very much of it, I sat down on the couch beside him when he requested.

"You remember the importance of keeping secrets. Don't you?" he inquired, placing his hands on my shoulders.

I tensed.

"You're a remarkably special boy. I'd like to offer you a delightful gift. But promise that you'll not mention it to anyone," he said.

"Why?" I asked.

"Because it's exceptional, and I wouldn't want many people asking for it. It will cease to be special. Don't you think?"

I wondered what kind of present this priest had in mind. Simão and I were content with our lives and what we had at the convent. We weren't worldly, and that was fine with us, I determined. But I couldn't express my thoughts. The nuns had brought us up to be kind and respectful, specifically to our priests and people older than us. The more I reflected on this special gift, the more unsettled I became, especially when Father Thrilho rubbed my shoulders. No one ever touched me that way. I attempted to get up, but before I could do so, I found the priest's hands down my shorts. I froze. The next thing I knew, he was kissing me on the mouth. He pinned me down despite my efforts to push him away. He was bigger and much stronger. Swiftly he had drawn down my undergarment and turned me over. A searing pain ripped through my bottom. I shuddered. After what seemed like an eternity, Father Thrilho drew out of me. I pulled up my shorts and limped out of the living quarters.

I averted Simão's gaze when I entered the room I shared with him next to the pantry. Despite the close quarters in which we lived, I took care of hiding from Simão what had taken place. I realized much later that I should have shared with him what Father Thrilho had done. Had I, he wouldn't have gone through the same experience. We said nothing to each other or to anyone, but our instincts told us that Father Thrilho had robbed us of our innocence. The candle no longer burned as it had done. Amelia sensed something was amiss with us. She prodded, but we couldn't find words to express ourselves. We still believed it was a mortal sin to share secrets with others. The priest had prepared us well in advance for raping us. But he couldn't take away our sense of self-protection and preservation. Somehow, Simão and I knew we shouldn't be alone with Father Thrilho.

Father Tomas Veloso recovered and returned after three months. It wasn't long before he noticed that something had changed. He had nurtured us since our infancy and as any good father, he knew us more than we knew ourselves. We felt safe and comfortable in his presence. It wasn't as though we couldn't confide in Amelia or in any of the nuns who played motherly roles for us. It was just that Father Veloso exuded a saintly disposition. There was something uniquely special about this man with an ingrained gentleness, a quiet dignity. I don't remember how it all happened, but Simão and I told him at the same time about our experiences with Father Thrilho, who left before our kindly priest's arrival from the hospital. Father Tomas Veloso wept. I've never seen a man weep that way since. But he also helped us to heal. He pushed us to recuperate the inner strength that he told us we both had. Above all, he encouraged us to understand that it wasn't our fault. We were victims.

I enrolled in the *Seminário São José* in Rio de Janeiro when I turned seventeen. Having lived in a convent, the way of life of withdrawal that allowed for the contemplation of God in solitude suited me. A year later, recollections of my experience with Father Thrilho intruded on my daily activities. The demon I thought I had buried made an unwelcome visit. Ashamed of what had happened to me eight years earlier, I couldn't share my inner turmoil with anyone at the seminary. *Cachaça*, that most potent and addictive drink, became my escape. I left the seminary before the rector heard of my plight.

For the uninitiated, the world outside cloistered spaces could be outright dangerous and frightening. My secluded living at the convent and the religious school hadn't prepared me to confront a world in which I needed to fend for myself as a jobless young fellow. With only my clerical garb on my back, individuals provided me with meals and a place to sleep. Somehow, those I met found a soft spot in their religious and sometimes secular souls to open their doors and purses to a youthful man who claimed to be a priest in training. But I couldn't hold on to the vestiges of my past history for long. I rapidly became a nuisance to my benefactors in the markets and on the streets of Rio de Janeiro. I didn't help myself with my drinking. The initial generosity of the few soon turned into the scorn of the many. I had embarked on a program of self-destruction.

During one of my daily wanderings on a Saturday afternoon, I found myself in *Passeio Público*, a public park in the middle of Rio de Janeiro. A traveling circus, *Circo do rei Galtero*—King Galtero's Circus—had set up several tents and was entertaining a large crowd. One of the major attractions was a boxing ring in which anybody from the audience could challenge a circus boxer to a boxing match. The winner walked away with a handsome prize. It was a rigged system where only a few challengers won their bouts against the veteran boxers. The throng cheered these disadvantaged volunteer fighters, underdogs. I hadn't eaten in over two days. Hunger pangs, jointly with the urge to drink *cachaça*, thus satisfying that addiction that coursed through my mind, my veins, my kidneys, and poisoned a body that young women contemplated in my ragged ecclesiastical outfit, forced me to jump into the ring and to offer my services as a boxer. The crowd shouted.

My challenger was a foot taller than me and had consumed, perhaps, more food that afternoon than I had in a week. I had hit nobody in my life, let alone had I been in a fight. Yet here I was, ready to tussle with a man in a circus whose job it was to pummel idiots such as me for the crowd's entertainment. Human beings, I reckoned, would do the stupidest things when deprived of the caloric intake that they needed to counteract earth's magnetic pull that would otherwise flatten them to the ground. Someone looking at the stage from afar would have concluded that I was part of the circus parading as a spectator. The frayed monastic rags and unkempt hair were convincing. I put my hands up, covering my sides and face when the referee announced the fight. My opponent looked at me with a smile laced with pity. Instinct told me not to move towards him. I took a few steps back. The crowd booed. The other pugilist laughed and encouraged more boos from the crowd. He made his way towards me as I backpedaled to one part in the ring. I had cornered myself. A trapped, helpless animal thrills the unsporting hunter. And that was who my opponent was. The first punch landed midriff and delivered a burning sensation throughout my entire body. A second one followed that sent me crushing to the floor. My opponent stepped back as the referee counted. I got up by the count of six. I stood erect despite my wobbly feet. My opponent came towards me again with a straight punch aimed at my jaw. I ducked, and he missed. The second blow that followed found a moving target and missed. I don't know how, but I became nimble on my feet, ducking, bobbing, weaving, and avoiding my opponent's blows. The crowd cheered. Other circus boxers joined in the cheering. This infuriated my opponent, who sought to end the whole spectacle with a knockout punch. He rushed towards me. I had taken temporary refuge in one corner. I slid to the side, allowing him to occupy that space. The only blow I landed caught him smack on the jaw and dropped him to the floor. I won my earnings for the day. Galtero Carvalho, the circus owner who had seen the fight, recruited me there and then.

Our circus arrived in Salvador da Bahia two years after I had joined it. Galtero Carvalho loves this place because, unlike others, Salvador has real boxing aficionados, many of whom are prominent individuals in the city. It was a fine Saturday morning, and the square where we had pitched our tents teamed with visitors. Reserved front ring seats for the city's elite surrounded the makeshift boxing ring. The air smelled of meats sizzling on charcoal burners and on open-pit fires. Itinerant vendors offered an assortment of delicacies. For the famished, it was a miasma of pleasant smells hovering over the park like a thick fog, enticing them and urging them to dig into their purses to put to rest their hunger pangs. Led by the police chief, who made his presence known through his haughty, peacock-like gait and knowing smile, the Civil Police made a powerful presence.

I was the first boxer to step into the circle, waiting for the dim-wit from the crowd, willing to have his hide tanned. As I peered at the throng, my gaze fell upon a dignitary in the front row. I froze. Eighteen years and his face looked the same. Time, it appeared, had stood still for him. Traces of that elegant look yet still held his face hostage. I noticed a large middle ring finger on his left hand, along with the color of his cassock— purple color—Archbishop! A sinking feeling hijacked my stomach, weakened my limbs, and sucked my energy. So many years! I thought I had moved on, but a hitherto repressed fury, in its rawness volcanic, possessed me when I saw him among the city's upper class with his refined air.

I climbed the stairs from the circle and made my way towards that man of God. Nobody had volunteered to go with me in the arena, making the spectators restless. The crowd observed my every movement, wondering whether this was part of the show. I carried a smile when I got to the archbishop. I leaned into him, offered my palm, and whispered into his ear.

"Thanks for volunteering to do in public what you did to me in Father Tomas Veloso's quarters during your visit to *Igreja Santo Domingo* in Belo Horizonte eighteen years ago. Remember?"

His body shuddered with shock and panic. Without giving him any chance to recollect himself, I lifted him up and carried him into the arena. This was entertainment of the highest order, the throng thought as it cheered. The crowd, recognizing the archbishop, must have wondered whether he intended to invite potential challengers to take me up on my offer. For others, the specimen of a shocked prelate in his informal apparel was part of the act. A quizzical look flashed on Ladislao Delgadinho, our referee's face. A nod and he announced the fight. I walked over to Archbishop Eusebio Thrilho, for that was the motherfucker's name, and landed a perfect right hand on his mouth, dislodging several front teeth before he and the spectators grasped what had transpired. A left hook broke his nose. Another disengaged his jaw. Everything occurred in rapid succession. When the eminent archbishop hit the floor, his face, which had refused to succumb to time and had kept its elegance, underwent a metamorphosis which time, with its potency, couldn't carry out.

The applause was mixed: cheers from those who enjoyed the brutal clobbering, alarm, and disbelief by those who knew Archbishop Eusebio Thrilho. Paulo Álvares de Andrade, that bastard who has been the bane of your lives here in *Refugio Pacífico*, formed part of the latter group. He and his deputies wasted no time in hauling me to *Refugio Pacífico*. I've spent three weeks here. They haven't charged me yet. I don't know what has become of Archbishop Eusebio Thrilho.

"So, my dear Mácula, here we're together, and this is the long version of my story I've told no one until today," said Salvador Viegas.

Nobody spoke. An unusual silence filled the cell. The raucous noise that came from the adjoining cells before Salvador Viegas' story started had muted. After a while, Arsenio Da Luz, a convict, asked. "So, what now?"

"That's a dumb question," responded Macario Figueiredo, the third prisoner in our chamber. "Can't you see the calm that surrounds Salvador Viegas? He's accomplished what God himself would have sanctioned. Didn't he say somewhere in the Bible that 'vengeance is mine'?"

"Yes, but God also added that we shouldn't take revenge but leave that to his wrath," suggested Salvador Viegas.

"But you did, and you must feel good," replied Macario Figueiredo.

"Do I? I wonder if one can ever forget what happened to these young boys and me. Does retribution, even if exacted in the manner in which I did with Archbishop Eusebio Thrilho, heal? I'm not sure," asserted Salvador Viegas.

"Pummeling that son of a bitch to a pulp solves it for me. If you were to ask me, I like that 'an eye for an eye' thing. No fucking around it," stated Macario Figueiredo.

"Yeah, me too," responded Arsenio Da Luz.

Given our recent collective experience, our shared response was a straightforward decision: we too.

*****

"Two things make for an excellent boxer. First, exorcizing the demon that torments him and knocking the hell out of that demon in the ring irrespective of his size or color," Salvador Viegas said as he started coaching us. He continued. "In your case, the demon includes the abuses you've endured in this shithole of a place and at the hands of these bastards."

With this unvarnished preamble, Salvador Viegas set to change my life and that of my fellow gang members. He tutored us first on the various boxing styles, including what it meant to be a pure boxer, counterpuncher, boxer-puncher, brawler, or slugger. We learned how to deliver punches: jabs, crosses, hooks, uppercuts, and overhands. Salvador Viegas was an excellent teacher. He knew we couldn't absorb everything under the circumstances. We learned basic defending and attacking techniques. He teased out our strengths and weaknesses and natural inclinations. Five weeks later, we could take out adversaries who hadn't had exposure to this fisting art.

They released us without charges after nine weeks. As we walked out of our cells, I realized Paulo Álvares de Andrade and his fraternity of violators had picked us for their sexual appetites. A fit of sulfurous anger overcame me, reflecting on my experiences as a freed slave who had sustained brutal physical harm from my former master and sexual violation as a homeless boy. Salvador Viegas' story rang in my ears. With the deep affinity I felt for him, I resolved that those who had wronged me needed to pay.

"Let's talk about our next move before we return to the alleyway," I suggested to the entire group after the Civil Police had dropped us in a park two miles from *Caminho Novo de Tabuão*. Somehow, I could tell that an incipient feeling of equality had emerged in the ranks following our experiences at *Refugio Pacífico*. I was ready to exploit it.

"Why?" Trunk demanded.

"Because the rules of the game have changed," I responded.

"I don't understand."

"Yeah, me too," Brute chimed in.

"We cannot go back to the streets and *Camino Novo de Tabuão* and fend for ourselves as we used to," I suggested. "The merchants are familiar with our tactics. Virgilio Da Cunha, that crippled bastard, would have shared our fate with most of the vendors. They'll be on the lookout. For that reason, we cannot count on what sustained us weeks ago."

"Well, we could find jobs," Trunk stated.

"Who'll hire us? And what work can we do? We cannot be porters like the black slaves. We're not big and strong enough," asserted Runner.

"Yes, you're right," Emilio Quadros chimed in.

"Couldn't we ask for alms?" Brute inquired.

"That is a recipe for starvation. We tried it in the past: it offered nothing but howling stomachs," answered Trunk.

The exchanges confirmed what I had suspected all along. Because survival had been of the utmost importance, the Cabula members left little room for deliberation and planning. Otherwise, how could they be talking about leaving our fate to alms, occasional work, and infrequent proceeds from stealing? How could I blame them? Nobody in the group had had close contact with powerful people to understand that exploitation and abuse made up the scaffold upon which they wrought their wealth and power. The new order was in place about street boys, and our experiences at *Refugio Pacífico* called for a different survival. I laid the groundwork.

"Let us begin first by expanding our turf," I said.

"Why the fuck should we?" Trunk asked.

"Yeah, why?" Dreamer demanded.

"Because it will offer more territory from which to work," I answered.

"How's that going to help?" Emilio Quadros inquired.

"We'll no longer have slim pickings."

There was silence.

"Let us take over the Raposa gang's territory, and let's kick the shit out of Rafael Texeira for ratting us out to the Civil Police. Let's settle the score of Thinker's death and the burning of *Palácio*," I declared, very much aware that I was stoking the ferocious flame that I knew was lurking just below the surface. It took little to convince the group.

*****

Rafael Texeira and his gang members had annexed our turf. They had filled a vacuum. They were in our *Palácio*! The Raposa team came out when we approached our alleyway. Without waiting for Trunk's instructions, I walked over to Rafael Texeira and stood ten feet from him. I signaled the Cabula band to stand behind me. Everyone, including Trunk, did. I turned around, looked at my crew, and shadowboxed before speaking. After a minute, I said, "Rafael Texeira, you're a *viado*, a *bicha*. A fucking snitch. A coward who doesn't have the balls to look a man in the eyes and tell him what you will do."

Rafael Texeira burst into laughter. "Did you just return from the clown training school?"

His band of space usurpers exploded into laughter. Beyond the gathered bunch in front of the *Palácio*, I remembered Thinker and felt a knot in my stomach. I swallowed and cleared my throat.

"Rafael Texeira, you son of a whoring *Peixe-Boi*, I'm asking you and your tribe of jokers to leave our territory and yours by the count of ten."

Silence fell on the Raposa group.

"What the fuck did you call my mother? And who the fuck are you, anyway? Where's Trunk, your wimpy leader who's allowing a pansy to be the spokesperson for his sorry ass?" Rafael Texeira asked. As he did so, he pulled out his blade, tucked behind him.

"*Puta merda*," I said to myself. Our boxing lessons didn't include fighting with a blade expert.

Trunk made a move towards Rafael Texeira, but I held him back.

"Trunk wants the wimpiest member of Cabula to knock the shit out of you, and I'm that pansy," I declared.

"O-o-o-h! I'm trembling, my teeth are chattering, and my knees are knocking," Rafael Texeira announced in mock terror, shaking his knees, and flapping his hands in the air like a bird and spinning. With a lightning movement, I closed the distance between us and landed a power punch to his stomach. Swift combinations of a cross and a hook sent him sprawling on the ground. Brute took possession of the blade.

Rafael Texeira's two lieutenants stepped forward. Runner and Emilio Quadros produced the same result as I did with their chief. Trunk took care of Zé Cantarelli, the boy who never felt pain. He was flat on his tail. Rafael Texeira attempted to get up, but I slugged him again and put my foot on his chest. This was the ultimate insult and disrespect among all of Salvador's homeless clan members. Word would soon spread that an obscure Cabula member had defanged Rafael Texeira. That this individual had single-handedly breached the demilitarized zone between both gangs and had prompted territorial surrender without opposition from Rafael Texeira and his clan would be legendary. At least, that was what I had imagined, but Brute had other ideas. With the knife in hand, he approached the stunned Raposa gang leader, who was still on the ground. In a swift move, he cut off Rafael Texeira's ear. The scream was piercing and bestial. Zé Cantarelli made no sound when Brute harvested him as well. Events had unfolded, leaving the Raposa in a state of shock.

Lifting Rafael Texeira up by the blood-soaked collar of his shirt and pushing him towards the street leading up to *Rua do Taboão* and onwards to *Igreja de Nossa Senhora do Rosário dos Pretos*, Trunk said, "Now, get the fuck out of here and never come to this neighborhood. With each of your ears gone, maybe you'll listen closely before you go accusing people of the exact thing you did to us." There was silence. After a pause, he added, "Next time, we'll not be this generous."

With their tails between their legs and hunched over as dejected soldiers pummeled into submission, Rafael Texeira's regiment followed him as he made his way out of the *Palácio* and onto the adjacent turf that used to belong to the Raposa. I'm not sure whether one would characterize my display as sheer bravery, recklessness, or pure stupidity. I hadn't been certain about the outcome of my challenge to Rafael Texeira. He was older and bigger than me. But my actions set into motion an internal dynamic within the Cabula gang. An inevitable shift had taken place. Brains and a little of audacity trumped brawn. I was younger than all the Cabula troika, but age had nothing to do with laying out a strategy to ensure our post-*Refugio Pacífico* survival. I had usurped the group's leadership.

Chapter 9

"Why should I take you on? You don't have any skills. You will cost me more in your upkeep than anything else you can do for me," Galtero Carvalho said as he dipped bread into a bowl of *feijoada*. He was burly and stacked low to the ground, with a thick head colonized by dense red hair. He wore a permanent tan.

"Because you won't regret it," I responded, staring straight into the eyes of *Circo do rei Galtero*'s owner.

"Tell me more," Galtero Carvalho stated, followed by a loud burp that almost shook the crate that served as his dining table. His assistant, who had granted me an audience with him, entered the tent to clear the dishes.

"I'd want to work for you as a boxer."

"Oh?" he replied, raising up an eyebrow. The other stayed in place, offering his wrinkled face the look of crookedly heaped pancakes. "What do you know about boxing, and who suggested I'm hiring?"

"Salvador Viegas."

Galtero Carvalho stopped wiping his hands with the handkerchief he had pulled from his side pocket and looked at me.

"How do you know Salvador Viegas?"

Despite his appearance and manner, something about him prompted me to share confidences. Having concluded that being homeless would not help me fulfill the resolution that I had made, I told Galtero Carvalho about *Refugio Pacífico*, the circumstances that led the members of the Cabula gang and me there, and our unspeakable experiences. I wasn't seeking sympathy. I was hoping for a new direction that would lead me to my goal of *senhorhood*. I shared with him our interaction with Salvador Viegas, informing him about his efforts to protect us and the brief boxing lessons. I, however, left out his story. Galtero Carvalho was quiet for a while.

"Salvador Viegas is not only one of my best fighters, but still the most honest and kindest man I have ever met. I don't know why he assaulted the archbishop. It is not in his nature to do such a thing," Galtero Carvalho paused and continued. "We are a travelling circus and should be on the road. But I'm staying until they settle his case."

A pained look crossed his face. I retold Salvador Viegas's story. As he listened, Galtero Carvalho's eyes burned with rage. "Salvador Viegas should have killed that motherfucker."

I wondered if Galtero Carvalho hired me because of his soft spot for Salvador Viegas and the communality of our experiences. I convinced him to employ Trunk, Brute, and Runner. Between the four, the circus, I argued, could draw persons in their teen years into the ring. Wasn't brash and insubordinate bravado the hallmark of most self-indulgent young boys wanting to show off and impress their friends? One accomplished goal led to another quest.

Dear Archbishop Eugenio Thrilho,   *April 15, 1807*

I hope this note finds you in satisfactory health, despite your unfortunate "assault" in the boxing ring at the circus. The shocked expression on your faithful followers' faces, the elite Salvador caste's indignation, and Paulo Álvares de Andrade's swift action against Salvador Viegas suggest they aren't privy to the reason behind your "assault." But I am. How could anyone forget what happened to Salvador Viegas in Father Tomas Veloso's quarters during your brief stay at Igreja Santo Domingo in Belo Horizonte eighteen years ago? And your relationship with Senhora Fidelia de Barbosa? How are your children, Agostinho and Adelina? Wondering how I know? I have in my possession Senhora Fidelia de Barbosa's letter sent to you on March 21, 1804. Given your unscrupulous nature in such matters, you must have kept the original copy. Do you suppose Senhor de Barbosa has his? You might wonder about this note's purpose.

Two requests: announce that as a perfect Christian (we both realize you're the worst kind to have considered taking the vow of licentiousness) you've forgiven Salvador Viegas; you'll use your position to ask for his pardon and release from Refugio Pacífico. Let me spell out the consequences if you don't comply. Salvador Viegas will complete his unfinished business after his incarceration if that comes to pass; I will make public Senhora Fidelia's letter. I'll know you have complied if they release Salvador Viegas in the next few days.

   Sincerely,

     From someone who knows the actual person hidden under that undeserving cassock.

They released Salvador Viegas a week after I had, under cover of darkness, slipped my letter beneath the familiar door that I used to traverse when I made my morning deliveries. I had made discreet inquiries regarding the archbishop's condition. Reports showed he had become a changed man. I didn't know what that meant. His compliance mattered, and it provided me with yet another insurance policy for future draw.

*****

Salvador's center city woke up to smoke billowing through *Armazém Geral Amado*, one of the most popular stores that sold food, clothing, building materials, and slave trade-sustaining items such as sugar, tobacco, rice, rum, and cotton. As others made efforts to contain the blaze, our gang lurked in the shadows and looted clothes, shoes, and food that we needed to sustain us for two weeks. Smaller stalls surrounding *Largo do Pelourinho* suffered a similar fate a few weeks later. A sustained attack on these commercial enterprises soon became routine. Try as much as they did; the governor, along with the civil police, could not apprehend the arsonists. We were nightcrawlers, and we could ferret out the detectives and agents they planted in locations the authorities believed to be attacked. Sitting ducks, countless stores beckoned, and we obliged.

"You're a genius, Mácula. This scheme of yours has developed into our mainstay to living as kings in the *Caminho Novo de Tabuão* alleyways," Trunk spoke to me as we dined on fare we had stolen from a local shop that went up in blazes in a different part of the city. We had an extensive landscape at our disposal after occupying Rafael Texeira's turf.

Despite our successes, I wondered how long we could continue to preserve that effort. I shared my inquietude with Trunk and the group. Trunk's response explained why I had turned into Cabula's indisputable leader without him or others recognizing my plot.

"Why stop if they have not captured us?" Trunk demanded.

"But what if we're arrested?" I challenged him.

He shrugged his shoulders.

"I'll tell you what. They will skin us alive. Our experience at *Refugio Pacífico* will resemble a picnic.

"So, what do we do?" Brute inquired.

"Let's quit the arson for a while," I announced.

"Are you out of your mind? And eat what?" Runner asked.

"Trust me," I responded.

Normalcy returned to Salvador with no reported fires. We had stocked enough fare to sustain us for two weeks. Rafael Texeira and his gang had paid for sending us to *Refugio Pacífico*. I set my sights on Virgilio Da Cunha. Paulo Álvares de Andrade's fate would come later, but I knew I had to bide my turn. I left Virgilio da Cunha a message in the middle of the night.

Dear Senhor Da Cunha,   *April 14, 1807*

I have received information that the arsonists plan to burn your store next. The perpetrators demand five hundred réis. If you don't fulfill their demand, your warehouse will go up in flames. Bring the payment in a small pouch and deposit it at Basilica Esperança's entrance at midnight on Saturday. Come alone, deposit the cash, and leave. They promise to torch your shop and home if you inform law enforcement or anyone. Burn this note after reading it. Put its ashes in the pouch along with the pay.

Yours, a friend who works with the Civil Police

At midnight of the scheduled time, Trunk, Runner, and I watched in the shadows of *Colégio dos Jesuítas de Salvador*, a building next to the cathedral, after having scouted the premise to make sure that nobody lurked anywhere at the *Terreiro de Jesus* plaza. We didn't have to wait long. Da Cunha arrived from the opposite end of *Rua Saldanha*. We had transformed the entrance into a threshold to execute our extortion. It no longer offered hope for those who believed crossing the gate guaranteed a positive audience with Saint Peter. Da Cunha made a sign of the cross and knelt as if in prayer. A few minutes later, he stood up and hobbled away, his unsteady walk reminiscent of a condemned sailor dangling on a gangplank. We remained for another half hour before Runner sprung up towards the gate. He returned a few seconds later, the envelope tucked into his underarm. We vanished from our safe perch and melted into the dark night with enough cash to sustain us. When we ran out of funds, we burned a shop opposite Virgilio Da Cunha's. It had been months since we struck. I left Virgilio Da Cunha another letter: he must deliver one thousand *réis* at the same place and time the next day. The inferno opposite his shop showed we could do the same thing to him if he refused to keep to the first letter's terms. He delivered. My plan to seek retribution from Da Cunha through monetary ruination was on course. I wanted to see how far I could push him before he broke. If, and when, he did, I would dispense the death blow. I upped the ante and asked for fifteen hundred *réis*.

Except for Cabula's troika, over which I had effective control, none of the Cabula gang members knew about our fraud. They were more than content to have their stomachs stuffed. They didn't have to experience the injustices of asking for alms or embark on the same hazardous activity that led to our detention at Refugio Pacífico. Sentries took up key positions along *Rua Pe Agostinho Gomés*, *Rua Ribeiro Dos Santos*, and *Ladeira de Carmo* the day after I left the third note for Da Cunha. They were to report any sightings of Paulo Álvares de Andrade at *Armazém Geral da Cunha*. The exchange between the shopkeeper and the police chief that fateful dawn when they rounded us up in the Basilica alley was still fresh in my mind. As I had presumed, Paulo Álvares de Andrade showed up.

We weren't anywhere near the cathedral where Da Cunha dropped off the cash. We used with stubborn efficacy our diversionary tactics. The early group surrounded Armazém *Geral da Cunha*. The second found its way to Virgilio da Cunha's home in São Bento. Both places went up in flames at midnight.

Early the next morning, I went to inspect what kind of wreckage the meek, who also needed to inherit part of Salvador, albeit differently, had generated. A thick crowd gathered around *Armazém Geral da Cunha* and *Rua Pe Agostinho Gomés*. As I pulled closer, Virgilio da Cunha's grating voice saturated the air. "Why are we paying fucking taxes to the King if he cannot protect our properties?" he lamented. Distress etched its tentacles on his red face as he raised his hands.

They could salvage nothing from his store. The fire flattened his home, we learned later. Although nobody in Da Cunha's family died, they would be homeless for some time, even if their homelessness did not take them to the back alleys.

*****

Ten weeks after our confinement in *Refugio Pacífico*, we joined *Circo do rei Galtero*. Prior to our enlistment, the team's extortionist and arsonist ways that I launched and guided offered us a pleasant existence. We didn't run into the risk of following the multitude of street boys that were being carted off to *Refugio Pacífico* to satisfy the city's establishment. Endeavors to clear Salvador of its undesirables continued as plotted. When the body meets its physical needs, the mind allows itself to reflect. In those moments, the brain could either become a close ally, or a savage beast and adversary when Pandora's brooding box opens. For those who have suffered unmentionable, outright horrific experiences as we had, the repercussions can be catastrophic.

Dreamer noticed first the urine pool under Cutpurse's possessions.

"What is wrong with you, Cutpurse?" Dreamer asked. "Why didn't you get up and pee outside the *Palácio* like everybody else? Why are your pants wet?"

The lad, who had a rebuttal for every question and could turn matters into verbal jousts and flippant whimsical exercises, was calm. Cutpurse had been keeping to himself after we returned from *Refugio Pacífico*. He went out on his own. He ordered me to piss off and leave him alone when I inquired about Sinha Olinda in the Lower City. And pissed off I was.

"Cutpurse. For all I know, you can eat crap," I said. "If it hadn't been for your foolish obsession with that dumb *Candomblé* nonsense, I wouldn't have met Zé Cantarelli," I added.

I was ready to blame anyone, especially Cutpurse, for those nightmares I thought I had banished from my brain. Runner had shaken and woken me up several times. Since my ascent to the gang's pinnacle, I occupied a space at the altar of the raised platform and slept next to Runner.

"Man, you've been talking shit, screaming, kicking, and flailing hands in your sleep as if the devil were after you. Who are Manoel Bagulho and Jorginho Carragoso?" he asked me. I ignored him. Restlessness settled on the Cabula team members. We forgot our reading ritual. Fights broke out for no reason. One was an exception. Emilio Quadros crossed a line and called Cutpurse, Six Fingers to his face. Graduates from the two-month boxing academy in the *Refugio Pacífico* cell, the pugilists put on a match that became legendary in the Cabula gang annals.

"Beat the crap out of him," I yelled and encouraged Emilio Quadros. Much older, taller, and bigger, Emilio Quadros won the fight. That night, Cutpurse didn't return to the *Palácio*. A few days later, they found his body hanging from a tree near Sinha Olinda's *terreiro* in *Piedade*. Perhaps he was with his *axé*, his protector both here and beyond, as Sinha Olinda had made us believe.

Chapter 10

Emilio Quadros assumed Cabula's leadership when Trunk, Brute, Runner, and I took off to join *Circo do rei Galtero*. Nobody expressed sentiments. We didn't have disposable emotional currency. For the next six years, we worked in the *Circo do rei Galtero*. Salvador Viegas taught us, and we became well-versed fighters. As I had predicted, as young boxers, we attracted many more challengers. We garnered more experience the more we fought. The circus traveled to several cities in Brazil, but we always returned to Salvador. Here, we had followers, among them Antonio Guimarães, who always showed up with some of his *capoeira* students. He approached me once and said,

"Keep it up, son, you inspire my *capoeira* trainees."

That was the strongest compliment I could have ever received. And it was from Antonio Guimarães of all people! He introduced me to Jacinto Cardoso, one of his best *capoeira* students with whom, a year later, I would share a room in a tenement in the Lower City. The Cabula tribe attended our fights.

"Mácula, *Nocauteá-lo*—knock him out—" they shouted, and sure enough, that was what I did with any opponent who climbed into the ring. It gave them a warped sense of satisfaction that I pummeled stupid white boys to a pulp.

We made an honest living as boxers. Fistic art became our passport, our letter of transit out of the slums and poverty of the *Caminho Novo de Tabuão* alleyway. At last, we had a family. The circus members cared for each other. Galtero Carvalho was a good employer. Yet I was restless. I hadn't forgotten my singular goal to become a *senhor*, a dignified freed slave, to live in comfort, and to take care of my own affairs. Life as a boxer in the *Circo do rei Galtero*, I reckoned, couldn't lead to that goal. On my twentieth birthday in 1813, I quit the traveling circus to set up my business. I had to find somewhere to stay in Salvador. I thought of Antonio Guimarães. The man didn't disappoint. He asked Jacinto Cardoso, who lived in the Lower City, to house me. I had somewhere to lay my head in Salvador, a place I could call my home, even if nothing but a rental.

Jacinto Cardoso and I had parallel stories: he was a freed slave, and his mother came from Dahomey. Quiet, he wasn't keen to talk of his past life. I surmised he preferred to expunge from his memory details of his history best left in the dustbin. If he could remove the debris of unpleasant recollections, why stay hostage to them? Yet Jacinto Cardoso differed from me in one way: he loved visiting brothels to cavort with black, biracial, and white prostitutes. His favorite bordello, *A Casa da Senhora Eulalia* on *Ladeira da Palma*, was an old colonial building that had seen better days. Despite feeble efforts to resuscitate its vanished splendor, it was still a failed cause. It had polychromatic salons and rooms divided into small partitions where Dona Eulalia's girls provided exigency sex and passion to many clients, including stevedores, vendors, and sailors passing through the city. Jacinto Cardoso invited me to go with him, but my response remained a resolute no. My nightmarish experiences at *Refugio Pacífico* had deactivated any natural sexual inclinations that I might have had.

Thanks to the experience garnered from robbing several shopkeepers in Salvador's market districts, I knew wares that moved fast and locations for brisk business. With the money saved, I invested in red roof tiles modeled on the thighs of slave women, ready-made windows and door frames, hinges, nails, locks, keys, and painted floor tiles. Other products included flowerpots and vases, fabric for window curtains, and a few wooden chairs. I set up a stall in *Largo do Pelourinho*. Any other person in my shoes would have shunned the landmark that carried horrid memories. Public flagellations still were the order of the day. Yet here I was, six and a half years later, doing quick transactions on days they flogged slaves. What would someone who knew my life story think of me? A survivor? An ambitious bastard who didn't give a damn about anything? A profiteer of a system that stood on the scaffold cobbled together on slaves' backs? A pragmatic entrepreneur providing goods in high demand? These reflections occupied me late one morning after the floggings when I heard a voice behind me.

"*Homem jovem*,"—young man—the voice said.

I turned around and saw a fellow in his late thirties to mid-forties staring at me. His accent suggested he must have just arrived from Portugal with many of the Portuguese who fled to Brazil in 1807 with King John VI. Fine-looking, he was of medium height but well proportioned. A pair of most curious and bright blue eyes embossed his shallow red face. His long black cassock reminded me of Father Fernando Santos Candido from *Fazenda Barbosa*. I could see he was not your run-of-the-mill Catholic priest. He rattled my central nervous system and triggered multiple warning flags. I became cautious and suspicious. I had heard of a radical group of priests within the church that had taken it upon themselves to proselytize in Brazil. Fifty years earlier, Marquis de Pombal, Portuguese Secretary of State, had planned to supersede state power over religious orders. Having failed in his efforts, members of the Society of Jesus considered it their religious duty to expand their evangelistic efforts in the New World. I thought theirs was a lost cause to spread the word of God to so-called condemned souls of *mestiços*, indigenous people, and African slaves in Salvador: they had seen enough condemnation on earth to believe that the same God that damned them to their miserable plight could offer any meaningful sanctuary when they were dead. At least, in my case, I had stopped believing in that God when the whip started crushing my tender skin when I was seven years old.

"*Homem jovem*," the father repeated after I had made a mental note of him without responding to his first utterance that sounded to me more than a greeting.

"Does any merchandise interest you? *Dom*...

"José Nuno da Silva Mendes. *Dom* José Nuno da Silva Mendes," said the fellow.

"Ah," I responded.

"So, what do you think about *Pelourinho*?" he asked.

The question stunned me. What the fuck? I said to myself. Did this man mean the slave whipping that just took place? The *Pelourinho* neighborhood? About how my business was doing in *Pelourinho*? And, if he was referring to any of these, why the hell, I asked myself, should I spend my time with a fucking priest. I wanted to sell my fucking goods and nothing more. Without giving me time to respond to his first question, the *Dom* of the kingdom of God on earth said, "Must be hard seeing your fellow blacks getting the short end of the stick."

"The short end of the stick?" I seethed. What the hell did this man mean? Did he have any fucking clue what it was to be a slave? The short end of the stick, eh? Not even close. Those who shoved and continued to shove the literal and metaphorical stick into our asses didn't intend to offer us any crumbs.

"What is it to you, my thoughts about *Pelourinho*?" I asked *Dom* José Nuno da Silva Mendes, barely able to contain my fury.

As if he kept a script with a list of questions that needed asking in quick succession, lest he forgot them, the priest shot another query at me. "Are you aware of *a abolição do comércio de escravos*?" This was another shocker. Abolition of the slave trade? How could one abolish slavery in Salvador and in Brazil? Hell, Portuguese and Brazilian authorities did everything they could to prevent Brazilians from doing something akin to those godforsaken Haitians who sent pikes through the asses of their bastard French colonizers. I had heard of a treaty that Portugal signed with Britain in Vienna on 22 January 1815. In the said accord, the Portuguese crown pledged itself to a limited dissolution of the slave trade. The treaty stipulated that the Portuguese government would forbid its subjects from acquiring slaves or engaging in the trade in Africa north of the equator. Regardless, I played my cards close to my chest and showed disinterest in any further exchange.

"Look, *Dom* José Nuno da Silva Mendes," I replied. "I don't appreciate what you are up to. I recognize that folks from your church have had and still have slaves in Bahia. You and your goddamned brethren profit using slaves on your own plantations. And you're here telling me of *a abolição do comércio de escravos*? Who the hell do you take me for? A slave I was once, but that does not make me dim-witted. Understood?"

"Yes, yes, you're right, *Senhor*. . . ?"

"Mácula de Souza. *Senhor* Mácula de Souza," I responded, inventing a new identification for myself. Somehow, being called a *senhor* sounded extraordinary. Almost magical. It was the first time anyone had applied this honorific tag to my nickname. I softened.

"Ah, yes, *Senhor* Mácula de Souza, you're correct. Some of my fellow clerics haven't been admirable in their ways."

I got worked up again. "Admirable in their ways!" What an insult! A gross understatement! A fucking delusional distortion of perfect Jesuitic crookedness! I thought.

"So, you newly arrived Portuguese monks are different? Didn't most of your Brazilian brothers-in-cassock come from the Iberian Peninsula?" I asked.

"We're not distinct, but some have taken on *a abolição do comércio de escravos*. That's why I am here," he stated.

I told myself that this man was a brazen fool with the naiveté of a clam. I knew profiteers of the trade would eat him alive. "How do you intend to do your good deed in Brazil?" I asked, making sure that my skepticism and indifference were as plain as the cassock he was wearing.

"We've set up the *Fraternidade Cristã*—Christian Fraternity—an organization designed to educate people in the evils of the slave traffic. Representatives work to abolish the business," *Dom* José Nuno da Silva Mendes said.

"Good luck," I announced, intending to turn on with my business. As though a bulldog not willing to let go, an albatross that had finagled its way around my neck, *Dom* José Nuno da Silva Mendes stuck to me like a leech.

"We want members such as you," he said.

Nearing throwing up the *acarajé* I had eaten earlier in the day, I felt my facial muscles tightening. Standing up, I took two steps towards him and hissed.

"Beat the hell out of here. I'm not interested in saving any goddamned slaves only to find myself enslaved again by the likes of you."

Unfazed, *Dom* José Nuno da Silva Mendes said, "We're meeting this evening in a greenhouse opposite *Igreja de Nossa Senhora da Glória e Saúde* at the crest of *Largo da Saúde*. Enter through the side door on *Rua Jogo do Cameiro*. We plan to build a center that will need extensive building materials. We'd like to do business with you. As good faith, here are one thousand *réis* in advance payment for some of your building supplies."

He walked away.

One thousand *réis* was no paltry sum, and nobody in their right mind, I thought, should part with this money with the carelessness with which *Dom* José Nuno da Silva Mendes had just done. As he walked away, I looked at him in the distance, and his silhouette, wrapped in a black cassock, evoked images of the Devil that I had seen in books in *Senhor* Felipe de Barbosa's house. I learned from an early age that everything associated with black was evil. How else could one explain expressions such as *Tão negro como o diabo*—as black as the devil, *Ovelha negra*—black sheep, *Magia negra*—black magic, *dia negro*—black day? Entrenched in this mindset of black toxicity, I wondered whether the fading black-cassocked figure was not the Devil himself in disguise, determined to ruin my life and to re-enslave me in another fashion. The coins in my hand, coupled with the prospect of even making more, forced me to throw caution to the wind. Nothing could stop me from attending this meeting. It didn't matter if I came face to face with the Devil himself. The promise to make more money mattered. That damned demon of desire, greed, and hope was nipping at my heels as though an angry dog, and I had no choice but to run towards it and embrace it.

*****

From the outside, the greenhouse on *Rua Jogo do Cameiro* was nondescript. Yet a closer look showed it was a *sobrado*: instead of one floor, it had two. They didn't use the ground floor for commercial business purposes. The owner of the house must be well to do, I thought. The roof had red clay tiles, the same color as the eaves extending beyond the walls. Wooden windows and the side door I had to use had elegant arches painted white at the top. A tall black slave with striking features greeted me at the entrance. He looked at me with suspicion. Sure, freed slaves abounded. Slaves like me in Salvador could show up and go as we pleased. The fellow who opened the side door to me appeared mistrustful. How did I get my freedom, and at what price? Did I sacrifice someone for my liberation? These questions didn't concern me.

"Good evening," I spoke.

The man studied me over without responding.

"I am here for the *Fraternidade Cristã* meeting."

"Follow me," he answered.

I found myself in a large internal courtyard that formed a spacious patio with the distinct sweet smell of plumerias and hancornia shrubby bushes impregnating the air.

"Wait here."

The man's brusque nature contrasted with that of a young woman who materialized from nowhere. She was slim with a narrow face, soft light brown wavy hair, and a small, full mouth. About twenty years old, the biracial woman introduced herself as Lucinda. Her elegant neck sat on a torso that announced, in advance, spectacular curves that defined her hips and lower body. Every limb of hers shouted out her femininity. I swallowed hard.

"Come with me, please," she declared.

For a minute, I stood motionless. I couldn't help but look at the way she swayed as she walked. She appeared to own the ground on which she trod. I hadn't been a lifelong prisoner of admiring elegant women, but in that very hour, I thought it would be a sentence to serve if Lucinda was in the mix. She turned around and eyed me when she realized that I wasn't following her. In my confusion, I tripped and almost fell as I attempted to follow. I'd have preferred to stay put and to admire that elegance. Lucinda chuckled. I speculated whether she had bewitched other fellows. In my entranced state, I imagined Lucinda as an eminent component of my imaginary world of *senhorhood.*

Lucinda led me to a living chamber, where I found ten people around a long desk. But for *Dom* da Silva Mendes still clad in his black cassock, the other well-dressed men were older. I fidgeted. *Dom* José Nuno da Silva Mendes broke the awkward silence that had accompanied my entrance.

"Welcome, *Senhor* de Souza," *Dom* da Silva Mendes announced, extending his hand to me, and pointing to an empty seat beside him. "Thank you for responding to our invitation to this evening's session," he added.

The possessive determiner "our" didn't escape me. How did one person's invitation morph into the plural? I remained mum. A man at one end of the table cleared his throat, reminding the cleric to get on with introductions.

"Oh! Pardon my manners. Let me introduce you to the group," *Dom* da Silva Mendes stated.

"At the head of the table is *Senhor* Cristiano Ronaldhino Coelho. He arrived from Rio de Janiero a month ago as King John VI's special envoy. To his right is *Dom* . . ."

I tuned *Dom* da Silva Mendes out. Was this a joke? I asked myself. How could King John VI, who, following the other fucking Portuguese kings before him that had profited from the slave traffic and had transformed Portugal into one of the most powerful nations in Europe, call for *a abolição do comércio de escravos*? I was no idiot. Something wasn't right. I couldn't remember when the monk ended his presentations. But I recalled hearing *Senhor* Cristiano Ronaldhino recount that with the treaty that the Kingdom of Portugal and Britain signed earlier in the year, Portugal agreed to end its slave traffic everywhere north of the equator. I wondered what the hell this had to do with me. *Senhor* Cristiano Ronaldhino Coelho must have read my mind.

"Now, you may wonder why we've invited you to this meeting," he returned to me.

"Please, enlighten me," I replied, making sure not to give away my skepticism.

Senhor Cristiano Ronaldhino Coelho stood up and walked to the end of the room. He had white hair and a bulbous nose that gave his face an odd, malignant look. He picked three oranges from a small basket that sat on a carved chest. It hushed the others. The *Igreja de Nossa Senhora da Glória e Saúde* bells tolled. Dogs in the neighborhood barked as though in response to the bells urging them to remind their owners that vespers were an indispensable Christian obligation. They made signs of the cross. I didn't.

"His Majesty, King John VI, is keen on implementing this treaty," *Senhor* Cristiano Ronaldhino Coelho said, making his way back to his seat and throwing, at the same time, the oranges into the air and catching them with the dexterity of a juggler.

"He's very much aware that it will meet with resistance in this colony. That's why he's setting up several branches of *Fraternidades Cristãs* across Brazil to inform and to educate people about the treaty as well as *a abolição do comércio de escravos*."

I said to myself that if the king's envoy was using the art of juggling as a metaphor to tell me about the challenges facing his fucking majesty and his fucking kingdom in implementing a fucking *abolição do comércio de escravos*, my sympathies were the last thing he could expect. My mood didn't include generosity or forgiveness. As a former slave, I had seen the legendary nature of Portuguese greed, guile, inhumanity, ruthlessness, and Christian hypocrisy. It occurred to me that the treaty and *Fraternidade Cristã* were a farce. The crafty Portuguese wanted to hoodwink the British into believing they intended to carry out their agreement with them! How could they? So high were the stakes with their kingdom and the colony's lifeblood dependent on black slave labor. Three hundred years of earnings from the trade etched into their very blood. Only a miracle could extract those profits, I reflected. I realized the Portuguese shuddered at the image of the mighty British naval force intercepting and destroying their slave ships. The British had destroyed Spain's ships when they declared unilateral antislavery.

My expression must have prompted *Dom* da Silva Mendes to stop the king's representative. He understood from our meeting that I didn't relish long-winded speeches, nor did I accept shit from anyone. He misread my thoughts. I had hatched my schemes.

"*Senhor* Ronaldhino Coelho, if I may break in," *Dom* Mendes maintained in a firm voice. "*Senhor* de Souza already knows of *Fraternidade Cristã* and the *abolição do comércio de escravos*. We should tell him of the critical role that we anticipate he can play."

It tempted me to say that if my task was to supply them with building materials for their *Fraternidades Cristãs*, it wasn't necessary to know their beloved King John VI's plans. Holding my tongue, I waited for my fertile mind to continue processing what was taking shape. Whatever transaction emerged had to help me, I said to myself. A faint grin replaced the disapproving look that crossed *Senhor* Cristiano Ronaldhino Coelho's face when *Dom* da Silva Mendes interrupted him.

"*Senhor* de Souza, on behalf of everyone gathered here, I would like to confess, and I count on you to forgive us," *Senhor* Cristiano Ronaldhino Coelho declared.

"What the fuck!" I said to myself. From a slave to a freed slave, I had become a lay confessor to these assholes who still hadn't revealed why I was here. I kept my cool.

"I'm afraid *Dom* da Silva Mendes approached you this morning under false pretenses. We're not interested in buying your merchandise," the monarch's envoy reported.

I shot up, ready to drive for the door. If I had picked up something after the experiences I had throughout my twenty-two-year-old life, it was never to allow anybody to take me for a ride or to require my subservience as long as I obeyed the laws of the land. *Dom* da Silva Mendes gently put his hand on my arm and said, "Please, hear us out."

I hesitated and sat down. The faint smile on *Senhor* Cristiano Ronaldhino Coelho's face still lingered. A few of the men shuffled uneasily in their chairs. The envoy continued.

"King John VI resolves to show Portugal's good faith to Britain by holding firm to the treaty. He plans to emulate the British by abolishing slavery in Brazil as well. The first step is to present a few freed slaves from Brazil to testify at the British parliament. *Senhor* de Souza, hence your role," said *Senhor* Cristiano Ronaldhino Coelho.

My facial muscles tightened, and my eyes narrowed to crinkled slits. I didn't know whether to burst out laughing at what I thought was both a cruel joke and an affront to my dignity as a human being, as a freed slave, or to walk over to the *filho da uma puta* who just delivered King John VI's fucking message and punch him in the face. I took a deep breath, weighing my response. The mere presence of Salvadore de Vila Nova, head of Bahia's Civil Police, who I had never met, was enough to make anyone in my position think twice before doing anything rash.

I got up from the table and paced the floor, all eyes glued to me. *Senhor* Cristiano Ronaldhino Coelho confirmed my first hunch that the whole idea of the *Fraternidade Cristã* and the treaty were nothing but a charade. I hadn't expected the extent they would go to execute this farce. If the elaborate scheme that was unfolding before me was a sham, and I knew that it was, then the questions in my mind were now irrelevant. These men scouted me out and wanted to enlist me as an unwilling recruit. No ordinary person could bring such a thing to fruition. A lopsided negotiation, I reckoned. I still had lingering questions. Why me? How did they find me? I resolved to find answers to these questions. I forgot the blatant hypocrisy and paradox that ensnared the men. The fellow who opened the gate was a black slave. Lucinda was another one. How many more labored elsewhere? For the gentlemen gathered in the house on *Rua Jogo do Cameiro*, the mere talk of *a abolição do comércio de escravos* somehow exonerated and exempted them from slave ownership and human brutality. It was a microcosm of the big lie sanctioned by the bloodthirsty, slave-trading, women-raping, and cock-sucking Portuguese royal mongrels determined to keep the status quo. It appeared this was an excellent opportunity to extract the most from these bloody hypocritical bastards as I waltzed into the world of *senhorhood*. At least, that was what I thought.

"What testament am I supposed to give to the British Parliament?" I asked, still attempting to unravel how to exploit my advantage.

"It's very simple," reported a man at the table who, as I later found out, was *Senhor* Federico da Facinda, one of the richest slave owners in Salvador and the largest tobacco producer and exporter to Europe via Portugal.

"You'll merely bear testament you are free because of the Portuguese king's magnanimity and that Portugal is dismantling the slave trade south of the equator," *Senhor* Federico da Facinda added.

"Ah, I see," I replied, trying to play dumb. Wasn't one premise of the slave trade grounded in those senseless and false beliefs that blacks were inferior to whites?

"*Senhor* Mácula de Souza, because you're a freed slave, your passion in conveying that information to the British would be critical," the king's envoy spoke.

I thought if these were the brightest men and the best ideas that Portugal had to hoodwink the British, God misplaced his infinite wisdom when he allowed the Portuguese to become the first to engage in the 16th century New World slave trade. The more I contemplated their offer, the more I understood theirs was an act of desperation. From what I heard, the powerful British navy was gearing up to intercept Portuguese slave ships if the treaty failed. If it wasn't despair, how else could they overlook one of the most important details of their plans? Didn't they know the British were cognizant Brazil had many freed slaves through different forms of manumission in which slave owners freed their slaves? How would they prove a few "freed" slaves hadn't got their freedom before the negotiation?

It occurred to me that had they considered more wisely their scheme, they would have realized the British government's futility of enforcing the so-called settlement. Maritime geography pointed to the challenge of patrolling the seas. Didn't the wise Portuguese know? I decided it was no concern of mine and opted to stick to the plan in my head, which took shape.

"So, *Senhor* Ronaldhino Coelho," I responded, turning to the king's emissary, "You're urging me, as his Majesty's subject, to do the great King John VI and Portugal a big favor. Is that so?"

My question provoked murmurs at the table. It was easy to notice the palpable sense of relief in the room. Their minion, they determined, would acquiesce. *Senhor* Cristiano Ronaldhino Coelho raised his hand, requesting silence.

"*Senhor* Mácula de Souza, the answer to your question is yes," said the king's envoy.

"What do I get?" I inquired.

All was quiet. If *Senhor* Cristiano Ronaldhino Coelho and his group hoped I would do charitable work for their monarch, their kingdom, their power, and glory, forever in the name of the *status quo*, my question told them otherwise. *Dom* da Silva Mendes cleared his throat and announced.

"We expected you to perform this duty as the king's faithful servant and hadn't considered a request from you. But I believe we can accommodate your needs." He looked at the men around the table. They approved, nodding.

Duty? My foot! I'm not doing the son of a bitch monarch any favors, I repeated to myself. And trusty servant? Tell me how anyone could make an upright servant out of a slave and an emancipated one who has suffered abuse and indignity? Yes, you could flog people, maim them, take away their human dignity and pummel them into submission and believe that because they serve you without complaining, they're dependable. If you've tracked in my shoes and those of millions of brutalized slaves forced into subservience, the word faithful is a slippery and dangerous one.

"How much for my services?" I inquired.

"How much do you think you'll need?" *Dom* da Silva Mendes asked.

"Fifteen thousand *réis*."

The men gasped.

"Are you out of your mind?" shouted *Senhor* Federico da Facinda.

Senhor Ronaldhino Coelho smiled.

I stood up, and looking at *Dom* da Silva Mendes, I said, "I'm ready when you are."

Silence. I stepped out of the room. Nobody stopped me.

Chapter 11

'Good morning, young man"—the now familiar voice called out from the entrance to my stall.

'Good morning, "I responded, looking at *Dom* da Silva Mendes, whose wardrobe had undergone no noteworthy changes since the previous night. He had the air of someone who carried good news, but I didn't want to jump to any conclusions.

"Have you had time to consider our offer?" asked *Dom* da Silva Mendes.

"I believe I was the last person to put an offer on the table, or am I mistaken?"

"Oh, yes," asserted the Jesuit priest. "I suppose you are interested in our project, aren't you?" he demanded, managing a deadpan expression.

From my prior day's meeting with him, I understood *Dom* da Silva Mendes's bargaining style. His technique wasn't a bait and switch. It was something akin to a bait and bite. He proposes, lures the unsuspecting customer in, and alters the merchandise on sale. But the suckered buyer, such as yours, who has decided, finds that he cannot walk away because he has over-committed. *Dom* da Silva Mendes's cabal could get me to do whatever it pleased, yet I didn't want to concede just yet.

"It depends, *Dom* da Silva Mendes. My offer to take part yet stands at fifteen thousand *réis*," I said.

"Fifteen thousand *réis* is a significant sum. Don't you think?" he challenged.

"Not for the work you want me to do," I responded, although they hadn't explained their project's full details.

"Could we entice you with something less?" he inquired.

"I'm listening," I retorted.

"Five thousand *réis?*" he suggested.

"Make it ten thousand, five hundred."

"You're a hard bargainer who knows what he wants."

"Why do you think I'm into trading?"

A freed slave. Failure didn't attract me.

"All right," the priest acknowledged with a smile.

*****

The devil is always in the details. They invited me back to the house on *Rua Jogo do Cameiro* the following day. The same black slave met at the gate.

"Good evening, *Senhor* Mácula de Souza," he announced with a beam on his face.

I waited for a minute before I reacted and went through the door. I suspect people who change like chameleons. At least with chameleons, you knew they changed their colors to show their moods and, by doing so, send social signals to other chameleons. I wondered about this humanoid chameleon's mood and what social signal he was sending. It didn't take long to find out.

"Good evening," I responded. This time, he didn't ask me to wait for Lucinda. Eduardo Braga, for that was the black slave's name, led me to the living chamber where our earlier meeting had taken place. Only three of the ten fellows that I had met were present: *Dom* da Silva Mendes, *Senhor* Cristiano Ronaldhino Coelho, and *Senhor* Pedro Batista Braga. A fourth person joined them: *Senhor* Felipe de Barbosa.

"*Puta merda,*" I added under my breath. I hadn't seen my old master in over six and a half years. He aged, but that singular look was ever-present: whatever he wanted was at his disposal, no matter the cost. I hadn't thought of him in years. His sight prompted me to wonder about the letter that his wife wrote to the Pious Thread.

"Hello, Pedro," he announced when I entered the chamber.

What the fuck! Why was the man here? The questions I had been asking myself became clear. Of the thousands of freed slaves in Salvador, I had speculated about why these men chose me. I asked myself if their cynical and diabolical plot involved someone from my past. The answer to that question was clear with *Senhor* Felipe de Barbosa's presence. It intrigued me how my old master and his accomplices found me. What was in it for him? *Senhor* Felipe de Barbosa must have read my mind.

"You assumed you could hide behind your new false name. Didn't you? Mácula de Souza. What an interesting name," said *Senhor* Felipe de Barbosa.

I remained silent.

"I admired you in the ring. You were a fine boxer. Thanks to the late Paulo Álvares de Andrade, I discovered that you had been in the Cabula gang before joining *Circo de Gaitero*," he continued.

Paulo Álvares de Andrade, that son of a bitch, knew who I was in *Refugio Pacífico* when he and his subordinates raped me and the others. I wished I could bring him back to life and kill him again.

"What the fuck do you want?" I asked *Senhor* Felipe de Barbosa. The manner I addressed him must have shocked him.

"Don't forget you're still my slave," said *Senhor* Felipe de Barbosa.

"I'm no one's fucking slave. I'm free, and there's nothing you can do," I said.

Senhor Felipe de Barbosa let out an unconvincing dry laugh.

"Hold it," *Senhor* Cristiano Ronaldhino Coelho intervened. "We're here on a mission, and we need to carry that through," he announced.

"I won't undertake any fucking mission," I said, rising from my chair. As I was doing so, Salvadore de Vila Nova arrived with four new players. I would soon find out that these accompanying black bodies formed part of the human cargo that would corroborate the lie. Like me, the cabal planned to send them to the British Parliament to assuage the nosy British. One of two of the men included Eduardo Braga. The other two were biracial women, including Lucinda.

As though the exchange between *Senhor* Felipe de Barbosa and me hadn't taken place, *Senhor* Pedro Batista Braga began introducing me to the newcomers. There was Constância, a tall, affable, shy woman with a smile that could disarm even the most ardent misogynist, Eduardo, the tall thirty-year-old fellow who greeted me and whose face told the story of someone unused to being paid attention, and Affonso, a lanky man who, as I found out later, was a practical joker. Everybody, including Lucinda, bore the same last name: Braga. Next, the core mission of my employment.

"*Senhor* Mácula de Souza. Or is it, Pedro de Barbosa? You'll be traveling to London with everybody in this room except me. *Senhor* Cristiano Ronaldhino Coelho, the king's envoy, and *Dom* da Silva Mendes will lead the delegation. For this trip, because you're the only freed slave, we've determined that you'd be the spokesperson when you meet with the British officials," *Senhor* Pedro Batista Braga said after the introductions.

They tied me up in knots, unsure about how to respond to what was unfolding before me. For *Senhor* Felipe de Barbosa, I was still his property. The men orchestrating the lie considered me a freed slave. I thought I was selling my spirit to the Devil, but it turned out the Devil had taken possession of it before I even elected to follow that cleric in the black cassock. I smiled. It was one thing to sell one's soul to the Devil. It was another matter not to let him know that one transacted business with him, knowing one understood the details before he showed up to collect his due. Uncertain of what role *Senhor* Pedro de Barbosa played in the whole drama, I resigned myself to the fraudulence surrounding the entire enterprise. I had no illusions about my ethical and moral bankruptcy. I looked out only for myself. Yet whatever little conscience and self-respect I had kept needling me to call out *Senhor* Pedro Batista Braga on the web of inconsistencies that he and his companion spurious abolitionists had spawned since I first met them less than forty-eight hours earlier. I surmised that if the pseudo-abolitionists knew I was on to their game, then the subtle nod that *Senhor* Pedro Batista Braga made when he referred to me as the "purely freed slave" was as great as a wink and that I understood their charade and was a willing collaborator. Isn't it true that the Devil sometimes speaks the truth? I looked around the chamber and rested my gaze on the human specimens provided as evidence and directed my question to the white men in the room.

"*Senhor* Batista Braga, with due respect, may I ask when the *abolição do comércio de escravos* begins? Could you please, sir, explain what you mean that I'm the only freed slave? Does it mean Lucinda and the others are still slaves?"

There was silence. Lucinda and her companions fidgeted in the seats lining the wall next to the long table in the middle of the room. They sat, unsure of their forced enlistment into a well-orchestrated fraud minted at the doorstep of the highest royal order. I caught Eduardo's stare. His brows knitted into a frown as though to announce I do not fuck up the opportunity being presented for him and the rest to travel to London. Like he and many slaves in Brazil, he must know they had abolished slavery in England several years ago. Which slave in Eduardo's boots wouldn't dream of traveling to a place where freedom awaited? I wondered if he had a hidden agenda as I did, but I dismissed the thought. No one besides me, I believed, could be as cynical and as callous as I was in obtaining their life's objectives with no scruples.

Senhor Cristiano Ronaldhino Coelho spoke. "*Senhor* de Barbosa, there's something you need to understand. *Senhor* Felipe de Barbosa may take you back any time he wants. He's within the law. You can't prove your status. I'd be careful with what to say if I were you."

My re-enslavement! I noticed a smirk on my former master's face and resisted the urge to wipe the sneer off that nauseating look with a solid punch.

"Besides, we're paying you to do a service for the king of Portugal. Yours is to do your job and shut up. Do you understand?"

"Oh, yes sir, I do," I replied. "But," I continued. "It's just that with the talk of the *Fraternidade Cristã*, and the *abolição do comércio de escravos* and all of *Senhor* Batista Braga's slaves, I am a little confused. To perform a service for the Portuguese monarch, don't you think it might be helpful to understand the situation?"

Senhor Pedro Batista Braga clenched his jaw, fastened a gimlet eye upon me, pounded on the table and declared. "Son of a bitch! How dare you?"

Dom da Silva Mendes stepped in. He asked Lucinda and the others to leave the chamber. As they streamed out, I wondered whether the man of God was executing his call as a peacemaker or was trying to prevent the slaves from smelling the rot emanating from the beast's underbelly. With the chamber emptied of the slaves, *Senhor* Cristiano Ronaldhino Coelho spoke.

"*Senhor* Pedro de Barbosa, I need not point out you've agreed with the Portuguese king. Breaking that contract will have its consequences. I also don't have to remind you that Salvadore de Vila Nova's office can enforce the law over slave possessions."

The repercussions of breaking my verbal undertaking with a bloody stuffed Portuguese king did not perturb me. The mention of Salvadore de Vila Nova's name, within the context of my supposed indenture, was, however, another matter. It was a sufficient warning shot with a simple message. They wanted to clamp down on my queries and musings. But I had already made my point. They knew I was aware of the farce, and that was all that mattered to me.

*****

I surprised Jacinto Cardoso, my roommate and fellow trader, when I urged him to acquire the contents of my shop. He wanted to know why. I informed him of *abolição do comércio de escravos*, my recruitment by *Dom* da Silva Mendes, and the powerful cabal sponsoring my trip to London. He was quiet when he heard what I planned to do with my ten thousand, five hundred reis. After a while, he suggested, "If I were in your shoes, I'd put that fund to a more lucrative use."

"What's better and more profitable than becoming a slaver at the quays in Salvador?" I asked. Before Jacinto Cardoso could answer, I expounded further on my interest. "My work will differ from other dealers. I don't aim to shout myself hoarse, angling to buy the most desirable slaves. I'll create a niche market, inquiring ahead of time from interested parties, specific details about the slaves they prefer. Made To Order—that will be my trademark."

"There's something bigger," Jacinto Cardoso said.

"What?" I inquired.

"Go to Dahomey."

"Dahomey. What the hell am I going to do there?"

"Acquire the slaves there and send them to Salvador," Jacinto Cardoso replied without blinking an eye. "You'll make more money that way."

That thought hadn't crossed my mind. Despite my proclaimed callousness and strong wish to become wealthy at any cost, Jacinto Cardoso's proposal disconcerted me. Heck, I was once a slave and recognized what it meant to be enslaved. I heard from other captives brought from Dahomey of the savagery, the inhumanity, and the barbarity of the traffic. I was sure Jacinto Cardoso was also familiar with these tales. His experiences wouldn't have been so unusual from mine. Why then would he suggest I go to Dahomey? Jacinto Cardoso's unvarnished counsel reminded me of those slaves on some plantations who, once promoted as overseers, became the worst of their type. Because they themselves sustained savagery, they were more inclined to duplicate that barbarity and to inflict even more violence. Was Jacinto Cardoso the breed of slaves whose fortunes, having changed, now assumed the attitude of an overseer? How could he be so obdurate? I quizzed myself, only to realize I possessed no moral authority to judge Jacinto Cardoso. Hadn't I resolved to turn into a dignified *senhor* irrespective of what it took? What about the niche market for slaves upon my return from London? How different was it from going to Dahomey? Hadn't I committed to the elaborate lie the Portuguese were constructing?

Something else kept gnawing at my conscience if I still had any left at all. I realized deep down my path to *senhorhood* was indelicate, and my resolution would confound anyone with a sense of empathy and who appreciated my history. Jacinto Cardoso was the first person with whom I shared my designs. On some level, I hoped he would serve as a sounding board to unmask my flawed intentions to become part of a system constructed on violence. But

Jacinto Cardoso didn't do so. I wondered why he failed to invoke the moralistic implications of my proposals and asked why I wanted to pull off such a stunt. Somehow, I was hoping he would ask these questions and others. For example, what did it mean for one man to enslave another? It wasn't as though I didn't know the answers. I understood the economic pressures that underpinned the trade; I recognized the savagery of the individualistic spirit and knew that barbarous and debauched forces installed themselves in each slaver's and benefiter's soul. Slavery was an act of terrorism of the individual spirit.

Despite these reflections and my conundrum, I was reluctant to reappraise my life goals, my strategies. I couldn't tame the internal demon nudging me towards a future of *senhorhood*. Like ticks adept at finding nooks and crannies in hard-to-reach unmentionable body parts, the singular wish of *senhorhood* continued to implant itself in that primitive part of my brain programmed for survival. Had Jacinto Cardoso asked me the same questions, I doubted the outcome would have been any different. So, Dahomey it was!

I gathered whatever knowledge was available on Dahomey. It was a hellhole; I learned. One could make a fortune in a short time if one didn't succumb to tropical diseases. I found out that freed slaves had returned to places such as Ouidah and other parts of West Africa. It was a return to their homeland. Armed with this knowledge and the decision made, I resolved to set into motion my plan.

*****

As preparations for the trip took shape, I visited the house on *Rua Jogo do Cameiro* street. These calls enabled me to understand the two Portuguese men leading the group. *Senhor* Cristiano Ronaldhino Coelho worked in King John VI's court and was among his influential advisers who left Portugal with the monarch for Brazil in 1807. He was Portugal's envoy to Britain in 1812 and joined the delegation that signed the Vienna treaty on 22 January 1815. *Dom* José Nuno da Silva Mendes, I found out, was a spiritual guide to

Felipe IV, the king's first son. Rumors circulated later that the two men who led our mission to England had a romantic relationship. I couldn't care less.

I assumed a most agreeable disposition during my visits and spent hours with *Dom* José Nuno da Silva Mendes and *Senhor* Cristiano Ronaldhino Coelho. The two men coached us on our body language and what to say if the British asked of our condition as "freed slaves." They provided us with new clothes befitting our so-called liberated status. Spokesperson of the "emancipated" slaves, *Dom* José Nuno da Silva, and I practiced much the speech for the British parliament.

It wasn't difficult to gauge my enslaved companions' sentiments. I noticed anticipation mixed with trepidation. It was clear they had bought into the lie. But had they? Did they have a choice? Liberated merchandise for display in London. That was what they were. Armed with scripted roles in England, they must return to Salvador and continue from where they had left: nothing but slaves owned by that son of a bitch, *Senhor* Braga. They weren't even *negros de ganho* or *ganhadores*, Salvador's urban slaves who moved about, earned a living, and paid their owner a regular fee. This thought angered me, forcing me to contemplate my status. If I changed my station, there was no reason I shouldn't change theirs, I reasoned. I suggested to *Dom* José Nuno da Silva Mendes and *Senhor* Cristiano Ronaldhino Coelho that to cultivate a sense of naturalness and familiarity between me and *Senhor* Braga's slaves, I needed to spend time with each one of them for us to better know each other. I proposed taking part in their various chores and accompanying them on their scheduled errands around Salvador. My motives weren't altogether altruistic: I wanted to be in Lucinda's company. Already sculptured into my mind, into my soul, she became the air I breathed. The more time I spent with her, the more I became weak-kneed. With my lamentable inexperience being around women as attractive as Lucinda, I couldn't interpret her feelings for me. She didn't flaunt her beauty, yet it made her unreachable, separate. The more I agonized over how to declare my love for her, the more I realized she was leaving in her wake emotional wreckage. I shared my turmoil with Jacinto Cardoso, who, as I had expected, had a response.

"For goodness' sake, Pedro de Barbosa, Lucinda does not differ from any other woman. Tell her how you feel without lying to her. Flatter her, tell her you cannot breathe in her presence because she takes your breath away, and don't forget to tell her of her unparalleled charm."

"It's easier for you to say that, Jacinto," I responded and added, "You don't know how it is to become tongue-tied with a goddess since all the women you've ever encountered are those housed in bordellos."

Jacinto Cardoso was silent.

"I'm sorry," I declared. "That was unkind of me."

Jacinto Cardoso shrugged and said, "Yeah! Whores. It is less complicated with them."

Although I wasn't sure if Jacinto Cardoso provided me with the weaponry required to sweep Lucinda off her feet, I took his advice.

"Wouldn't it be an act of mercy if you married me?" I asked Lucinda the first time I accompanied her out of the house on *Rua Jogo do Cameiro*. We headed towards the outdoor market of a large plaza near *Igreja de Nossa Senhora do Rosário dos Pretos*. If this was what I thought Jacinto Cardoso meant by flattering girls, I was off to a pathetic beginning. My inept wooing efforts didn't escape Lucinda. Yet she surprised me with a generosity. Rather than point out my acute shortcomings in that arena of courtship, she teased me about my initial interaction with her.

"Didn't realize you could walk without tripping."

That she recalled our early meeting was both embarrassing and exhilarating.

"I borrowed new legs so I can walk with you," I replied.

"I think they are hideous," she reacted, studying me.

"Girls go crazy over them. They're always stumbling into each other, trying to get a glimpse of them and to touch them.

"I don't see any girls now."

"It is because I am walking with one who intimidates the shit out of them. They recognize she is protective," I responded.

"Is that how to talk around ladies? Vulgarity terrifies me," Lucinda suggested.

"I'm not great at talking to ugly girls," I answered, only to cringe. "Dumbass," I told myself.

"Neither am I perfect at walking with terrible legs. Now that I am inspecting them, they remind me of those of a wooden puppet," Lucinda added as she burst into laughter, revealing those white teeth in that well-shaped mouth. This was a woman with a wonderful sense of humor, a naked spirit devoid of malice or depravity. My attraction to Lucinda only deepened.

For weeks, I got to know well my proposed traveling companions. Constância was taciturn, a strong believer and practitioner of *Candomblé* who didn't fancy anyone who contradicted her. Affonso, a harmless prankster, had dreamt of becoming a Catholic priest. He frequented the *Igreja de Nossa Senhora da Glória e Saúde*. He became disillusioned and irreligious when they told him a black slave couldn't serve as an altar boy, let alone do any chores for free in the sacristy. Eduardo was a grave, thoughtful individual. Lucinda, I've introduced. I must add that, as was Affonso, she had no patience for religion, a quality that endeared her to me more.

Chapter 12

We set sail from Salvador in the early hours of June 10, 1815, on the Clipper *Cisne Vermelho*—the Red Swan. Our first port of call was Lisbon, from where we would take another ship to London. Several of the passengers on the *Cisne Vermelho* were Portuguese merchants, others with family members returning to Portugal with merchandise, including *cachaça*, tobacco, manioc, dried fish, sugar, and much more. They divided the passengers on the ship into four groups: cabin; saloon, or house on deck; second cabin between deck; and intermediate or third-class passengers, who were sub-divided into enclosed and open berths. I thought, given his vocation as a priest, *Dom* da Silva Mendes would have remained with his flock to offer it with spiritual succor when needed. Instead, he took a place in the cabin, along with *Senhor* Cristiano Ronaldhino Coelho.

They put Eduardo, Constância, Lucinda, Affonso, and I in a sectioned-off intermediate compartment for ten people. The cubicle had a partition that offered the two women in the group little privacy. Our space suited me just fine. Whereas we couldn't congregate in Salvador, not only did we have room in the *Cisne Vermelho*, but also, I had time to unfold my plans. Our Messman was Ronaldhino Ferreira. He was a cantankerous Portuguese who had convinced Regolio Umberto, the Italian captain of the *Cisne Vermelho*, that he could make a living not as a paid steward but as an unofficial Messman who catered to the needs of those who occupied the bottom of the totem pole on the ship—intermediate or third-class passengers. For his recompense, he had full room and board on the ship and a stipend that he spent on whores at the ports that the *Cisne Vermelho* anchored before setting sail. Ronaldhino looked as though he could double for the ship's mast in the event it broke. Hair covered every part of his body, especially his massive head and his mustache that resembled the tail of a mangy dog. His responsibility as a Messman included carrying water, provisions, and other items to the cabins of the less illustrious passengers on board. Ronaldhino brought us our food but wasn't responsible for cleaning our cabins. First and second cabin passengers enjoyed that service. The giant of a man didn't hide his scorn for us when he understood he was serving us: *pretos*—niggers— he called us when he first entered our berth.

Our cabins weren't the best. The food was abysmal. The claustrophobic Constância came down with seasickness, and God knows whatever disorder she may have picked up in those squalid cabins. The ship's doctor recommended she spend a few hours in the sun on the deck. Constância's health concerned *Dom* José Nuno da Silva Mendes and *Senhor* Cristiano Ronaldhino Coelho, who accompanied the physician. She couldn't sabotage their well-orchestrated plans. As the days passed, we learned more about *Dom* José Nuno da Silva Mendes: the cleric was a dishonest bastard and a closet gambler.

Except for the brief appearance with the ship's doctor to examine Constância, *Dom* José Nuno da Silva Mendes had made no contact with us in our indecorous third-class cabin during the one and a half weeks we had been sailing. When he reappeared later, he smiled and grinned from ear to ear like a capybara eating ipomoea batatas. I thought the good priest came to say he had made provisions to improve our situation, having seen our derisory condition. No, *Dom* José Nuno da Silva hadn't arrived with news to ease our pathetic living state. He had come with a business proposition on the ship. A passenger in the first-class quarters of the *Cisne Vermelho* who had seen me in a few boxing matches in Salvador when I was with *Circo do rei Galtero,* suggested to Regolio Umberto and to *Dom* José Nuno da Silva that the ship's patrons could use some entertainment in the form of a boxing match between me and Ronaldhino who, in another life, was a champion boxer in the slums of Lisbon. They would place bets, with the winner receiving ten percent of the proceeds. At the prospect of seeing a black man crushed to a pulp by the gargantuan Ronaldhino and picking up extra *réis* along the way, the captain embraced the idea.

"So, what do you think?" *Dom* José Nuno da Silva asked after informing my cabin mates and me about the proposition. Before I could respond, Affonso burst into hysterical laughter. All of us turned to look at him as he continued to laugh, holding his sides, with tears streaming from his eyes.

"What in the world is so funny?" I inquired.

"I can already see the shit coming from your rear end," Affonso stated, still laughing.

"Who said I will fight?" I demanded.

"Oh! You will, and you know it," replied Affonso. "Can't you understand that these white folks want to get a nigger whipped up like they do on land? They're craving for it on the sea as well. The only difference here is that there might be some rules," he continued.

"There're no rules. It permits all fighting techniques. The last person standing wins," announced the priest.

"Premeditated murder, that's what it is," said Eduardo in a soft voice.

"Oh! C'mon. No one is talking about killing anyone," responded *Dom* José Nuno da Silva. "It's nothing but entertainment for everyone on the ship. Besides, *Senhor* Barbosa may win a handsome prize. The captain has promised to move you to the second cabin, where conditions are much better if all of you agree to fight. It might help Constância's delicate constitution. Don't you think?" *Dom* José Nuno da Silva asked, as he looked around our cabin.

"I'll not take offense at some luxury," Affonso declared. "Heck, if the giant will not whip my black ass, I'm for it," Affonso stated with a wink.

"You're such a bloody lout, Affonso," responded Constância, who had built an impenetrable fortress of isolation and quietude around herself since the voyage began.

Nobody spoke for a few minutes. Lucinda, who had been watching what was going on from the cabin's far corner, walked to *Dom*

José Nuno da Silva. If she owned the ground on which she trod on land, her calculated gait towards the priest confirmed she dominated the watery space underneath her. With brows knitted in a frown and standing with arms akimbo, she declared.

"*Dom* José Nuno da Silva, you should be ashamed of yourself. Have the seas driven you out of your mind? Should that be the case, that God of yours who created the white man, and I mean the white man and not the white woman, black man, or black woman in his own image, must be a depraved, reprehensible being. Pedro de Barbosa will not fight."

Lucinda dumbfounded us. Where did she find the voice to confront one symbol of her enslavement and dehumanization? Before *Dom* José Nuno da Silva could react, we heard the familiar and unmistakable sound of Ronaldhino's feet descending with an ursine heftiness down the stairs leading to our cabin. The look of surprise when *Dom* José Nuno da Silva saw Ronaldhino's towering figure told us he hadn't met him before. From his facial expression, it was easy to guess what was going through the preacher's mind: the clarity of Eduardo's statement that the fight was nothing but a planned murder. Was extreme unction perhaps among the Father's thoughts as well? The Messman had a sardonic grin on his face as he looked at me. His daily schedule didn't bring him to our cabin at this time of day, yet here he was. To evaluate his prey. The contest was inevitable. I felt the same way when *Senhor* Braga and his pseudo abolitionists asked me to be a spokesperson for the so-called freed slaves. In both instances, an indisputable compensatory allure cohabited with a subtle threat. Refusal to comply had probable consequences.

I drew a long, hard look at Ronaldhino. I had fought people of his stature, weight, and demeanor in boxing rings and won. Those fights had set guidelines. My bout with Ronaldhino would adhere to no rules. Jacinto Cardoso introduced me to Antonio Guimarães' *capoeira* club in the Lower City when I quit boxing. Grounded in dance, acrobatics, and music, I reckoned that blending boxing with *capoeira* could prove decisive against Ronaldhino. Potential gains from the fight appealed to me. Three hundred fellows on board. If each of them placed a bet of 500 *réis*, proceeds could be close to fifteen thousand *réis*. Ten percent of that sum, and I might walk away with 3000 *réis*. Not bad, but not enough for my efforts, I thought. But I saw the advantages of changing cabins, especially for Constância's sake. My shrewd business mind argued for a better deal.

"I'll fight, but only on three conditions," I said to everyone's consternation.

"David versus the ugly Goliath," Affonso said, laughing. "I get to witness the day when that stinking Bible story is unmasked for the fraud for which it is."

"Oh Lord, give me the chance and strength to slay myself before I murder this idiot," Lucinda said, looking at me. "Pedro de Barbosa, you have the brains of a dimwit. I would also add that your stupidity is unparalleled. Look at that mountain of flesh. Do you think your pitiful tiny ass can turn that pile? Even if you had a million mustard seeds, I doubt they would generate enough faith to move this shit of a mountain."

"Watch your dirty mouth, young woman. Shitty mountain, I ain't. What I am, though, is a bloody crusher, and I can't wait to earn easy money at the expense of this little nigger," Ronaldhino responded.

I ignored our friendly giant and, turning to *Dom* José Nuno da Silva, I declared.

"The first of my three conditions is five percent of the proceeds as my appearance fee. Second, I'd like twenty-five percent of the earnings if I win and twenty if I lose. Before the bout, I'd like you to move us to the second cabin.

"Fantastic!" shouted Affonso. "I'd prefer to be in an extra space on the ship before the fight. I would hate for your ghost to come haunting us down here after they throw your body into the sea. When do we pack?"

The older Eduardo smacked Affonso on the head. "Will you quit being the clown you've been since you were born?"

Dom José Nuno da Silva cleared his throat and replied, "I'll see about your terms."

He clambered up the stairs and disappeared from our cabin. Ronaldhino followed suit, but not before glaring at us. "You're dead meat." He spat on the floor. The stairs creaked, protesting the mass.

"Dead meat you are," said Lucinda. "So, you used to be a boxer, eh? What more is there you haven't revealed about yourself?" she demanded.

"Lucinda, leave the poor fellow alone," Affonso said. "He is a kind man, and he's already on his way to improving our living conditions. The best thing to do is to pray his death isn't painful," Affonso added.

"Affonso, why in God's name are you so obsessed about Pedro de Barbosa's death? The last time I checked, God hadn't commissioned you as his messenger to identify who is dying and when," Eduardo said.

Constância once again broke her impregnable bastion of silence and inquired, "Why isn't anyone here talking about our trip? Have you all forgotten its importance? Of what use will it be if something happened to Pedro de Barbosa?"

It occurred to me that this was the most opportune moment to tell my companions what I thought to be our trip's true purpose. I expressed my suspicions about the treaty and the real motives behind King John VI's decision to dispatch so-called freed slave to England. The cabin became quiet when I finished.

"Whoa! A few minutes ago, I didn't consider you a fool. Now, I see why Lucinda suspects you're an imbecile," declared Constância.

"What has Pedro Barbosa mentioned that makes you conclude thus?" Eduardo asked Constância.

"Because his explanation about this, our journey, doesn't add up," she stated.

"How so?" Lucinda interjected.

"Let me get this right," Constância began. "So, Pedro de Barbosa thinks *a abolição do comércio de escravos* is a farce; Portugal and King John VI plan to deceive the British they're upholding the treaty; they send a few freed slaves from Brazil to England as testimony that they are implementing the agreement; they want the British warships attacking Spanish ships not to decimate Portuguese vessels since they wouldn't be carrying slaves from West Africa to Brazil;

in reality, though, the Portuguese aim to continue trafficking; and
. . ."

"Yes, yes," Affonso spoke, interrupting Constância, "That's
what Pedro Barbosa stated, and if you plan to tell us you don't
trust him, you're the moron."

"You can call me whatever you want, but I believe in *a abolição
do comércio de escravos*, and that is why I'm on this voyage," Constância declared.

"I don't remember an invitation to a party to celebrate your
freedom from *Senhor* Pedro Batista Braga, our own and truly esteemed *filho da uma puta*" Affonso said.

"I've something else to report," I announced to the group.

"About your cleverness in figuring out these bloody Portuguese
and appraising how you will die at the hands of one of them?"
Affonso asked.

"No, Affonso. It's about my intelligence in liberating you from
Senhor Pedro Batista Braga, your own and esteemed *filho da uma puta*,"
I responded.

"There we go again. The idiot spews nonsense once more," stated an even angrier Constância, who couldn't understand how everyone accepted my hypothesis about the journey.

"What're you waiting for? Let's hear your brilliant idea, Mr.
Liberator," Affonso said.

"I'm not returning to Salvador. You shouldn't either," I stated.

Affonso's high-pitched laughter rang throughout the cabin again.

"So, our Toussaint L'Ouverture's splendid idea to liberate us is
to decline returning to Salvador. The fine liberator you are, Pedro
de Barbosa," Affonso scoffed.

"Have you forgotten we're still *Senhor* Pedro Batista Braga's
slaves?" Lucinda asked.

"No. But I know we're traveling to a country where slavery no
longer exists. Its laws apply to anyone who's there, which means you
will no longer be under Portugal's legal jurisdiction," I answered.

There was silence.

"What the hell will we do in England? Thought of that too?"
Affonso asked.

"I plan to go to Dahomey and to set up a trading business. A lot of freed slaves have repatriated to Dahomey on the West African coast. I understand most of them are doing well. You're welcome to come with me, but if you decide not to do so, I have saved money for each one of you to begin a new life as a freed slave in England," I announced.

"Your offer is generous, but I reject it," declared Constância.

"Servitude and bondage become you, Constância. What are you afraid of?" Affonso asked.

Constância was silent.

"What's your angle?" Eduardo asked in a manner that insinuated he had incriminating evidence against my honesty.

"I am in love," I replied.

"What in God's name does love have to do with this?" Affonso asked.

I looked at Lucinda.

"Oh! I see. You are in love with Lucinda. I thought it was with Ronaldhino," Affonso stated.

Everybody laughed.

"And what makes you think a lovely lady such as Lucinda will fall for an ugly, lousy bastard like you?" Affonso asked.

"Lucinda likes my gorgeous legs. So, she told me," I responded with a smile.

"No, I did not," Lucinda replied.

I walked towards her and, with one knee on the floor, I pulled out of my shirt pocket a small box and offered it to her. It contained a silver ring I had bought from a jeweler in *Pelourinho*. Everybody was silent as Lucinda opened the package. An opal stone in the middle, she put the ring on and announced, "Yes!"

"Oh! How wonderful. He is the sweetest and most romantic fellow in the world. Isn't he? But, Lucinda, you're saying 'yes' to nothing. The man didn't even propose. Make him grovel and ask for your fabulous hand," said Affonso.

"Oh! shut your big mouth up, Affonso," Constância declared.

"Thank you," Eduardo said.

"Lucinda, will you please marry me?"

"Now, the real liberator speaks," Affonso declared.

"Yes, I will," Lucinda answered, the fullness of her indisputable beauty and femininity enveloping the entire group.

Despite the eminent contempt I had built up for *Dom* José Nuno da Silva and the institution he represented, I asked him to wed us on the ship. It was a solemn ceremony, and I must confess that although I had banished my Catholic faith to purgatory, there was something charming in that timeless ritual of vow-taking that I embraced it with serenity and solemnity. Lucinda was the most beautiful bride one could have contemplated, both on land and sea. With the tailored dress that she was to wear to the British Parliament, Lucinda radiated an infectious glamor that overwhelmed everybody. Constância was her bridesmaid. Affonso and Eduardo were my groomsmen. *Senhor* Cristiano Ronaldhino Coelho served as a witness. A befitting celebration awaited us in Lisbon, we decided.

*****

They set the boxing match for a Saturday evening, a week and a half before our expected arrival in Lisbon. I had four days between when they settled on the fight conditions and the fight day. Under the agreement, they moved us from our third-class, enclosed berth cabin to the more luxurious second cabins. Instead of a messman, we had stewards. Ronaldhino was no longer a regular feature. I turned Affonso's and my room into an improvised gym. We turned empty bags into punching bags, which we tied to a rafter. I trained for hours before the event. Eduardo and Affonso sparred with me. I shadowboxed the air and went through *capoeira* moves, starting with *balança,* which, mixed with boxing, combined feint movements side to side to deceive the opponent. I concentrated on *cocorinha* and *esquival de baixa,* defensive and escape moves, and *esquival lateral,* deployed to protect oneself from the opponent's kick or other attacking moves. Given his gargantuan form, I worked on *rasteira* and *negativa* used to take an opponent down to the ground. I spent a while on *bananeira,* a move I thought I could use as a last resort. The intensity of my training, confidence, and focus took away the apprehensions that my companions had harbored.

They put together a makeshift ring on the ship's upper deck on the fight day. Slaves who did most of the grueling work on the vessel brought chairs from cabins to the deck. The front row around the ring belonged to the most esteemed passengers on the ship and those who had placed higher bets. Among them were our dear priest, *Dom* José Nuno da Silva, and the king's representative, *Senhor* Cristiano Ronaldhino Coelho. The late afternoon weather was perfect. Even waters replaced the Atlantic Ocean's high winds and turbulent waves. Still as a millpond, an even surface provided for a flat boxing ring. No errant clouds appeared in the sky to disturb the fine, striking blue.

From the lower deck, we could hear the crowd that had filled the seats. Affonso and Eduardo were to be in my corner. We all gathered in our cabin. Constância insisted we invoke *Oludumaré*, the Supreme Creator, his lesser deities, *Orixas*, and my *axé* before going up. I consented with little conviction. Lucinda hugged me and gave me a full kiss on the lips. I melted. Paradise awaited, and I would not miss it. A knock on our cabin door signaled it was time for the contest. I tensed. Affonso planted his hands on my shoulders and massaged them.

"You'll be fine if you stick to our fight plan. Trust yourself as we all count on you," Affonso said.

A boisterous crowd greeted us when we got to the deck. Hoots, hisses, catcalls, and whistles came from all sides as I approached the ring. I wore red trunks with socks and leather boots. The fans came to witness a massacre. They had informed me before the contest that the bet was 20 to 1 in Ronaldhino's favor. I mounted the ring and began shadowboxing. The heckling continued. The crowd went wild when Ronaldhino's imposing figure made its way into the ring. As he clambered into the makeshift ring, the planks of wood creaked and sagged, paying homage to my opponent. He blew kisses at the adoring throng and pointed to his trunks and stockings: Portugal's national colors—red and green. The spectators were ecstatic.

Ronaldhino's features, which I described earlier, came into sharper focus in the ring. As I contemplated him, the immensity of his enormous chest, coupled with bundled, suntanned arm and leg muscles, stood out. The mustache on his thin upper lip, lodged on a face fixed to a massive head, took on a sinister shape when he smiled. A scar gracing the left side of his ear down to the chin was enough to send petrified children scurrying to find refuge behind their mothers' skirts. Meanwhile, as I continued shadowboxing to contain my nervousness, I mean fear, Ronaldhino paced like a confined tiger, his muscles tight and his eyes blazing.

Regolio Umberto, the referee, entered the ring and announced the rules of engagement: they permitted any kind of fighting techniques. Each round would last three minutes with a minute of rest. Whoever kept standing won. The fans erupted in cheers. As the ship's captain, turned referee, went to one side of the ring to begin the fight, I suffered a panic attack. If the stomach is fear's preferred permanent residence, my buckling knees on the makeshift scaffold of a ring were its summer home. When the bell rang, I stood in my corner shadowboxing the air. The crowd booed. I cut a pathetic figure for myself.

"What the fuck are you doing?" Affonso cried. I didn't hear him.

Ronaldhino wasn't in any hurry. The crusher had a while to do his job. He could have ended the contest had he strolled over and punched the bloody hell out of me. But he waited, and that was his mistake.

"Pedro de Barbosa, do you have a death wish or what? If so, why did you marry me?" That cry pulled me out of whatever stupor in which I was trapped. I recognized it, and with the sound of that voice, the experiences of the many fights I had fought throughout Brazil and the adrenaline that I had always harnessed and deployed moved through my body. Ronaldhino must have sensed the change in me because, in an instant, he stood in front of me delivering a right hook I avoided with a *balança*. The power with which he delivered the blow, and its inability to hit the intended target, forced Ronaldhino to spin. Before he could recover, I used a *negativa* that sent him sprawling on the floor. The wooden planks creaked, the crowd gasped, but my opponent got on his feet in an instant. His immediate reaction came as a warning shot: if I or the spectators thought this corpulent Messman was indolent and in poor shape to give a good account of himself, he wasn't.

Ronaldhino took an upright boxing stance and reached for me with a straight jab. His height gave him an advantage with a longer reach. Even though I backed up, he still caught me on the forehead. The force of the jab almost snapped my head off and sent me to the ropes. The son of a bitch was quick and good. He followed up with body punches to my ribs that knocked the bloody wind out of my sails. The bell rang. It saved me.

Eduardo and Affonso climbed into the ring and helped me to my corner. As Eduardo gave me water, Affonso said, "Don't engage in a boxing match. He will kill you if you do that. Use *balança* for this round. Don't throw any punches. Let him chase you. Let him tire himself out. That's what you need to do to survive this giant of a man."

The bell rang, and before I could get out of my corner, Ronaldhino Ferreira was once again in front of me. I followed Affonso's advice. As I made feint side-to-side movements, from one leg to the other, not only did I deceive Ronaldhino, but I also made it difficult for him to track each of my next moves. The more he swung and missed, the more frustrated and tired he became. At the tail of the second round, I landed several quick kicks and an unexpected head butt that dazed him. *Rasteira*, a final capoeira move, sent the giant crushing on the floor again. Yet again, the Portuguese brawler, the ship's passengers' white hope, got up before the bell sounded for the end of the second round. He went to his corner, his eyes blazing with anger and partial humiliation like an injured predator forced to hobble back to its lair.

The crowd was becoming agitated. I saw frantic heavy betting going on all over the deck among the merchants and the businessmen. *Dom* José Nuno da Silva Mendes and *Senhor* Cristiano Ronaldhino Coelho were full participants. My stock was undoubtedly rising. Astute gamblers knew where to place their bets. It certainly wasn't on Ronaldhino. Amid all that action, I noticed a man in the front row, next to *Dom* José Nuno da Silva Mendes and *Senhor* Cristiano Ronaldhino Coelho, studying me and relishing, perhaps, my wit and craft. I had seen him earlier, sharing a few words with *Senhor* Cristiano Ronaldhino Coelho.

I went into an attack mode when the bell rang for the third round. Ill-advised, Ronaldhino rushed in. I negated his incoming attack, lowering my body to the ground and moving aside. I hooked his leg with mine, and with the other, I aimed at his groin. It was a perfect *vengativa* move. Its suddenness and the pain sent him slamming onto the floor. The throng went silent. Cheers from my corner and the slaves from the far reaches of the deck filled the air. As I turned around to acknowledge the applauds, Affonso leaped into the ring. His eyes brimmed with fear.

"Duck, he's got a knife in his . . ."

Ronaldhino swung at me, and as I crouched, the six-inch dagger found its way straight into Affonso's throat. In an instant, he was in the middle of the ring, blood gushing from his trachea. He was dead in a flash. The wail that echoed throughout the deck rose out of both Lucinda and Constância like a tempest assailing their souls. The shock, rage, tears, and anguish all coalesced in a visceral and violent eruption in our hearts. Captain Regolio Umberto ordered Affonso's body removed, and the ring moped. He announced, delaying the fight for twenty minutes. The spectators cheered. The announcement stunned us. I had no urge to fight. Emotionally and physically drained, we converged at my corner, hugged each another and cried. The man I had seen earlier approached the captain. He shook his head. It appeared he was the only spectator who disapproved of the referee's decision. I wondered who he was.

"That's it for me. I'm not fighting," I said between tears. The unspeakable dreadfulness of losing Affonso had unanchored me.

"I don't blame you. There's nothing they can do if you decide not to fight," Eduardo said.

"And Affonso? Would he have died in vain?" Lucinda challenged, looking at me with tears in her eyes. "Affonso was more than a friend. He was a brother," she added.

"That offspring of a bitch should pay and pay dearly. The only way we exact revenge for Affonso is for you, Pedro de Barbosa, to go back into that bloody ring and beat the shit out of that bloody son of a bitch who murdered the most wonderful person in the world. You hear me, Pedro de Barbosa?" Constância asked.

Constância's order to battle should have been my clarion call. As I contemplated the fact that Affonso had saved my life, I harnessed the raw emotions that were gelling into an intense urgency to retaliate on Affonso's behalf. Ronaldhino's brutal act told everybody that fair fights weren't his cup of tea. He had lived his entire life by cheating. I wasn't in any position to claim I was any better. But I hadn't taken another man's life when presented with the same set of circumstances as Ronaldhino. I resolved to resume the contest. As we continued to hug each other, our cries converged into a solo voice, bellowing a message of unambiguous vengeance.

After twenty minutes, we climbed into the ring again. Regolio Umberto stated the rules once more. Before we restarted the match, he made sure that none of us had any knives or objects tucked into our boots or stockings. I wondered why it hadn't occurred to him to have done so earlier. As we shook hands to wait for the bell, I looked straight into Ronaldhino's eyes and said, "Little coward, you're dead meat."

He smiled, but I could see the fear in those eyes that pretended a false sense of calm. I knew with no doubt that it was the danger he felt as he returned my gaze. Before the bell tolled for the inevitable fourth round, Lucinda, Constância, and Eduardo burst into a *capoeira* song called *A Bananeira Caiu*—The Banana Tree fell.

> *The Banana Tree fell*
> *My machete struck low*
> *The banana tree fell*
> *The machete struck low*
> *The banana tree fell*
> *Fall, fall, banana tree*
> *The banana tree fell*

The song saturated us with an unbridled emotion akin to the songs that compelled men to take up arms. Its subtext was evident to Eduardo and me. I had practiced the *bananeira* move, which I had planned to use only as a last resort. This was the moment. I took the handstand pose when I heard the tune. The spectators gasped at the rapidity with which I went from my feet to my hands. The bell rang, and in a few seconds, Ronaldhino understood why *bananeira* was one of the most unpredictable and deadly *capoeira* moves. I somersaulted several times and stopped. Just when he rushed in, I flipped up again and flew as high as I could, towering over him as though I was a peregrine falcon ready to dive for its prey. I aimed the forefingers of both hands at his eyes. The impact produced a loud popping sound. Ronaldhino shrieked as he put his hands to his eyes. Vitreous gel and blood bathed his fingers. He flopped in the ring, and in a split second, I had his thick neck locked between my thighs. The laws of self-preservation abandoned him when he needed it most. He couldn't decide which part of his body to protect: his mutilated eyes or his neck, which was in a tight vise, courtesy of my robust thighs. As the coup de grâce, I inserted my fingers into his nostrils, blocking any errant air determined to enter his lungs. Ronaldhino fought for dear life, but I was in no mood for beneficence. A few minutes afterward, they removed a limp and lifeless gigantic body from the makeshift ring, which they dismantled in a hurry.

The four of us held a memorial in our cabin for Affonso that evening. They buried him at sea the following morning. As they laid his body to rest, Lucinda, in a haunting, plaintive voice, broke into a familiar song etched in our collective memory that spoke of the odyssey that bounded Affonso's life and ours.

Boa Viagem	*Bon Voyage*
Boa viagem	*Bon Voyage*
Adeus, adeus	*Goodbye, Goodbye*
Boa viagem	*Bon Voyage*
Eu vou	*I'm going*
Boa viagem	*Bon Voyage*
Eu vou, eu vou	*I'm going, I'm going*
Boa viagem	*Bon Voyage*
Eu vou-me embora	*I'm going to leave*
Boa viagem	*Bon Voyage*
Eu vou agora	*I'm going now*
Boa viagem	*Bon Voyage*
Eu vou com Deus	*I go with God*
Boa viagem	*Bon Voyage*
E com Nossa Senhora	*And with Our Lady*
Boa viagem	*Bon Voyage*
Chegou a hora	*The hour has arrived*
Boa viagem	*Bon Voyage*
Adeus...	*Goodbye. . .*
Boa viagem	*Bon Voyage*

Chapter 13

"I'm sorry for your loss," declared a voice behind me as I stood on the ship's deck, contemplating the great Atlantic Ocean. There was sunshine on the ocean, and the intensity of the waves that plunged and spattered on the sides of *Cisne Vermelho* was cobalt blue. In the distance, a pod of dolphins jumped out of the water, and as they dipped back into the watery surface, the little waves they created merged into wider ones, furnishing them with greater buoyancy on the horizon. It had been two days since we lost Affonso. I turned around to discover the fellow who had stared at me during my fight with Ronaldhino. He was the same person who protested the continuance of the contest after Affonso's homicide.

"*Governador* Ladislao Belarmino," the man declared, presenting his hand. He was short and of hardy frame, freshly shaven, with a bulky, twisted nose, and glistening and discerning eyes that kindled his face.

"*Senhor* Pedro de Barbosa," I replied, shaking his hand.

"I know who you are and the purpose of your trip," he stated, beaming.

For a minute, I was silent. I pride myself in my excellent memory, and never overlook the names or the faces of the people I meet, even if that encounter is only once. The features and the name of the man standing in front of me didn't set off any such recollection. His title: Governor also astounded me. Of what and where? I deliberated. My interlocutor disrupted my thoughts.

"Your trip to England with *Dom* José Nuno da Silva Mendes and *Senhor* Cristiano Ronaldhino Coelho is a very important service to the Kingdom of Portugal. I'm playing my part as the designated governor to Dahomey," *Governador* Ladislao Belarmino spoke with controlled force.

"Ah, I see," I reacted. "Why does Portugal need a governor in Dahomey if they're ending the slave trade?" I quizzed him. My skepticism must have caused dismay because it took him a moment to counter.

"Oh! We prefer to maintain our alliance with Dahomey," the minted governor replied without conviction.

"Yes," I acknowledged and proceeded, "And we're shipping to London folk who're still in servitude and professing they're free? Isn't it?"

"You're a brave and accomplished fighter. It fascinated me how you disposed of Ronaldhino. I detest men who don't engage in a fair fight," *Governador* Ladislao Belarmino responded, as he settled beside me and observed the horizon and the dolphins that were yet expressing their breathtaking maneuvers.

"Do people fight fair?" I asked the governor, conscious that he had switched the terms of our discursive conflict to another area that wasn't a rebuttal to my previous claim.

"I should expect that most do. I am sure both of us do."

I was silent.

"I want to make you a proposal."

"What kind?"

"To employ you as my assistant and bodyguard."

"Oh?" I reacted, lifting my eyebrow.

"*Senhor* de Barbosa, the man I had selected for that position, changed his mind just before I left Salvador. There wasn't sufficient time to consider a replacement. I was aiming to enlist someone in Lisbon. I think you'll make an excellent substitute," responded the governor.

"You've just met me. You don't know the slightest detail about my story and my ultimate ambitions. What causes you to think I'd like to surrender them and retire to Dahomey?"

"Because like you, I trust in the Royal cause."

I grew tired of this farce and decided not to dance along any longer. I considered the governor's offer a most promising introduction to Dahomey under the Portuguese royal banner. I reckoned it was a sign that madam fortune was welcoming me into her friendly arms, paving the path to accomplish my secret mission. I surmised that my official capacity as the governor's assistant would grant me an instant connection to those who transported human merchandise from the interior to the coast for transaction and for transport to Salvador. I pushed home my advantage, given *Governador* Belarmino's handicap.

"*Governador* Belarmino, there might be an overlap between my particular interests and those of your sovereign, King John VI. If I were to travel to Dahomey, however, I would play by my own rules."

"I am sorry I don't follow," *Governador* Belarmino said.

"Oh! Let's quit playing games. You and those whose interests you serve in Brazil and Portugal are not eager to end slavery. You realize it, and so do I. Heck, I am not interested in terminating it either. I foresee my ultimate success in the trade."

Governador Belarmino studied me, unaware that I had already weighed the benefits of going to Dahomey under the Portuguese monarchy's patronage.

"I may have underestimated you, *Senhor* Barbosa. What place could be better if your future rests in the traffic?" the governor inquired.

"What are the terms of your offer?" I asked.

"You'd be my special aide and security guard. You'll learn more about your compensation after I've consulted with King John VI's bureaucrats in Lisbon. They represent the monarch on the peninsular while he is in Brazil, said *Governador* Belarmino.

I accepted *Governador* Belarmino's proposal. Delighted, he revealed more about himself. He had received his initial order and memoranda of appointment as governor of Dahomey from King John VI in Rio de Janiero. The monarch and his government had retired to Brazil in 1807, following the imminent arrival of Napoleon's troops from Spain. *Governador* Belarmino had been born in Lisbon, read law at the University of Coimbra, and had been in Brazil for the preceding three years as legal counsel for the Braganza Royal court in Rio de Janeiro. The *Governador* invited me to dine with him and his family in the first cabin the ensuing evening to celebrate our new partnership. I informed him I had just married and planned to accept his invitation if Lucinda came along. He assented.

First cabin passengers like *Governador* Belarmino and his folk occupied one of the most luxurious spaces on the ship. The governor, his wife, *Senhora* Matilde Belarmino, and their twelve-year-old girl, Terezinha Belarmino, greeted Lucinda and me. I've always wondered how ugly husbands such as the governor end up marrying women as remarkable as Matilde. Complete disclosure. I would count myself in the community of brothers such as the governor if you saw me standing beside Lucinda, who wore the same immaculate dress as the day we wed. It would be hard for all who met *Senhora* Matilde Belarmino not to memorize the charming details of her profile. With eager warm eyes, she caught her brown, luxuriant hair in tight curls at the forehead and on both sides of her head. Her solid-colored silk overskirt or *manteau* had an open face that created a train at the back. Padded at the hips, the waistline appeared high, offering a complete, flowing expression. Despite her elegance, there was something quiet and genuine about her. The strong resemblance between *Senhora* Matilde Belarmino and her offspring foreshadowed what Terezinha would look like when she came of age.

"Congratulations on your wedding. Ladislao told me about it," said *Senhora* Matilde as she held out her hand to Lucinda. She had a natural smile.

"Thank you," Lucinda replied. There wasn't anything in Lucinda's demeanor that would have shown she was a slave. From what I had noticed from her encounter with *Dom* José Nuno da Silva, I recognized she carried a calmness and tenacity that didn't pay homage or play second fiddle to anyone.

"What next? Lucinda? Are you coming along to Dahomey with Pedro?" *Governador* Belarmino asked.

"Ladislao!" Senhora Matilde Belarmino said, glaring at her companion. "They just got married. I doubt they've had the chance to work out their future. Am I not right?" she inquired, looking at Lucinda.

Matilde was intuitive. I hadn't formulated a narrative for Lucinda concerning my true motives for traveling to Dahomey. And Dahomey? Would I go with Lucinda or play as the advance party and prepare the way and place for her later arrival? The governor's question and Matilde's reproach brought into sharpened focus the fact that I could no longer think only about myself. I had become a new tenant in the community of the hitched. There was no going back. *Governador* Belarmino interjected before Lucinda responded to a future that, like me, she had yet to contemplate.

"After your trip to London, perhaps, Lucinda can remain with Matilde and Terezinha in our home in Lisbon until we're both ready to receive all of them in Dahomey."

"What a brilliant idea, Ladislao," Matilde stated before we could respond. The couple's generosity touched me.

"That's settled then. Now, let's celebrate," *Governador* Belarmino said as he led the party to the dining table and the waiting feast.

*****

We arrived in Lisbon a few days after our evening with *Governador* Belarmino and his wife. *Dom* José Nuno da Silva had made lodging plans for us in the capital for a week before our passage for London. But the governor requested that Lucinda and I, along with our colleagues, spend the week in his home in Lisbon. In Baixa Pombalina, his house was a classic *Pombalina* style, planned to resist shocks after the 1775 seismic catastrophe that demolished part of Lisbon. *Governador* Belarmino's home had a facade with small, yet interesting ornamental details that suggested the edifice belonged to a well-to-do family. Next to the building was another one that belonged to the governor's parents. Our guest's mansion had four levels with a merchant shop on the ground floor. Balconies on the second and third floors overlooked *São Cristóvão* street. *Governador* Belarmino and his household stayed on the second floor with three chambers, a bath, and a gallery. Constância and Eduardo had rooms on the third floor. Newlyweds, they offered Lucinda and me the part with a cavernous and adorned attic.

Our time in Lisbon would turn into the most enduring experience in my life. With her affinity for religious architecture, despite her uncertain faith, Lucinda, following *Senhora* Matilde Belarmino's advice, recommended that we see the *Mosteiro Jerónimos* and the *Torre Belém*. There were no such constructions with historical and architectural elegance in Salvador, and the *estilo manuelino*—the Manuelin style—that defined both buildings dazzled us. It was a style of architectural embellishment that combined naval elements and images of the discoveries, or should I say plunders, from the voyages of Vasco da Gama and Pedro Álvares Cabral. We went on an adventure through Lisbon's narrow streets. Because ours was nothing but a visit, a pass-through, an exploration, we had the leisure to take in the details of buildings bulging with colorful balconies bursting with flowerpots and caged birds that hummed along with their fluttering uncaged brethren that carried news from distant places. We stopped at the shores of the blue Tagus estuary, jammed with ships and *fragatas* reminiscent of the Phoenicians who conquered these geographies centuries earlier. The noise and hubbub of fishermen selling their day's catch to *varinas*—female fish vendors—who we would meet later in the streets, clad in long black skirts and carrying their wares in baskets on their heads— reminded us very much of Salvador. From small bars, we smelled garlic and onions simmering in olive oil that constituted the base of dishes such as *Bacalhau com broa*, *Cataplana de Lagosta*, and *Arroz de Mariscos*. We inhaled from wide windows the aromas of Iberian lamb and pork made from recipes conceived years ago and passed down from generation to generation. We held hands as we strolled. When we got to a flower booth, I purchased a single purple rose and offered it to Lucinda. She asked the vendor, an elderly woman, to place it in her hair. Her response revealed it wasn't the first occasion people had implored her to do such a thing.

"*Que beleza*"—what beauty—," she announced after she had dethorned the rose and fixed it in the large multicolored head tie that Lucinda wore.

I couldn't help the irresistible impulse to catch glimpses of Lucinda's face. Confident in her striking looks, she was self-effacing and accepted complete responsibility for her charm. I tickled the inside of her palm several times, and the result invariably was the same: her face crumpled with laughter.

Our walks all ended the same way. We sheltered ourselves in our attic where our bodies consumed one another's with careless abandon as if our very lives and happiness depended upon offering ourselves our souls on the shrine of lust and desire. With Lucinda's naked body against mine, her tongue seeking mine, wriggling, and interweaving, her hand guided me to that wet spot of hers. We saw ourselves floating and slipping into a chasm. An ancient wisdom inscribed in our bodies lured us into a space filled with shivering and intertwining membranes and shafts determined to suck the air out of us, only then to offer a lifeline to cling on to untold pleasures.

On the fifth day after our arrival in Lisbon, *Dom* José Nuno visited to reveal that they had delayed our trip to London. *Senhor* Cristiano Ronaldhino Coelho had been taken ill. This news pleased me. I was falling deeper and deeper in love with Lucinda, and Lisbon served as the backdrop, the cradle that harnessed those forces that rendered men weak-kneed and coerced them to pay ultimate homage to the love of their lives.

Governador Belarmino and his spouse suggested we visit their modest ranch in Sintra, a small town in the foothills of the Sintra mountains, an hour and a half away from Lisbon. The governor's parents, who were spending their summer and part of the autumn at the estate, met us at the property even before we stepped out of the carriage. In their mid-seventies, *Dom* Gregorio Belarmino and his wife, *Senhora* Lucrecia Belarmino, looked robust and walked with a spring in their respective steps. *Dom* Gregorio Belarmino, a retired judge, was passionate about raising horses and making wine from the vineyard beside the country home. *Senhora* Lucrecia Belarmino, from whom the governor got his luminous and attentive eyes, had been a teacher in a parochial school in Lisbon. The couple couldn't avoid kissing their granddaughter, whom they hadn't seen in over three years.

"Terezinha! How wonderful you've grown," *Senhora* Lucrecia Belarmino declared as she held her granddaughter as though she was afraid of losing her once again.

Dom Gregorio Belarmino embraced Matilde, her daughter-in-law, held her, closed his eyes, and inhaled in the pure country air and the balsam in her hair.

"Welcome home, sweetheart," he announced. "I hope that rascal of a son doesn't take you and Terezinha away from us again. I'm happy he's continuing to Dahomey, but I'm not confident it's a place for such elegant women like you and Terezinha," he maintained.

"Don't put any crazy ideas into her head," *Governador* Belarmino said. "If you were to ask me, I'd tell you that Matilde and Terezinha are much stronger than I am," the Governor continued as both father and son embraced and kissed each other on the cheeks.

Governador Belarmino introduced Lucinda and me, along with Constância and Eduardo.

"*Senhor* Pedro de Barbosa and Lucinda were married on the ship. They're so much in love. Isn't it so Lucinda?" Terezinha asked, holding Lucinda's hand. Both had become fond of each other after Lucinda began teaching Terezinha how to cook dishes with their origin from Africa. They included *acarajé* and *moqueca aos ovos*—spicy egg stew. The young girl enjoyed cooking and sampling all kinds of new delicacies.

"Ah! Newlyweds. I have the perfect gift for you two," *Dom* Gregorio Belarmino said with a glimmer, showing that *Governador* Belarmino had already told him about us.

"Oh, no! Don't tell us you've an attic tucked somewhere on this estate. We haven't seen these two lovebirds since the governor made the mistake of offering them the attic in their home in Lisbon," Constância said, grinning.

"Thunder and lightning have been fighting on Mount Olympus, and we, the poor souls at the base, have had to plug our ears," the soft-spoken Eduardo stated with a straight face.

The adults burst into laughter, prompting Terezinha to ask why everyone was giggling.

"Oh! It's nothing," her mother declared. "Just adult talk," she added.

Gardens, flowering plants, and lush vegetation surrounded the five acres on which the home stood. Tall European pine trees stood as sentinels lining the path to a building not noticeable from the front of the dwelling. It was the quarters of Daniel Vasconcelos and his wife, Maria, custodians of the estate. A barn next to that building was home for *Dom* Gregorio Belarmino's horses. Further away in the distance, a vineyard came into view that boasted of rows upon rows of vines that produced the finest grapes including *Aragonês*, *Castelão Frances*, and *Touriga Francesa*, used for red wines, and those such as *Códega*, *Malvasa Real*, and *Fernão Pires*, dedicated to white wines.

The double-story, hundred-year-old estate had a roof of red tiles. Neo-classic etchings and several engravings adorned the four columns leading to the structure's primary door, the window casements, and the balustrades spiraling to the second floor.

"Welcome to our refuge from the city," *Dom* Gregorio Belarmino said after Maria had opened the door to the building's main hall.

After we had cleaned up, we went to the dining room for a sumptuous lunch of *caldo verde*, made with potato, shredded kale, and chunks of *chouriço*—a spicy sausage; *cebolada de bacalhau*, a cod and onion dish; and *arroz doce*, a rice pudding decorated with cinnamon and caramel custard that was served as dessert. We would have observed a siesta, but *Dom* Gregorio Belarmino was impatient to shower us with our wedding gift. He led the entire party to the estate's entrance and ordered his son to blindfold Lucinda and me.

"*Avô*, can you whisper in my ear what the wedding present is?" Terezinha asked her grandfather as her father tied a red scarf around Lucinda's eyes.

"No, Terezinha. From the little I have observed, you and Lucinda are good pals. I cannot trust you," *Dom* Gregorio Belarmino said.

"Aw! *Avô*! I have never met that lady in my entire life," Terezinha responded, smiling.

"Ah! Yes! That's true. Did I just recall that an intelligent little fibber told me a short while ago that two strangers got married on the ship? I wonder who that liar is," responded *Dom* Gregorio Belarmino with a deadpan look.

"OK, *Avô*, if you won't, Vovô will. Will you Vovô?" Terezinha urged, as she strolled to *Senhora* Lucrecia and gripped her hand.

"Of course, love," *Dohna* Lucrecia responded as she stooped down and murmured something in Terezinha's ear.

The young girl was bug-eyed. "Really?" she exclaimed.

"Oh yes," said the grandmother.

"Can I teach Lucinda how to ..."

Before she could finish, *Senhora* Lucrecia placed her index finger on Terezinha's mouth, charging her granddaughter to be silent. We didn't have to stand by long for the surprise. After they blindfolded us, we heard the dull drumming of hoofbeats arriving from the back of the house.

"A horse?" I asked myself. What an unusual wedding present. I thought. Once they removed the blindfold, our eyes caught a breathtaking sight as they adapted to sunshine that glistened the mahogany-bay glow of a stallion best defined as regal. For a few moments, an unpardonable crime of speechlessness struck me when what I desired at that moment was a full-throated expression of appreciation.

"If you will be my son's aide and security guard, you'll require your own horse. He's planning on taking *Trovão* to Dahomey. You should take *Arion* with you," *Dom* Gregorio Belarmino suggested.

"Thank you, *Dom* Gregorio," I uttered. Terezinha saw my uneasiness.

"*Avô*, but *Senhor* Pedro de Barbosa doesn't know how to ride a horse," Terezinha said. "Do you?" Terezinha asked me.

"I'm afraid not, Terezinha," I replied, feeling embarrassed.

"And Lucinda? Do you?" the young girl inquired, turning to my wife.

It took Lucinda a few minutes to respond. I wondered what passed through her mind. The gift's incredulity? How far she had come in a matter of weeks? What was apparent was Terezinha's innocence of the conditions under which Lucinda and I had re-mained since childhood. Lessons in horseback riding, and its culti-vation as a hobby, didn't factor in the job description of any slave I had come upon. The twelve-year-old may have seen slaves. But had she come into close contact with any of them? If she did, they might have been servants in her parents' home when they were in Rio de Janeiro. It was easy to pardon the innocent.

"No, Terezinha, I don't," Lucinda responded.

"I will teach you," Terezinha said, jumping up and down and flapping her hands. She had a thing to offer Lucinda in exchange for her African culinary tutelage.

"Terezinha is an excellent horse rider. I taught her myself and am certain she will be a wonderful teacher for you, Lucinda," *Dom* Gregorio Belarmino declared, glowing with a smile. "Pedro, I will be your tutor. I would have suggested Ladislao but, even though an expert rider, he is a terrible instructor," the older Belarmino contin-ued as he winked at his son.

"He is yours, *pai*," replied Governor Belarmino.

Amid the excitement during the gifting, I detected a faint shift in Lucinda's disposition. She had grown subdued and somewhat disengaged from all that happened that evening. I ventured into her closed world after we had dinner and retired to our cozy guest room.

"It's been a fantastic day, hasn't it?" I declared as we rested in bed.

"Uh-huh," she muttered.

"Aren't *Dom* Gregorio Belarmino and his wife remarkable hosts? And our wedding present? Such a gift! Who could have come up with such an idea? I wager it was the governor," I mused.

"I guess so," Lucinda responded.

"What do you think about it?" I inquired as I reached out and kissed Lucinda on her lips. She turned her back to me.

"What's the matter, *meu amor*? I inquired.

"Did you ever inquire whether I wished to go to Dahomey?" Lucinda asked as she sat up with her back against the bedpost and arms crossed over her chest.

"Why did I have to ask? I thought I had mentioned it to you and everyone else on the ship."

"Is that what you call asking? You consider telling an entire group of people your plans the same as asking me?"

"Well," I started, but Lucinda interrupted.

"Well, what? First, you said you wanted to move to Dahomey to set up a trading business. You didn't provide details. The next thing, you will be the aide and bodyguard to a governor whom you met on a ship. A merchant or a lackey? Which is which? And, oh, I am expected to stick around in Lisbon until you and your governor determine when I am to join you in Dahomey. Did I have a voice in this? Lucinda seethed.

I was unprepared for Lucinda's outburst and questions. I had thought that she would go along with my arrangements. Wasn't that what women did? No one had ever subjected me to this line of questioning as related to my intended ultimate objectives. I became flustered and understood that I had two options. Stamp my authority and state that the decisions I had made were final and non-negotiable and that, as my wife and as a woman, Lucinda needed to agree and do whatever I determined was best for two of us. My other alternative was to show my true intentions regarding Dahomey. Such a disclosure would lead to my discussing my subsequent dreams, of which she had now become an eminent part. I found both choices noxious and opted to straddle a fine line between the two. I'd provide half-truths, as I was wont to do under these kinds of circumstances. But I was about to learn that I had married a woman with an acute mind who could discover the most concealed intentions and fantasies blazed in one's brain.

"Lucinda, *meu amor*, what made you think I was abandoning my plans to be a merchant? Working as *Governador* Belarmino's aide will strengthen my position," I argued.

"Do you recall what you told us on the ship? You said the Portuguese aren't interested in *a abolição do comércio de escravos* and that they're only keen on getting the British off their backs? Lucinda asked.

"Yes," I replied.

"Do you still believe what you said?"

"Yes."

"So, isn't it why the Portuguese are assigning a governor to Dahomey?"

I fidgeted, foreseeing already where Lucinda's line of questioning was heading. Like a litigating attorney, my bride was making a case. I inhaled hard.

"I presume they intend to continue their alliance with Dahomey. At least, that is what *Governador* Belarmino mentioned," I responded.

"So, the alliance is not devoid of slave trading, is it?" Lucinda inquired.

Fury engulfed me at this moment in our conversation or, better still, my interrogation. I recognized from where came the anger. Lucinda was peeling away the layers to unveil the agenda I had concealed from her. I didn't imagine confronting the inconvenient truth so soon, and it was this prospect that both angered and terrified me.

"I was wrong in assessing the situation," I said.

"How so? That the Portuguese want to devote themselves to the abolition but want to maintain their alliance with Dahomey?" Lucinda demanded.

"Good God! Will this woman back off?" I asked myself.

"Maybe," I said.

"Maybe? Hmm," Lucinda muttered.

"What's that supposed to mean?"

"Nothing," Lucinda said. She slumped and turned her back to me again.

An awkward silence followed. Lucinda was no fool. I needed to dig myself out of the gaping hole that threatened to consume and expose me.

"Listen, Lucinda," I said. "I will make you a promise. If I get to Dahomey and find out that Governor Belarmino is nothing but the monarch's agent, whose role is to sustain the slave trade, I will stop working for him. Who knows? I might even begin a campaign to end the trade," I added.

"And what will you do if you cut your ties with him?"

"I'll trade."

"In what?"

"In cotton cloth, brass pans, glass beads, and guns," I lied.

"Aren't these the same items used in the slave trade?"

"What do you want of me, Lucinda?" I raised my voice. "Do you want us to go back to Salvador? You want to remain *Senhor* Pedro Batista Braga's slave? Maybe that's what you desire. Perhaps, like Constância, servitude and bondage have become you, as Affonso told Constância. And me? What prospects does a freed slave have in Salvador?"

"I don't know, Pedro. I don't know."

"What I hope for us, Lucinda, is a future in which we're not enslaved. A future where nobody can violate our children's' bodies. I fancy walking the streets with my children without looking over my shoulder. A life in which I wouldn't look on the ground as I communicate with another man because my skin differs from his."

"That sounds marvelous, Pedro. I likewise wish for those things. But not at the expense of a fellow human being."

I got out of bed and paced the floor. "How does one survive a storm of this magnitude that has swept and continues to tear everything in its wake?" I asked.

Lucinda was mum. The storm of which I spoke wasn't foreign to her or to any freed slave. Haiti was an exemplar. If Portugal signed a treaty with England, it meant the days of the trade could be numbered. Wasn't the British navy annihilating Spanish slave ships? Something was afoot to stem the tide of the traffic, its power. I determined that force didn't include me. Neither was I interested in being part of it. My life's ambition was still unscathed. I undertook to make the best out of the prevailing condition before that force became impregnable. I considered naïve and improbable Lucinda's efforts to hold a high moral ground and to appeal to what she hoped might be an ethical compass imprinted someplace in my soul. Lucinda shattered the quiet moment.

"The world might go insane, but that doesn't mean you should likewise follow the crazies to their asylum," my wife pronounced.

"Yeah," I said, keen to change the topic to something less depressing. I came back to Lucinda and tickled her on the most sensitive part of her body: her long, elegant neck. "How come the most gorgeous woman in the world married the ugliest man on earth?"

"Stop it," she said, giggling.

"No, I won't."

She shielded her neck with both hands, leaving vulnerable other parts of her body that soon gave in to the passion that had become familiar and inviting to both of us.

Chapter 14

I discovered a heretofore unknown knack for horse riding in Sintra. *Dom* Gregorio Belarmino was a skillful rider and an exacting instructor. He required me to understand the essentials before our trip to Dahomey. Lucinda was not as animated a student as I, despite Terezinha's and her mother's best attempts to teach her. Something frightened her when she approached the mare on which Terezinha had mastered how to ride. For the next ten days we spent at the estate, I worked my best to build a bond with *Arion*, a stallion that, as Governor Belarmino said, would be steadier and more faithful to me than my wife if I treated him nicely. I wasn't positive about that, but I took pains to learn as much as possible everything to do with horses, horseback riding, and horse care.

We returned to Lisbon after a fortnight in Sintra. *Senhor* Cristiano Ronaldhino Coelho had bounced back from his ailment and was fit to set sail for London to carry out our mission. Before our departure, I opened a bank account and deposited the cash I had brought from Salvador. I opened another for Eduardo and Constância. It included funds from various origins: the sale of the items from my stand, payment for undertaking the trip to London—I had insisted on compensation before leaving the shores of Salvador—earnings from the fight on the ship, and monies from other sources that I prefer not to reveal. I had ample reserves to begin my slave-trading enterprise in Dahomey and enough to split with Eduardo and Constância if they made London or Lisbon their new home.

Our trip to London from Lisbon was unremarkable. Having lived in the capital as Portugal's representative, *Senho*r Cristiano Ronaldhino Coelho knew the place well. We arrived late at night. A horse-drawn coach drove us from the port of London to the Durrants Hotel, a Georgian Townhouse on George Street in Marylebone. Dark wood paneling and heavy furniture from the 18th century surrounded the hotel's lobby and the adjoining coffee rooms. Military engravings and paintings of the English countryside pasted the walls. A persistent scent of tobacco smoke from the coffee areas flowed into the foyer as we entered the reception. A porter carried our trunk and admitted us to a chamber with a gigantic bed that devoured most of the space. Two straight-backed chairs stood at the foot of the bed. They decorated the plastered walls with vibrant blue and crimson wallpaper, the same color for the chairs, bedcover, and curtains.

After an English breakfast of bacon and eggs, roast beef, ham, hot chocolate, and a roll with butter, along with tea and toast, we ventured out into the English autumn morning. The overpowering stench from urine, clogged sewers and cesspools below houses accosted our noses when we emerged from the coach that welcomed us to George Street. People and an endless number of working horses crowded the route. Smoke and soot filled the air. What appeared to be mud covering the carriageway turned out to be horse manure. An unseemly sight unfolded as young boys darted in and out of the traffic, scooping horse dung. Pedestrians jumped off the streets to avoid carriages and wagons. Women crossing the streets or going alongside the carriageways wore shoes that looked seemingly designed to muddle through the muck. Several of them drew their long garments with both hands to avoid the delicate tips from hauling strewn rubble. With their purses dangling in their elbow crooks, they looked like amateur equilibrists unsure of their next steps.

I realized if Eduardo and Constância entertained any wishes of residing in London, what we saw on our previous day, coupled with our later communications with the British, might instead persuade them to make Lisbon their new home. Besides, they wouldn't have to cope with a new language and alien cultural norms in the Portuguese capital. But still, as *Senhor* Braga's slaves, they might run into legal troubles. Our handlers designed our London trip to be short, with minimal exposure to British representatives who might ask questions and detect inconsistencies in our scripts and those of our handlers. Our initial meeting took place two days after we arrived. We met with Mr. Charles Abbot, the Speaker of the House of Commons, Lord Castlereagh, the Foreign Secretary, The Right Honorable Earl Bathurst, the Secretary of State for War and the Colonies, and The Right Honorable Henry Addington, Home Secretary. They called the meeting in a vast oval office adjoining the House of Commons chamber. Several bright, opulent paintings depicting past kings, queens, and distinct English landscapes hung from the fifteen-foot beam to the floor. The portraits warded off the room's somber mood, courtesy of the black coat on wood that marked the walls. A long table circled by fifteen chairs on a bright green rug dominated the middle of the room. Thirty people sat in the chamber when we entered. Several of them, junior officials, came along with their secretaries and aides. Lord Castlereagh spoke first.

"We're here to receive our Portuguese counterparts who're visiting us in the spirit of the treaty we signed earlier this year. His Majesty, King John VI, who, as I learn from the Honorable *Senhor* Cristiano Ronaldhino Coelho, organized their visit. He is eager to notify the British State that Portugal has moved beyond the Treaty's agreement and has started to dismantle slave traffic in Brazil."

"I'm honored you've welcomed me back to London, to the seat of the Great British Empire," *Senho*r Cristiano Ronaldhino Coelho began. "I bear you greetings from his Majesty, King John VI, who, along with the people of Portugal and Brazil, its colony, are thankful for the £300,000 in cash and the £600,000 in loan forgiveness that your government has promised Portugal in our push to abolish the slave trade."

"Holy Mother of God!" I whispered under my breath. I was now comprehending the treaty's details they had withheld from us. We were actors in a drama in which they had provided us with nothing but a blank script.

What was in it for the British? I asked myself. *Senho*r Cristiano Ronaldhino Coelho's voice penetrated my thoughts.

"I'll be dishonest if I said vehement protests from some quarters haven't followed King John VI and his government's resolution to abolish the slave trade in Brazil. His Majesty and his government are, however, determined to carry through with his plans. I must add, as you'll gather from a few freed slaves that came on this trip, that some slaveholders have released their property."

*Senho*r Cristiano Ronaldhino Coelho was paving the way to present us as exotic specimens thrust into the public eye to lend credence to an accord minted in the hallways of the masters of a commerce that calculated the value of merchandise of a contrasting color, of a unique texture, of a curious race, of an unusual provenance. I had inferred the criminality of the entire enterprise. It was another matter to observe its articulation by nobody other than a state official associated with the illustrious Portuguese court. As I looked at *Senho*r Cristiano Ronaldhino Coelho in disbelief, Lucinda whispered in my ear.

"But that's a lie, isn't it, Pedro?"

I had to consider my response to Lucinda. If I concurred too, my house of cards would come tumbling. She had breached its walls in Sintra, and although I had pre-empted a logical conclusion to the exchange we had had the night they gifted us Arion, I noticed it had left Lucinda perturbed.

"It's conceivable to wrest something beneficial from a despicable lie," I answered Lucinda, who gaped at me, baffled. "The lie we're living right now has pulled you, Eduardo, and Constância out of bondage. It has provided me with the opportunity to marry the most beautiful woman I have ever met. I'd prefer that on this day, at this moment, we think of ourselves instead of carrying the entire world's burden on our shoulders," I added.

"You want us to put our heads in the sand while the universe goes bang! Is that what you mean?" Lucinda asked.

I couldn't get the chance to answer my wife's question. It was my time as leader of the freed slaves to deliver. As planned, they designated me to introduce my companions. It was *Senhor* Cristiano Ronaldhino Coelho's idea. My introductions, he said, would carry more power: for the first time, nobody would speak for the natives but themselves. The brief conversation with Lucinda was on my mind as I cleared my throat. The lesson in tenacity that I had learned from the *Camino Novo de Tabuão* alleyway matched her persistence in questioning my moral compass. It had become the unsigned agreement between myself, my conscience, and my actions. Still, I was unsure of how to deliver my well-rehearsed speech. Should I expose the blatant web of lies that the Portuguese King's envoy continued to spawn? Of what use would it be if it jeopardized my own plans? I felt as though I was being given yet another opportunity to come clean and assuage my conscience. Once again, I quarantined the conflict that was rearing its ugly head in my mind. *Senhor* Cristiano Ronaldhino Coelho, having raised the curtain and executed to perfection the first act, it was my turn to take off from where the leading actor had left. As I stood up, however, I realized I was no longer just a part of the supporting cast. I had assumed a principal role in which I could stray from the script if I chose to.

"Esteemed officials of the British government," I started as I plucked from memory the speech our handlers had prepared. "We're here to signal to you the extraordinary developments that are taking place in Brazil as I speak to you. Less than three months ago, I, along with Lucinda, who is resting next to me, Constância, and Eduardo, who are sitting across the table from me, were all *Senhor* Pedro Batista Braga's slaves."

Eduardo and Constância shifted in their chairs. I doubt if people in the place noticed. I went on. "Today, I am glad to report to you we are free. They put no strings on our freedom. Nobody demanded manumissions. A loyal servant of the Portuguese king who ordered the elimination of the slave trade, *Senhor* Pedro Batista Braga, our master, is among the many slaveholders in Brazil who have heeded that call," I revealed. I felt the impulse to improvise my prepared speech. Additional flavor wouldn't hurt, I thought and digressed.

"Lucinda and I got married on the ship on our way to London. Although he wasn't in our company, I'm sure *Senhor* Pedro Batista Braga would have given us his full blessings. This, my friends, proves the extent to which conditions are altering for slaves in Brazil. There is gaiety on the faces of many a freed slave who now wander the streets with their heads held high. A new dawn has arrived on the horizon in Brazil, and we've all embraced it to better humanity," I announced and sat down.

"When did you pick up a head injury? Oh! Let me see, you just dropped to earth from another world. What the hell was all that about?" Lucinda asked, peering at me as though she was experiencing me for the first time.

"I am nobody but a character performing his act," I told Lucinda.

"And I curse the heavens for having placed me in this drama," Lucinda hissed.

Our session ended after an hour. Lucinda refused to talk to me. Two hours afterward, we sat in the public galleries of the House of Commons. It was Question Time when members of Parliament of the House of Commons questioned government officials regarding matters connected to their departments. The Speaker of the House, Mr. Charles Abbot, had briefed the Chamber on our visit and meeting. He recognized Lord Castlereagh.

"Thank you, Mr. Speaker. I would want to comment on the treaty we signed with Portugal earlier this year."

"What treaty? We've signed so many of them I bloody can't remember which!" shouted a voice from the Tory opposition faction of the Chamber. Members of that party roared with laughter.

"Order!" yelled the Speaker.

"If my distinguished colleague from the other side of the House had paid any consideration to what's been going on this year, he would have learned that bringing up 'Portugal' and 'treaty' in the same sentence meant simply one thing," Lord Castlereagh retorted. The Whigs cheered. The Tories booed. Mr. Charles Abbot called for order. Lord Castlereagh proceeded.

"We just met the Honorable *Senhor* Cristiano Ronaldhino Coelho, emissary of his Majesty, King John VI, along with four freed slaves who traveled here on their own volition to this our great Chamber to corroborate what is taking place in Brazil," he paused. "I'm honored to report to you that Portugal is enforcing the treaty, and its government has abolished the slave trade in Brazil," the Foreign Secretary continued.

"And the Whig Party's pigs can fly," a voice hollered, followed by boisterous laughter.

"Does the Honorable Member have a question for the Secretary?" the Speaker asked, directing his query to the area of the Chamber from where the question came.

"Yes," said a man with a long nose, blonde hair, and a heart-shaped face crowned with a smirk that made you know his question would not be a friendly one.

"Has the Honorable Secretary gone to Brazil to confirm what the Honorable *Senhor* Cristiano Ronaldhino Coelho said?" he asked. Several members in the Chamber giggled.

"Did the Honorable Mr. Collins Jenkins from Islington North constituency go to Ceylon to confirm that the cup of tea he had this morning came from there?" Lord Castlereagh inquired. More laughter filled the Chamber.

"*Senhor* Cristiano Ronaldhino Coelho is an honorable man. So is his Majesty, King John VI. Neither do I doubt the compelling account that *Senhor* Pedro de Barbosa, one of the freed slaves, who is sitting in the public galleries, gave us this morning," Lord Castlereagh said.

"Something doesn't add up," Jonathan Rawlings of Lochaber constituency said before they recognized him.

"Have the slave owners in Brazil decided on their own to free their slaves with no compensation? If so, why is this chamber contemplating compensation for British slave owners in the Caribbean? Is it because we have influential slave owners such as Charles Blair, John Gladstone, and Henry Lascelles who need recompence?" he asked.

Mr. Jonathan Rawlings' question shocked me. So, the British were thinking about compensating slave owners who made their fortune by exploiting the Africans they imported to work as slaves on Caribbean sugar plantations. Somehow, there was something wrong with this. I waited to hear more. I was no longer interested that as the members of the Parliament asked poignant questions, they would uncover the web of Portuguese royal maneuver: soften the British but remain behind the scenes and the oceans and continue with that addictive, wealth-generating, and empire-building project on the backs of black slaves. It didn't appeal to me to learn whether the members of Parliament would uncover this scheme. If they discussed compensation, I needed to see what was in it for the slaves. Would they reward them as fully? Was afoot any payment to them? To my biggest disappointment, no discussion of that nature developed during the full span of the Question Time.

What became clear as I remained in the public galleries was that while the Portuguese resorted to trickery to hoodwink, the English had the infinite facility to deploy their language to project altruistic sensibilities while using that same language to vindicate with pious reverence, recompence for those who had thrived on the trade upon which they frowned. I wasn't sure what was behind the movement to abolish the slave trade in England. However, I understood afterward that it emerged from the resistance to the trade by slaves in Haiti, Jamaica, Barbados, Brazil, and other places. Some reported that sectarian groups were behind it, while others maintained a phenomenon called the industrial revolution played a role. What I knew yet was that if the British contemplated offering reparations to their nationals who held slaves but considered doing nothing for the slaves, they didn't ground abolition in humanitarian concerns. As I pondered my intentions in the galleries, I understood that I, along with the Portuguese and the English, formed a guild of charlatans, con artists, and beguilers more attentive to economic benefits. A few of these villains had their plans in plain sight. Others had theirs shrouded in mystifying jargon and deception. I was in decent company; I felt. The internal voice that confronted my conscience receded. In the grand scheme of things, my hypocrisy was no longer obnoxious when juxtaposed with the deceit playing out on such a vast scale.

*****

Lord Castlereagh invited us to his home for supper that evening. Lucinda refused to talk to me. Neither did Eduardo nor Constância. The people I loved had shunned me. I wasn't inattentive to the fact that not everyone might agree with what I plotted to carry out to fulfill my life ambitions. To shatter the awkward silence that imprisoned us, I thought revisiting my offer to help resettle Eduardo and Constância in London or Lisbon, thus unfastening them from the vicious tentacles of enslavement, could break the impasse.

"We're about to carry out our mission," I announced, addressing no one in particular as the four of us lingered in the Durrants Hotel lobby for the horse carriage to Lord Castlereagh's residence. *Dom* José Nuno da Silva Mendes, whose role since our arrival in London remained hazy, had left the hotel earlier with *Senhor* Cristiano Ronaldhino Coelho. For someone I assumed to be quiet and reserved, Constância surprised us with salacious gossip about the prelate and the diplomat: *Dom* da Silva Mendes and *Senhor* Cristiano Ronaldhino Coelho lodged in the same room with a single bed. Guests complained of rhythmic grunts, loud audible moans, and other kinds of sounds from their chamber every night. Given the hotel's reputation for guarding information about its guests, we wondered whose Constância's source was and how she even met this person. Yet, as with all gossip, one enjoys it without troubling with the subtle details. According to Constância's source, objects the room's occupants had requested prior to our arrival suggested *Dom* da Silva Mendes' business in the chamber wasn't to provide his companion with spiritual guidance. When pushed to define what were those so-called objects, information dried up. My three companions' imaginations traversed both plausible and fantastic landscapes with this chatter. Our handlers' secret affairs didn't excite me.

Obtaining no response from my companions, I asked Eduardo when he and Constância planned to return to Salvador. When I realized I had indecorously framed my query, Lucinda snapped in response.

"Pedro!"

"What?" I rebutted. "Is it an abomination to ask what their plans are? They are conversant with ours. Isn't it entirely fair they informed us about theirs?" I demanded, exacerbating the situation.

"I've suspected you were a weasel and a son of a bitch. I recognized it the first day I met you, and I was right," Eduardo said with an expression of resentment swamping his face.

"You want to know our plans, Pedro de Barbosa? I'll tell you our plans," Constância chimed in with remarkable swiftness and in a sarcastic tone.

"We're traveling back to Brazil where a new dawn has risen on the horizon, where conditions have changed for slaves so our owner, *Senhor* Pedro Batista Braga, can welcome and embrace us as his equals. We're returning to a Brazil, where according to the gospel of Pedro de Barbosa, there's gaiety on the faces of many freed slaves who wander the streets with their heads held high. This is the Brazil we're turning to. Are you content?" Constância asked.

The acerbity of the sudden explosion shocked me. If this was how Eduardo felt, he did a great job to suppress that emotion; I thought. And Constância and her contempt? I sought to untangle what was developing. After a while, I determined Eduardo and Lucinda felt the way they did because they presumed I plotted to reverse the pledge I gave out on the ship. Another thought invaded my mind: my traveling companions were furious with me for my blatant lies at the British Parliament House. As I pondered this prospect, I recognized I formed many assumptions concerning their realities as *Senhor* Braga's slaves. I universalized my personal narrative as a slave and foisted it on them. Yes, we shared a commonplace reality because of the consistent, widespread concepts that bolstered slavery. As slaves, we were capital; and we were equity because we were black. Violence, whether real or presaged, formed our condition. Still, Lucinda and the others couldn't have gained the same survival instincts and strategies that circumstances levied on me. We were of the same tribe but with distinct stripes and colors.

Another element had also eluded me until now: given slavery's narrow limits, the fundamental human relationships embedded in it could span the spectrum from benevolent to contemptuous. I was ignorant of how *Senhor* Braga treated his captives. Did he care for them adequately? Did he and his slaves care for each other even though such friendship might have been moderated and bounded by the inherent power inequality in such an exchange? I decided that since none of my travelling companions had displayed any explicit sentiments towards their master, there might be a benevolent relationship between *Senhor* Braga and his slaves. But I realized that if that were the situation, Lucinda, Constância, and Eduardo could never ignore their condition as property, no matter how *Senhor* Pedro Batista Braga treated them. With these considerations, I concluded that I didn't have to overplay Constância's and Eduardo's reactions to my query.

"I'm sorry my question caused you any pain," I announced, contemplating my companions. "My experiences as a former slave, coupled with the time I spent on the streets, taught me that to survive, one deployed every weapon in one's arsenal without hesitation. What you saw earlier this morning came from those realities. Am I glad that my liaison with facts and truth is sparse and spurious? No. Am I proud I lie and distort the truth when forced by circumstances to do so? No. Will I tell a lie again? You bet I will if it means watching out for myself and for my loved ones." After a few minutes' pause, I added, looking at Eduardo, Constância, and Lucinda, "I've opened a bank account in Lisbon for the two of you. You'll have ample funds to find a new life here in London or in Portugal. Salvador isn't the place for any of us."

I noticed a softening in Lucinda's and Constância's faces. Eduardo's was blank.

"I know that Pedro and I aren't returning to Salvador. I realize I have sold my soul to a son of a bitch, and there's no going back," Lucinda said, rubbing my face with tenderness.

"My apologies for calling you a son of a bitch though occasionally, that label fits you like a glove," Eduardo said, eliciting laughter from everybody. "I think you've a kind heart, *filho da uma puta*," he continued, evoking more glee.

"Do you recall when *Senhor* Pedro Batista Braga became violent and called Pedro, *filho da uma puta*?" Constância asked, cackling.

"Who could forget that?" Lucinda chuckled. "It was the first time anybody had mentioned his hypocrisy and double-talk. He couldn't believe a *preto* did so. The ferocity in his eyes looked as though those eyes were nursing criminal motives."

"I thought *Senhor* Pedro Batista Braga was going to yank off his head. This must be a fucking *filho da uma puta*, I said to myself. Of course, my use of the term differed very much from *Senhor* Pedro Batista Braga's," Eduardo said, chortling.

"It was at that juncture that you fell in love with Pedro. Wasn't it? Constância asked Lucinda.

"Yes. I told myself that a fellow with such balls needed someone to secure them, and here we're," Lucinda said, laughing as Constância joined her.

I didn't mind that my companions laughed and had fun at my expense. We were joking once more, and our relationship hadn't suffered from what had just transpired between us. As if on cue, one of Lord Castlereagh's attendants entered the lobby and welcomed us into the horse carriage. The Minister's house stretched along fashionable and elegant Piccadilly Street. Ladies didn't have to cross the street lifting their garments to avoid importing horse dung enmeshed with the miasma of offensive putrefying smells that hovered over other parts of the capital.

One entered the courtyard from the street through wrought-iron gates decorated with the Castlereagh family crest held in place on both sides by brick walls. Enormous ivies clothed the house's massive red-pink brick walls and attempted to etch their stubborn vines into the brick. Unsuccessful at this undertaking, they latched on by twisting and intertwining themselves in a macabre yet tasteful dance on the surfaces. Acres of gardens and well-maintained lawns sprinkled with lush trees and flowers surrounded the mansion.

Lord Castlereagh's major-domo, Charles Adderley, met us at the entrance. He wore a brown wig, and his coat had the same family crest as on the gates. He escorted us into a foyer that could accommodate some tall flowering bushes in the garden. A maroon-colored carpet dominated most of the floor. Two rooms on adjoining sides of a corridor led to a central area serving as a drawing room. It was enormous, with four large windows with crimson draperies held back by tassels of thick white thread. Patterned paper depicting pastoral fields with men hunting wild game decorated the walls. The area had several pieces of furniture, including three ornate armchairs arranged to allow one to walk around the room and admire many of the paintings that hung on the sides. *Dom* Silva Mendes and *Senhor* Coelho, who had arrived earlier, relaxed in one armchair with glasses filled with wine. Lord Castlereagh and his wife sat on the opposite settee. The couple stood up to greet us as we entered the room, led by Charles Adderley.

After a few drinks, they brought us to the dining place, where a veritable feast awaited us. The pleasant smells of roasting poultry and goose already baited our senses. Dinner didn't disappoint. Amidst the ebullient chatter that accompanied the clinking of knives, forks, spoons, and expensive china, not to mention the exquisite wine that the maids served, Lord Castlereagh stood up and cleared his throat.

"I'd like to make a toast," he announced, looking around the table and at the four of us.

"I'd like to thank *Senhor* Cristiano Ronaldhino Coelho, *Senhor* Pedro de Barbosa, and the rest of you for making the long trip from Brazil to inform the British people on how Portugal is carrying out the fine treaty we signed earlier this year. I want to acknowledge his Majesty, King John VI, for promoting the tour. My family and I, along with the British State, wish you a safe and expeditious return to Brazil. Cheers," Lord Castlereagh said as he raised his glass.

"Cheers," we responded.

Before *Senhor* Cristiano Ronaldhino Coelho could react to Lord Castlereagh's compliment as custom demanded, I rose up, looked around the lavish dining place, and spoke.

"On behalf of the four of us who arrived here on our own accord as freed slaves, we want to thank you and the British people for your magnificent hospitality. We've very much enjoyed seeing parts of the famous city of London and meeting good English individuals who've accepted us with open arms. We have felt special." I calculated the effects of my comments. *Senhor* Cristiano Ronaldhino Coelho and *Dom* José Nuno da Silva Mendes, both had an incredulous look on their faces. My traveling companions looked at me with a knowing smile. I could read their minds. The *filho da uma puta* must be up to something.

"We have enjoyed our stay here so much that we're planning to make London our next home. With your support, I'm confident we'll be able to secure the required documents to make our stay here legal," I concluded.

"Are you out of your mind?" Lucinda hissed.

"*Tranquillo*," I said to Lucinda.

A grin crossed Eduardo's and Constância's faces. They were on to my game.

"Absolutely," Lord Castlereagh answered with vigor. There's a large Portuguese community in London that, I'm certain, will welcome you.

Senhor Cristiano Ronaldhino Coelho clenched his jaws, as did his sidekick and lover. His face flushed with wine and suppressed indignation. I had set into motion an inevitable process of unshackling my companions from bondage. *Senhor* Cristiano Ronaldhino Coelho would have to tell *Senhor* Pedro Batista Braga his coveted slaves had become their own masters. How he would manage it was of no concern to me. After a few tense moments, the illustrious head of our contingent stood up to respond to my speech and to Lord Castlereagh's toast. He had no choice. Remaining mum would have been as awkward as undiplomatic.

"Thank you, Lord Castlereagh," he uttered. He paused and added, "I'm confident my traveling companions will discover their new home welcoming."

A short while afterward, we bid the Castlereagh family farewell. Although the colt carriage which brought us to Piccadilly Street accommodated only four individuals, *Senhor* Cristiano Ronaldhino Coelho insisted he and *Dom* José Nuno da Silva Mendes ride in the same carriage to the Durrants. The genuine aristocrat and nobleman, Lord Castlereagh, wouldn't hear of it. *Senhor* Cristiano Ronaldhino Coelho was unrelenting, and our host yielded.

We wedged into the carriage. Lucinda, Constância and I remained facing Eduardo, sandwiched between *Senhor* Cristiano Ronaldhino Coelho and *Dom* José Nuno da Silva Mendes. A moment of frozen, awkward silence filled the carriage, and nobody attempted to break it. But just as we turned on to Piccadilly Street, which was busy, *Senhor* Cristiano Ronaldhino Coelho unleashed an outburst of imprecations.

"Who the hell do you think you're, you stinking *preto*?" He screamed into my face. "How dare you ask Lord Castlereagh to help you procure documents to remain in London when you're still *Senhor* Pedro Batista Braga slaves?" *Senhor* Cristiano Ronaldhino Coelho demanded.

Although I couldn't see his face in the dim coach, I imagined in my mind's eye the bulging blue veins that crisscrossed his flushed face, which, if I wasn't mistaken, threatened to explode. People have called me several names in my life, courtesy of Andreia's rich glossary of expletives she had fashioned for me. It had been a long time since anybody called me a *preto*, a nigger. This insult wouldn't slide by without retaliation. But others more capable were quicker in the draw before I could react.

"And who, you bloody idiot and son of a bitch, do you think you're to call us slaves?" Lucinda shrieked at *Senhor* Cristiano Ronaldhino Coelho. "You realize who's a slave? It's assholes such as you, along with your bloody priest lover and tramp, who lie through their teeth and peddle their souls on the stupid altar of loyalty to their stinking monarch. Yes, *Senhor*, son of a bitch, you're the fucking slaves," Lucinda said.

What followed next occurred as though in a dream. *Senhor* Cristiano Ronaldhino Coelho lunged at Lucinda. The coach's motion, along with the force of the charge, pushed Lucinda out of the carriage door that they hadn't latched properly. Immobilized, I could not break Lucinda's fall. As she landed, I heard the distinctive trot of a carriage's horses behind us. I cringed. By the time Lucinda hit the ground, the other coach was upon us. The driver struggled to draw his horses to a stop. Spooked by the impending crash, two of the horses broke loose and trampled Lucinda. She was dead before I got to her on the pavement.

I felt my veins swell up with indescribable agony, anguish, and irrepressible rage.

"Oh, God!" I said to myself, "Is this your idea of punishing a self-professed con artist and lover who, having fallen in love for the first time with his soul, must confront a malevolent force that comes along to spoil it all?"

As I held Lucinda's savaged remains tight to me, Constância's ear-splitting wail pierced the night air and stopped all movement around us. It was a wail that had as its genesis the shores from which her forebears had been ripped. It was a primal scream that had as its fountain, a Salvador da Bahia that had an allure, even if the wretched of the earth were in bondage and couldn't have the leisure to enjoy it. A cry that radiated out of Constância like a thunderstorm assailing her heart, her soul. A cry that told me I was going to carry with me for the rest of my life, an irreversible pain.

PART II

Kingdoms of Dahomey, Ouidah, and Allada
1788-1825

Forewarning: A Word from the Narrator

Dear reader, before you proceed on this word journey, I want to alert you to a few details. As you're about to discover, Pedro de Barbosa is no longer the chronicler of the second part of this narrative, much as it is his story. This reversal has a good reason. The omniscient narrator of this novel, I surrendered my position to allow Pedro de Barbosa to pen his memoirs, trusting he would reveal the truth about his life in Salvador and his ventures in the Kingdoms of Dahomey, Ouidah, and Allada as a slave trafficker. Thus, as I read his diary, I expected to discover the true Pedro de Barbosa. But how mistaken I was! Like many a reader, it wasn't long before I became drawn into his gripping tale. The further buried I got into his autobiography, however, the more I understood Pedro de Barbosa had several objectives in mind: to hoodwink me despite the terms we had settled upon, to falsify his story, and to imbue it with such anecdotes that were I to intervene, as I'm doing now, you, gentle reader, would be confused in deciding whose account of this story is the most accurate.

Let me reassure you that I don't intend to dispute Pedro de Barbosa's accounts of himself. Although he doesn't state it, his recourse to autobiography should offer a clear proximity to truth, as it provides an authority. But truth-telling could justly be an undertaking to thwart it when dealing with a character such as Pedro de Barbosa, who, from the beginning, made his intentions known. I suggest to you, dear reader, that Pedro de Barbosa filled his autobiographical narrative with fantasia since he used his chronicle as an auspicious place to produce and to reproduce his own identity, his story, and his own agenda. In doing so, he has seduced his readers into accepting his truth. It is for this reason, and many more, that I have reclaimed the narrative authority that I so invested in him and to narrate the second part of this story myself. Until my present intervention, Pedro de Barbosa rigged his story, purging insalubrious actions and facets of his conduct that could have proved further his declared position as a con artist.

First, did he mention he had drawn on his promised insurance policy on Archbishop Eugenio Thrilho? He dispatched three separate notes to the cleric and demanded payments of a thousand *réis* in each of them. He sent these letters many years after the prelate had complied with his request they release Salvador Viegas from *Refugio Pacífico*. Neither did Pedro de Barbosa mention that despite the priest's compliance, he delivered anonymously *Donha* Fidelia's letter, along with the one he, Pedro, had written to the Archbishop to *Correio da Bahia*. For the life of me, I find it odd Pedro de Barbosa didn't discuss the sensation that gripped Salvador's elite establishment following the letters' publication. Curious still was his omission that a week after he had delivered these missives, he followed up with another spellbinding tale: *Senhor* Felipe de Barbosa contracted him to kill Paulo Álvares de Andrade during the *Entrudo popular* carnival to silence him and to put an end to his blackmailing of the wealthy and respected *Senhor* de Barbosa. Paulo Álvares de Andrade's blackmail? Disclosing that two of *Senhor* de Barbosa's children belonged to Archbishop Thrilho, as reported in the published letter that *Senhora* Felicia had sent to the priest.

Isn't it confounding Pedro de Barbosa didn't tell the outcomes of these revelations and of his master's later change in status after they charged him with Paulo Álvares de Andrade's murder? And speaking of his homicide, who do you think was its architect? Although Pedro de Barbosa alluded to his desire to bring the police chief back to life and kill him again, he left that statement hanging; ambiguous. Let me indulge your patience and take a few minutes of your precious time to tell you what happened.

After ensuring Virgilio da Cunha's financial ruin, Paulo Álvares de Andrade became Pedro de Barbosa's target when he returned to Salvador. Through Jacinto Cardoso, he learned that the detective chief was a regular visitor to *A Casa da Senhora Eulalia*. Dressed in his official police attire, many clients despised him at the bordello. He ordered them to buy him drinks. Almost always drunk, he wound up with Elisabete, the prettiest and youngest prostitute in the enterprise, and retired without paying for her services. Despite his resistance to visiting *A Casa da Senhora Eulalia*, Pedro de Barbosa frequented the bordello, ending up befriending Elisabete. He chose carefully when to interact with the police officer: the *Entrudo popular* carnival, which took place during the early three days before Lent. It was an occasion when revelers who wore costumes had their faces painted and threw flour and balls of scented water on people who filled Salvador's streets.

With his face powdered and wearing a stevedore's costume, Pedro de Barbosa approached Paulo Álvares de Andrade at the bar. Claiming it was Lent and generous because it was his birthday, Pedro de Barbosa invited the chief to a drink. An ardent and impatient glutton, Paulo Álvares de Andrade quaffed his drink in a hurry, as though he needed to do so before the distillery from which the brew came went out of business. Having paid Elisabete a large sum of money earlier that evening, he asked that she leave the backdoor to the chamber open and the place empty when the law enforcement chief made a port of call at her shrine. He needed privacy with Paulo Álvares de Andrade to discuss a matter of utmost importance, he said. Pedro de Barbosa had already sprung up the stairs behind the establishment and entered the room when the top policeman got to the semi-dark chamber that Friday night. He had changed into a new *Entrudo popular* carnival costume with a Salvador Civil Police outfit.

Everything happened fast. With a sharp knife, Pedro de Barbosa forced the police chief to consume copious amounts of *cachaça* and *cravinho* that he had spiked with an herb that itched the skin like pinpricks. Paulo Álvares de Andrade passed out. Pedro de Barbosa carried the police chief out of the chamber through the backdoor onto the streets filled with drunken men leaning on one another as they plodded along the cobblestones. *Entrudo popular* brought out many more such companions, of which Paulo Álvares de Andrade and Pedro de Barbosa were now an integral part. Two days later, they found a lifeless, mutilated, and naked body in an alley where *Ladeira da Palma* and *Largo do Palma* split. Although the body was bloated, it wasn't difficult to know whose it was. Several witnesses testified to seeing a Salvador Civil Police officer carrying the police chief along *Ladeira da Palma*. The police officer's identity has remained a mystery.

Pedro de Barbosa's third and egregious omission in his memoirs was his failure to tell his readers what transpired with the mangled bodies of a priest and a Portuguese diplomat that was found floating in London Docklands a week after Lucinda's death. Did you notice the hasty fashion in which Pedro de Barbosa ended his recollections after Lucinda's death? With the many traces peppered throughout his narrative warning that those who had wronged him paid, why was he reticent on *Senhor* Cristiano Ronaldhino Coelho's fate? After all, wasn't he the author of Lucinda's death? Let me ask your goodwill and relate what transpired.

It was easy for Pedro de Barbosa to discover the large Portuguese community in London to which Lord Castlereagh had alluded during their visit to his home. From Lisbon, Oporto, Funchal in Madeira, and the Azores, these Portuguese settlers lived in the London Docklands area. For a character who had survived on the streets, it wasn't difficult for Pedro de Barbosa to detect hardened criminal elements in the neighborhood. Two nights at *Taberna Tosca* were what he needed to uncover his man. He had learned that the sight of money, its cold feel in the hands, and the promise of earning more produced desired results. Pedro de Barbosa didn't have to convince Eberardo Judas and his men.

Under the guise of desiring his aid to co-sign a housing contract because they had made London their permanent homes, Pedro de Barbosa invited *Senhor* Cristiano Ronaldhino Coelho and *Dom* da Silva Mendes to *Taberna Tosca* to meet the rental home's proprietor. Having saved his neck by contending that Lucinda's death was a mishap, *Senhor* Cristiano Ronaldhino Coelho and his associate granted his request.

All was in place when Pedro de Barbosa and his two traveling companions arrived at *Taberna Tosca* the next night. It was a raucous bar with patrons dancing, drinking, and eating authentic Portuguese dishes found nowhere else in London. A lone fellow sitting at a table beckoned to Pedro and his retinue.

"There he is, owner of the rental place," Pedro de Barbosa told *Senhor* Cristiano Ronaldhino Coelho above the din, as he pointed to the fellow at the table who stood up and shook Pedro de Barbosa's hand and those of *Senhor* Cristiano Ronaldhino Coelho and *Dom* da Silva Mendes.

"Eberardo Judas," he declared.

A server brought them fresh jugs and a magnificent bottle of Port as they sat.

"On the house," the server announced.

Not long after, the same server came back with plates of meat stuffed pastries, deep-fried meat patties, salt-cod fishcakes, and salt cod hash. The server filled their glasses and plates as they emptied them. Eberardo was an exceptional conversationalist who regaled Pedro de Barbosa and his companions with Portuguese immigrants' stories in London, their *saudade*, their desolation, their hankering for a Portugal which wasn't by any stretch of the imagination, remarkably distant from England. Such was the revelry of the occasion that by midnight, they hadn't broached the subject of their visit to *Taberna Tosca*. Since all glorious moments must end, Pedro de Barbosa suggested they return to their hotel. The inebriated priest and his companion raised no objections. Eberardo gestured to three men next to his table. It took the Durrants Hotel guests a few minutes to adjust their eyes to the semi-dark street on which the tavern was located. Four masked men emerged from the shadows and stopped them before they could get to a corner street to take a coach. In a split second, they whisked away *Senhor* Cristiano Ronaldhino Coelho and *Dom* da Silva Mendes. The next evening's *The British Evening Post* reported the police found two mutilated bodies floating in the London Docklands waters. They identified one of them as *Senhor* Cristiano Ronaldhino Coelho, Portugal's former ambassador to England. The other body was that of a priest dressed in his informal attire. The article in the report suggested it wasn't clear how the remains had ended up in the Docklands. It stated that Senhor Coelho had arrived in London on a diplomatic mission for his Majesty, King John VI of Portugal. Investigations were ongoing, and the newspaper asked that anyone with any information about the case contact the London police.

In view of the above omissions and deletions, could one conclude that Pedro de Barbosa's accounts make up nothing but the truth? His ability to beguile is the only thing consistently truthful regarding his memoirs. By excising and banishing unflattering and yet crucial details from his autobiography, couldn't Pedro de Barbosa be manipulating readers to curry favor with them? Having left an impressive trail of settling scores with those whom he believed had wronged him, why not leave a few traces of his benevolence as well? Isn't it common knowledge that talented writers portray compelling villains as humans, or at least with human characteristics? Couldn't Pedro de Barbosa have done the same about himself if he thought readers might find his actions objectionable? Even if it were the case, couldn't it be feasible that Pedro de Barbosa designed his plain act of altruism to mislead his readers as he remains faithful to his declared objectives? When a burglar says he's a reformed thug but regales you with this message while nursing an item purloined from your own home, you'd better set up whatever defenses you have before he strikes again. One of those walls I have mounted for myself is to refuse Pedro de Barbosa's fascinating and soul-wrenching accounts to dupe me. Reclaiming my narrative rectifies my faux pas, thanks to the con artist.

As I set to re-introduce Pedro de Barbosa into his story, however, I call for your patience since you wouldn't see much of him until later in the second part of this narrative. The reason for this choice will become apparent. As a character in this novel counsels us, the patient individual cooks stone until he or she gets broth.

My final forewarning: You will come across a couple of exchanges between Pedro de Barbosa and the author who has deployed me to tell this story. Should you be confused, you would be in good company. But rest assured that this isn't the first occasion that an actual writer has engaged his characters. Other more eminent authors have employed an analogous device to achieve outcomes not too dissimilar to this one who has used me as his narrator to carry forth this narrative.

Chapter 15

Three significant events affected Ena Sunu's life. The first took place in 1798 when she was ten years old and overhead the heated exchange between her father, King Daguenon of Allada kingdom, and his counselors in the Chamber of Oration. Next to one of the palace's public halls, this was where the monarch's closest advisors debated pressing issues and expressed whatever was on their minds, with no fear of retaliation. It was a threshold once crossed that all, including the king, jettisoned their power. From where she sheltered, Ena Sunu could hear Bekou, the king's oldest counselor's hypo nasal speech.

"Who among us is an alien to slave trading? Didn't this practice flourish in our land and in other kingdoms long before the arrival of those goddamned Portuguese *yovos*—white men—who corrupted our leaders with trinkets, mirrors, guns, and strong drinks that turn one's head from something into nothing?" He paused and continued. "But ours was different. We integrated them into our society, into our culture, offered them our men and women to marry, and made them part of us. We didn't put them in chains. In fact, we valued those slaves who came from the noble families that we conquered. Some of them even rose to become important courtiers and kings. And what do these accursed *yovos* do to the slaves we sell them?"

Gahnwa, Allada's illustrious historian, interrupted Bekou.

"Bekou, what you've suggested is true. Yes, we offered them our men and women to wed. We gave them plots of land to cultivate yams, cocoyams, plantains, and cassava. But were they integrated?

Did we ever consider them our equals? If so, why did we add the *kluvi* tag to their names? Wasn't it meant to remind them and everyone that they and their progenitors had been slaves? Otherwise, why do they have names such as *Avavikluvi*—Slave of the small penis—*Avagakluvi*—Slave of the big penis—*Kologakluvi*—Slave of the big vagina—*Kolovivikluvi*—Slave of the sweet vagina, and *Kolokuatikluvi*—Slave of the hanging vagina?"

"Yes. Yes. I appreciate where you're going with that," Bekou responded with a shrug.

"No, you don't," declared Gahnwa. "What I'm saying is that as slavers, we do not differ from the Portuguese, French, Dutch, Spaniards, English, and many others who have taken slaves to wherever they take them. Don't tell me we should celebrate our benign slavery. It was wrong on all counts, and we should be ashamed and responsible for selling our own to those goddamned *yovos*," the royal historian added.

"Gahnwa, your role as royal historian has gotten into your head and is fogging it with baseless generalizations," Bekou responded.

"How so?" Gahnwa asked.

"Tell me, aside from the psychological scars that the slaves and freed slaves might bear because of their names—which in most cases, are tied to penises and vaginas—I don't know which genius came up with these names unless he's consumed with naming private parts in public—what physical damage did they encounter?" Bekou asked.

"Slavery is slavery," Gahnwa responded.

"It may be so, but you're misguided," said Bekou.

"How am I?" asked Gahnwa.

"I'll tell you. The *yovo* slavery is in an extraordinary world. It violates what we interpret as slavery. Theirs is evil embodied. Otherwise, why would they brand the slaves we sell them? Why would they put smoldering hot rods on the skins of their fellow beings and brand them like horses? Can you explain to me why an individual can put shackles on the necks and legs of another human being? And, while you're at it, can you explain to me how and why a living being can string another being up a pole and thrash him because he wishes to break his spirit to have him do whatever he prefers? I'll tell you what, it is evil and depraved souls capable of executing such heinous deeds. There are no terms to describe the *yovos'* inhumanity, savagery, and callousness. So, when you tell me we marketed our own, yes, we did, but let's be circumspect," declared Gahnwa.

"So, we're having this conference because some of these slaves who've returned from Salvador say their brothers and sisters in Brazil are experiencing a torrid life, and we should consider ending the trade. Am I right?" asked Akoli, the royal treasurer.

"Yes, and no," King Daguenon spoke for the first time. "Yes, because Francisco da Rocha's and some returnees' reports on slaves in Brazil are chilling. No, because this isn't the first occasion we've heard of the tribulations of those we've sold in the past. With these stories, however, one cannot help but think of the moral undertones of our collaboration in this entire business."

"We've turned ourselves into a bunch of malcontents. Haven't we?" Akoli asked. "If you sought my opinion, I don't regret selling those who we capture in warfare to the *yovos*. That is just the nature of things. We want their goods; they need ours. Did you ever ask why our enemies and neighbors haven't attacked us in these past decades? Because they know we have the European guns that are more potent than those made from the iron ore we buy from the Akpafu people in Awubeame Mountains," added the royal treasurer.

"I acknowledge what Akoli says," responded Yessu, one of the kingdom's sharpest minds. When Yessu spoke, everyone listened.

"Introducing the *yovo*'s guns changed all. We fought with bows and arrows in our wars. But now? We purchase the *yovo*'s damned guns to defend ourselves from our enemies and neutralize the mercenaries that these same *yovos* formed, outfitted with their guns. Thanks to those damn guns, we can now invade other tribes, acquire slaves, and sell them to the *yovos*. They destabilized our way of life. We've evolved from something into nothing. I admit with Gahnwa that we need to be circumspect when we talk about our role and the *yovos* in this trade."

"Aren't we losing sight of something significant in this?" asked Akoli?

"What isn't obvious from what I expressed?" asked Yessu.

"I'm talking about the trade. Are we forgetting that the guns, metals, cotton cloth, and the other goods we buy from the *yovos* play a crucial role in our kingdom?" Akoli asked.

"Akoli, can you stop wasting our time and state what you have in your bloody mind?" Gahnwa asked.

"We have suppressed political and tribal dissentions by redistributing the goods in which we trade with the *yovos*. Think about it. When was the last time we had internal uprisings and conflicts?" Akoli asked.

"Akoli, are you and Yessu suggesting that we're not vulnerable, as in the past, because we've hitched our fortunes on our foreign connections, our dealings with the *yovos*?" asked King Daguenon.

Many of the men in the Chamber of Oration muttered a collective "yes."

"Can someone tell me what would happen if these transactions end? What if the *yovos* say they're no longer interested in our merchandise because they've found another way to do things without it? What then?" the monarch asked.

There was silence.

"I'll tell you what," suggested King Daguenon. "When the dust settles, they we will consider us the immoral bastards who sold their own to the *yovos*. What do you suppose the *yovos* will do? They'll pretend as if it wasn't their greed and insatiable demand for slaves that made us dependent on it. I suggest we put a closure on it before it comes to that," King Daguenon added.

"The head that wears the crown has lost his head," said Akoli. "Has the king forgotten our history before we signed treaties with Dahomey and Ouidah and before we developed our foreign relationships with the *yovos*? Doesn't he remember that they took his great-great-grandfather and his great-grandfather prisoners and executed them after those marauding bastards from the north overran our kingdom and wanted to enslave us and to convert us to Islam? But because we were much further south from the north from where they came, and also that we could use our landscape to thwart their endeavors, we would have been kneeling with our foreheads pointing to God knows where."

King Daguenon's face erupted with fury. Akoli had offered him the nasty hand of insult and dishonor, but he could do nothing about it. This was the Chamber of Oration's purpose.

"You're not supposed to be here," a voice behind Ena Sunu startled her. It was one of the palace guards doing the rounds. She scooted off with her cousin, Azonton.

Ena Sunu had seen long lines of men, women, and children brought to Allada and housed in the barracoons outside the Allada palace. She knew they sold them as slaves, but she wasn't certain who purchased them or where they took them. What did her father mean by chilling stories about the slaves? And Brazil? Where was that? She had seen the Portuguese *yovos* who showed up at the king's court to talk to him. Were they the traders? She remembered Akoli's words. The slaves were products, goods sold to buy many things, including guns. They bartered them.

The second event occurred five years afterward, in 1802, when Ena Sunu had just turned fifteen. She received the news that King Daguenon's twenty children dreaded: her father planned to gift her to the Dahomey kingdom and throne to fulfill a long-maintained tradition that continued diplomatic alliances and avoided war among the disparate realms. The ramifications of being gifted were familiar to her and her siblings. The gifted royal family member lost links with his or her home and started life afresh in a foreign land. If he was a boy, he had no chance in hell to ascend to the Allada throne. As a female, they groomed her according to the customs of her new kingdom to prepare for her marriage to either the monarch or to any of his heirs in her new home. Because gifted children were noble, they recognized them in their new land, but for such individuals, it was nothing shy of expulsion.

Anger filled her face when Queen Lawani, Ena Sunu's mother, disclosed the news.

"How did the king decide that of his twenty offspring, I, Ena Sunu, should be the gifted one? Is it because I am different from the other princesses who waste their life thinking of who they would marry and serve? Why didn't the king have the dignity and courage to consult me before he made this arrangement?" Ena Sunu asked her mother.

Queen Lawani weighed her words and said, "I know you're upset, but I am afraid that's the order of things."

"Of all women, I can't believe this is coming from you," Ena Sunu declared.

The queen was silent. Her daughter's remark didn't shock her, and she didn't feel disrespected or insulted. None of Ena Sunu's siblings would have dared to challenge the king's verdict, let alone to raise their voices at their mother. Not Ena Sunu. They reputed Queen Lawani herself among King Daguenon's wives for her unrivaled disdain for their husband's authority. A fierce critic of Allada customs in its treatment of princesses at court, Queen Lawani had advocated equal treatment of the king's children. Nobody paid heed to her, a woman of all people. But it didn't mean she couldn't bring up her daughter the way she thought fit.

Akin to her mother, there was nothing complaisant or conventional about Ena Sunu. As an adolescent, she violated rigid customs and etiquette the court designed to prevent her or any princess from participating in the same activities that her brothers, half-brothers, and her many male cousins at court relished. Most of her sisters and the other princesses occupied themselves with tasks devised for their gender. Ena Sunu kept company with her brothers and boy cousins. She played and wrestled with them and never missed their hunting escapades with their counselors. Much to the chagrin of the women in her father's harem, Ena Sunu took considerable pleasure in wearing the same clothes the lads wore, making it impractical to find her among her male siblings. She learned Allada's history and customs and cherished her kingdom's rich history. Its customs were a different matter. She hated most of them, including the one soon to define her future. Her brothers and half-brothers, potential kings, and court dignitaries regarded her with amusement and tolerated her. As a female, she posed no threat to their ambitions as they plotted and positioned themselves for the most desirable ranks at the Allada court. Of the lot, Azonton was the closest to Ena Sunu.

As the report of her gifting sunk in, Ena Sunu couldn't help but evoke the parallels between her fate and that of the many female slaves that she had seen passing through Allada to distant lands, never to return. She recognized her position at the Dahomey court was better than the slaves shipped to Brazil. But weren't they hauling her away as well? Wasn't she being bartered? Wasn't she a product? If slavery meant subservience and absolute subjugation, what made her different from the female slaves and her father's wives and concubines and those of his courtiers and other powerful men in Allada?

*****

Five years later, after they had groomed her to become King Gesa's third wife, Queen Ena Sunu experienced first-hand the potency of those powerful forces that would establish her place as nobody but a traded property. This experience, and what took place a few years afterward, transformed her and set the stage for a calculated long-term campaign. Less than a year after she married King Gesa in 1807, Ouidah kingdom's crown prince, Dozan, visited Dahomey on a diplomatic mission directed at strengthening ties between the two kingdoms. Ena Sunu had just turned nineteen. The Ouidah kingdom had previously named Prince Dozan successor to the Ouidah throne, even though it was the sole kingdom that didn't confirm the sovereign's first boy as a natural heir. Although King Tezifon of Ouidah had four wives and fifteen children, Dozan was the only male, earning the king the moniker, "The millet stalk that produced merely one grain." Prince Dozan was that single grain. Thus, when the twenty-two-year-old, Prince Dozan, showed up at the Dahomey court, he received the pageantry befitting a visiting monarch.

"We have to prepare you properly for the Ouidah prince. He must recognize that the Dahomey king is offering his prime and most intimate property to his esteemed royal guest," said *Kpojito*—queen mother—Nene Mojissola, the monarch's mother, as several maids bathed Queen Ena Sunu with black soap and scrubbed her sweet tender brown skin with shea butter oil. She looked as smooth as a gleaming black stone plunged into palm oil, removed, burnished, and left out in the sunlight to dry.

"Why me? Why should any woman?" Queen Ena Sunu asked.

"Because that's your duty," replied *Kpojito* Nene Mojissola.

"And the king? Does he know about this?" Queen Ena Sunu asked.

"Your king is following tradition and protocol," said *Kpojito* Nene Mojissola.

"This practice and protocol, did you, *Kpojito* Nene Mojissola, or any royal female, have everything to do with it?" asked Queen Ena Sunu.

"Ai, my little queen. So many questions you always ask the old woman. So many questions that she cannot answer. When was the last time you saw blood?" *Kpojito* Nene Mojissola asked, sitting close to Ena Sunu. "We must make sure you don't have any blood down there," the *Kpojito* continued.

Queen Ena Sunu hesitated. She studied *Kpojito* Nene Mojissola's friendly and wrinkled face that paralleled the crinkles of wilted, dry passion fruit. The generous gray hair on her chin reminded her of elegant silk strands exploding through a corn husk. The breath from her toothless mouth smelled like the failed attempt at tanning an animal pelt. Queen Ena Sunu moved aside from the *Kpojito*. Who is brave enough to tell the lioness that her breath stinks? *Kpojito* Nene Mojissola waved at the maids to evacuate the area and didn't notice.

"I ceased seeing blood five days ago," Queen Ena Sunu said.

"Good," *Kpojito* Nene Mojissola said. "All must be clean down there. You must regard yourself as lucky the king chose you to share the Dahomey people's property with the Ouidah kingdom," she continued with a smile.

So that was who she was! A piece of property, Queen Ena Sunu thought. Hers was a body that they hauled away without her approval, as her father had done. A body traded between two influential men serving two powerful kingdoms. An open body, a parchment, a palimpsest one can etch upon without recognizing the agony of the scratches at the juncture of inscription and after.

Both kingdoms had minted her like a coin useful in the barter of what she considered specious alliances. And she had been right about the spurious rapprochement between the kingdoms because, in 1810, three years after Prince Dozan's visit and after the birth of her identical twin boys, the unimaginable happened.

*****

Azonton burst into Queen Ena Sunu's separate quarters. This was extraordinary for a man who never wore his emotions in his sleeves. Bronzed and burly, he carried his weight and strength as mere appendages to other physical attributes that warned people to keep away. King Daguenon had ordered Queen Ena Sunu's cousin, Azonton, to go with the youthful princess to Dahomey when he gifted her to the Dahomey throne. The queen's two-year-old twins, Sossa and Favi, scurried around the living area, knocking over toys made from raffia palm leaves, bamboo branches, and coconut shells when Azonton entered the room.

"*Ylon* Azonton," they cried and flew to the door when they saw the man whom they called "Uncle Azonton."

"What did you bring us?" Sossa said as he held on to the visitor's massive leg.

"Something nice, but I'll show it to you later," he responded.

"No! We want it now," said Favi.

Queen Ena Sunu observed the look on her cousin's face and detected something was awry. His face spelled urgency and distress. She knew him well enough to understand that he attempted to engage her children.

"Hosu," Queen Ena Sunu called out to one of her many servants. "Take the children out and play with them," she ordered.

"We're doomed," Azonton blurted out before the twins, and their caretaker had left the room.

"What's it, Azonton?" asked Queen Ena Sunu.

"The kingdom has fallen. They've captured them and will trade them as slaves. Ena, they're all gone," Azonton said, unable to contain his composure.

"Azonton, you aren't making any sense. Who did they capture? What kingdom fell?" asked Queen Ena Sunu.

"Allada," said Azonton.

"How?" Queen Ena Sunu asked in a hushed voice as she slipped into an armchair.

There were a few moments of silence.

"My younger brother, Mausi, who escaped, brought me the news a short while ago," said Azonton. "Ouidah's and Dahomey's joint armies attacked Edome, the Allada capital, at dawn yesterday and seized our parents along with their spouses and several of the king's envoys and courtiers. They rounded them up along with hundreds of slaves and Allada citizens and sent them to *Forte São João Baptista de Ajudá* dungeons in Ouidah. Plans are afoot to ship them off to Brazil."

Queen Ena Sunu sat paralyzed as a wooden effigy and stared into a void. Chaos ambushed her mind as thoughts and questions galloped through her head, ignoring chronology. She was mindful of the fifty-year-long treaty between Allada, Ouidah, and Dahomey. They invented the gifting of princes and princesses, official state tours, and many goodwill gestures to prevent what had just fallen Allada. Hell, she herself was a product of that very project. Why did the Ouidah and Dahomey kings attack Allada? What changed? Had her father and the Allada throne warranted such violence against them? Queen Ena Sunu wondered what plot was unfolding next. Who was behind this? Why hadn't King Gesa called to tell her the news? Did he think as a gifted royal, she had forgotten her roots, her parents, and her people? Dahomey was now her home, her kingdom, and she was its queen. She hadn't forgotten that they had bartered and traded her as though a slave. She had resented it. Did that pain rise to a level for her to celebrate her father's and his kingdom's downfall? Each question she asked opened a new crater of unsettled questions. Azonton's voice pierced the madness that threatened to explode in her mind.

"What are you planning to do?"

"Save them," responded Ena Sunu.

"How?"

"I don't know."

"I'm afraid there's no turning back the minute one crosses the portal that leads towards slavery. Once one enters *Forte São João Baptista de Ajudá* dungeons, one is doomed to go through the door of no return," declared Azonton. "The combined forces of two kingdoms are a formidable obstacle," he added.

A somber silence prevailed.

"Why didn't we know of this plot?" Queen Ena Sunu asked her cousin.

"I don't know. Even if we did, what could we've done?"

"A lot. I could've convinced the king. We could've notified my father."

"That's why they kept it under wraps."

Azonton, who had been standing, stepped over to the queen and sat on a bench facing her.

"Ena, what has happened to our kingdom and to our families distresses me as much as you. But what troubles me now is you and your children. I'm more worried about the present and the future than about a history over which we've no control."

"How so?"

"They've seized your father and will sell him as a slave. I'm uncertain of what will come of your position as King Gesa's spouse."

Queen Ena Sunu hadn't thought that far. She shivered at that knowledge and its ramifications. Unlike the other kingdoms, Dahomey customs and practices forbade the king and members of the royal family from physical contact with slaves and their relatives. Was this the reason King Gesa hadn't summoned her? Had she turned into a *kluvi nɔví*— a slave's relative—and hence a pariah? She rose up and wandered around the living room. A shrine dedicated to several of Dahomey's deities occupied one corner. Among them was *Nana Buluku.* At her foot was a basin full of cowry shells, kola nuts, and preserved leaves from a jumble of trees. Other gods, garbed in expensive fiber and garments, staked the special area in the living suite. They included *Mawu-Lisa,* creator goddess identified with the sun and moon, *Ogun,* god of iron and warfare, and *Ake,* the patron god of hunters, the forest, and the animals within it. The noisy shriek of the queen's two boys playing in the adjoining room interrupted her movement. A visceral rage overwhelmed her. Was the fury founded on the fear and uneasiness of a future that has befallen her? Somehow, the singular contempt to authority that she had learned from her mother and had deployed in ingenious ways in the king's court consumed her. The recognition validated her disdain, her loathing of authority that her father and King Gesa wielded. It was a puissance constructed of violence and greed in both kingdoms.

"My position hasn't changed, and it will not alter," Queen Ena Sunu said, more to herself than answering Azonton. "I was a gifted princess and am now a monarch of the Dahomey kingdom."

Azonton nodded, although skeptically. He'd seen first-hand enough political machinations and the rapid shift in fortunes to conclude that the status quo would remain in place for his cousin and her children. Yet he knew Queen Ena Sunu better than anyone else, indeed better than she knew herself; the look in her eyes, the tightened jaw, and the flaring nostrils. That sufficed to tell him that the woman sitting in front of him would embark on something poignant. What it was, he wasn't sure, but he recognized it. Queen Ena Sunu knew how, where, and when to cut deepest to wound a system constructed to extract from the body of the other. Her process was going to be as tenacious as it was decisive. And resolute and efficient it was.

*****

As she sat distilling her conversation with Azonton and reflecting on her resolution to defend her status and that of her sons', Queen Ena Sunu couldn't help recalling her mother. What would the Alladan queen have done if she had been in her daughter's shoes? Queen Ena Sunu wondered. The more she mulled over this question, the more she thought about their conversations. "*You must attend to your business with the vendor in the market and not to the noise of the market,*" her mother often told her. She wished she had taken the time to ask her to explain further that aphorism's significance. If they hadn't dragged her away so soon in her young life, she could have discovered what she meant. In her present circumstance, she was at liberty to construe that maxim on her own terms as she thought, which was the merit of these adages. For Queen Ena Sunu, it meant that her initial course of action would be to meet with her husband, the merchant, the purveyor, the guarantor, the arbiter of what remained mutable or immutable. The noise in the market, as of vultures circling around carrion, would soon descend, but the good soldier knows to secure the perimeter first. As a result, when Queen Ena Sunu entered King Gesa's chambers, she banished the ragged breathing and sweaty palms that became uninvited companions when she left her living quarters. She rehearsed and played out in her mind how to control this first meeting with the king after the attack on Allada. Queen Ena Sunu reckoned she had two options: fight a lost cause of saving her father and his kingdom or accept an irreversible historical reality and deploy whatever resources she could marshal to carry out her goal of dismantling the scaffold upon which the human body became a commodity for use and abuse by those who possessed the economic, political, and social gravitas and clout. The queen reminded herself of the promise she made to Azonton and to herself and relaxed her clenched jaw and unbarred her bared teeth that had forced the king's personal guards at the chamber's entrance to draw back as she entered a space that very few people in the kingdom ever traversed.

It was a large oval room, the east end of which had a platform on which stood the king's carved mahogany wooden stool with an oval seat and a high back. Two armrests shaped like the front legs of a lion with paws made of ivory, jutted out from each side of the stool as though fit to pounce. An enormous cushion, its coat made from leopard skin and stuffed with soft compact raffia grass, sat on the seat. From the front of the stool, leopard skins spread towards the principal part of the room. Where the leopard skins ended, those of other animals took over, enclosing the entire space and converting it into a motley patchwork of shapes and sizes.

King Gesa stood in front of the wooden stool when Queen Ena Sunu entered. Dressed in a crimson tunic shirt with matching trousers, different animal symbols and images covered the batik fabric that formed his outfit. He wore cowhide sandals adorned with cowry shells and heavy woven fabric dyed in gold, yellow, and maroon. Although he exhibited hints of old age, it was easy to perceive that at one point; he'd had a powerful, muscular body. It was a body that had seen action in several battles. It was a body with scars, akin to a jigsaw patched together as if to catalogue all the battles in which he had fought.

"*In the moment of crisis, the wise build bridges and the foolish build dams,*" King Gesa said, by welcome. "You're a shrewd woman, and I hope you haven't arrived to shatter our bridges."

Queen Ena Sunu broadened her smile and, replying in kind, said, "*By the time the fool has learned the game, the players have dispersed.* I haven't come begging you to reverse what we have done. I will miss my parents but am foremost Queen of the Dahomey kingdom. And it will remain so."

The Queen's response confirmed King Gesa's sentiment that his wife's intelligence and fortitude would triumph over whatever reservations she might have when she discovered what had developed in Allada. Yet his wife's reaction took him aback. She was practical with the new state of affairs and, although grieved, she had accepted it. How many women could have done the same thing? Not his first two wives, who seemed more interested in the luxury that their positions offered them at court. Could he have acquitted himself with such royal dignity as Queen Ena Sunu had done? He wondered and, as he did so, his mind went back to the youthful, gifted fifteen-year-old princess who had shown disdain for some of Dahomey's customs and etiquettes upon her arrival at the court. Her striking disposition, the monarch thought, was a means to survive leaving her home, her own kingdom. She would settle down once the nostalgia passed, he speculated. But he was mistaken.

When she turned into his third bride, Queen Ena Sunu's autonomous and recalcitrant streak, and her contempt and mockery of Dahomey's many practices, only heightened. Her refusal to be submissive as a spouse to the most powerful man in the land became an open secret. She was aloof and loving when she chose and refused to capitulate to protocol. Exasperated, King Gesa still found these lineaments in his new bride offensive and enchanting. Besides, she had given him identical twin sons, a sacred gift from the gods. Their delivery wasn't only about to augur prosperity for the kingdom, but the ascension of one of them to the Dahomey throne when he died meant that the gods would shower his kingdom with their blessings: women would give birth to healthy children, impotent men would become potent once again, the rains would come on time, crops would do well, famine would be but a distant memory, domestic animals would produce strong offspring, hunters would be successful in their hunts, peace, and stability would belong to the order of the day.

There was something else about the young Queen that none of his two wives, courtiers, and consuls could offer the king. Within fewer than ten years in court, Queen Ena Sunu had learned and known more about Dahomey's history, economy, and culture than most of the monarch's confidants who pranced about the palace feeling grand. Through her network of chosen loyal informers, she had her pulse on all courtly intrigues, illicit liaisons, hidden ambitions, and financial malfeasance in the kingdom's treasury. Such was the case of the murder plot against the king that Queen Ena Sunu's informers had unearthed. They seized the traitors and hung them. For failing to discover the plot, they executed Minister Akohouendo, liable for security, along with several of his deputies.

The excited chirping of blue-spotted wood doves and the animated twittering of whistling cisticolas flickering on wide plantain and banana leaves by two wide-open windows broke the king's thoughts.

"Any other reply from you, Queen Ena Sunu, would have been uncharacteristic of who I believe you are," King Gesa answered.

Queen Ena Sunu grinned. She had pulled off her immediate mission and didn't have to learn from the horse's own mouth what had hastened his judgment to cooperate in the raid of her former kingdom. She had learned that the Portuguese Governor, Federico Soares de Souza, and King Tezifon of Ouidah orchestrated the scheme. The governor discovered that King Daguenon had diversified his kingdom's economy. He planned to keep slaves to work on his sprawling palm oil plantations. The British, who already had a powerful presence in the palm oil trade in the southern Niger Delta, wanted to expand the trade to Allada. British palm oil merchants had visited the Allada capital and had convinced the king to consider supplying them with the coveted product. The proceeds from the trade, they argued, would be substantial. Governor Federico Soares de Souza considered the Allada situation a blatant economic threat to his country's interests. He feared it might also tempt the Ouidah and Dahomey kingdoms to enter the palm oil trade, rendering untenable a well-oiled and well-orchestrated mechanism that had sustained Portugal's and Brazil's economic verve, forged on the backs of African slaves. The only way to end the threat was to attack the Allada kingdom and capture King Daguenon along with the entire royal family members and the hundreds of captive slaves that worked on the king's palm oil plantations. With the tantalizing promise of enhancing the price paid for each slave, along with the opportunity of raiding the kingdom of Allada at will to take even more slaves, King Gesa, whose royal treasury was in dire financial straits and was keen to replenish its stock, turned into a co-conspirator.

*****

Queen Ena Sunu told herself her husband may have had all the reasons in the world to launch the violence he had unleashed on her family and her former kingdom, but she remembered a powerful saying among her people: "*The ax forgets what the tree remembers.*" She would remember but ensure whatever ax she wielded in her quest never forgot why she had deployed it. Having secured the perimeter of her battleground, Queen Ena Sunu set to render void Dahomeyan customs that regarded her sons *kluvi nɔvíwo*— relatives of a slave. By Dahomeyan tradition, only two individuals could invoke the clause: Langanfin, the palace's soothsayer and Voodoo chief priest, and Montcho, Dahomey's royal legal master.

She visited Langanfin's sprawling compound in the palace complex. It was one among several at King Gesa's palace, which was more than a large town surrounded by a wall interspersed with wooden pillars capped with pointed cast copper, not too dissimilar from the one which surrounded the entire city of Abomey. They divided the palace into several splendid houses and apartments that contained members of the king's royal family, his courtiers, and their family members, along with the military brass. They sprinkled the palace with several round and rectangular halls with walls decorated with pictures of Dahomeyan conquests and battles.

"Welcome, my queen," the Voodoo chief priest said after several of his acolytes had met Queen Ena Sunu at the compound's entrance and led her into a spacious visitors' room.

"My apologies for showing up unannounced," Queen Ena Sunu said after High Priest Langanfin had offered his visitor a piece of kola nut and had spilled water from his calabash on the ground.

"The queen needs no explanations, after what has happened to her family in Allada and how that development might play itself out here," replied the Voodoo chief priest, a tall, sinewy, gray-bearded man in his mid-fifties.

"That's why I'm here to see you," said Queen Ena Sunu.

"Oh," responded Langanfin. "And how can I help?"

"I want your support. I want you and Montcho to not invoke the *kluvi nɔvíwo* clause on my sons and me."

Langanfin was silent for a few minutes. He didn't like the youthful queen at all. She had defied the kingdom's customs and had advocated dedicating fewer resources to the profligate Vodoo religious ceremonies. The king had concurred with Ena Sunu. For Langanfin, that meant less money to maintain his lavish lifestyle as the kingdom's most powerful religious figure. Getting rid of Queen Ena Sunu was a straightforward way to restore the status quo.

"I'm afraid your petition will be difficult to undertake. You know, we have our own customs here in Dahomey, although people I know don't subscribe to them," said the chief priest. "Besides, nobody can tell Montcho what to do. *Kluvi nɔvíwo* is both cultural and legal. Very tough, my queen, extremely difficult."

"What if the king doesn't approve?"

"He may be king, but he doesn't rule in a vacuum. You should know that."

"Do you realize that he who other people's clothes cover is naked?" Queen Ena Sunu asked.

"I beg your pardon."

"You heard me."

"I don't follow."

"Queen Noanti," said Queen Ena Sunu.

Langanfin shuddered, sucked in a quick breath, and started sweating as the queen's proverb gained full meaning.

"You thought no one knew, didn't you? I suppose you've forgotten that he who shits on the road meets flies on his return," said Queen Ena.

Langanfin remained dumbfounded. How could the youthful queen have discovered that he had been carrying an ongoing illicit liaison with Queen Noanti, the king's second wife? Sure, the queen visited his shrine. Consulting the Voodoo priest was par for the course for most of the royal family members and the dignitaries at court. Except for a few women, no one learned that the shrine's inner sanctum was a hideaway for encounters. None of those women who had crossed that threshold would've uttered a word. The consequences would've been too ugly for them. It appeared that wasn't the situation with Queen Noanti. But why would she share this knowledge with her rival? Queen Ena Sunu's voice startled him.

"Listen, High Priest Langanfin. You're going to do as I ask and get Montcho on board. The repercussions should King Gesa hear about you and Queen Noanti are clear. Yes?" Queen Ena Sunu asked.

Chief Priest Langanfin shook his head. The prospect of that head bumping along on the durbar grounds wasn't a scene that he could consider, given his influence, position, and all that grew with it. The nonverbal agreement between them satisfied the monarch.

Chapter 16

In the complex and convoluted world of Dahomey's internal politics, Queen Ena Sunu knew daggers were being unsheathed and aimed at her and her children. She remembered the saying that vultures always showed up at the place where they slaughtered the goat. Queen Kin-Ha, the king's first wife, was one person to prowl the periphery of influence and power and do whatever it took to accomplish them at whatever cost. Her son, Agossou, had been the heir to the throne. That changed when Queen Ena Sunu delivered her twins. By Dahomeyan customs, they would choose one of them to replace King Gesa. Queen Kin-Ha and her son stood to profit from Queen Ena Sunu's expulsion from the court, should they enforce the *kluvi nɔvíwo* clause. The young queen couldn't afford to wait for her adversary to set her plans into motion. She called on her, as she had done with the chief priest. Queen Ena Sunu took Queen Kin-Ha by surprise when her servants announced her visit. The young queen hadn't visited her since she became King Gesa's third wife and rival. The unexpected call vexed her because she had sent for *Migan*—the king's principal consul—Nagoba for a confidential consultation. She maintained a forced excitement upon seeing Queen Ena Sunu.

"What prompts one of my favorite rivals to my modest quarters?" Queen Kin-Ha asked as she welcomed her visitor into her parlor. She was adroit with little lies that could have devastating results and also impress the uninitiated. Queen Ena Sunu didn't fall for any of them.

"I realized recently that I haven't paid a courtesy call to her

Royal Highness in a while. The king's younger wives ought to pay their respects to their elders. Don't you think?" Queen Ena Sunu countered with her own set of prevarications.

"Ah! I'm honored. How're are Sossa and Favi? They are growing so fast, those boys," said Queen Kin-Ha with a half-smile.

"Yes. And they're quite a handful too. You appreciate how little boys can be. It wouldn't shock me if Agossou was the same too at that age. They all take after their father, don't they?" Queen Ena Sunu asked.

"Oh, yes." Queen Kin-Ha replied and switched the subject. "You seem in good spirits given what happened to your kingdom and to your parents just a few days ago."

"Appearances sometimes can be deceptive, can't they? I am most distressed about what fell to my old kingdom and my parents. Our duty as Dahomey queens is to keep a royal cheer, isn't it?" Queen Ena Sunu asked the older woman.

Queen Kin-Ha didn't reply, parsing the young queen's words. She was struck by how she had referred to Allada as her old kingdom. It might not be that easy to pull off the plan that had been forming in her mind, for which she had sent for *Migan* Nagoba.

"Is there anything I can do to help?" Queen Kin-Ha asked, regretting to have done so.

"Yes."

Queen Kin-Ha sat up straight. She had long black braids lying loose on her shoulders, enveloping a plump face, active eyes, and thick lips, outlined by the mesocarp of *efor*, a black plum. For some inexplicable reason, she found her defenses heightening.

"What's it, my dear?" she declared, recognizing to her horror that the word "dear" carried no sentiment. If Queen Ena Sunu noticed, she didn't show it.

"How does one react to events that might alter one's world, one's beliefs, hopes, and aspirations?"

"What do you mean?"

"Just what I meant by that. For example, everyone expected Agossou to ascend to the Dahomey throne, but then come along Sossa and Favi, who, by Dahomeyan customs, have displaced your offspring because they're identical twin boys. How did you and do you deal with something like that?"

Queen Kin-Ha seethed with anger. Had this woman come to mock her? Was she oblivious to her bitterness? Didn't she know she cursed the gods for what they had done to Agossou? Why was she asking her this question today of all days? She and *Migan* Nagoba were already plotting to recover what they understood was their right: reinstating Agossou as the legitimate successor to the throne since Queen Ena Sunu and her sons had become *kluvi nɔvíwo.*

"You're asking this question because you expect your world, your beliefs, hopes, and aspirations are about to turn?" Queen Kin-Ha asked.

"Yes, and no. Yes, because no one can foresee one's future. No, because for now, I believe nothing is about to change."

"How can you be that confident?" asked Queen Kin-Ha.

"Because I'm not the woman who acquiesces and succumbs. If there's anything I've learned, it's using whatever mechanisms I have at my disposition to fight," said Queen Ena Sunu.

"What might that be?" Queen Kin-Ha asked, allowing her curiosity to get a better part of her.

"I know there're several people itching for a quarrel. It would tempt Voodoo High Priest Langanfin, for instance, to explore the *kluvi nɔvíwo* clause because of what's happened in Allada."

"If I'm to understand, you've deployed one of your so-called arsenals against him?"

"I have. I shocked him when I mentioned his dalliance with an important royal family member. Should this affair become public, who knows what will transpire?"

Queen Kin-Ha shivered. She understood the entire purpose of the young queen's visit. Yet she craved to push the limits. She wanted to find out what Queen Ena Sunu knew.

"I presume there might be other people itching for a fight?"

"Yes. You, for example."

"Me? You must be joking."

"No, I'm not."

"Let's assume it was true, which I'm not saying it is. What would be your weapon?"

"You, *Migan* Nagoba, and Agossou."

"Come again?"

"I don't suppose King Gesa knows about Agossou. If he did, you and *Migan* Nagoba would have been long dead. Don't you think?"

The older queen was quiet. In a few minutes, everything had come tumbling down. How in the world did this young woman know about Agossou's lineage? Who else knew? What if she denied it? Of what use would that be? It was true. Wasn't it? She'd been in love with *Migan* Nagoba before she married King Gesa. Her mind was in turmoil. Just when she thought she had advanced a clever scheme to secure the throne for her boy, this woman had come along to spoil it all once more.

"You need not fret over it," declared Queen Ena Sunu. "So long as you and *Migan* Nagoba don't do anything underhanded, your secret will remain where it's been all this while."

As a last line of defense, Queen Ena Sunu sought three of her husband's most influential counselors. The first was *Migan* Hounsa, responsible for the royal treasury. She had discovered that he had been siphoning money from the royal coffers for his personal use to construct a palace in Ikpinle, his remote village. The two other men included *Migan* Mizéhoun, Minister of War and Defense, and *Yovogan* Nondichao, Minister of the Slave Trade. Both men had been conspiring to dethrone the king just before the Allada invasion. The assault on Allada had upended their plans, but they hadn't suspended their plot. Queen Ena Sunu didn't mince words when she admitted to the three men what she knew about them. In return for keeping their secrets, she wanted their unqualified support, should they advance the *kluvi nɔví* clause. Well-versed in Dahomey customs and traditions as well as in its laws, the three individuals knew that discovery of their offenses and abuses meant instant decapitation.

*****

Having ensured a secured position at court, Queen Ena Sunu

embarked on her long-term goal. She reckoned that if she couldn't abolish slave trading in Ouidah, she could, at least, stem its flow in Dahomey. That would be the beginning. Ouidah would be next, and she already had a plan etched in her mind to accomplish that. Sintana Fansinnou, leader of the *N'Nonmiton*—Our Mothers—was her initial recruit.

The *N'Nonmiton* was an all-female military regiment that the Europeans, upon their first encounter with them, called Amazons because of their striking similarity to the semi-mythical Amazons of ancient Anatolia on the Black Sea. Dahomey's women soldiers were foreign captives and recruits from within the Dahomey kingdom. Ruthless and having learned survival skills and apathy to pain and death, the *N'Nonmiton* was the perfect fighting machine the Dahomey king deployed in his raids for slaves. All virgins, they couldn't marry or have children. In theory, they were married to the king. Disciplined to the core, service in the *N'Nonmiton* offered these women the chance to accrue wealth and occupy prominent positions in Dahomey. Reputed to be fierce, they were as powerful as their male military counterparts.

It surprised Sintana Fansinnou when Queen Ena Sunu summoned the warrior to her separate quarters. She found the monarch sitting on a long bamboo couch in the middle of the living room in her suite. Her light brown, soft skin matched her large brown eyes. Her dark hair sat on a well-sculpted head, and her face revealed a modest bump of a nose situated just above a mouth adorned with luscious lips. Queen Ena Sunu wore a wide neck blouse that unloaded firm, full breasts, a bounteous sample of which was noticeable as one contemplated the silver necklace with three studded gold beads around her neck. Queen Ena Sunu stood up to welcome her guest, a remarkable gesture since, as one of the kingdom's queens, custom dictated that she remained seated when she greeted and welcomed visitors. Sintana Fansinnou took notice. Almost of the same height as Queen Ena Sunu, Sintana Fansinnou was dark, muscular, and imposing. Her vigilant eyes illuminated her face because of the agility of her movements, although she was a large but not a fat woman.

They captured Sintana Fansinnou, along with her family, when the Dahomey army raided her village. Six feet tall at fifteen, the fight she put up to the invasion when the Dahomey soldiers raided her father's compound was exceptional. Armed with a pestle used to pound yams and root crops, Sintana Fansinnou broke the skulls of five soldiers before they subdued her. She spat into the troop leader's face. Such a daring and most denigrating act could have had calamitous repercussions, but General Novi Sia, who led the raid and recruited foreign captives for the *N'Nonmiton*, recognized that Sintana Fansinnou was no ordinary girl. Her recruitment into the *N'Nonmiton* was inevitable, but the rest of her family suffered the destiny of all the vanquished: they auctioned them as slaves and shipped them off to Brazil. In ten years, Sintana Fansinnou had turned into the *N'Nonmiton* leader, an influential position that permitted her to amass wealth and influence in Dahomey. Despite her situation, however, something disquieting gnawed at her.

Queen Ena Sunu surmised that while it appeared as though the *N'Nonmiton* leader had exorcised the excruciating experience of separation from her own family, buried in her subconscious mind must be unspeakable rage and loss. Akin to the birthmark delicately etched on one of her own breasts that she couldn't jettison no matter how many rivers and mountains she crossed, Queen Ena Sunu saw in Sintana Fansinnou a kindred spirit who couldn't wish away her imprisoned subterranean bitterness and anguish. This was their first private encounter, and the queen had her choice of weapons well laid out.

"Welcome, my dear Sintana Fansinnou," Queen Ena Sunu said as she held out her hand and took the warrior's in hers. The *N'Nonmiton* leader's calloused hand, which felt like a wilted and shriveled coconut husk, swallowed Queen Ena Sunu's. For a few seconds, they remained quiet and looked into each other's eyes. After a while, Sintana Fansinnou replied, "It's an honor to respond to my queen's summons."

Queen Ena Sunu pointed to an armchair next to the long bamboo couch on which she had been sitting. Her guest surveyed the room. Several potted plants stood beneath a large window overlooking the palace's most important public space: the central courtyard to receive foreign dignitaries, to install chiefs, kings, and their elders. The intensity with which her guest gazed at the shrine in her living room intrigued Queen Ena Sunu, who was watching Sintana Fansinnou closely.

It wasn't as though her visitor saw such a shrine for the first time. There wasn't any private or public space in Allada, Ouidah, and Dahomey that didn't have similar shrines that cohabited with their eager or reluctant worshippers. Was her guest judging her on the size, design, and the shrine's placement in her living room? The queen wondered. Two maids emerged from a side door bearing bamboo trays crammed with fruits and two gourds filled with water and palm wine. When they set both trays on a low center table, one maid offered empty calabashes to Queen Ena Sunu and her guest. The other poured water, first into the queen's calabash and next into Sintana Fansinnou's. The maids exited. Lifting her filled calabash, Queen Ena Sunu looked at the *N'Nonmiton* leader, poured water on the ground, and took a sip. Sintana Fansinnou followed suit, but she did something unusual: she didn't pour libation, the requisite ritual that served as a sign of reverence for the gods, friends, or departed relatives. A few moments of silence followed. None of them felt awkward with the silence.

"I don't remember the last time I neglected to pour water on the ground in homage to the gods before drinking," Queen Ena Sunu said with a smile.

"I didn't forget."

"Oh?" Queen Ena Sunu said, raising an eyebrow.

"Overrated," said Sintana Fansinnou.

"What is?"

"This whole ritual thing. I've never believed in it and never will."

"Are you informing me you don't believe in our gods?" the queen asked her visitor, doing her best to maintain her voice as disinterested as possible.

"Why should I?" Sintana Fansinnou asked.

"Should I assume you don't have a shrine in your quarters as ordered by the statutes of the land?"

"I have one to keep appearances. But I spit on it when I wake up every morning and before I go to bed."

"You must have some strong views. I wonder from where they came," Queen Ena Sunu said. She paused and proceeded. "Aren't you risking sharing this information with me? What you've told me is sacrilegious, and if Langanfin, the palace's soothsayer and Voodoo chief priest should find out about this, the repercussion could be catastrophic for you. You know that. Don't you?"

"I would relish a debate with that charlatan along with his many acolytes and his enablers."

Queen Ena Sunu smiled and switched the subject.

"I respect what you and your fighters do for the Dahomey kingdom. King Gesa cannot fail to mention your name any time we're together. If I didn't know him, I would've suggested he was in love with you," Queen Ena Sunu lied.

"Oh?" the *N'Nonmiton* leader declared, shifting in her chair.

"Oh yes. But you wouldn't understand how it feels to fall in love or for someone to love you because of your position. What a pity. To carry such a heavy weight on your shoulders and never to have experienced the joys of intimacy."

Sintana Fansinnou was quiet.

"They expect all *N'Nonmiton* warriors to be virgins and unmarried. Is that true?" Queen Ena Sunu asked.

Sintana Fansinnou nodded.

"What irony! To think those who endanger their lives raiding towns and villages for slaves to generate wealth for this great kingdom cannot come home from the frontlines to loved ones who would welcome them, kiss them, and make them forget the pain of losing their dear warriors in battle," Queen Ena Sunu said, as she stood. After a brief pause, she continued, "Yet it isn't the same with the men. Isn't it right?" the queen asked as she sat next to her guest. She planted her hand on the warrior's. Sintana Fansinnou remained quiet and thoughtful. She didn't move her hand.

"Tell me about your people," Queen Ena Sunu said. "They must be proud that you've risen to such a prominent position in Dahomey and that you have a secret lover in the king of the land," she added with a smile that appeared innocent and charming.

An anguished look flushed through Sintana Fansinnou's face. She assumed everybody at the palace knew of her history. If Queen Ena Sunu was inquiring about her family, it could mean one thing: her recruiter, General Novi Sia, and those soldiers who captured her must have vowed to reveal nothing about her past. Wouldn't the Dahomey people prefer that their *N'Nonmiton* leader come from the Dahomey kingdom instead of the backwoods? Wouldn't young girls who aspired to join the elite female warrior group fancy a role model whose family they didn't capture in a raid and sold as slaves? No, Queen Ena Sunu knew nothing about her, she determined. Sintana Fansinnou reckoned this was the first time that anybody had asked her of her family and had taken an interest in her personal story. Most people in the palace and beyond cared only for her position in the *N'Nonmiton*, their exploits, and what it meant to be equal, in theory, to Dahomey men soldiers.

Sintana Fansinnou looked into Queen Ena Sunu's eyes. She had learned of her powerful will and her insouciance towards all that smacked of authority. She hadn't reacted in the manner most people would have responded if they heard she spat on *Nana Buluku*. Wasn't this female Supreme Being the creator and was, therefore, protector of beings, especially the *N'Nonmiton*? The queen stoked something that she hadn't acknowledged: coming back from a campaign to an empty house without an awaiting partner. She wondered why they robbed the *N'Nonmiton* of what the men warriors had had for years. If they could marry, have close companions, and still fight as they did, what prohibited the *N'Nonmiton* fighters from achieving the same? Queen Ena Sunu's remarks came thundering through her ears, and she echoed them verbatim to herself:

"What irony! . . ." Sintana Fansinnou thought. They hailed them as the *N'Nonmiton*—Our Mothers—yet they required them to be virgins, unmarried! The queen had kindled feelings that Sintana Fansinnou had banished from her mind: anger and sadness. She had refused to reminisce the day they captured her family, and her village razed to the ground. She had refused to accept that her inscription into the *N'Nonmiton* extended that violence that they had unleashed and inflicted on her body; a body that now served as an instrument fashioned to wreak yet again havoc and violence on others. For the first time, she was confronting imprisoned feelings and thoughts. She shuddered at what that meant. After what seemed a long time, Sintana Fansinnou responded to the queen's query that had set her mind tumbling through a hitherto barricaded memory lane. "I don't have a family. They captured us in a raid. They bartered my people, except me, and sent them to Salvador," Sintana Fansinnou said, doing her best to stifle the tears.

"I'm so sorry to hear that," Queen Ena Sunu said, tears sparkling in her eyes. Both women were hushed for a while, each of them receding into their own separate spaces of loss and anguish.

"You must think of your folk. Don't you?" Queen Ena Sunu asked her guest, rubbing her upper arm.

"As often as I try, no day passes without wondering where they might be. Did they make it crossing the ocean? What could they be doing now? Are they still together, or did they separate and trade them to different owners? These questions course through my mind every day," said Sintana Fansinnou.

"I'm sure I would ask myself the same questions if I were in your shoes," declared Queen Ena Sunu.

"But you do, don't you? They shipped your parents to Brazil. Haven't similar thoughts accosted you?" Sintana Fansinnou asked.

"Yes. You're right," asserted Queen Ena Sunu. "But I've told myself that I'll never standby and let that happen to my children or any child in this kingdom."

"What?" the warrior demanded in horror.

"My body has been a product traded and abused through the violence spawned by those who have power in our and other kingdoms. I intend to stop that from happening to other women," said Queen Ena Sunu.

"Queen Ena Sunu, with all due respect, I think her royal highness must be out of her mind. How're you going to do that? You asked me a short while ago if it wasn't risky sharing my thoughts about the gods with you. Aren't you doing the same with me? Isn't what you're saying blasphemous?"

"Maybe, I'm crazy. Maybe, I am taking a risk talking to someone who they have trained to use her body as a weapon to do what they did to her family and to mine. Perhaps the next thing I know, the leader of the *N'Nonmiton* will orchestrate to have my head rolling on the durbar grounds because she thinks she must obey the rules that others have set and because she believes that Dahomey and Allada women are helpless."

An uncomfortable silence replaced the warm one that prevailed when they first met. Queen Ena Sunu got up after a few minutes and stood in front of the still seated soldier. She hadn't repelled the young queen's physical touch. Queen Ena Sunu held Sintana Fansinnou's head and pulled her towards her midriff. She didn't resist. Nobody had held her that way before. Neither had she been in such intimate contact with anyone, a woman. She had had close encounters with men on the battlefield. It wasn't a place to experience the fire that seemed to course through her body as she found her head wedged between two voluptuous breasts. A sweet, distinct, and intoxicating perfume of a body that was ripe and luscious overcame her. Sintana Fansinnou's arousal intensified as the queen touched her between her thighs. She opened her legs. This was a place, a space, a sanctuary, an altar at which no human being had ever paid homage. A place that had laid dormant for the past twenty-six years. The fury with which her body erupted terrified her as it plunged into an abyss that engulfed her with pleasure. She murmured, not believing that her body could be a fountain, a repository that spouted such intense, almost paralyzing spasms. She stood up and kissed Queen Ena Sunu and pulled her to her powerful body, but the monarch drew back.

"Why did you summon me here?" Sintana Fansinnou asked. She was neither angry nor embarrassed. The encounter with the queen seemed natural and quite normal even though she knew that as a *N'Nonmiton*, to be intimate with anybody, and especially with a woman, was taboo.

"I need your services," said Queen Ena Sunu, who also appeared at ease. She had known only two men in her life. One of those encounters was a forced one that she'd sooner forget. As for King Gesa, she could tell many stories about his visits if she wanted to, none of them stirring. She had never been with a woman, yet her brief experience with Sintana Fansinnou seemed to have unleashed a heretofore hidden passion.

"What services?"

"If King Gesa and King Tezifon attacked my father's kingdom because they wanted more slaves from the Allada kingdom, along with those from other towns and villages, to be sent to Brazil, they'll be in for a shock. I plan to sabotage those efforts. That's where you come in."

The *N'Nonmiton* leader was silent for a few minutes. "How're you going to do that?"

"I'm already doing that with your presence here. But I'd like to know whether you'll join me," Queen Ena Sunu said, walking towards the female warrior and extending her hand to touch Sintana Fansinnou on the shoulder.

"Yes," said the *N'Nonmiton* leader.

*****

The Dahomey kingdom ceased to be the same fifteen years after the invasion and ransacking of the Allada Kingdom. To understand the present, it might be useful to highlight a few things that transpired during the interceding years.

A week after Queen Ena Sunu had summoned her to her living quarters, Sintana Fansinnou stormed General Novi Sia's compound in the royal complex where he lived with his two wives, two concubines, and several children. This was surprising for the *N'Nonmiton* leader, who embodied military discipline that demanded absolute deference to one's superiors. General Novi Sia was one of King Gesa's most powerful army generals who commanded the *N'Nonmiton*. He had aged considerably since he first met Sintana Fansinnou. He remembered her conscription and admired her. She was more capable and formidable at war than most of his men and was the perfect soldier who took orders and followed them to the letter. The five thousand *N'Nonmiton* fighters under her command submitted to her will. For Sintana Fansinnou to barge into his private quarters without following standard protocol, she must have something terribly urgent on her mind, Novi Sia thought. And urgent were the things that assailed her mind.

"How many *N'Nonmiton* fighters lost their lives in the last raid compared to the men fighters?" Sintana Fansinnou asked General Novi Sia without observing traditional protocol that required salutations.

Sitting on a stool surrounded by two of his youngest children, the army general ordered them to withdraw from the room. He was of average height, slim but solid–built, and his black skin looked supple around his eyes, mouth, and neck. The *N'Nonmiton* leader's question had taken him by surprise. A thoughtful man who weighed his words before he spoke, Sintana Fansinnou's uncharacteristic and unprecedented behavior shocked General Novi Sia.

"Can you sit and allow me to serve you with water, as our custom demands? You know, we regularly welcome visitors by pouring libation to our forefathers to help us deliberate on whatever we may have in our minds," said General Novi Sia.

"I've heard enough about libation and our ancestors," Sintana Fansinnou replied, still standing at the entrance to a room layered with animal skins and baskets full of several dried flowers arranged around two large windows overlooking the compound of the general's concubines.

"Oh, I see. You must have been speaking to many people then, I assume?" asked General Novi Sia.

"It's neither here nor there," replied Sintana Fansinnou. "I asked you a direct question."

"Alright, I'll answer you, even though I admit your question proposes a fundamental flaw in its premise."

"How so?"

"You're not considering proportions and percentages. More men took part in the raid than women. As a result, more of them died."

"You might be right, but you're wrong in your calculations. Two thousand men and a thousand *N'Nonmiton* fought in the war. Five hundred men died. Eighty women died. You lost twenty-five percent of your men and I, eight percent of my women fighters. Your math and your assumptions aren't logical."

"What are you getting at?" General Novi Sia asked, with irritation.

"That the *N'Nonmiton* soldiers are as formidable, if not more, than the men," replied Sintana Fansinnou.

"So?"

"So, we need to rethink *N'Nonmiton's* role in the Dahomey army and society."

"What do you mean?"

"Let's put it this way. If men can do what custom grants them and yet can fight in battles, there shouldn't be any reason women couldn't do the same."

General Novi Sia burst into laughter. "This is the best joke I've heard in a long time," he said, holding his sides.

"The *N'Nonmiton* refuse to remain virgins. God knows they've starved us long enough. Like you and the men warriors, who have wives and concubines, we wish to marry."

"Has a rabid dog bitten you? Where did you get this stupid idea? Do you understand what this means? It means we'll be working against nature and the gods. That will be the end of Dahomey customs as we know them."

"Going against nature and the gods, you say? What about the secret rituals some of your men perform on one another before every battle? Isn't that going against the world and the gods?"

General Novi Sia surged from his stool and charged at Sintana Fansinnou, but the soldier held out her long brawny arm and parried away the general as though she was brushing off a fly. Shocked and livid, the man hollered. "Get out of my house!"

Sintana Fansinnou got a stool and sat.

"Go on, call your guards, and, while you're at it, summon your wives and your concubines. It might interest them to learn about those customs that fortify your men's manhood. I, along with my *N'Nonmiton* fighters, have seen them, and we don't give a damn. Perhaps others could tell if those habits do or don't work against nature, thus transgressing the hideous laws of your toothless gods."

General Novi Sia felt dazed and confounded. Tongue tied.

"Since *Migan* Mizéhoun, Minister of War and Defense, was once a soldier, it would behoove you to confer with him on our demands," suggested Fansinnou Sintana.

"And what the hell are they?" General Novi Sia spat out.

"We should wed whoever we choose, even if that person is a woman."

General Novi Sia leaped up again. "Now, you've lost your mind. I was getting the logic of what you claimed were your demands until you added marrying women into the mix. Oh, the scourge that will come upon Dahomey should that come to pass!"

"What calamity has befallen this kingdom, despite what your male warriors do? Doesn't that warrant the curse of your gods? Yet I have noted no scourge on Dahomey, which prompts one to draw two conclusions: either your gods are feckless and helpless, or they themselves engage in some unutterable acts in private."

General Novi Sia was apoplectic but remained mum. As the *N'Nonmiton* warrior stood up and was about to walk out of the room, General Novi Sia said, "You know you are a *kluvi nɔví*. Right? All that I've got to do is to invoke that clause and, if you are lucky, they will banish you from the kingdom. I could also ask that they decapitate you."

Fansinnou Sintana became quiet and pensive. After a few moments, she smiled.

"Go ahead. Invoke the clause. But you must explain to the court why you recruited a *kluvi nɔví* who's now head of the *N'Nonmiton*. Let's see which of these infractions of yours is more egregious, or do you want me to tell you?" she asked.

The *N'Nonmiton* leader walked out. A few months after her clash with General Novi Sia, a vigorous debate occurred at court. The General had told *Migan* Mizéhoun about his encounter with Fansinnou Sintana. He underscored the *N'Nonmiton* leader's knowledge about some Dahomey soldiers' pre-war acts. Fearing public exposure, the Minister and his General advanced Sintana Fansinnou's requests. Despite vehement opposition, the military's puissance prevailed, and for the first time in Dahomey's history, *N'Nonmi-*

ton soldiers could marry and still fight. However, *Migan* Mizéhoun and General Novi Sia considered women marrying other women as untenable. But it was of no particular concern to the *N'Nonmiton* fighters: they had been performing their own rituals out of sight long before the men.

During those same intervening years, Ena Sunu accomplished one of her goals: to curb the slave trade in Dahomey, snuff it out, and replicate a similar strategy in Ouidah. She reckoned that dwindling resources and pillage at the royal treasury prompted King Gesa to co-conspire and loot her father's kingdom fifteen years earlier. Dahomey's economic system, she concluded, needed a complete overhaul. With King Gesa under her thumb, she advocated revamping and streamlining the kingdom's internal revenue and tax structure. *Migan* Hounsa, Minister of Finance, who stopped syphoning money from the state coffers, became involved in enforcing these reforms. She exposed illegal financial dealings at the kingdom's treasury. In short, the hemorrhage of the royal coffers ceased. It wasn't long before the kingdom's treasury became robust. King Gesa now had ample funds to launch projects to benefit the Dahomey people.

As Queen Ena Sunu had expected, diminished financial pressure on King Gesa resulted in a decline in slave raids. Dahomey's novel approach to the slave trade emerged. The queen understood she couldn't stop outright the traffic, but she could have a voice in who they traded. She instituted and ensured that they enforced a new protocol in the raids, which were no longer indiscriminate. During their sorties, Dahomey fighters now brought back from their invasions, criminals, and men abusive of their wives and children.

Despite the internal economic reforms and the strategic changes in slave acquisition, Queen Ena Sunu knew they couldn't sustain the new normal for long. Inevitable pressures from within and from the European slavers were a matter of time. She recalled the stormy debate she overhead in the Chamber of Orations as a fourteen-year-old girl. Strong proponents of the trade in the king's palace couldn't allow Dahomey to wean itself of slave trafficking. Queen Ena Sunu did what her father had attempted doing: diversify the Dahomeyan economy and embrace palm oil manufacture. Prior to providing her spouse with a thorough comparative evaluation between slave trafficking and palm oil production, she sent Azonton to the Delta Region, east of Dahomey, to learn about the industry and consult with British merchants. In high demand for lubricating machinery and as a key ingredient in margarine, candles, and soap, palm oil production proved more lucrative. Its manufacture didn't require capturing slaves and sending them across the Atlantic.

In presenting her diversification plans to her husband, Queen Ena Sunu didn't neglect to remind him of the fate her father suffered when Governor Federico Soares de Souza noticed a reduction in the number of slaves that her father sold to the Portuguese slave traders.

"I'm not perturbed about suffering an identical fate, like your father. I don't have any Portuguese Governor with whom to do business. Pedro de Barbosa, that black merchant now in *Forte São João Baptista de Ajudá*, doesn't control me. Besides, I've a great treaty with the Ouidah kingdom and an outstanding relationship with King Dozan," King Gesa had declared.

"So was my father's situation," Queen Ena Sunu replied.

"What do you mean?"

"When one blows up a treaty, it is easier to break another. King Dozan has a warmer rapport with Pedro de Barbosa than you. The slave fort lies on the Ouidah coast. It is in the Ouidah king's interest to preserve slave trafficking."

"What're you proposing?"

"If we're to pursue the same route as my father did, we must strengthen our defenses against any future attacks. I suggest we shift our army's focus from offense to defense. I advocate the *N'Nonmiton* fighters no longer take part in raids. They should become a core defense entity."

King Gesa remained thoughtful. Queen Ena Sunu wasn't done.

"We should plant several spies in the Ouidah court and in the kingdom. We ought to have a pulse in whatever happens there."

With her proven record of providing the monarch invaluable

advice and aiding him to remodel his kingdom's economy, King Gesa consented to Queen Ena Sunu's propositions. Thus, it was that within fifteen years, Dahomey had become a kingdom that stopped depending on the slave trade. Sure, slave traffic still took place, but they only sold criminals and unwanted elements in the kingdom and beyond. With all these changes, Queen Ena Sunu secured a powerful position in Dahomey. Although the king's third wife, she wielded tremendous influence over her two older rivals. Queen Kin-Ha loathed with an intensity the young queen and had been biding her time to unleash her rage. The time arrived when Queen Ena Sunu launched the second chapter to dismantle the slave trafficking on that part of the West African coast.

Sossa and Favi turned seventeen in 1825, and either of them was ripe for her project. As expected, she had been deliberate and had considered her plans with Azonton's advice.

"I understand there're disagreements between King Dozan of Ouidah and Pedro de Barbosa," Queen Ena Sunu told her husband during one of their few and rare intimate moments in the queen's quarters. It was on these occasions she made notable requests.

"What is the basis of these disagreements?"

"I hear the Ouidah king isn't delivering as many slaves as the trader wants. They say King Dozan doesn't want to succumb to the pressure of selling his own people."

King Gesa remained quiet.

"I'm worried," said the queen.

"Why?"

"One cannot say the extent to which these slavers will go to secure their merchandise."

"Come now, you're not thinking they will be stupid enough to invade my kingdom. Are you?"

"Worse still, they could connive with King Dozan."

"But we have a treaty with Ouidah."

"Didn't you have one with Allada before you and King Tezifon attacked my father's kingdom?"

"Don't remind me of my nightmare," said the king.

This was the first time Ena Sunu heard her husband refer to his co-scheme as a bad dream. She let it slide and concentrated on her agenda.

"We should neutralize King Dozan and gift one of your twin boys to Ouidah."

"Why would you wish to subject one of your sons to the same experiences that you had as a gifted princess? They treated you as the royal you were, but you loathed your gifting. How do I determine which of the twins to gift? Wouldn't I be robbing one of them on a path to the Dahomey throne?"

Queen Ena Sunu was silent for a moment. She had expected these questions. But her husband's perspicacity surprised her. For the first time, he had remarked on her early years at the court. In addition, he showed remorse for having looted the Allada kingdom.

"Gifting Sossa or Favi could settle a succession issue in Dahomey. It raises the opportunity for the gifted son to become an Ouidah king. As you well know, unlike Dahomey, gifted princes can ascend to the throne in Ouidah. Having both Sossa and Favi as Dahomey and Ouidah kings would augur well for sustained peace and progress between the two kingdoms. Given what I've learned, the most likely contender to the Ouidah throne may not have the requisite temperament for ascension," said Queen Ena Sunu.

King Gesa looked at his third wife for a long time and said, "You carry a brilliant mind in that head of yours, don't you?"

Queen Ena Sunu smiled. She had just laid the groundwork for her Ouidah plans, and her husband had just sealed the foundation.

Chapter 17

"That bitch had everything worked out from the beginning. Didn't she? The king proposes to gift Sossa to the Ouidah kingdom. You realize what that means, don't you?" asked Queen Kin-Ha.

"Yes," responded *Migan* Nagoba.

"What are you going to do about it? Where does our Agossou fit into all of this?" inquired a furious Queen Kin-Ha.

"The king determines which of his sons or daughters to gift to another kingdom. One cannot do anything about that."

"Oh, I'll be dead before that arises," announced King Gesa's first wife.

"What do you intend to do?" asked the king's consul.

"Go back to the plan we had before the bitch of a queen outmaneuvered us many years ago," said Queen Kin-Ha.

"You know it is virtually impossible. Their uncle and counselor, Azonton, shields them like a hawk. Nothing goes into their mouths without a taster," said *Migan* Nagoba.

"Oh, there're other ways to snip the bitch's wings, bring her down to earth, and have her banished from Dahomey," said Queen Kin-Ha.

"Is there something you know I don't?"

"As usual, I do," said the queen.

"Pray, tell me, my love. I cannot wait to hear it," said *Migan* Nagoba with a grin on his pocked face.

"Sintana Fansinnou."

"You want the *N'Nonmiton* leader to kill your rival?" demanded the confused consul.

"No. There's something happening between her and that bitch," said Queen Kin-Ha.

"What?"

"Do I have to spell out everything to you? What do you think two bitches do with each other in the same bed at night?"

"You don't mean . . ."

"Yes, I mean that," said the queen.

"That's blasphemous and treasonous. How did you find out?"

"Two sources: the sorcerer in Ikpinle and one of the bitch's own servants."

That Queen Kin-Ha vented her ire in her parlor in eunuch Hounsa's presence was of no significance either to the queen or her lover. Like any eunuch in the king's court, Hounsa was a servant whose position was above that of a slave's. Like the others of his ilk, his task was to serve the king's wives, concubines, and ministers. Castrated, their manhood taken away from them, everybody assumed their tongues had become muted, making them the finest secret keepers. That idea, held by many, suited the eunuchs just fine. What Dahomey's haughty political establishment and social elite didn't know, however, was that the eunuchs possessed a wealth of information about everybody and all that ensued at the court.

Hounsa had heard and seen a lot during his thirty years of service at King Gesa's palace. He was familiar with the plots, the murders, the backstabbing, the illicit affairs, and the thirst for power which people had pursued with reckless abandonment and met with decapitations. The conversation that he had just overhead, however, couldn't have been more dramatic. What stood out in this case, though, had to do with the person involved: Queen Ena Sunu. Hounsa shuddered. He continued his tasks as though he had just discovered two people talking about the weather. Yet he boiled with rage. The exchange involved the murder of a future king and, above all, Queen Ena Sunu's son. That thing about the queen and the *N'Nonmiton* leader? He wondered who in Dahomey cared except those hypocrites who pretended that such a thing didn't exist. Didn't his eunuch friends leave the court to do things with nanny goats in the fields? Queen Kin-Ha epitomized what Hounsa despised with the king's older wives. They feigned love for one another at court, yet the norm behind the scenes included venomous tongues, malicious hearts, and mouths filled with lies. There was no way in hell, he repeated to himself, that he wouldn't alert Queen Ena Sunu.

As Hounsa reflected on his resolution, he couldn't help himself from chuckling when he recalled the prank the youthful Princess Ena Sunu pulled on the eunuchs, less than a month after she had arrived from Allada. Bored, homesick, and feeling constrained, she conspired with one of her closest servants, and disguised as a eunuch, entered their eating and living place. Close to fifty eunuchs ate, drank, laughed, and told crude jokes about the counselors they served. Princess Ena Sunu learned the eunuchs were a repository of valuable insight regarding what ensued at the palace. They bore grudges against those who maltreated them and discovered little ways to seek revenge. As she spent time with the eunuchs and listened to their stories, she remembered a saying: "*Those whose palm-kernels a benevolent spirit cracks for them should be humble.*" She resolved never to conduct herself like the courtiers and royal family members who despised the eunuchs, the benevolent spirits who made their lives better than most of Dahomey's citizens. After several incursions into their area, Princess Ena Sunu revealed her identity. Mortified, she assured the eunuchs they had nothing to fear. Over time, she won their confidence, transforming some of them and her maids into potent allies when she became King Gesa's third wife. Hounsa was one such supporter and informer.

*****

The trial of members of the Dahomey royal house was an extraordinary phenomenon. Tribunals took place in an open courtyard surrounded by walls decorated with allusive images in bas-relief that served as a record book of the major events that marked the history, customs, rituals, and military exploits and victories in which the Dahomey people took pride. The courtyard featured a prominent live pond with tropical water lily day blooming plants, African feather fin catfishes, albino cory catfishes, red and green tiger lotuses, water sprites, and giant hair grasses. Tamed cattle egrets, hornbills, and colorful ducks spread across the pond. The palace laborers covered the grounds with a low grass lawn with flower-beds dotted with giant lobster claws, miracle fruits, variations of yellow, pink, orange, and red volcano flowers that attracted butter-flies, long-beaked regal, olive-bellied, red-chested, and black-bellied sunbirds.

A three-foot scaffold stood at one end of the pond. On the platform, the requisite number of chairs for the accused and their complainants and witnesses sat facing each other. Dahomey customs dictated that defendants and their accusers sat on the same platform to look one another in the eye when they made denunciations. For the sake of fairness, they didn't allow anonymity when someone levied charges against an individual in court. On this occasion, five women sat on the scaffold: Queen Ena Sunu, Sintana Fansinnou, Queen Kin-Ha, Ladipo, the sorceress from Ikpin-le, and Mindivi, Queen Ena Sunu's servant. Montcho, Dahomey's royal legal master, Langanfin, the palace's soothsayer and Voodoo chief priest, *Yovogan* Nondichao, Minister of the Slave Trade, *Migan* Mizéhoun, Minister of War and Defense, and courtesan *Migan* Nagoba sat in front of the platform. The six would determine the accused persons' destiny. The gossiping jealous women of the court who had milled around the courtyard like a gang of squawking buzzards, primed for what they hoped would be one of the biggest trials in decades.

Montcho got up to address the court after King Gesa, and all the palace dignitaries sat. He had been furious since the day Langanfin came to his compound and demanded that he not enforce the *kluvi nɔvi* clause against the young queen and her sons. That was fifteen years ago. Although the powerful Voodoo chief priest hadn't told him why, he had complied. This trial, he thought, provided him the chance to redress what he deemed a long overdue infraction against the Dahomey people.

"His Royal Highness, King Gesa, conqueror of the wind, sun, and the rain," Montcho began. "We're assembled here today because Her Royal Highness, Queen Kin-Ha, is accusing her rival, Her Royal Highness, Queen Ena Sunu, and Sintana Fansinnou, leader of the *N'Nonmiton*, of an infraction that, if found true, would be the vilest crime ever committed within the walls of this palace."

Whispers punctured the silence that followed Montcho's opening statement. The alleged crime of the young queen and the warrior had already circulated in the palace and beyond. Several variations of the same theme had morphed and intertwined with one another, paving the way for easy digestion and regurgitation.

"Pray, Montcho, can you call on Her Royal Highness, Queen Kin-Ha, to tell us what the alleged crime is?" asked *Yovogan* Nondichao. "I'd suggest the illustrious royal legal master refrains from labeling the supposed crime of which Queen Ena Sunu and Sintana Fansinnou are being accused as vile or otherwise. We make that decision, not an individual," added *Yovogan* Nondichao.

Queen Kin-Ha chewed on her bottom lip. She and *Migan* Nagoba met with the *Yovogan* after the king named the jurors. Aside from agreeing they wouldn't order her to make the accusations, *Yovogan* Nondichao had concurred Queen Ena Sunu and Sintana Fansinnou committed a reprehensible crime. What changed? Was her devoted friend reneging on their arrangement? She wondered. She had met with *Migan* Mizéhoun to persuade him of a swift and guilty verdict. Now, she wasn't sure about this arrangement either.

"Queen Kin-Ha, can you inform everyone assembled here about the crime your rival, Queen Ena Sunu and Sintana Fansinnou committed?" Montcho asked.

It hushed the crowd and tamed the whispers. Queen Kin-Ha fidgeted in her chair. How was she to recount something she hadn't seen? How was she to reveal what Ladipo, the sorceress, said she saw in a trance when she herself hadn't? And Mindivi, the maid? She seemed so nervous. Who could blame her? She was nothing but a servant who found herself on the same scaffold as the kingdom's most powerful women. The sorceress's testimony, Queen Kin-Ha reasoned, would appeal more to Langanfin than anybody else.

Like Ladipo, he was a soothsayer, and, as a Voodoo chief priest, he wouldn't condone what she, Queen Kin-Ha, had concluded was sacrilegious. Besides, she was cognizant that Langanfin didn't take to Queen Ena Sunu. Before she could answer Montcho's question, *Migan* Mizéhoun rose to his feet. Everybody shifted their attention to the war and defense minister. His ministry carried out punishments, including executing those found guilty. He cleared his throat and swung around to face King Gesa and the court's dignitaries. His gaze didn't end there. He fixed his eyes on the women on the scaffold. A knowing smile, which Queen Kin-Ha noticed, crossed Queen Ena Sunu's face.

"Queen Kin-Ha," he began. "You understand that by Dahomey law, accusers have the chance to withdraw their charges before they open their mouths to make the accusations. Yes?" he asked, staring at the king's first wife. The queen nodded.

"Censurers must have incontrovertible proof against their accusers before they summon a proceeding such as this one. Am I not right?"

Migan Nagoba shot up from his chair. "I don't understand where the king's honorable minister is going with these questions. Montcho asked her royal highness a simple question. Let's hear her response," declared the pocked face counsel.

"Our laws allow any member of the jury to ask the questions I'm posing during such a trial. Am I mistaken?" *Migan* Mizéhoun asked, looking at the royal legal master.

Montcho had a pained and angry read on his face. He hadn't expected this snag in the proceedings.

"Yes," said Montcho.

Migan Nagoba, still standing, sat. His twitch was now more pronounced, as the muscles in his pocked face run amok. Although one of the king's closest advisers, there was something overweening about *Migan* Nagoba that the monarch, along with many ministers, distrusted.

"Could you answer my question please, your royal highness? Or do you want me to repeat it?" *Migan* Mizéhoun pressed.

Queen Kin-Ha was quiet. She no longer sat with a straight back.

She slumped.

"You're aware that by Dahomey law, whoever accuses a member of the royal family mustn't have any hidden agenda behind the accusations. In addition, such a plaintiff themselves mustn't have committed any egregious crimes against the king and the people of Dahomey. Isn't that right?" *Migan* Mizéhoun asked.

"Yes," said Queen Kin-Ha.

"Given your response, do you want to go ahead with the charges?" asked *Migan* Mizéhoun.

An expression of bitterness colonized Queen Kin-Ha's face as she stared at Queen Ena Sunu. She carried spitefulness in her eyes. "The bitch has put me up anew," she said under her breath as several thoughts scurried through her mind. How could she have been so naïve and stupid? She wondered. Her rival must have shared her secret about Agossou's paternity with the minister. He wouldn't have otherwise posed that question. "Oh! that bitch, how I hate her so!" she muttered. She surmised that whatever Queen Ena Sunu did with that woman warrior was not as egregious as carrying the son of another man in her womb and deluding the king that the child was his. "I must withdraw my complaint," she thought. What a humiliation! What will become of her? And Agossou? She speculated about the adage that a stone thrown in one's rage never hit the target. Had she been in a rage? Yes, of course, and for a good reason. And that stone? Why didn't it for once find its target to render that aphorism stupid? Her fate now settled in that bitch's hands. She shuddered. A distant sound liberated Queen Kin-Ha's highjacked mind that had splintered into several directions. It was Montcho's voice.

"Queen Kin-Ha, we're waiting for your response."

"I withdraw my charges," said Queen Kin-Ha.

A collective gasp erupted among the assembled. Was the queen retracting her accusations for lack of evidence, or was it because she had committed some abominable crimes against the king and the people of Dahomey? Would they force her to articulate what those transgressions were, as the law required? Would King Gesa intervene? How would Queen Ena Sunu respond to what had been developing so far? It was her prerogative under the law to prescribe the punishment they would mete out to her adversary for bringing up a charge that she had failed to press. What would it be? Many in the crowd wondered.

After a long interval, Queen Ena Sunu stood up. She knew beforehand the outcome of the proceedings and had prepared for this moment. She reckoned that, like her, Queen Kin-Ha had been playing all along, a game with rules set by the men sitting in front of the platform and those beyond. To denounce her opponent, she thought, wasn't to condemn the older queen but herself as well. It would be tantamount to dancing to a tune that none of them had crafted, composed. Her tune and that of Queen Kin-Ha's would be their own, a composition devoid of structure, arcane notes, textures, and references to unwritten verbal texts.

"His Royal Highness, King Gesa, conqueror of the wind, sun, and the rain," Queen Ena Sunu began, following a page of Montcho's script. "The ruin of a nation, they say, begins in the homes of its people. If there's no ruin in our homes, as Queen Kin-Ha has pointed out, it means our nation's foundation stands firm. It is immutable. And because Sintana Fansinnou and I don't have such devastation in our homes or in my rival's, it makes that foundation even stronger. Milk and honey, they claim, have contrasting colors, but they share the same house in peace."

Queen Ena Sunu descended from the scaffold. The other women followed, leaving the jurors stunned. In just a brief speech, the monarch had scuttled what could have been an inscrutable sanctioning of the king's first and third wife.

*****

Rumors about the gifting of a Dahomey prince to the Ouidah kingdom had been swirling for six months. Both kingdoms had witnessed substantial changes since their joint armies ransacked Allada fifteen years earlier. The architects of that raid were long dead. Governor Federico Soares de Souza died in 1812, two years after Allada's fall. Five years later, in 1816, King Tezifon passed. Only a trickle of slaves arrived from Dahomey beginning in 1821. The Allada Kingdom, which for several years had had a puppet king installed by Ouidah's late king and his Portuguese partner, had reduced the number of slaves traded to the European traffickers. Instead of a Portuguese Governor, a black Brazilian slaver named Pedro de Barbosa now carried out slave trading activities on *Forte São João Baptista de Ajudá* premises.

Dahomey contingent's arrival in its traditional garb confirmed the gifting rumors. They validated Queen Yiram's worst fears. King Dozan's first wife, she felt an urgency to see her husband to find out if the rumors were true. Something precipitated even further her eagerness: the conversation that she overheard between her two rivals who had been exulting over the information that her boy, Akonde, could no longer assume the Ouidah throne following the death of Akonde's most potent challenger. Queen Yiram waited until mid-afternoon when King Dozan had lunch with his courtiers and any important visitors at the palace. Because of her status as the first wife, she could see her husband whenever she chose, unlike her rivals, who had to wait their turn to spend their designated seven nights with the monarch.

Among those dining with the king that afternoon were the Dahomey delegates, who arrived to complete preparations for Sossa's gifting. The guards who prevailed at the banquet room's entrance nodded as the queen approached. It animated the room when they announced Queen Yiram's arrival. Several diners rose and bowed. A surprised look crossed King Dozan's face. His wives didn't join him on such occasions. The guests continued feasting after the queen sat beside her husband, who stared at his wife and said, "What's the Queen's agenda this time?"

"I don't understand his Majesty's question," Queen Yiram responded.

"Why would she understand? I suppose it's fortuitous that of all days, she joins me."

"I don't recall losing the right as first wife to keep his majesty's company as he plays host to his dignitaries. Or did I?"

"I'm not falling for your ruse, Queen Yiram. This is about

Akonde, your worthless offspring. Isn't it?"

"How can you describe your own son in such a fashion?" Queen Yiram replied, seeking to keep her smile.

"I would have considered him differently if you allowed him to be himself."

"Any decent mother would do what I'm doing for Akonde: to prepare him to be as good a king as his father, should the gods resolve he succeed him."

"And I presume the gods require a little of help from you, don't they?" King Dozan said, without disguising his sarcasm. He was aware of his wife's many visits to Yakumi Atrivi, the famous *Voodoo* priest's shrine in Azamati, a village ten miles outside the palace.

Queen Yiram did not reply. Although King Dozan's first offspring, Akonde's ascent to the Ouidah throne was not a foregone outcome. To strengthen her son's prospects, the queen had prepared a calculated and systematic purge of potential rivals to the throne. The result of her efforts was the murder of Ganji Sindje, Akonde's most powerful competitor. Just when she hoped she had cleared the way for her boy, here she was with yet another prospective challenger to the coveted Ouidah throne. The new prince's arrival would complicate matters.

*****

Queen Yiram wasn't the only person interested in the news of a potential prince from Dahomey. The distance between *Forte São João Baptista de Ajudá*, the slave fortress in Ouidah, and King Dozan's palace was just over one mile. Pedro de Barbosa usually went to the palace on foot, but not today. He traversed the distance, riding *Arion*, his favorite stallion. From over a quarter of a mile, the king's sentinels could hear *Arion*'s thunderous gallop and the cloud of dust that he left in his wake. Pedro de Barbosa was no ordinary visitor to the palace. The typical entry etiquette didn't apply to him.

"*Senhor* Pedro de Barbosa, welcome to King Dozan's palace," said Kole Dassa, the fellow responsible for the palace's protocol.

Pedro de Barbosa grunted as he dismounted from his horse.

"I must see the king," he announced as he brushed his clothes and made towards the palace's inner compound.

"The king is attending to some guests," Kole Dassa said as he caught up with Pedro de Barbosa.

"Are these visitors more important than me?" Pedro de Barbosa asked, narrowing his eyes to crinkled slits. He was the viceroy of Ouidah, a prominent position that gave him easy access to the king.

"No, Viceroy Pedro de Barbosa, but these visitors are not from these parts. They've come from afar," said Kole Dassa.

"Ah, so the rumors are true," Pedro de Barbosa said to himself. Molten anger rolled through him. He sensed unknown and uncertain forces were about to disturb even further a familiar order. And that, for Pedro de Barbosa, would not be acceptable. They led him to the waiting room, where he paced back and forth. In spite of the subdued voices, Pedro de Barbosa could still make out which one belonged to King Dozan. It was an unmistakable deep, booming, baritone voice. The other voices were unfamiliar and undoubtedly not from Ouidah. From the accents and inflections placed freely on certain words and phrases, Barbosa knew these were Dahomey envoys. The door to the waiting room opened.

"The king will receive you now," announced Kanfon, the monarch's spokesperson.

Pedro de Barbosa entered the familiar throne room, the largest of the palace's audience halls. They lined the walls with batik fabric in contrasting colors and sizes, depicting various battle scenes and portraits of animals such as elephants, eagles, and lions that enjoyed special meaning for the Ouidah people. Several life-size statues of gods and goddesses flanking both sides of the chamber assaulted the visitor entering the throne room from the waiting room. Turning right, the guest faced the entire length of the place toward the seated King Dozan and his attendants.

"Welcome, my dear friend," said King Dozan, as he extended his hand to Pedro de Barbosa.

"Thank you, your majesty," he replied, shaking King Dozan's hand.

"May I know to what we owe the honor of the Viceroy's visit?"

Pedro de Barbosa looked around the room. As usual, the king's ten advisers were present. Five seated on each side of the king's throne, forming a semicircle. Visitors rested on chairs positioned in front of the throne.

"My dear King Dozan," Pedro de Barbosa began. He hesitated, cleared his throat, and continued. "I've heard a rumor that, if true, could be detrimental to our enterprise."

"What kind of rumor?"

"I hear that your highness is receiving a gifted prince from Dahomey."

"Ah, I see. They say news travel faster than fire. If I hadn't known you, I would have considered your call today a courtesy call," said the king, with a faint smile on his face. He knew Pedro de Barbosa well, perhaps too well to know that although in his presence he always appeared extraordinarily respectful, charming, and gazing with those purportedly affectionate eyes, Pedro de Barbosa was never to be trusted. His sycophancy and modesty concealed a most devious nastiness, of which the king had first-hand knowledge through several of his ministers who interacted with him regularly.

"Yes. King Gesa of Dahomey is generously gifting us, Sossa, one of his sons. Isn't that extraordinary?" the king asked. "To part with Sossa, one of his twin sons, when he could have done so with his other sons is a sign of great friendship, don't you think?"

Pedro de Barbosa remained quiet with narrowed eyes. He bit his lips.

"And our plans?" he asked through a clenched jaw.

"In time, Viceroy Pedro de Barbosa, in time. The patient man cooks stone until he gets broth from it. Having King Gesa's son here couldn't have been better for our cause," said King Dozan, rising from his stool, signaling that the meeting between him and Pedro de Barbosa was over.

*****

Pedro de Barbosa's mood was no different after his meeting with King Dozan. If anything, it worsened. *Caralho! monte de merda!*

filho da uma puta!—Fuck! Piece of shit! Son of a bitch!—Pedro de Barbosa cursed as he galloped away, uncharacteristically kicking *Arion*'s sides harder than he had ever done as he made his way back to *Forte São João Baptista de Ajudá*. Who the fuck did King Dozan think he was? Had he forgotten that without him, he wouldn't have ever become the king of Ouidah? The fucking son of a bitch has such a short memory! What nerve! Pedro de Barbosa said to himself. The sound of Arion's flying hooves almost produced a tempo for his endless curses.

Tlot tlot! tlot! tlot tlot! tlot tlot!
Caralho! filho da uma puta! monte de merda!
Tlot tlot! tlot tlot! tlot tlot! tlot tlot!
Caralho! filho da uma puta! monte de merda!
Tlot tlot! tlot tlot! tlot tlot! tlot tlot!
Caralho! filho da uma puta! monte de merda!

The sole factor that relieved Pedro de Barbosa's condition when he found himself in this kind of state was to carry out a prompt entry in his journal. More than a diary, the thick leather-bound notebook he had locked up in an enormous mahogany desk drawer in his study served as a memoir of sorts that chronicled his life as far as he could recall. Still bristling from his meeting with the king, Pedro de Barbosa poured himself a glass of *Vinho do Porto*, made himself comfortable in a chair and lit a pipe. He was about to record his encounter with King Dozan when he realized he had neither the narrative authority nor the privilege he had enjoyed writing his own memoirs.

"Fuck you! Yaw Agawu-Kakraba," he shrieked and threw the half-empty glass at the wall. He recalled with fury his encounter with the author who, without warning, had taken away the narrative rights that he, Pedro de Barbosa, had negotiated with the author's narrator. If he had a score to settle, why not go to the lying source itself instead of that toothless narrator? he asked himself.

"How dare you suggest I falsified my story? And a con artist? You have the gall to call me a trickster? Humph! I'll tell you what?

It's hucksters like you who're impostors."

"*Tranquillo*—calm down—Pedro de Barbosa," responded the author. "I didn't call you a con man. You did. Remember when you referred to yourself as a con artist?"

For a few seconds, Pedro de Barbosa remained tongue tied, recalling the initial paragraphs of his memoir: "My name is Pedro de Barbosa. I'm an ex-slave, a con artist, a slave trader, a warmonger, and a lover . . ." He shook his head and confronted the author.

"Don't fucking *tranquillo* me, you understand? I can refer to myself however I wish. You don't have the right to do the same. And *bandalho*—punk— your attempts to wipe me out will fail."

"How?"

"Because when you're dead and gone, I will continue to live on in my pages."

"If I allow you to do so."

"What do you mean?" Pedro de Barbosa asked with alarm.

"Because I invented you."

Pedro de Barbosa disintegrated into a peal of frenzied laughter.

"What is so funny?"

"You're no fucking Miguel de Unamuno."

The astonished author sputtered, "But, but."

"Ah! I've shocked you. Haven't I? Do you think because I'm from a distant century, I don't know the abuse characters suffer at the hands of asshole creators like you and Miguel de Unamuno? We literary types keep good company in the present, past, and in the future. It is a privilege you cold-blooded and hardhearted writers can never enjoy."

It took the author a while to collect himself and overcome his confusion. He expected none of his many characters to leap out of his story and confront him with such ferocity. Turning to Pedro de Barbosa, the author said, "Miguel de Unamuno didn't mistreat Augusto Pérez in his *Niebla*. He told him he was nothing but an imaginary character he had created."

"Piss off. This is truly cruel, and you know it. As we speak, that son of a bitch of a monarch might be reneging on our arrangement. I'm the only person capable of hurling insults at him and stopping him. Not you, impostor!" said Pedro de Barbosa.

"What agreement did you make with King Dozan?"

"Kiss my fat ass. Aren't you the narrator, author, charlatan, or whatever role you fancy ascribing to your sorry self?" Pedro de Barbosa asked as he turned his back to the author and walked out of the study, slamming the door behind him.

The barking of a neighborhood dog jolted the writer from his short snooze. Although brief, he remembered Pedro de Barbosa's animosity towards him in his dream. He rubbed his eyes. "Bah! It was just a daydream," he told himself, setting out to continue writing about the most intriguing character that he may, perhaps, ever write about. As he had done with a part of his story, he called upon his narrator's services.

Chapter 18

Pedro de Barbosa was accurate when he declared that King Dozan wouldn't have been a monarch without him. Before turning to that, however, let's pick up from where his memoirs ended in early October 1815.

Pedro de Barbosa was a broken man when he returned to Lisbon along with Constância and Eduardo. With Lucinda's untimely death, a vital piece of the future that he thought he had constructed came tumbling down like a house of cards. As painful as Lucinda's death was, he refused to use the tragedy to change his life's goals. Lucinda's death, he thought, was nothing but one of the many lousy hands that God, in his tyranny, dealt and foisted on his creatures. He reckoned the only way he could show disdain and contempt of God was to forge ahead with his mission. He would exorcize any self-pity that would undermine his inimitable march towards *senhorhood*. It didn't matter where, when, or how this quest would unfold.

When Pedro de Barbosa returned to Lisbon, *Governador* Belarmino had received from the king's bureaucrats the provisions they needed. King John VI had offered the governor a new ship, *Alma Valiente*, for the voyage to Dahomey. In addition, the king's officials recruited a seasoned captain and fifteen former Portuguese army soldiers to accompany the governor. Several slave merchants booked passage on the ship. Dockworkers loaded the vessel with the building materials needed to refurbish *Forte São João Baptista de Ajudá*, which had been abandoned for over a decade. Wooden doors and windows, locks and keys, furniture for bedrooms, living rooms, and a study were some of the many items that found their way into the ship's hold. Others included kitchen utensils, cotton fabric, *cachaça*, sugar, wine, brass pans, glass beads, and two hundred guns. They loaded *Trovão* and *Arion* onto the ship.

Alma Valiente left the port of Lisbon on the 15th of October 1815 and arrived in Ouidah on January 10, 1815. It was Pedro de Barbosa's twenty-third birthday. No Portuguese ship had anchored off the Ouidah coast in a long time. News of the boat's arrival reached King Tezifon. The peculiar red and green colors of the Portuguese flag hanging on the ship's mast were recognizable. In 1806, King Tezifon sent messengers to King John VI in Lisbon, pledging to maintain Ouidah's friendship with Portugal and continue as the European nation's sole slave supplier. Governor Federico Soares de Souza, with whom he and King Gesa invaded Allada, had died three years earlier. The Portuguese sovereign hadn't sent a replacement. With the new agreement, King Tezifon would gain slaves through warfare and raids into neighboring kingdoms, including Allada, that had a puppet king who answered to the Ouidah monarch. In response to King Tezifon's offer, the Portuguese monarch promised to send a new governor. Although King John VI hadn't pledged to provide the gifts King Tezifon had sought, the Ouidah king had been expecting them. King Tezifon believed the presents would ratify the deal and signal the dawn of a great friendship.

A tall man who wore what turned out to be a threadbare uniform of a midshipman of the Portuguese Navy led one of the five pirogues that approached *Alma Valiente*. It comprised a dark, dirty, long-skirted coat, a waistcoat, and a tricorn hat that had lost its luster and color. What passed for gaiters was torn fabric fastened to the ankles and legs by twine. From afar, he could be mistaken for a scarecrow or a castaway that a benevolent spirit had dispatched to warn the sojourners of the imminent danger awaiting them when they set foot on land.

"Bem-vindo a Ouidah,"—Welcome to Ouidah—said the marooned-like midshipman who flapped his hands with excitement.

Governador Belarmino was in his governor's outfit: a green coat with red collar and cuffs, silver turnbacks, white piping outlying the coat front, gold epaulets, blue breeches, and a crimson sash with silver tassels. He acknowledged the fellow and climbed the rope ladder into the pirogue. Pedro de Barbosa followed the governor. He wore green pleated with crimson, a silver cape, and blue-colored cuffs along with a white waistcoat and blue breeches. Several of the men from the ship followed suit. Fully loaded, the pirogues headed towards the beach. The sound of the waves, along with the wind, made communication futile. As he caught sight of the sandy shore in the distance, Pedro de Barbosa felt as though he was in a strange yet familiar place. The cry of circling seagulls, whirling above the coconut trees, and swooping for crabs, reminded him of Salvador. He felt a pit in his stomach, but he suppressed it.

Kosi Aholuvi, for that was the name of the marooned-like midshipman, prostrated in front of *Governador* Belarmino as soon as they landed. His head on the ground, he declared, "I've waited so long for this day. The gods have brought you back as I knew they would."

Perplexed by this strange welcome, *Governador* Belarmino asked Kosi Aholuvi to explain himself. In perfect Portuguese, tinged with a heavy accent, he announced he had been an assistant to Federico Soares de Souza, the late Portuguese Governor, who had died of unknown disorders. As he reported the former governor's anguish before he passed, Kosi Aholuvi made the sign of the cross. Pedro de Barbosa wondered if Kosi Aholuvi intended the gesture to bolster the departed governor's chances at Heaven's Gate or to stave off for them a recurrence of the same misfortune. Further revelations followed. Kosi Aholuvi had taken care of the abandoned fort after the natives had looted it and desecrated the graves of many of the *yovos*. Many voodoo priests believed the bones of the white men brought more potency to their soothsaying prowess. Kosi Aholuvi was an excellent storyteller. He warned *Governador* Belarmino and Pedro de Barbosa about King Tezifon's temperament and cautioned them of the powerbrokers in the kingdom. He advised them on how to navigate Ouidah's treacherous monarchical and political minefields. To garner more respect from King Tezifon, he suggested the newcomers keep the king waiting. With such unsolicited vital information,

Kosi Aholuvi talked himself into being hired and writing his own job description.

Forte São João Baptista de Ajudá sat on the coast overlooking the Atlantic Ocean. Surrounded by solid thirty feet high embankments, the entrance to the fort had a massive drawbridge over a dry moat. The ground floor of the fort's three levels contained several clammy, dark, and poorly vented dungeons that held over one thousand male and female slaves at a time. With their abysmal sanitary conditions, the dungeons' floors were still strewn with human excrement. The rooms above the dungeons where Portuguese soldiers and the governor's aides lived were vast, airy, and devoid of the stench that pervaded the cells below. *Forte São João Baptista de Ajudá*'s most luxurious section was the third floor where Federico Soares de Souza lived. From here, the magnificent sight of the blue Atlantic Ocean waters came into view. From their configuration, it was easy to surmise that the ten rooms were well vented and decently furnished with beautiful wooden floors. Pedro de Barbosa couldn't contain his shock when he saw a modest chapel on the east side of the fortress. Realtor Kosi Aholuvi's vigilant eyes didn't miss the dismay on Pedro de Barbosa's face. He intervened quickly.

"The governor and his assistants prayed at the chapel before dispatching their slaves on their voyage to Brazil. They wanted God's help to deliver them to their buyers."

With no response from *Governador* Belarmino and Pedro de Barbosa, Kosi Aholuvi added.

"That changed when the number of slaves brought here increased. They didn't care any longer how many perished on their way to Brazil."

Governador Belarmino and Pedro de Barbosa listened, but the urgent task of refurbishing *Forte São João Baptista de Ajudá* absorbed them. The ceiling on the third floor revealed an uncovered roof. Forcefully wrested off their hinges, most of the rooms had no windows. A few that didn't suffer the same fate had slanted and unstable windows. On the ground rested the flagstaff, which used to carry the Braganza flag with its "five shields." Five gigantic, rust-coated cannons laid strewn on the third floor. From the governor's area, the newly arrived visitors noticed wide crevices between the cobblestones lining the first-floor compound. They hosted spirited, fast-growing weeds and trees. With the fort's extensive damage, *Governador* Belarmino and Pedro de Barbosa wondered how long it would take to make *Forte São João Baptista de Ajudá* habitable. The thought of staying aboard *Alma Valiente* until they completed the work was unappealing. As though reading their minds, Kosi Aholuvi said, "This place looks like shit now. I'm certain we can fix it in no time under his honor's capable direction," Kosi Aholuvi nodded at *Governador* Belarmino. "In the meantime, I'm sure you can find temporary accommodations in *Casa da Silva*," added the realtor-scarecrow-castaway-host.

Kosi Aholuvi had had a long time to figure out these things, given his conviction that a new governor would appear shortly on the horizon to help restore his position as the link between the Ouidah people and the *yovo* world. Pedro de Barbosa and *Governador* Belarmino looked at each other. *Casa da Silva?* If keeping King Tezifon waiting only reinforced their importance as Kosi Aholuvi had stated, seeking a place to stay should take precedence, they thought.

*****

Casa da Silva was a bar, restaurant, whorehouse, hotel, and trading post situated a mile and a half from *Forte São João Baptista de Ajudá*. Like many of the dwellings one encountered in any village or town in Ouidah or Dahomey, *Casa da Silva* had over thirty round mud houses with thatched roofs scattered around the property. Low windows in the huts offered guests an elegant view of the extensive Atlantic Ocean. The force of the breeze slitting through them served as a natural repellent against mosquitoes. Antelope skins layered the floor of each lodge. A massive rectangular structure with adobe walls and white stucco stood in the middle of the thirty huts. One entered the building through a large door that led to a sprawling room that doubled as a bar and a restaurant dining room. A long wooden counter sat in a corner. Behind the bar shelves of contrasting heights and sizes housed bottles of rum,

Portuguese *porto*, Brazilian *cachaça*, English gin, and French wine. A hallway beside the counter led to twenty rooms where *Casa da Silva*'s proprietor, Silvio da Silva, stayed with his prostitutes.

From Portugal, Silvio da Silva moved to Dahomey to partake in the slave trade. He immediately found out that the intense competition between slavers mitigated against any lofty dreams of amassing enormous wealth quickly as a middleman. He chose, instead, to open *Casa da Silva* to cater to the many European traders on the West African coast. A tough crowd, they were as ferocious in their dealings with the slaves they bought as they were with other fellow traders. They came to *Casa da Silva* to eat, cavort, fornicate, and sleep with whores Silvio da Silva had imported from bordellos in Lisbon, Amsterdam, Cadiz, Liverpool, and Nantes. Gamblers, thieves, and drunks, these men they knew who to consult and how to access their human merchandise. They were brokers between the Dahomeyan and Ouidian kings and slavers with their ships anchored on the coast glutted with rum, tobacco, guns, silks, and calico.

As they drew closer to *Casa da Silva*, the aroma of grilled meat and fried fish from Jorginho d'Almeida's kitchen assailed Pedro de Barbosa and his companions. The Portuguese cook worked on a slave ship until he lost an eye in a fight in a Lisbon bar. The newcomers hastened their steps. Three months at sea would make even those with discriminating palates seek anything besides what a ship's kitchen offered.

Everything came to a standstill when Pedro de Barbosa, *Gobernador* Belarmino, and the crew arrived at *Casa da Silva*. They didn't need any introductions. Their official uniforms conveyed a simple message: a new Portuguese governor had come to Dahomey, and the order of things would have to change. A prostitute dashed into a rear room to alert Silvio da Silva. With a thin white cotton shirt in a concession to the heat, the proprietor burst into the dining area. Swatches of sweat layered his chest and underarms. His long grey-blonde hair parted in the middle, he had the look of those cheap, mournful paintings of Christ.

"*Bem-vindo meu Governador,*" Silvio da Silva said, offering a hand that was missing two fingers. "Silvio da Silva at your honor's service. Of what help can I be to you?" he asked.

"*Primum cibum*,"–Food first–said *Gobernador* Belarmino, recalling his university days where the study of Latin was essential to studying law.

After conversations that followed a satiating lunch, they arranged temporary lodging at Casa da Silva for Pedro de Barbosa, the governor, and several merchants from the ship. Silvio da Silva was euphoric. A new governor meant ratcheting up slave commerce: it augured well for business.

*****

One detail struck King Tezifon when he saw the two men who walked towards the throne, along with Kosi Aholuvi. They didn't arrive with a line of porters toting guns, a throne like the one on which King John VI sat in Lisbon, mirrors, tobacco, liquor, and an all-white Iberian horse that he had requested as gifts. His expression was tense. His broad lips, clamped together, established a serpentine line that curled and ended at the base of both ears. It wasn't a welcoming face. Before the new governor could begin the exchange of salutations, King Tezifon's voice rumbled. "Where're the presents?"

Kosi Aholuvi was an able interpreter. The king's question and its implications took *Governador* Ladislao Belarmino aback. Gifts? King John VI's functionaries in Lisbon had mentioned nothing about gifts when they provided him with the ship and accompanying supplies. The two men recalled what Kosi Aholuvi had told them about the king. They had heard stories about the Ouidah king's ruthlessness. Rumors had it he required a distinct human skull of enemies killed in battle for each kind of liquid that he consumed. An uncertain look on the visitors' face prompted the king to add, "The gilded throne, guns, the all-white Iberian horse. Where are they?" King Tezifon asked as he rose from his wooden stool and paraded in a heavy, calculated pace towards the governor. His face now looked stony in indignation. Somehow, his puckered lips took on a different shape, looking thicker as though sculpted to underline the thundering voice that came from the depths of his thick-necked muscles. Governador Belarmino was tongue-tied, but Pedro de Barbosa, who never let an opportunity slide when he got one, pounced. He remembered Cutpurse as the prevarications escaped from his mouth.

"Your Majesty, King John VI sends his warmest greetings to you," Pedro de Barbosa said, buying time to consider what to say next. After a while, he continued, "King John VI didn't forget your gifts. He was reluctant to send your presents without the magnificent all-white Iberian colt that he had chosen from his stable for you. The horse needs time to grow stronger before it can cross the ocean." Pedro de Barbosa paused. A look of bewilderment flashed through Governor Belarmino's face. He whispered, "That's false, Pedro de Barbosa. I hope you know what you're doing."

"Buying time, *Governador*, buying time and saving our hides," Pedro de Barbosa said, as he turned his attention back to King Tezifon, whose facial features had mellowed slightly.

"A year from today, he will deliver your all-white Iberian horse, along with the presents you requested from his majesty. In the interim, we have on our ship a few presents for his eminence. We shall bring them when we make a second official visit to the king's palace."

"That's not the plan," Governor Belarmino hissed.

"I'm afraid now it is. Good dancers who improvise force seasoned drummers to modify their rhythms," Pedro de Barbosa said.

"Never heard of such a simple adage. You're not proposing that an orchestra playing José Mauricio Nunes Garcia's *Zemir Ouverture* for instance, abruptly changes the tune's rhythm to fit the caprice of a superb dancer. Are you?" the Governor asked.

"I said, drummers. Not an orchestra," Pedro de Barbosa replied.

King Tezifon, who followed the exchange between his two visitors, broke into a smile that soon spiraled into laughter.

"I knew King John VI would keep his word," the monarch said.

His visitors were uncertain of the abrupt switch in the king's demeanor. Kosi Aholuvi's warnings still lurked in the back of their minds. "You're welcome to Ouidah. Because you showed up without the offerings that your sovereign had pledged, Portugal will not have exclusionary rights to the slaves in my kingdom or the Kingdom of Dahomey. Conditions might change when the presents arrive," the monarch said as he left the throne room.

*****

Jean-Marie Bernheim couldn't help eavesdropping on the conversation between Pedro de Barbosa and Governor Belarmino in *Casa da Silva*'s bar a few days after their arrival in Ouidah.

"I cannot believe that King Tezifon just walked out on us without making a firm commitment to Portugal," Governor Belarmino said, looking at Pedro de Barbosa, who held a glass of wine in his hand.

"And what did he mean Portugal wouldn't have exclusionary rights to slaves in his kingdom? That has been the situation in the past. Hasn't it? Besides, he agreed with King John VI."

"Well, Governor, the Portuguese are not the sole entities who have deals with the king of Ouidah. Several Dutch, English, German, Spanish, Italian, and French slavers have made *Casa da Silva* their home."

"I know," said *Governador* Belarmino. "It's the damned French that I'm worried about and cannot stand," he continued.

A grin spread over Jean-Marie Bernheim's face. He was a veteran French slave trader who worked for a selling company out of Bordeaux. Although France didn't have a fort or treaties with Ouidah, Dahomey, or Allada, the country took an active part in slave trading along the West African coast. It prospered from selling and shipping human cargo to the French West Indies. Between 1738 and 1745, Nantes, France's leading slave port, carried 55,000 slaves to the New World in 180 ships. In 1768, Louis XV stressed Bordeaux slavers' role in the trade. Bordeaux Port merchants, he asserted, zealously trafficked black slaves. A Portuguese governor's absence in Ouidah meant that slavers such as Jean-Marie Bernheim and those from other European countries purchased slaves with no constraints and marketed them to merchants on slaving ships anchored off the coasts. During the past ten years, Jean-Marie Bernheim had handled over ten thousand slaves to several French slave ships, including prominent ones such as *Amitié* and *Liberté*.

The conversation that Jean-Marie Bernheim had overhead between Pedro de Barbosa and the governor excited the Frenchman because it meant France, which had overtaken Portugal in buying slaves and forwarding them to the French Antilles, would continue to keep its enviable status. In addition, Portugal wouldn't have a monopoly over slaves from Ouidah, Dahomey, and Allada. Pedro de Barbosa spun around and noticed Jean-Marie Bernheim staring at them. The governor's observant deputy knew the Frenchman had been listening to their conversation. It occurred to Pedro de Barbosa that to make any headway to fulfil his aim in Dahomey, he must disentangle himself from the Portuguese administrator and find an effective way to compete, stifle and eliminate his rivals. He must familiarize himself first with the ground rules before he could accomplish such a bold move. He smiled at Jean-Marie Bernheim, who returned Pedro de Barbosa's smile with a weak one and turned around. Excusing himself from Governor Belarmino, Pedro de Barbosa went over to Jean-Marie Bernheim's table and asked if he could join him. The Frenchman consented.

"Looks like you're an expert in these parts of the world. You look comfortable in your own skin," Pedro de Barbosa said by introduction.

"One gets used to this hell of a place," answered Jean-Marie Bernheim, extending his hand.

"Jean-Marie Bernheim. And I have the pleasure of knowing?"

"Pedro de Barbosa."

"You arrived just a few days ago, didn't you?"

"Who could've missed our entrance to *Casa da Silva*? With Governor Belarmino bedecked in his official uniform, a blind man could've seen his outfit's bright colors a mile away."

"So, what brings you to Dahomey?"

"Same thing as you. Although you've had a head-start. How long have you been at it here?"

"Ten years."

"And business has been good?"

"So-so," the Frenchman lied and said, "It might get worse now that your Portuguese king has sent a governor to Dahomey. Soon, your monopoly will return, right?"

"I'm afraid I am a master of my own."

"So, how come you're attached to the governor's hip?"

"Because it facilitates my agenda."

"Oh? What kind of agenda?" asked Jean-Marie Bernheim, who took a sudden interest in Pedro de Barbosa.

"To turn into an autonomous slave merchant and not tied to anybody's hip."

"How do you plan to achieve that?"

"I'm a patient and a quick learner. It'll happen sooner than you realize."

"You're confident in your abilities. I applaud that. But tell me. You're from Brazil and not from Portugal. And you're black. Aren't you?"

"Yes," declared Pedro de Barbosa. "And you're a Jew. Right?"

"I don't understand how pertinent being a Jew is."

"I don't know how pertinent being a black is. What I recognize is that we're in this despite our particular and partially comparable histories. Aren't we?"

Jean-Marie Bernheim didn't reply.

*****

Forte São João Baptista de Ajudá opened for commerce. The fort's refurbishing took a mere two weeks, thanks to the tireless efforts of the former soldiers who came to the West African coast with the governor and dozens of natives that Kosi Aholuvi had rounded up with promises of payment in cotton fabric and brass pans. They re-thatched roofs, whitewashed the thick black walls, and cleared up the clogged cistern. The Braganza flag, which fluttered as it did in the past, quivered later again on the repainted flagpole, heralding the fort's reopening for business. Slaves were available for sale!

Pedro de Barbosa and the governor called on King Tezifon's palace soon after settling into *Forte São João Baptista de Ajudá.* They brought ten guns, several bottles of Portuguese wine, sugar, *cachaça*, and glass beads. The monarch's reception was not as frosty as the first time. But his lack of interest, when his visitors presented him with their gifts, showed he would have preferred his gilded throne and white stallion from King John VI.

"I hope the next time you show up bearing gifts, it would include one as pretty as those two I've been told you brought along for yourselves," said King Tezifon.

Pedro de Barbosa and Governor Belarmino looked at each other. They had taken *Arion* and *Trovão* ashore from *Alma Valiente* two days earlier and had ridden them that morning before their visit. That King Tezifon was aware of this event was revealing. That didn't bother Pedro de Barbosa. What irked him was that the gifts, which circumstances had coerced them to produce, had come from his own inventory of merchandise. He had paid for them. They were to help him launch his own trading business. Another thing that weighed on Pedro de Barbosa's mind was the steady change in his affair with Governor Belarmino. It was a shift that reminded him of how he had usurped Trunks' place as the Cabula gang leader. When he took his current post, his goal was to support the governor setting up whatever slave trading schemes Portugal intended in Dahomey. He would sever his relationship with the king's deputy and strike out on his own when they realized that goal. But the governor's performance had exposed his unsuitability for the job. Pedro de Barbosa found himself once again in the familiar position of being at the helm of a project, except that, in this case, he hadn't sought it. But for his prompt intervention, the Portuguese administrator would have crumpled in King Tezifon's presence the first day they met him. The governor's incessant whining that Portugal wouldn't be given exclusive rights to Ouidah slaves didn't portend well for someone tasked with defending his kingdom's interests.

Although none of them had expressed it, both newcomers were conscious of the subtle change that was taking place in their relationship. It wasn't as though Pedro de Barbosa was in a submissive position concerning the governor. He had declared from the beginning that he would not play second fiddle to him or to the Portuguese monarch. Pedro de Barbosa had had to concede that, for the people in Ouidah, an incontestable hierarchy existed between them. The deferential treatment Governor Belarmino received from King Tezifon and the other slavers in *Casa da Silva* reinforced that reality. That suited Pedro de Barbosa. From the shadows, he would pull the strings of a stooge who must play by his rules. Damn the Portuguese monarch, he thought.

When Governor Belarmino didn't respond to King Tezifon's comment about their horses and future visits, Pedro de Barbosa intervened.

"Dear King Tezifon, the next time we come bearing gifts, they would be those that King John VI had pledged. Like you, he's an honorable man who keeps his promise."

"I'm counting on that," replied the king.

After a few moments of silence, Pedro de Barbosa said, "We want to let you know that *Forte São João Baptista de Ajudá* is now ready to receive slaves. We're eager to do business with you and other kingdoms. We understand the kingdom of Dahomey has hundreds if not thousands of slaves they plan to send to *Forte São João Baptista de Ajudá*," Pedro de Barbosa said, knowing well that the latter part of his statement was a blatant lie. Hardly did he suspect that this flagrant fabrication, and the one he had told so easily a short while ago, would catch up with him.

King Tezifon grinned. It was a grimace familiar to the courtiers in the throne room. Several of them shuddered, but neither Pedro de Barbosa nor Governor Belarmino noticed. If they had paid heed to Kosi Aholuvi's warnings and had asked him to tell them more about the Ouidah king, the two newcomers standing in front of the monarch would have taken a much different tack in their dealings with the king. They would have understood that this was a fellow who changed his mind on an impulse. This was a monarch who suffered periodic mental breakdowns and would order raids into centers and decree that they captured a specific number of slaves. When that didn't happen, he would flog all his Ministers publicly and have their wives sent to his harem, where he would enjoy them for weeks. When Damashie Kouakuvi, Ouidah's

Voodoo chief priest, foresaw drought, he had his throat cut, and his blood spilled into the Vuvuli river because he, King Tezifon, had fantasized otherwise. This was a king who burned down the Python Temple and the pythons dedicated to *Danh-gbi,* the powerful Voodoo god thought to be a divine intermediary between the spirits and the living, and purveyor of wisdom and bliss. His reason? He, King Tezifon, had dreamt that a python had swallowed him whole. Many of his subjects thought his reign would end following that unprecedented action. Yet that never happened. The most scandalous of all transgressions, however, was King Tezifon's decision to sell large numbers of his own people and pillage his own towns and villages to procure slaves. That act contravened the normal practice that prohibited the sale of his native Ouidians as slaves.

When one put into context these unutterable infractions against his people and the imprisonment in the palace's squalid prison of four of the former Portuguese governor's men because he claimed the governor had defaulted on payment of slaves yet to be delivered, one got the picture of a man who any sensible person would keep at arm's length. This was where Pedro de Barbosa and Governor Belarmino found themselves in the company of King Tezifon. Would it have made any difference if King John VI had received, prior to Governor Belarmino's appointment, the report Governor Federico Soares de Souza had prepared to describe the Ouidah monarch's instability? It was hard to say.

With a face still plastered with a grin that the visitors thought was benign, King Tezifon said, "*Senhor* Pedro de Barbosa, transporting slaves from Dahomey, Allada, and elsewhere through Ouidah, which would be inevitable, will cost you more. Besides the royal tax and the final export tax, we'll also levy a duty on each individual captive that is supplied to you outside of this kingdom. But I haven't said the kingdom of Ouidah will not trade with you. All that I mentioned was that Portugal wouldn't have absolute rights to our slaves."

Pedro de Barbosa and Governor Belarmino had no clue about these duties, but that didn't deter them from glossing over such a crucial detail.

"Then let's start first with Ouidah. We will see how our relationship develops," Pedro de Barbosa said.

*****

Pedro de Barbosa was awoken by an uproar of screams and whiplashes. The racket came from the north side of *Forte São João Baptista de Ajudá*. Peering through his bedroom window on the third level, he saw what appeared as dots of tiny ants in the distance. It was a chain-gang of men, women, and children with iron collars around their necks and ankles being driven like cattle by overzealous slave drivers who didn't hesitate to flog those who couldn't walk fast enough or had been taken ill during the long trek from their homes in the hinterlands. The first batch of slaves had arrived in *Forte São João Baptista de Ajudá*! It had been six weeks since Pedro de Barbosa disembarked in Ouidah. The comparative advantage that the Portuguese had over the other slavers would quickly become evident. Unlike their competitors, they had *Forte Sao Joao Batista de Ajudá* to hold their slaves for extended periods until they made shipping arrangements. Many burning questions galloped through Pedro de Barbosa's mind as he got dressed. As the human merchandise snaked its way towards the fort, he wondered who brought the captives. How were they going to feed them? They would send them to Salvador. But how and to whom? They hadn't worked out those details with the merchants who had traveled with them from Lisbon. It dawned on Pedro de Barbosa that, yes, they opened *Forte São João Baptista de Ajudá* for business, but they weren't prepared.

"Who're these slaves, and who sent them?" Pedro de Barbosa asked Kosi Aholuvi when he entered the main living chamber from where the ten rooms on the fort's third floor converged.

"They're King Tezifon's," said Kosi Aholuvi, who squinted to see the slaves who were now less than two hundred yards from the front entrance. "I recognize a few of the slave drivers. They're the king's soldiers," he added.

"King Tezifon didn't notify us he was bringing in any slaves," Pedro de Barbosa protested.

"He didn't?" Kosi Aholuvi asked.

Pedro de Barbosa couldn't help noticing consternation on Kosi Aholuvi's face.

"What's it?" Pedro de Barbosa asked.

"Not good," said Kosi Aholuvi.

"What do you mean?" asked Pedro de Barbosa.

"You have money? Good, good money?" Kosi Aholuvi asked.

"What're you talking about? asked Pedro de Barbosa, who was becoming alarmed, following the uneasiness and terror grouted on his aide's face.

Before Kosi Aholuvi could answer, Governor Belarmino burst into the living room, endeavoring to button his still-open shirt.

"What is all this ruckus?" he asked.

Pedro de Barbosa and Kosi Aholuvi were silent. Their gaze through the north-facing window answered the governor's question.

Chains holding the slaves' ankles connected them to one another. The dungeon doors were low, and most of the captives had to bend at the waist to enter them. Because they were at the fort's lower level, its thick walls repelled the welcoming breeze from the Atlantic Ocean. Pedro de Barbosa knew that in no time, the dank and dark spaces would turn fetid and malodorous, thanks to the bodily secretions that wouldn't have any place to go other than on the floor and on the bodies that generated them.

"King Tezifon has brought you four hundred men, one hundred and eighty women, and twenty children," Togbega Ahialu, King Tezifon's royal accountant, began after they had deposited the slaves in the dungeons.

"We know that a strong slave in Salvador da Bahia is worth £45. We will charge you a flat fee of £10 per slave. That should total £6,000. With the royal tax, the payment you must pay royal officials who would handle the movement of slaves to the ships, and the final export tax, we're expecting £6,500," said the Ouidah official.

Silence.

After a minute, the illustrious accountant added, "King Tezifon also expects the gilded chair and his horse along with the payment."

Pedro de Barbosa and Governor Belarmino had identical gapped-mouth stares. After what seemed an eternity, Governor Belarmino said, "I'm sorry, but we didn't ask the monarch to bring all these captives. Besides . . ."

Kosi Aholuvi forced a big sneeze and signaled the governor to stop. An awkward hush followed.

"Did I hear you say you didn't ask the monarch for slaves?" Togbega Ahialu inquired, brows bumped together in a scowl. "If you're not ready for slaves, then what the hell are you doing here? Didn't you inform the king you had opened *Forte São João Baptista de Ajudá* for business? Listen, you know what you owe. By our customs, you've a week to settle the debt. If you don't, Kosi Aholuvi will tell you the consequences."

Togbega Ahialu left *Forte São João Baptista de Ajudá* with ten Ouidah soldiers armed with spears and knives tucked into their leather skirts. Kosi Aholuvi shivered. The meaning of the royal accountant's last comments was all too familiar. He couldn't help but conjure the image from over a decade earlier of four of Governor Federico Soares de Souza's men in King Tezifon's prison cells.

"Not good," Pedro de Barbosa recalled Kosi Aholuvi's words. There wasn't any need to ask him what that meant. How could they come up with £6,500? And the gilded throne and Iberian white horse? Nothing made sense to him. He called for *Arion* and galloped off to *Casa da Silva*, where he located Jean-Marie Bernheim with no difficulty.

*****

"So, you need my help?" the Frenchman asked Pedro de Barbosa after he had told him about the plight in which he and Governor Belarmino found themselves.

"We'd be very gratified if you could provide some help," Pedro de Barbosa said.

"£6,500, a gilded throne, and an Iberian white horse. One cannot easily get these in a matter of days, even for veteran traders like us who've been here longer," said Jean-Marie Bernheim.

If he was delighted at his competitors' looming quandary, he never showed it. Why should he save the Portuguese when their ultimate goal was to dislodge him and the other slavers from the trade and region? Didn't this arrogant fool sitting before him declare that he was a patient and fast learner and would turn into an independent slaver before he, Jean-Marie Bernheim, knew it? And suggesting that because he was a Jew, he shared similar histories with him, Pedro de Barbosa, a black? What nerve? Jean-Marie Bernheim thought. A smile cut across his face, but a preoccupied Pedro de Barbosa lost in his thoughts failed to notice. If this wasn't a God-sent opportunity, what could be? Jean-Marie Bernheim asked himself. It would be stupid not to grab it. The slave ship, *Amitié*, which his employers in Bordeaux had dispatched three months earlier, had just arrived and anchored off the Ouidah coast, one nautical mile away from the *Alma Valiente*. He had all he needed to execute the plan that was already crystallizing in his mind.

"I could help by providing you half of the £6,500. But that wouldn't do you any good. Would it? Once King Tezifon makes a decision, nobody can change his mind," the Frenchman lied. Sure, the Ouidah king was temperamental, but there were ways to assuage and to contain him if one knew how. But Jean-Marie Bernheim wasn't about to disclose such critical information.

"Is there anyone who could intervene on our behalf?" Pedro de Barbosa asked desperation lodged in his voice.

"I'm afraid not," Jean-Marie Bernheim said, rising from his chair.

Chapter 19

"He who has the sovereign's ear picks up the largest harvest." Jean-Marie Bernheim understood this Ouidah axiom and applied it. He couldn't have been the prosperous slave trader that he was in Ouidah during the Portuguese governor's absence without finding out how things worked in the kingdom. In the course of his ten years' sojourn in Ouidah, the Frenchman had cultivated the king's ear, and the outcome had been his country's disproportionate share of the slave market on this West African coast. As was his practice when he sought an unplanned audience with King Tezifon, Jean-Marie Bernheim didn't come to the palace empty-handed. He visited a day after he met with Pedro de Barbosa, bearing gifts for the king and many of his ministers and subordinates. But aligning oneself with a monarch who had turned into a tyrant meant that those who fraternized with him and curried his favor became targets of the incipient resistance that had emerged following King Tezifon's attempt to assassinate his only son, Prince Dozan. "The millet stalk that produced only one grain" had now embarked on a campaign to crush that grain.

It all started when Prince Dozan had opposed the Python Temple's destruction and the pillaging of a town in Ouidah that supplied the best annual tribute of goats, millet, and other food crops to the Ouidah capital. The regent's open criticism of his father earned him the king's instant ire and fury. But it won the young prince widespread support and admiration in a disillusioned and tyrannized Ouidah ruled by a leader whose irrational behavior had become the norm. Prince Dozan's staunchest allies were Voodoo priests. Never in Ouidah's history had they encountered a ruler who so went against the will of the gods. If he had faced no wrath from *Danh-gbi,* for destroying the Python Temple, it strengthened their resolve as intermediaries between the people and their gods to start a clandestine campaign against the monarch. When they uncovered the plot to kill the young prince, it was some Voodoo clerics, along with several mutinous Ouidah soldiers, that whisked him from the palace. King Tezifon was a powerful king with a retinue of sycophant courtiers and many spies. But the bourgeoning opposition, spearheaded by Agameli Kouakuvi, son of Damashie Kouakuvi, Ouidah's late Voodoo chief priest, also had spies in and out of the royal court. Thus, when Jean-Marie Bernheim walked into the throne room that afternoon, others, besides the king and his enablers, would be attentive to what he had to say.

"Ah, here comes the Frenchman who never disappoints," said King Tezifon as Jean-Marie Bernheim approached the king's throne and prostrated in front of the monarch theatrically. A *yovo*'s apparent complete servility in the king's presence was all that it took to break down barriers.

"No, no. Get up, my friend. You don't need to prostrate," said the king.

"I bear greetings from his Majesty King Louis XV. French citizens call him *le Désiré*–The Desired, just like your people refer to you," said Jean-Marie Bernheim as he rose, bowed, and looked into the king's eyes.

"Ah, he's a fellow after my own heart," King Tezifon responded.

The Frenchman motioned to the ten young girls who carried on their heads presents of several muskets, beautifully embroidered silk, cotton, hardware, and iron. The monarch's eyes popped when they spread out the colored thread and trinkets on the floor. A smile lit his face. He can satisfy his wives' incessant cravings for imported fine fabric.

"These are gifts from his Majesty King Louis XV to his Majesty King Tezifon for allowing us to do business in Ouidah while the Portuguese were away. He wishes to know if we can continue to do so, even though the Portuguese have sent a governor here," Jean-Marie Bernheim said.

"Did you mention these are gifts from your king?" the Ouidah monarch asked as he stroked his chin.

"Yes. And unlike your other European friends here in Ouidah, we, the French, always make sure we carry out our king's orders. We've not kept any of the French king's offers on *Amitié*, our slave ship that arrived a few days ago," said Jean-Marie Bernheim.

"I don't understand. Is someone holding something that belongs to me on their ship?" the king asked with narrowed eyes.

"Oh, I'm afraid I might have revealed what someone told me in confidence," Jean-Marie Bernheim said with feigned remorse plastered on his face.

"Nobody holds nothing from me in my presence. Tell me what you found out," said King Tezifon.

Jean-Marie Bernheim hesitated for a minute and said,

"I understand Governor Belarmino and his assistant, Pedro de Barbosa, have the gilded throne and the horse that their king dispatched to his Majesty on their ship anchored offshore."

King Tezifon slammed his eyes shut and gritted his teeth.

"What you're telling me. Is it true?" the king asked as he looked at the Frenchman.

"Well, that's what I've discovered. I've not boarded their ship to see whether it's true. But I know that even though they have the £6,500 you're charging for the six-hundred slaves you sent to *Forte São João Baptista de Ajudá*, they plan to tell you they don't have the money. They want you to bring the cost down," the Frenchman said.

King Tezifon stood up from his throne and paced the floor. Everyone was silent. A minute later, Jean-Marie Bernheim added, "France will pay £7,500 for the slaves if the Portuguese don't want to pay, but I'll leave that to his majesty."

"The governor and his aide have one week to settle their debt. That's what our customs demand. Let's see what happens after that," the king said as he walked out of the throne room.

*****

"Back-stabbing-stinking-French-Jew-son-of-a-bitch!" Pedro de Barbosa shrieked after Kosi Aholuvi had relayed to him and the governor what his informant at the palace had overheard. Governor Belarmino, who hadn't realized that Pedro de Barbosa had visited *Casa da Silva* to solicit the Frenchman's help, was furious.

"You did what? How dare you go behind my back to make such a preposterous arrangement with that hideous Frenchman without consulting first with me?" the governor demanded. "You realize who's the back-stabbing-stinking-son-of-a-bitch? It's you, Pedro de Barbosa," Governor Belarmino added, his lurking resentment towards his deputy emerging from the shadows as he inched towards Pedro de Barbosa, who didn't budge.

"*Oh, seu senhorio*—Oh, Your Lordship—when did you make any decisions since we showed up here?" Pedro de Barbosa asked, making sure that the governor didn't miss the irony that belied the honorific tag and the question. He went on, "Have you considered how to settle our debt? If so, what've you done about it? Tell me. What about the slaves in the dungeons? Do you have any bloody idea about how we're feeding them and with what means? Any suggestions regarding what to do with them? I suppose not. Before you call me a back-stabbing-stinking-son-of-a-bitch, you might as well stare at yourself in the mirror because the governor I see is an incompetent wimp who's not cut out for the job."

For a minute, Governor Belarmino thought of jumping on his deputy, but his common sense prevailed. He realized he held no chance against Pedro de Barbosa. He was honest to concede that Pedro de Barbosa was better suited for the obligations they had tasked him as governor. Reluctantly, he admired Pedro de Barbosa's ingenuity in improvising, telling half-truths to get out of difficult situations. He had found out about the veteran slavers in Ouidah and their suppliers, the first step necessary to stifle competition. He already controlled and directed some of the ex-soldiers that came with them, except for Paulino Cabral, the highest-ranking former officer. These soldiers took Pedro de Barbosa's orders without batting an eye. He got on very well with Kosi Aholuvi, who provided them with whatever information they required on the West African kingdoms. The truth, Governor Belarmino reckoned, cuts deeper and is more uncomfortable when exposed to no palliative. But pride sometimes gallops ahead of reality.

"I will not cede my position to a freed slave who I met on a ship and offered a job," he told himself.

Governor Belarmino beckoned to Paulino Cabral and whispered something into his ear. Pedro de Barbosa failed to see what was going on around him. He sat with his head in his hands, considering how to get out of their dilemma. Four former Portuguese army soldiers surrounded him when he raised his head.

"Can someone explain what's going on?" Pedro de Barbosa asked.

"What's going on, back-stabbing-stinking-son-of-a-bitch, is that I haven't come to Dahomey to see a fucking *preto* dictate to me what my duties ought to be and how to carry them out," said Governor Belarmino.

"Oh, yeah?" asked Pedro de Barbosa. "Care to tell me what you're going to do?" Pedro de Barbosa asked.

"You'll soon find out," said the Governor.

Three ex-soldiers grabbed Pedro de Barbosa. The fourth pulled his hands behind his back and tied them with a rope. Quickly, they led him downstairs towards one dungeon that held several of the recently arrived slaves. Before opening the door to the cell, Governor Belarmino said, "Pedro de Barbosa, a slave you were, a slave you've been, and a slave you'll always be. You'll be going back to Salvador where you belong, and a new master will await you."

The dungeon gate opened before Pedro de Barbosa could respond. The stench knocked him over as the door closed behind him. It took him a few minutes to adjust to the darkness. With their feet in chains and attached to one another, some men in the cramped space sat with their backs leaning against the grimy walls. Others remained on the floor. Pedro de Barbosa stumbled, slipped, and fell. The shit and urine, combined with human sweat, had rendered the uneven surface slippery. As his face hit the surface and got plastered with the sticky substances on the floor, Pedro de Barbosa's mind scuttled back to the day his face became the cleaning object in *Senhora* Fidelia Barbosa's room. He retched. The bitterness of the vomit that lingered on his palate found good company with the bile that erupted from within his core. It came from a familiar place. He was no stranger to this visceral anger. He had found a way in the past to lay waste to its provenance. But, as he stretched on the floor, his hands tied, Pedro de Barbosa wondered if he could ever settle this score.

An eerie silence prevailed, despite the many slaves in the dungeon. Pedro de Barbosa imagined what was passing through the slaves' minds. He knew they fretted about their destiny, their destination. He reckoned that if he ended up like them, he would have an early advantage over them: he would return to a familiar place of bondage. The voice of the captive on whose naked torso he laid interrupted his thoughts.

"*Nin we é non yo lo wé do, Bo fi dé te nou we nou wé?*"—What's your name, and where do you come from? The man asked.

"*Eu não falo sua língua,*"—I don't speak your language—Pedro de Barbosa replied.

"*A sé yovo gbé a? Nou te wou we aka do fi?*"—You speak the language of the white people. Why are you here? The man demanded.

"*Eu não te entendo,*"—I don't understand you—Pedro de Barbosa said.

Suddenly, several of the men began shouting, "*Yovo! Yovo! Yovo! Mi nan hwoui!*"—White Man! White Man! White Man! Kill him! In an instant, many blows rained on Pedro de Barbosa. Hands looked for his face and his throat.

"What the fuck!" Pedro de Barbosa said to himself. "Why the fuck are they shouting *Yovo! Yovo! Yovo?* Is it so dark in here that they can't see that I'm a black man? I? a white man? What a joke!" Pedro de Barbosa muttered to himself, only to realize that his response to the questions that the slave had asked him was in Portuguese. It wasn't in any of the recognizable languages such as Fon, Gen, or Fulfulde. "*Puta Merda,*" he said, as the reality of his situation and its implications sunk in.

Outside the dungeons, Governor Belarmino breathed a sigh of relief. He'd gotten a grip on the situation, he thought. Pedro de Barbosa would not dictate the terms of engagement with the Ouidah king any longer. He wondered why it had taken him so long to act as decisively as he did. He felt grand. Henceforth, he would show everyone who was governor, the true representative of the Portuguese king in Dahomey! Kosi Aholuvi, who had witnessed everything, trembled. The look on his face, followed by his question, told the newly minted governor that his so-called victory might be nothing but pyrrhic.

"Your lordship has the money. Yes? To pay the king, yes?" Kosi Aholuvi asked.

Governor Belarmino didn't respond.

"No money? Dead dog," said Kosi Aholuvi.

The questions Pedro de Barbosa asked the governor before they hauled him away came back to him vividly. He remembered Kosi Aholuvi's statement of King Tezifon's temperament, the different human skulls from which he drank. He found the king's demands and his ultimatum irrational. So was the transaction itself. The king carried it out without previous negotiation. Rumors of the Ouidah monarch's unstable disposition loomed as these thoughts ran through the governor's mind. He couldn't ensure his safety if he failed to settle accounts with the king.

"Bring him out," the governor ordered the soldiers.

Had they delayed any longer, the slaves would have wrung Pedro de Barbosa's neck like a hen. He gasped for air as the soldiers pulled him out, shielding his face and blocking the blinding sunshine that accosted his eyes. Pedro de Barbosa was in the dungeon for less than ten minutes, but it seemed to him as though they had locked him up for hours. Several things went through his mind, none of which carried a reflection about the status of the slaves with whom he had just spoken. He wondered why Governor Belarmino changed his mind. As he mulled it over, it dawned on Pedro de Barbosa that the Portuguese governor realized how bewildered he would've been without him. It also occurred to him that the man was terror-stricken! King Tezifon scared the shit out of the *yovo*! Pedro de Barbosa let out a burst of long and loud laughter. No one spoke. Whereas his reaction seemed incongruous with what he'd just experienced, for Pedro de Barbosa, the laughter underscored a significant shift in his relationship with the governor. The Portuguese had inadvertently openly declared an embittering war between them. He wasn't sure yet of the outcome, but he knew in his mind who would be the victor. A long, uncomfortable silence succeeded. It wasn't Pedro de Barbosa who was ill at ease. It was the governor and Paulino Cabral, who within the short span that Pedro de Barbosa was in the dungeon, fancied becoming the governor's deputy. Still wanting to keep the fleeting semblance of authority that he felt before reality struck home, Governor Belarmino said, "This is to teach you I'm Dahomey's governor."

"We've more important tasks to perform," Pedro de Barbosa declared, ignoring the governor's remark. "King Tezifon is awaiting our response," he added as he walked up to the fort's third floor to wash off the shit, urine, and vomit.

*****

The surf of the Atlantic Ocean lapped on the wharf that sat between the beach and *Forte Ajudá*. Pedro de Barbosa had come a long way and wasn't about to have all go awry. Yet he couldn't think of a way to counteract Jean-Marie Bernheim's cleverly executed move. He acknowledged his naïveté in believing that he could trust the Frenchman who had outmaneuvered them, placing them in a precarious situation with a monarch who, from what he had seen so far, they couldn't trust. As much as he loathed what Jean-Marie Bernheim had done, a part of him admired the veteran slaver. He acknowledged that he would have done something similar. It struck Pedro de Barbosa that their predicament required a unique response. He recalled their first encounter with Kosi Aholuvi. He had informed them of power brokers, insidious royal intrigues, and flagrant political animus in the kingdom. An idea solidified in Pedro de Barbosa's mind after Kosi Aholuvi updated him on the prevailing events at the palace.

"So, the monarch requested they execute his own offspring?" Pedro de Barbosa asked.

"Yes," said Kosi Aholuvi.

"And you say Prince Dozan has support?"

"Yes."

"Is he in the palace?"

"No. Voodoo priests rescued him and spirited him elsewhere," said Kosi Aholuvi.

"What's he plotting?" asked Pedro de Barbosa.

"What can he do when loyal guards, an entourage of backslapping courtiers, and many spies surround the monarch?"

"How can I reach Prince Dozan?" Pedro de Barbosa asked Kosi Aholuvi.

"Nobody knows. People say he's escaped to the kingdom of Benin. Others say he might be in Dahomey. But I doubt that very much. Ouidah has treaties with Dahomey, and its king would be obliged to hand him over to King Tezifon if he went there."

"So, you're suggesting there's no way to locate him?"

"He would have been dead if it was so easy to find him. But I know a way out. Money greases palms in Dahomey," said Kosi Aholuvi.

Two days after their conversation, Pedro de Barbosa, Kosi Aholuvi, ten mutinous soldiers from the king's army, and four former Portuguese soldiers walked for several hours through a jungle. The forest came to life with nocturnal animals protesting the invasion of their home and privacy. The Voodoo priest who led them ordered them to sit on logs built into stools when they arrived at a clearing in the middle of the forest. Light from the perfect moon, hitherto obstructed by thick canopies and foliage, now displayed its verve, allowing the visitors to see the Voodoo priests who emerged from four huts clustered around a tall wooden statue. They proceeded towards the group in silence. Without saying a word, the head voodoo priest motioned to the group to follow him and the others.

At the entrance of another hut, further back in the clearing that the visitors hadn't seen, four mutinous Ouidah soldiers with long spears and Flintlock guns around their shoulders stood guard. It was a massive oblong hut with a floor carpeted with animal hides. In the center stood *Nana Buluku*'s statue. A dozen low stools formed a circle around it. A room partitioned by raffia palm leaves stood at the far end of the hut. Quietly, the chief voodoo priest said, "*Agodofi!*"

"*Amee!*" came a response.

Shortly after, Prince Dozan emerged from the hut's interior. Everyone prostrated. After brief introductions, Pedro launched straight into the purpose of their visit. He explained the situation with King Tezifon and his concerns: the king would renege on the arrangements between Dahomey, Ouidah, and Portugal; his request was, at best, unreasonable. From what he had learned, he could not escape a severe reaction if he failed to meet the monarch's requests. He had to prevent that at all costs.

Prince Dozan stayed focused. After a while, he replied. "Are you informing me you, *yovos*, have come here because you're afraid of what my father might do to you?"

"Well, I'm not a *yovo*. Am as black as you," Pedro de Barbosa protested.

Prince Dozan let out a deep laugh.

"My friend, it may be dark, but I can still see your skin. It is as black as mine, but you're no black man. I'd suggest we begin this conversation on a proper footing instead of insulting my intelligence."

"Not again," Pedro de Barbosa said to himself. No one had ever claimed him white except for the slaves in the dungeon and now the prince. All his life, they had referred him to as a *preto*, a nigger, a black. Yet here he was in Ouidah, where they called him *yovo*, a white man. Did being a foreigner make one a *yovo*? He wasn't sure. The people they had employed to cook the millet and corn gruel, with which they fed the slaves, came from places as distant as the Ashanti kingdom. And still nobody called them *yovos*. How was he to respond to this perplexing racial categorization in which they had inserted him, a black former slave, with no debate or previous consultation? Pedro de Barbosa thought about more pressing issues at hand. The *yovo* signifier business could rest for now.

"I am here to aid your honor in whatever manner I can, and to be frank, I am petrified of what your revered father may do if we don't settle bills," Pedro de Barbosa responded. For the first time in many months, it occurred to him he wasn't fudging the truth.

"I admire your honesty, *Senhor* Pedro de Barbosa," Prince Dozan said. "Now, how can you support me?" the prince asked.

"A palace coup."

"What's that?" inquired Prince Dozan.

"We overthrow the monarch and install you, the new king. Both of us are young, and we can work together to help one another," said Pedro de Barbosa.

"Ah! I understand. And what causes you to assume I'd choose to do that?"

"Because you'd have been dead if not for the Voodoo priests."

"True. True. But why do you believe I'd wish to assassinate my father?"

"I didn't say murder. I said depose."

"Then what?"

"Don't the Ouidah people have laws against their kings who have become tyrants and unstable?" Pedro de Barbosa asked in return.

"His wives will kill him before anybody gets to him," said the chief voodoo priest. "An ousted king unable to defend his throne is unworthy of living," he added.

With Prince Dozan's consent, they quickly made plans. Konda Alifo, the leader of the mutinous soldiers from King Tezifon's army, would return to Ouidah and recruit clandestinely as many soldiers as possible. Pedro de Barbosa would provide the soldiers one hundred Flintlock guns. The ex-soldiers from the Portuguese army would help with training. Movement of the recruited soldiers would take place at night. They would hold all exercises in the Siba forest. It was dawn when Pedro de Barbosa and Kosi Aholuvi, along with the others, came back to the fort. Following the exchange between Pedro de Barbosa and Governor Belarmino and what had occurred in the dungeons, the latter kept to himself. He devoted his time to his study, reading and writing. That suited Pedro de Barbosa just fine. He had taken his destiny into his own hands and was hesitant to share any plans he had with the governor.

At midnight on the third day succeeding their encounter with Prince Dozan, two hundred rebel soldiers from the Ouidah army led by Konda Alifo arrived at *Forte São João Baptista de Ajudá*'s entrance. They had collected supplies for the soldiers' upkeep before their arrival. Kosi Aholuvi proved to be a genius in working out logistics. This was no surprise, as he had single-handedly orchestrated the feeding of the six hundred slaves that showed up unannounced. By daylight, the group, except for Pedro de Barbosa and Kosi Aholuvi, arrived in the Siba forest. The Governor's deputy was to stay put at *Forte São João Baptista de Ajudá*, lest he drew attention to the plot they hatched a few days earlier.

*****

Pedro de Barbosa woke up with a start. For a moment, he was unsure of his surroundings. The combination of the stench of his excrement, urine, the smelly cobalt-colored liquid in the giant vat in which they had submerged him up to his neck, and the early morning sunlight piercing through the rafters of the semi-thatched removable roof, and the relentless chirping of birds perched on it, reminded him of where he was. On the fifth day of their one-week grace period to settle their accounts, Togbega Ahialu, the royal auditor, appeared at *Forte São João Baptista de Ajudá*. King Tezifon had decided five days were long enough and couldn't wait for a couple more. It was time to get his due. Naturally, there was no gilded throne or horse to be carted off to the royal palace. Neither was the tidy sum of £6,500 available for the royal coffers. Jean-Marie Bernheim had been right. Pedro de Barbosa and the new governor were taking him for a fool, thought King Tezifon, after his royal clerk had reported to the palace empty-handed. The king's response was swift. His special forces stormed *Forte São João Baptista de Ajudá*. They seized hold of Pedro de Barbosa and three of the fifteen former Portuguese soldiers who had stayed back at the fort. Except for Paulino Cabral, who took refuge in the governor's quarters, the other missing soldiers were already in Siba's deep jungles. Governor Belarmino had a month to settle, after which the king couldn't guarantee Pedro de Barbosa's fate along with the three Portuguese *yovos*. Neither could the governor's own safety in Ouidah be assured. That was three weeks earlier. Pedro de Barbosa felt as though his limbs were atrophying from lack of exercise. Through bribery, Kosi Aholuvi visited him the earlier evening, as he had done every day. He informed him of what transpired at the fort. Jean-Marie Bernheim offered King Tezifon £7,500 for the slaves. They had them moved to *Amitié* to be shipped off to Martinique in the French Antilles. Of the six-hundred slaves, ten died in the dungeons. Now in the Ouidah king's good graces, the French slaver, with the monarch's aid, took over *Forte São João Baptista de Ajudá*. Governor Belarmino sheltered in *Casa da Silva*. It appeared the irritable king, once again, couldn't wait for the one-month grace period before he allowed the governor to settle for Pedro de Barbosa's release.

Pedro de Barbosa seethed with rage as he recalled Kosi Aholuvi's report. His future and that of the three ex-soldiers who still floundered in their respective clay vats, bursting with substances not too dissimilar from his, didn't concern him. What infuriated him was that Jean-Marie Bernheim appeared to have lifted a page from his own playbook. And for that, he would make the Frenchman pay a stiff price when he got out of his current plight, which, for someone watching from afar, sounded hopeless. In two nights, they would test Kosi Aholuvi's liaising prowess, his knack for gathering intelligence from the palace, and share relevant information with Pedro de Barbosa, who synthesized the intelligence and sent instructions to Prince Dozan.

It was a simple plan. Kosi Aholuvi planted a rumor whose source was none other than one of the king's top spies, who was a double agent: Prince Dozan had aligned with Orire, the *Oba* or Emperor of the Kingdom of Benin, and was planning to attack in three days. The rumor produced the desired effect. King Tezifon gathered his ministers to consider how to respond. They agreed on a pre-emptive strike two days before they believed the Kingdom of Benin forces would descend on Ouidah. As King Tezifon's troops vacated the city's outskirts and marched east towards Edo, the Kingdom of Benin's capital, a smaller, nimble, well-armed group left the

Siba Forest in the west and headed towards the city.

Surrounded by few bodyguards and soldiers, King Tezifon was a sitting duck in his palace. Resistance to Prince Dozan and his men was nominal. In less than an hour, the powerful monarch surrendered. The Ouidah army was halfway to Benin when one of Kosi Aholuvi's and Pedro de Barbosa's agents caught up with the soldiers. News of a Benin attack, he declared, was nothing but a rumor. While the army general contemplated what to do with the latest intelligence, a messenger appeared on horseback from Ouidah with earth-shattering news: Prince Dozan was in the city they left behind and had deposed his father as king. Following tradition, the king's wives took him to the Python temple ruins and returned to the palace, leaving a naked, lifeless King Tezifon hanging from a tree on the temple grounds. As the returning troops drew near the city walls, the distinctive sounds of the *Ojakari* ceremonial drums thundered through the air. Their message was unmistakable. King Tezifon was dead. Ouidah had a new king: King Dozan, who had named Pedro de Barbosa Viceroy of Ouidah.

Chapter 20

Upon his arrival in *Forte São João Baptista de Ajudá* from his prison, Pedro de Barbosa ordered Governor Belarmino, Paulino Cabral, along with some of the ex-soldiers to go back to Lisbon on *Alma Valiente* with a message for King John VI in Rio de Janiero through his functionaries in Lisbon: King Dozan, the new Ouidah monarch named him viceroy of Ouidah and offered him the monopoly of slave trading in the kingdom; he, Pedro de Barbosa, will represent Portugal's interests but on his own terms; Portuguese slavers and slaving ships could come to Ouidah, but the same trading conditions would apply to them as any other European slave trafficker; he would pay the Portuguese government to lease *Forte São João Baptista de Ajudá* if they agreed on his rate.

Pedro de Barbosa's second act as Ouidah's new viceroy was to inform the European slavers in Ouidah about the new terms that would govern the slave trade, both in Ouidah and Dahomey. Before doing so, he sought Jean-Marie Bernheim, who slipped out of *Forte São João Baptista de Ajudá* before he and the ex-Portuguese soldiers arrived. The Frenchman took temporary refuge in *Casa da Silva*'s whorehouse. He didn't resist when two ex-Portuguese soldiers dragged him to the fort. Pedro de Barbosa had the same vat with its contents in which he spent the past three weeks brought to the castle and placed in the fort's center courtyard, not too far from the chapel. Stripped naked, Jean-Marie Bernheim found himself submerged in the fluids that the earlier occupant had left. Flies, maggots, and other curious tropical insects greeted the opportunity to visit with the Frenchman.

A week afterward, Pedro de Barbosa had a reception for the European slavers at *Forte São João Baptista de Ajudá*. Jorginho d'Almeida catered the event that took place on the pristine beach beside the fort. Guests found long tables covered with white tablecloths, napkins, elegant plates, and drinking glasses that *Senhora* Matilde Belarmino sent along on *Alma Valiente*. As they milled about the beach and around the tables, servers filled their glasses with French, Portuguese, and Spanish wines, British gin, and *cachaça*. Several of da Silva's prostitutes arrived in their numbers, some of them holding on to the arms of clients who must have paid extra to have their company outside of their place of employment. The extraordinary events of the past week were on the guests' minds as they talked about Governor Belarmino's return to Lisbon, King Tezifon's ignominious end, the ascension of King Dozan to the throne, and Pedro de Barbosa's new position as viceroy. The rumor mill in *Casa da Silva* had gone into extra drive. Speculations were rife, and people wondered how a black ex-slave from Salvador, a newcomer, could have risen to become such a powerful player in the trade in such a short time. Guests wondered why he had organized the reception. Jean-Marie Bernheim's absence intrigued many. Who ordered the Portuguese ex-soldiers that picked up the Frenchman from *Casa da Silva*?

Answers to these questions and speculations came sooner than most expected, but not before guests satiated themselves with Jorginho d'Almeida's exquisite assortment of dishes. Among them were grilled red snappers, fried calamari, marinated broiled guinea fowl, game meat, fried plantains, boiled yams, and fruits such as mango, papaya, guava, and pears. An hour later, Pedro de Barbosa called his guests' attention.

"Thank you for joining me this evening. I'm confident you've heard that Governor Belarmino has returned to Lisbon. I ordered him to do so because I didn't think he was up to being a governor," Pedro de Barbosa said. He paused. He wanted his guests to grasp the magnitude of what he had just expressed.

"I wanted to share with you that my appointment as viceroy of Ouidah comes with having full control of slave trading in Ouidah, Dahomey, and Allada."

"Who the fuck do you think you're, you nigger? I've been in Dahomey for over twenty years. Nobody has had the audacity to assert or to undertake anything so stupid, you shitty ape," shouted Jon Van den Berg, a red-faced-angry Dutch slaver. Others joined. Soon, the hitherto peaceful beach party turned into a raucous affair.

"Let's throw him into the sea and have him swim to Brazil where he belongs," exclaimed an enraged slaver.

"Yeah, yeah, yeah," several men in the crowd howled in a chorus.

Pedro de Barbosa didn't blink. He stood still and remained calm. What the guests hadn't detected was the discrete signal that he had given to six of the fifteen servers who slipped away. Just as the guest's vitriol was reaching a crescendo, a nauseating odor hammered them. Most held their hands to their noses as a large clay vat came into view. Pedro de Barbosa signaled the carriers to set their cargo down at the far end of one of the long tables. Submerged in the vat up to his neck was Jean-Marie Bernheim's unrecognizable face. Gasps, followed by a deafening silence, seized the crowd as Pedro de Barbosa walked towards the barrel, indifferent to the stench. Jean-Marie Bernheim clinched his visible jaw at the sight of his fellow slavers. This was a humiliation of the highest order, he thought. He curled his lips with icy contempt at Pedro de Barbosa.

"By God, I swear I'll kill you when I get the chance," he hissed.

"Given your present circumstances, I wouldn't make any threats if I were you," Pedro de Barbosa said.

"Go fuck yourself," the Frenchman spat.

"I admire your tenacity. I must admit that the more I consider your actions during these past weeks, the more glaring I find the similarities between us," said Pedro de Barbosa.

"We have nothing in common, you stinky nigger."

"Ah! my friend. You're mistaken. When I told you that as a Jew, you and I may be different but share parallel histories, I don't think I explained what I meant. Care to know?" Pedro de Barbosa asked.

"I could not care less," said the French slaver.

"When I was ten years old, an ex-cleric called Marcelo Resendes told me something that I've never forgotten. It involved the persecution of a people under the guise of religion. But it was more about their race. He recounted the story of how the Portuguese expelled his extended family members who were Sephardic Jews from Brazil. Those who remained, he declared, hid their identities and converted to Catholicism. His own parents became devout Catholics, and he planned to become a Catholic priest." Pedro de Barbosa said and paused. Before he could continue, Jean-Marie Bernheim interrupted him.

"Oh! Spare me your story. You're not telling me anything new."

"Maybe, but you've not heard the end. I hate to not finish a story once I've begun," Pedro de Barbosa said. "When the rector and his superiors at the Seminary found out about his Jewish ancestry, they kicked him out. Can you imagine?" asked Pedro de Barbosa.

"You're a pathetic and lousy storyteller," said Jean-Marie Bernheim.

Pedro de Barbosa ignored him and continued. "You know what else I learned from Marcelo Resendes? He told me how they persecuted your people in Europe in the past centuries and in the present one. Remember the Inquisition when they burned a lot of them at the stakes for refusing to convert to Catholicism?"

"Who the fuck cares? It wouldn't have been funny if you weren't so delusional. You started by talking of fucking persecution, and where do you end? With a fucking Inquisition. How the fuck are they related?" Jean-Marie Bernheim asked.

"Oh! They're very much connected. As usual, you're hot-headed and impatient despite the miserable state in which you find yourself. I was making a point about your people's persecution in which they burned many of them at the stake under false pretenses," *said* Pedro de Barbosa.

Jean-Marie Bernheim was silent.

"Black Africans are being enslaved and persecuted. The slave trade, of which you've been part is the persecution of a race. Isn't it? They've despised us for peculiar reasons. Your people, for not believing in the true faith, which was Catholicism during the Inquisition, and mine, the curse of Ham, which continues to endure as we speak. They amount to the same thing. Don't they?"

The Frenchman remained mum.

"You and I are most alike in one respect."

"In what fucking way?"

"They abused and enslaved us in the past and they continue to do so now. Yet we're willing to perpetuate the same violence on others. Don't you think that's why you and I are here?"

"If you're such a fucking philosopher who's figured everything out, why the hell are you here? Why are you a slaver? Why don't you do something different?" asked Jean-Marie Bernheim.

"Because, most times, when they unleash violence on you, you internalize it. When you combine that with two other factors, things become less obvious," stated Pedro de Barbosa.

"And pray, Mr. Socrates, what're those two factors?" Jean-Marie Bernheim asked with disdain.

"The inability to exorcize that violence, a resolution saying, given a chance, you'll never subject yourself again to that violence. It may be a determination not to become like the perpetrator but to adopt whatever means possible to secure a position of power and influence such that nobody ever fucks with you."

"This is a most convoluted and deranged way of thinking."

"It may very well be. But what's certain in my mind is that nobody fucks with me. And you, Jean-Marie Bernheim, have screwed me on a grand scale. So, let me tell you what you'll do. Inform your fellow slavers gathered here what you did and why I've housed you in this vat for a week."

"And if I don't?"

"I'll keep you in this barrel and reduce your daily ration. Your limbs will atrophy and wilt. Imagine what will happen if your legs cannot hold your weight when still immersed in this liquid."

The Frenchman didn't fancy that prospect. He nodded. Pedro de Barbosa climbed onto a table, cleared his throat, and appealed for attention. None of the guests left, despite the stench. It wasn't clear whether they lingered on because of the occasional relief they got when the sea breeze carried away the odor, or it was curiosity that got the better part of them.

"There's something your friend in the vat wants to share with you," the host declared.

The visitors became quiet as Jean-Marie Bernheim recounted how he had double-crossed Pedro de Barbosa and made a fateful deal with the late King Tezifon and the consequences of his decisions. When he ended, the viceroy addressed his visitors.

"I need not tell you how I attained the viceroy post. Rumors will take care of that. What I want to do is to establish the new terms of engagement for slave trading in Ouidah, Dahomey, and Allada. After consultations with King Dozan and Dahomey's King Gesa, all slavers on this part of the West African coast will pay a new local tax besides the existing taxes. A part of the revenue from that tax will come to me for facilitating its collection," he paused and continued. "To do business in Ouidah, Dahomey, and Allada, slavers must register with me, for which there will be a fee. I must house all slaves in the *Forte Sao Joao Batista de Ajudá* dungeons before their shipment. You will pay tax to use the fort and your slaves' upkeep. I'd also like to know who your suppliers are and impose a tax on them.

"Are you out of your mind? No nigger gives me any instructions," Jon Van den Berg shouted.

Pedro de Barbosa climbed from the table and strolled to Jon Van den Berg.

"Repeat what you just said," he demanded.

"I said no nigger gives me . . ."

Before he could finish his sentence, Pedro de Barbosa delivered a crunching punch to the Dutchman's midriff. As he kneeled, another uppercut followed that sprawled him on the sandy beach, rendering him immobile. Pedro de Barbosa wasn't done. He lifted the hefty Dutchman as though he were the branch of a tree limb, carried him to the vat hosting Jean-Marie Bernheim, and dipped his head into the fluid. Jon Van den Berg gasped and gulped, having swallowed the cobalt-colored liquid. The efficiency with which Pedro de Barbosa delivered the one-two-punch combination and Jon Van den Berg sprawled on the ground beside the vat, was more than a warning shot. The ex-slave who had attained in such a short time immense power wielded it with such naturalness that he confounded the guests. Most guests understood this wasn't a man with whom to meddle. Besides, several of the Portuguese ex-soldiers had his back.

"Anyone among you willing to repeat in my face what that son of a bitch said?" Pedro de Barbosa asked his visitors, pointing to the still inert Jon Van den Berg. No one moved. Guests, who a short while ago, were spoiling for a fight were tight-lipped.

*****

In no time, Pedro de Barbosa imposed his will on the slave traders in Ouidah and Dahomey. They grumbled in private, but the trade was lucrative, and they couldn't walk away from it. Despite the new taxes, they complied with the new order. Pedro de Barbosa built considerable wealth between 1815 and 1822, playing a significant role in the violence that generated his fortune. With King Dozan's consent, he and the four ex-Portuguese soldiers transformed the Ouidah army. Young and strong recruits, nimble on their feet, replaced the old, fat, lazy, and clumsy soldiers. The Dahomey army became adept with Flintlock guns. They learned surprise attack and ambush strategies along with combat formation. Pedro de Barbosa subjected himself to the training. A quick study, he soon understood warfare. Because King Dozan's army didn't confront another one of equal puissance, slave raids became ruthless and efficient under Pedro de Barbosa. He went along with the Ouidah army and bore the rigors of the lengthy trek through swamps infested with crocodiles, arid grasslands, and thick forests replete with venomous snakes and conniving mosquitoes. The ransacking of the towns and villages outside of the Ouidah and Dahomey kingdoms adhered to the same pattern. Pedro de Barbosa and the Ouidah army, which he now commanded, waited until dawn. Their superior firepower made settlements vulnerable. Pedro de Barbosa took part in these raids for one plain reason: because he acquired the slaves himself, he paid King Dozan minimum tax. The profit margin exceeded the hardships he endured in capturing the slaves. The European slavers shuddered at the thought that Pedro de Barbosa joined in these attacks. They favored *Casa da Silva*'s safe comfort and left slave acquisitions to their dealers, from whom they bought them and sold them to the Brazilian and European slave captains and merchants.

As he engaged in these invasions, Pedro de Barbosa saw the ruthlessness of the soldiers he had assisted in training. It wasn't uncommon to see them garroting infants after taking the parents prisoners. Sometimes, they cut off the heads of those whom they deemed too old for the long hike to *Forte São João Baptista de Ajudá* and bagged them in their satchels as souvenirs. Gradually, Pedro de Barbosa himself became as barbarous as his soldiers. The cries of toddlers and women in their burning huts didn't move him. By his own deeds, Pedro de Barbosa was fulfilling what he had shared with Jean-Marie Bernheim: he was unleashing the violence that he had internalized; he grew into a formidable force, and nobody, as he had stated, could fuck with him any longer. But did the innocent and powerless slaves that he captured fuck with him in any manner? Could one separate one form of violence from another? Doesn't violence, in its particular nature, come from that evil place implanted in the human spirit? Isn't history rife with the incontestable proof that one of humanity's sole existence is barbarity? Yet for Pedro de Barbosa, it appeared his version of violence gave cruelty a good name, in so far as he carried it out to further his goal. Yet beneath it all, what emerged was nothing but disguised sadism that lurked just below the surface. Had the landscape transformed Pedro de Barbosa, the man? Did telluric forces have a hand? It was difficult to tell. Amid the violence and human suffering, what mattered for the slaver was his resolute determination to attain the status of a *senhor* upon his return to Brazil. And, as he made it clear, the only way to realize this uncompromising goal was to accumulate as much wealth as possible. Anyone who stood in his way, or attempted to swindle him, did so at his own peril. Captain Romero Salgado and Captain Gaspar Martins learned that lesson the hard way.

Gaspar Martins, a Brazilian slave ship captain, sounded like a decent fellow, or so Pedro de Barbosa thought. He had crisscrossed the Atlantic Ocean several times with Pedro de Barbosa's slaves and always paid the slaver well. He was a superb source of information on ongoing events in Salvador. A native Salvadoran, Captain Gaspar Martins knew the city very well and traded with the most prominent slavers, including none other than *Senhor* Federico da Facinda of the spurious and infamous *Fraternidade Cristã* cabal. Captain Gaspar Martins understood Pedro de Barbosa's ultimate plans from earlier conversations. He had invited him and others to the fort for elaborate dinners, as he was wont to do, while the slave ship captains waited to fill their anchored ships with human cargo. Captain Gaspar Martins saw an opportunity: pick up an estate for Pedro de Barbosa if the slaver was so inclined. Several pleasant homes, he claimed, had come up for purchase in the São Bento neighborhood. Pedro de Barbosa considered the proposition. Purchasing an imposing home was the first step towards his goal. And what area could better that purpose than São Bento? The prospect of running into his erstwhile master as a wealthy and powerful *senhor* in the same locale tickled Pedro de Barbosa. It took little for Captain Gaspar Martins to extort out of the slaver, £18,500, to buy a non-existent property.

Six months later, Captain Gaspar Martins and his First Mate, Evaristo Caetano, came back from Salvador. His business partner's return elated Pedro de Barbosa. He organized an uncommonly large reception for them. Slavers and whores from *Casa da Silva*, King Dozan's Minister for the Slave Trade, *Yovogan* Abalo Bajani, and many other Ouidah state officials were among the guests. The evening's function wasn't exceptional. Pedro de Barbosa threw these parties for European and Brazilian merchants and Ouidah's elite, excluding King Dozan, who, by custom, couldn't be in the same place where they kept slaves before they shipped them away. These galas, always catered by Jorginho d'Almeida, allowed Pedro de Barbosa to keep a pulse on what went on in Ouidah. It provided him the chance to hear of events in Brazil and Europe.

Despite efforts to abolish the slave trade, French, Portuguese, Spanish, and, yes, English slavers were engaged in the market. As usual, Pedro de Barbosa opened his cellar to everyone. Servants provided copious amounts of exquisite wine from Europe's best wineries. As was the case, Pedro de Barbosa didn't drink. As the evening wore on, he left the party and climbed up to his study, which was still full of Governor Belarmino's books. The sale papers that Captain Gaspar Martins brought along sat carefully stacked in a leather paper-carrying bag on a large mahogany table. The viceroy removed them and began working through them. Laid out in the sale, Pedro de Barbosa found the property's location, size, the gardens, name of the former owner and the signature of the alderman, who validated the sale and transfer of the property to the new buyer. Pedro de Barbosa's name appeared on several sheets. His representative and agent, Captain Gaspar Martins, signed on his behalf below his name. Pedro de Barbosa looked for the bill of sale and the certificate of title. He didn't find them. Still absorbed in the documents, he heard the drunken voices of Captain Gaspar Martins and First Mate Evaristo Caetano. The party was over. Kosi Aholuvi had arranged for the guests a bedroom next to the study.

"You think he'll buy it?" First Mate Evaristo Caetano asked, slurring his speech.

"Shhhhhhh! Captain Gaspar Martins whispered.

Pedro de Barbosa stood up and tiptoed towards the wall dividing the study and the bedroom. In refurbishing the fort, Governor Belarmino ordered a small window cut into the wall separating the study and the bedroom. Through it, Kosi Aholuvi could deposit the Governor's drinks or whatever he required without disturbing him. Kosi Aholuvi had covered the window on the bedroom side.

"I'll be darned if the idiot *preto* didn't fall for it. Edir Neves, the best forger in the Alderman's office, put the documents together. Not even the devil will notice," Captain Gaspar Martins said, cackling. "He didn't even bother to read the papers. That would've been the first thing I would've done if I gave £18,500 to someone to purchase me a fucking house," First Mate Evaristo Caetano said, helpless to curb the giggles.

"What do these *pretos* know? They're all the same. A bunch of fucking apes," Captain Gaspar Martins said, snickering. "Wait till

I make him another offer. This time, it will acquire him an imaginary sugarcane *Fazenda*. I can't wait to see how he responds."

"How much will you ask him for it?" asked First Mate Evaristo Caetano.

"The fucking *preto* is squatting on a shitload of money. I doubt if he even realizes how much he has and of what significance," said Captain Gaspar Martins.

Pedro de Barbosa had heard enough. His knees wobbled as he walked back to the mahogany table. It took him a while to control his shaking limbs. Sulfurous rage burned through his body. He sat still for an hour, gathering his thoughts. He opened a cabinet that had blank papers of identical make, as those on which they had drawn up the fictitious property sale. For the next six hours, he copied the documents. The art of text reproduction hadn't forsaken him! Locking the study and leaving the papers on the table to dry, he moved to his bedroom, recognizing that he couldn't sleep.

It appeared as though the forces had lined up against Pedro de Barbosa. Just when he was about to fall asleep in the early morning hours, Kosi Aholuvi woke him. Captain Romero Salgado, the Portuguese slave ship captain, had arrived and sought his audience. With no money or goods to pay for them, the captain had implored Pedro de Barbosa to furnish him with a shipload of slaves for Salvador da Bahia, promising to repay him with a handsome interest upon his return. Like Captain Gaspar Martins, Captain Romero Salgado was a known quantity and had done business with Pedro de Barbosa a few times. The viceroy assented. Upon his arrival in Salvador, Captain Romero Salgado squandered the money made from the sale of the slaves. Broke, he did what he did best. He rounded up his crew and headed out to the West African coast to bring more slaves back to Brazil. He headed for Badagry; another slave port next to Ouidah. After landing, half of Captain Romero Salgado's crew he hadn't paid mutinied and almost hanged him. The captain escaped by the skin of his teeth with a few loyal sailors. Ouidah was the closest port of call beyond Badagry.

Pedro de Barbosa's spirits soared. He expected to receive adequate payment for his shipment and the generous percentage the

Portuguese captain had pledged. It didn't take Pedro de Barbosa long to realize yet another transaction had gone bust. An infant wouldn't have believed the captain's cock and bull story: a pirate vessel had raided his ship and made off with Pedro de Barbosa's payment. The slave merchant smiled to himself as he listened to the captain's tall tale. Captain Romero Salgado was about to suffer the same treatment that his fertile mind had devised for Captain Gaspar Martins just before he fell asleep. He welcomed the Portuguese with open arms. The captain, who hardly believed his good fortune, thought Pedro de Barbosa had swallowed his narrative line, hook, and sinker. His creditor showed no outward sign of anger or frustration. If he ever encountered a cretin, the captain told himself, Pedro de Barbosa must be a full-blown one.

*****

The sun was high up when Captain Gaspar Martins and his First Mate, Evaristo Caetano, got up. Kosi Aholuvi had set out brunch for them in the main living room.

"*Sehnor Barbosa* is expecting you in the study when you're done, "Kosi Aholuvi informed the guests.

Bookshelves filled with books on subjects ranging from law to the natural sciences lined the study's walls. Rosewood chairs and a sofa stood on one side of the study. Pedro de Barbosa sat in front of a wide mahogany table with two chairs behind it. A large window looked out at the sea. On the horizon, hazy silhouettes of several ships remained off the coast.

"I trust you gentlemen had a good night?" Pedro de Barbosa asked with a faint smile.

"There's nothing more pleasurable than setting one's foot on land after many months at sea and languishing in a bed that doesn't swing," Captain Gaspar Martins acknowledged, as both men sat.

"I had the chance to look at the documents this morning. The estate is magnificent. It is exactly what I required. The right location, adequate number of rooms for guests and for entertainment, vast gardens full of all kinds of flowers."

"You should've been there when Evaristo Caetano and I saw it. We couldn't believe the estate's architectural integrity and magnificence. Its location is remarkable. From the study, one could view the lower city and the docks," said Captain Gaspar Martins.

"I didn't find the bill of sale, though. The property was £18,500?"

Captain Gaspar Martins hesitated and answered, "Well, by the time I paid the taxes and the Alderman's services at the Municipal Council, I had to add £400 of my own funds to cover everything. I'm not expecting you to reimburse the £400. It's the least I can do to help a friend," the slave captain replied, grinning. He was bald and had a sharp nose and an anxious look that gave him an odd and malignant face which was deceptively affable.

"That's very kind," said Pedro de Barbosa. "I noticed the certificate of title wasn't in the documents. Did you forget it?"

"*Merda*," Captain Gaspar Martins muttered under his breath. The man sitting in front of him was more intelligent than he had imagined. How could he have learned about the details of purchasing an estate? Hell, he himself knew nothing regarding bills of sales, let alone certificates of titles and that sort of thing. "*Merda*," he repeated once again. Edir Neves should have included all these documents. The son of a bitch was so eager to lay hands on his money he failed to do what they expected of this sort of transaction. That prick. He would deal with him when he returned.

"Oh, I might have forgotten to include those documents. I had them, though. I can see them in my mind's eye. Yes, I left them in a drawer in my study. Not to worry, I'll return them the next time I come back."

Pedro de Barbosa smiled. It was the smile of the conman who knew when a fellow conman made things up as he went along, when the noose tightened around his neck.

"And this Alderman, what's his name again? Pedro de Barbosa asked.

"Monteiro Macedo," Captain Gaspar Martins replied.

Pedro de Barbosa drew a top drawer and spread out the reproduced documents.

"I hope my eyesight isn't deceiving me, but the Alderman's

name on these documents is Edir Neves. So are the signatures. In addition, I'm wondering why, even though I wasn't there, my signatures appear on the dotted lines," Pedro de Barbosa said, pushing the documents towards Captain Gaspar Martins.

A visible shudder ran through the captain's body as a look of incredulity spread through his face. Was he dreaming? He asked himself. These were the documents he had brought, he thought. Yes, Edir Neves had forged the papers and placed Alderman Monteiro Macedo's name where it ought to have been. Yet the documents in front of him now carried Edir Neves as Alderman. Besides, his name and signatures, which appeared on the original record, were nowhere to be found. By heavens! And how did Pedro de Barbosa's name and signatures appear?

"Is something wrong, Captain Gaspar Martins?" Pedro de Barbosa asked.

"Yes, No. It's just that. . ."

"It's just that what?" Pedro de Barbosa demanded with a firm voice.

"Oh, yes, everything is in order," Captain Gaspar Martins said.

"But Edir Neves isn't an Alderman. I have got a book here of government officials in Brazilian cities, including Salvador," Pedro de Barbosa said, getting up and studying both men. They squirmed. Despite the early afternoon breeze breaking through the open window, Captain Gaspar Martins felt perspiration on his forehead. His heartbeat had increased by a tempo. Everything was unraveling. He couldn't defend the indefensible, and he knew it.

"Do you want to tell me what's going on here?"

Silence.

Pedro de Barbosa walked towards the large window overlooking the Atlantic Ocean. His back turned to Captain Gaspar Martins and Evaristo Caetano; he said, "It might incline me to forget this whole affair if you came clean. You said last night that I'm sitting on a shitload of money without appreciating how much of it I have, let alone its value. Perhaps you want to tell me more about this property you bought and what I might not know about myself."

Captain Gaspar Martins and Evaristo Caetano looked at each other, slack mouthed. Those darned glasses of wine, gin, and God knows what else from last night! Captain Gaspar Martins said to himself, attempting the impossible possibility of recalling his conversation with his First Mate. As the silence intensified, they could hear the sea's incessant crash and roar on the fort's walls. Pedro de Barbosa spun around and rang a bell on the side of the mahogany table. Six of Pedro de Barbosa's personal guards invaded the room.

"You've left me with no other choice," Pedro de Barbosa said to the two still stunned men as he stepped out of the door.

Within moments, they led Captain Gaspar Martins and Evaristo Caetano to the chapel on the fort's ground floor. There, they found Captain Romero Salgado, who Pedro de Barbosa's men had corralled. As they made their way to the sanctuary, a familiar sight caught their eyes. Three seven-foot poles stood ten feet apart in the middle of the fort's courtyard. Beside each of them were long lashes. The image of Salvador's *Pelourihno* went through their minds. Pedro de Barbosa breezed in before they had the chance to sit.

"A decision I made when they crucified me on a pole in Salvador's *Pelourinho* was never to put anyone through that experience if I had the power to do so. I was twelve years old, innocent, and naïve. Seventeen years later. I've learned of man's ability to lie, cheat, and kill if he had to do so to get ahead," Pedro de Barbosa said, as he paused in front of the pews facing the three men, who his men surrounded.

"You will experience *Pelourinho* in Ouidah. But it isn't a fortuitous *Pelourinho*. You fucked with me, and nobody does. I'll give you a few minutes to pray to your God for intervention, although I am skeptical that he'll turn up soon," Pedro de Barbosa said, sitting on a pew with his back turned to the men.

A few minutes later, he motioned to his aides, who lifted the men off their seats and marched them towards the poles. The sun was high in the sky, hot. In no time, they stripped the men naked and tied them to wooden posts. Pedro de Barbosa sat on a chair as he watched three of his black, muscular attendants step forward. The long whips flashed through the air with speed, tearing into white skins. Blood oozed. The three fellows passed out. Captain Gaspar Martins was the first to recover consciousness. He found his feet in chains in a dungeon full of slaves. He wasn't sure what sped up his resuscitation: the stench? Humiliation? Unbearable pain that coursed through his body? Who could have dreamt that he, a slave's captain, would keep company with shackled slaves? And yet here he was.

"I'm in a fucking hell hole, a dog pit, a shit hole of a place," he said to himself. He doubted if God, in his cruelest moments, could have ever thought of casting his most unruly children into such a place. Even so, here he was. He hadn't embraced the chance to pray in the chapel when Pedro de Barbosa offered him the opportunity. His mind had been in turmoil. He couldn't remember the last time he had gone to Mass or even prayed. He agreed with Pedro de Barbosa's skepticism about God's intervention. Now, he wondered if even such a superior being who ascribed to itself or himself unproven omniscience and omnipresence existed. All he could think of was the fucking and fucked up humanity that still clung to the notion of a God that was benevolent and malevolent at the same time.

Pedro de Barbosa's aides carried on the *Pelourinho* ritual for seven days. They brought the men out of the dungeons each day at noon and whipped them. It wasn't clear why Pedro de Barbosa had chosen seven days. Perhaps, he recalled, it was the same number of days *Sehnor* Felipe de Barbosa strung his father up a tree on his *Fazenda*. On the eighth day, they took Gaspar Martins, Evaristo Caetano, and Romero Salgado to the shore. Their sailors stood on the beach. From the distance, four pirogues approached their ships. Flames engulfed them in a matter of minutes. Shackled, they could simply curse. Pedro de Barbosa turned and addressed his captives when both ships' last remnants sunk into the ocean.

"I'll arrange for your sailors to find new captains and ships. The three of you will remain in Ouidah. But you cannot stay in *Forte São João Baptista de Ajudá* or in *Casa da Silva.*"

Unshackled, one could hardly recognize the men who had arrived at the fort a week earlier. Word of how Pedro de Barbosa had treated them spread. When the natives found Gaspar Martins, Eva-risto Caetano, and Romero Salgado languishing on the beach and understood that their survival depended on Ouidans' generosity, they added an inevitable nickname to Pedro de Barbosa's title: *Yovo Mɔla*—The Whiteman's Fucker.

Chapter 21

The breaking day's faint glimmer permeated the morning September sky with its typical splendor of pink, violet, and yellow when Queen Yiram, in the company of her servants and eunuchs, left the palace. This outing wasn't abnormal. The queen had a propensity to stroll on the shore next to *Forte São João Baptista de Ajudá* and watch the sunrise as she dipped her feet into the warm and soothing Atlantic waters. What was unusual with this excursion, however, was who Queen Yiram was meeting. As she awaited her encounter with Pedro de Barbosa, she thought of past events that precipitated her request for this meeting, an encounter she hoped to enhance her son's ascension to the Ouidah throne. She recalled the conversation she had overheard between Fuseina and Afiriwa that had prompted her to crash the banquet in honor of the Dahomey delegates. It was a gleeful conversation, underscoring their delight that Akonde was to have a formidable challenger from Dahomey to the throne of Ouidah.

Despite her attempts to convince herself that her unutterable love for Akonde motivated her, Queen Yiram knew in a profound instinctual way that it was her own ambition to become yet the most powerful queen mother in Ouidah's history that propelled her. By tradition, the queen served as an advisor to the monarch and ruled with him in what one could term an informal diarchy. The king performed the day-to-day administrative functions, but the queen held the most powerful position at court. With King Dozan usurping all power and relegating his wife to a subordinate station, Queen Yiram relished the prospect of Akonde becoming king. He was her son, and she could control him and dictate social, political, and economic policies that included slave trading. It had been for her, a lifetime of scheming, lying, and killing, to pave the way to the mighty Ouidian throne. She was aware of her son's deficiencies compared to the other Ouidah princes vying for the throne. Despite those flaws, she vowed that her son's shortcomings wouldn't become an impediment. Didn't one of their proverbs say although a baby may be unpleasant to look at, his mother never refuses him? It was for this reason that she had arranged the murder of Ganji Sindje, her son's most potent challenger. Sossa's arrival could complicate matters. She was ready to strike again, deploying the same outside force that altered ten years ago, the course of the kingdom's history. The estrangement between Pedro de Barbosa and King Dozan offered a splendid opportunity, and Queen Yiram was keen to exploit it.

King Dozan and Pedro de Barbosa appeared secure in their respective positions. King Dozan's loyalists had replaced most of the ministers who worked under the late King Tezifon. The viceroy became the single most powerful slave merchant on the West African coast. Although both men continued to collaborate, tensions emerged between them. The king envied and disliked the rate at which Pedro de Barbosa prospered as he used his kingdom's army in the slave raids. Yes, the viceroy paid taxes, but Dahomey's coffers didn't grow at the same rate as the Brazilian's. King Dozan reckoned higher returns if his army carried out the raids and marketed the slaves to the slave traders. He decreed Pedro de Barbosa could no longer control his army. To siphon off the gains Pedro de Barbosa had made, King Dozan began ordering the slaver to offer him gifts, including guns, rum, iron, and other items used in the barter for slaves. The viceroy complied, but the more presents he delivered to the king, the more persistent the requests came. Pedro de Barbosa was losing money, and he wasn't happy.

Another schism between the two collaborators was King Dozan's resolute refusal to plunder any towns or villages in the Ouidah kingdom for slaves following the dramatic decrease in the number of slaves that arrived from Dahomey thanks to the long-term campaign Queen Ena Sunu had launched to end slave trading in her kingdom. King Dozan had learned his lesson well. His father had committed the abominable crime of selling his fellow Ouidians with a disastrous outcome. Pedro de Barbosa couldn't do anything to reverse the monarch's mind. The viceroy's fortunes were dwindling.

Pedro de Barbosa was at the designated place on the beach when Queen Yiram and her cortege arrived. Custom prevented the viceroy from speaking with King Dozan's wives, but it would have to change.

"I'm very much obliged and honored to meet the queen on such a morning. I hope my head will still stay in its place if the king were to find out I've spoken to his first wife," Pedro de Barbosa said, walking to Queen Yiram and raising his right hand in salutation.

"The queen has the power to ask for your head and to have it stay in its place. It looks well where it sits for now, and I'm sure it will stay there when we're all done," Queen Yiram responded.

"To what do I owe the honor of this encounter?" Pedro de Barbosa asked.

"I see you're not used to preambles. You go straight to the point. I admire that," Queen Yiram stated.

"Why dance around a fire ring if you don't want to feel the heat?" Pedro de Barbosa asked.

"I notice you're speaking like our people. I didn't think *yovos* were that clever with language.

"*Yovos* again!" Pedro de Barbosa muttered to himself, but he let it slide. "It's only a fool who closes his eyes to a brewing storm," said Pedro de Barbosa.

"A seething storm indeed because what you're about to discover foretells an approaching tempest. As they say, the wise always take inventory of their property before an equatorial storm strikes," said the queen.

A soft morning breeze blew past them as gentle waves lapped slowly and lazily on the beach. One wouldn't believe that in a few hours, these same waves would gain a ferocious disposition. Pedro de Barbosa's silence paid homage to the surrounding calm.

"I understand your inventory has been diminished lately. There's a way we could remedy that," suggested Queen Yiram.

Pedro de Barbosa was slack-jawed momentarily. He puzzled over why Queen Yiram sought their meeting. Of all the probable reasons he had considered, slave trade wasn't in the mix. The queen's proposal was attractive and couldn't have fallen at a better time. Yet he was suspicious.

"Her royal highness is well-informed," said Pedro de Barbosa.

"When one keeps one's ear close to the ground, one hears things," asserted the queen.

"The king has messengers and spokespersons. He's as invested in the trade as I am. He and I have been at this for years now, you know? I wonder why he sent you instead to discuss a solution to our problem," Pedro de Barbosa said.

"You're a sensible man, Viceroy Pedro de Barbosa. So am I. When an opportunity presents itself, one doesn't question it. It's only fools and cowards who do," said the queen.

"And what is the opportunity?" asked Pedro de Barbosa.

"To become even richer. The chance to thumb one's nose at so-called conventions that prohibit the sale of native Ouidians and Dahomeyans as slaves. An ability to sell vast numbers of our people and those from Dahomey to enlarge your profits and ours," Queen Yiram answered, although she wasn't keen on the slave commerce per se. The perks that came with being a queen mother mattered to her.

Pedro de Barbosa smiled. He proposed the same scheme to King Dozan, but he'd been adamant in his refusal. But he warmed up to Pedro de Barbosa's idea of attacking King Gesa, toppling him, and declaring Dahomey and Ouidah a merged kingdom under King Dozan. Much to Pedro de Barbosa's displeasure, the sovereign had recommended they bide their time, considering the gifting of the Dahomeyan prince. Queen Yiram's proposal was audacious. This was a pragmatic woman. But what was the catch? Pedro de Barbosa asked himself.

"Of course, you recognize that's not conceivable with the current monarch," Queen Yiram stated.

That was obvious to Pedro de Barbosa, but he wasn't about to verbalize it.

"How do you plan on doing so without the king's blessing?" he inquired.

"It's simple. We don't require his permission. We'll replace him with Akonde in the manner he took over from his father."

"I see," Pedro de Barbosa said. "You want your son to be a king without waiting until your husband is dead. A new prince from Dahomey is on the way, and his arrival might complicate matters for you and your boy. That's brilliant. You must have a plan, I suppose?"

"Yes," said the queen.

"And I imagine you're sharing this with me because your strategy involves me. Am I right?"

"Yes," the queen responded.

"And if I refuse?"

"You'll not because you're not stupid enough to let slip an opportunity such as this. Besides, King Dozan's army, which you've helped train, would invade *Forte São João Baptista de Ajudá* if he heard you've been plotting with agents from the Kingdom of Dahomey to overthrow him."

Pedro de Barbosa's eyes darted from the horizon and descended on the queen.

"You know that's a lie."

"Yes. But who do you think the king will believe? You or me?" Queen Yiram asked.

Pedro de Barbosa paused, wondering what all of this meant. Did the king accept whatever his wife told him? A few warning signs lit up in his mind. What if this was a trap? As a part of his virile mind contemplated this possibility, a separate part calculated the planned scheme's benefits. He would be in a stronger position to control Akonde, who, in his assessment, was nobody but a lout who took pleasure in visiting *Casa da Silva* along with De Adjara, his worthless second cousin. They were a few of the men from the king's palace who patronized the bordello. As royals who had access to influence and resources, Silvio da Silva and the other slavers treated the two with reverence. The queen's proposal to flout the conventions banning the sale of native Ouidians and Dahomeyans as slaves meant only one thing: the slave trade could flourish once more and increase his fortune anew after losing part of his accumulated wealth.

"So, what's your plan, and what's my task?" Pedro de Barbosa asked.

"I presume you're in?" Queen Yiram asked.

"Do I have a choice?" Pedro de Barbosa asked.

"We have choices. Don't we?" Queen Yiram said with a knowing smile. "I knew I could count on you. For now, we will limit your role. You'll serve as a backup if our original plan doesn't produce the desired results," responded the queen.

"You still haven't informed me what the plan is," said Pedro de Barbosa.

"Let's say you'll find out the day they present the so-called gifted prince from Dahomey to the Ouidah people," Queen Yiram added as she left the beach with her entourage.

*****

The whiff of sizzling goat meat grilled in large open pits infused the air. Elsewhere, on these expansive grounds next to an amphitheater, the distinct smell of hot palm oil in which swam *akkara*—black eye bean fritters, *aloko*—fried ripe plantains, *massa*—millet flour pancake, and *wagassi*—fried cow cheese—wafted into the afternoon air along with smoke emerging from makeshift hearths that bore these savory foods. Entrepreneurs in their improvised stalls offered eager patrons many drinks, including the ubiquitous palm wine.

But perhaps the stalls that appealed to most clients were those that sold *jukutu*. A misty and fermented alcoholic drink prepared from red extra-large millet grains, the liquor had the rare quality to provoke lethargy despite one's gallant efforts to avert it. Early patrons of these stands were drunk and sound asleep on the roadside, leading to the amphitheater. The smell of human sweat, urgent and potent, perforated the air like dense fog, reluctant to give to the sun's relentless onslaught. Hundreds of Ouidah citizens, who had lined up for hours along the road heading to Ouidah from the

Kingdom of Dahomey, bore the solar assault with uncharacteristic calmness, patience, and enthusiasm. And who could blame them? Very few would miss this memorable event: their new prince and possible future king's arrival. As the hours rolled by, musical and acrobatic troupes from villages and towns in both kingdoms performed and entertained the crowd.

The throng became animated when it saw the conspicuous red flag of a horse rider in the distance. It was the king's herald, prompting the crescendo of the drums to increase tenfold. They sprinkled the road leading to the amphitheater with hibiscus and bougainvillea flowers of different colors. By the time King Dozan and his entourage, along with King Gesa's representatives, entered the arena, the crowd's excitement had reached fever pitch. The people recognized how significant Sossa's gifting was to them. It heralded a new era of friendship with the Kingdom of Dahomey. The decades-old exchanges and the gifting of royal family members between the kingdoms had curbed Ouidah's warring habits.

The imperial dais at the amphitheater was teetering on the brink of collapse with the weight of the king's wives and their children, courtiers, various ministers, and members of prominent Ouidah families. King Dozan's stool, which they brought from the throne room, occupied the center of the podium. Two less gilded seats stood on both sides of the king's. Everyone on the platform rose when King Dozan reached his throne, followed by the cortege of aides. His quick and elastic movements stressed his tall, broad-shouldered, and statuesque shape. He seized a moment to study those on the stage and spun around to meet the throng that filled every seat at the amphitheater. He recognized the cheers with a calculated royal arm wave. With the golden crown on his royal head, joint with the long hand-woven colorful cotton cloth wrapped around one side of his shoulder to his feet, King Dozan cut the figure of a man who could be the king of not only one kingdom, but several, an emperor. He reckoned there were over five thousand of his subjects in the arena. Musicians, dancers, drummers, acrobats, wrestlers, and many performance artists occupied the amphitheater's center. Thanks to the rain that had poured a few days earlier, no dust arose to prevent spectators from seeing everything. It was a feast for the eyes.

With a nod from the king, the royal master drummer began striking the four *Ojakari* ceremonial drums with two long angular hooked wooden sticks. The drums ranged in size from the biggest to the smallest. Although their shapes were the same, large barrels with a cylindrical foot open at the base, they produced distinct tones. As the drums rolled, the cheering became deafening: the ceremony was to begin. With the arena cleared, Ouidah's Voodoo Chief Priest, Ikurisiare, invaded the center, accompanied by ten of his acolytes clad in white tunic shirts and briefs. One of them pulled behind him a large ram. Another had a gourd with a long neck like an ostrich's filled with palm wine. Once in the center of the arena, the Chief Priest bowed to King Dozan, who responded with a nod. An acolyte produced a calabash from a raffia satchel which they filled with palm wine. Taking off his sandals, the Voodoo priest poured a libation in a solemn voice.

Nouminsin vivenan, yolo
é lo gnin votata aa.
Azan é gbé ton gnin azan
dé kpo oun an.
Honton mi ton Dahomey ton lé
kpla vi yé ton wa nou mi.
Gni ko ton non gnin Sossa.
Vi mi ton we é gnin din.
Di déé mi do yi gbon we
kpo do alo wé kpo é yo,
mi lo bo yi gbon mon.

Dear Ouidah gods and ancestors.
Our calling is not frivolous.
Today isn't like any other day.
Our Dahomey friends and allies have brought us their son.
His name is Sossa. He's now our son.
As we accept him, we pray you also do likewise and protect him.

Hardly had Chief priest Ikurisiare finished with the libation when one of his acolytes slit the ram's throat. With its blood spouting out like a geyser, the chief priest cried,

"*Inh!*"

The crowd answered in one massive, fervent cry. Soon, the arena resounded with *Inh! Inh! Inh! Inh!*—Yes! Yes! Yes! Yes!—The *Ojakari* drums sounded again, and the call became silent when King Dozan stood up. He took a deep breath, cast his gaze on his family on the platform and on his subjects in the amphitheater, and, in a thundering voice, stormed out.

"*Agoo do fi,*"

"*Amee,*" the jubilant throng responded.

The king burst into a wide smile and addressed his people.

"The Ouidah and Dahomey people have a common saying: *To give thy friend is not to cast away, it is to store for the future.* Today, the kingdom of Dahomey is giving us Sossa. The people of Dahomey are not storing for the future. We all are. But it is we, the Ouidah people, they have blessed with a gift that will bolster our friendship and strong alliance for many years to come."

Moved by King Dozan's brief speech, the crowd cried out to Sossa. "*Awa do gandji bo mi yi wé kpo do alo wé kpo, Sossa, Awa do gandji bo mi yi wé kpo do alo wé kpo, Sossa,*"—*You're welcome, our very own Sossa. You're welcome, our very own Sossa.*

After a brief pause, King Dozan raised his hands into the air and, as if performing an imaginary offertory, he roared: "The people of Ouidah, I present to you Sossa, our new prince, our new son."

The pack burst into a raucous, thunderous cheer, bracing itself for the most expected moment: everybody at the amphitheater, except for the king and a few of his courtiers, would see Sossa's face for the first time. Custom required that Sossa enter the theater with a mask that concealed most of his face, except for the lower part of his chin. Akonde was to perform the mask removal ritual: he was not only embracing a new brother but a likely challenger to the throne. Akonde strolled to Sossa, who remained beside King Dozan. The crowd held its breath.

"Is he a girl?" one of King Dozan's youngest sons, six-year-old Ikuame, asked in a loud voice, much to the amusement of guests on the dais who couldn't help snickering.

"Shhh! quiet, Ikuame. He's our new prince," whispered Afiriwa, Ikuame's mom.

"Why is he wearing that thing like a princess?" Ikuame asked. Young Ikuame must have been thinking about his sisters, who wore veils whenever they were in their father's presence.

His younger half-brother's interruption angered Akonde. They had focused all attention on Sossa. This was the most important occasion for him to be in the spotlight. Yet Ikuame was wrecking it. He spun around and walked towards Ikuame and his mother, who sat at the podium's far end. Akonde smacked Ikuame and hissed at Afiriwa. "Can you, for once, be an exemplary mother and control that brat?"

Ikuame let out a muffled cry as Akonde returned to Sossa, whose mouth dropped. The spectators didn't see what transpired, and it delighted them when Akonde removed Sossa's mask. They cheered. Many on the platform remarked on how Sossa resembled the king. Akonde raised Sossa's right hand up with his left hand and spoke.

"Behold, Sossa, my new brother, and Ouidah's new prince."

A guttural roar of the frenzied crowd filled the amphitheater as they gave the prince a standing ovation. It went wild when they announced that in honor of their new prince, they would perform the *Miwui* sport, which occurred during the annual *Sese* festival. A bow and arrow contest on horseback, the event drew together King Dozan's finest and bravest slave soldiers, who were trained specifically for the gala.

From a holding pen, a hundred fighters in groups of ten broke into the middle of the amphitheater. The object of the contest was to establish which fighter in each group was the fastest and the most accomplished horse rider, capable of averting and firing arrows that either killed, impaired, or displaced his opponents from their mounts. Fighters who slipped from their horses stood no chance of survival. Steeds, hair-trigger, fearful, and panicky that came unglued immediately they entered the arena trampled fallen contestants. They declared the group's champion, the last combatant, who remained saddled on his stallion. As their reward, the ten winners became freed slaves and mobilized into King Dozan's elite military equestrian force. *Miwui* was a beloved and bloody sport, and the crowd's reaction when they declared the contest showed the people loved it.

They arranged the arena, and in a short time, the first batch of fighters appeared. The multitude thundered. In fewer than ten minutes, several bodies lay strewn across the ring. From the first set, only one fighter, with a bloody torso, sat on his horse. The crowd cheered when the announcer pronounced him the victor. "This is hideous," Sossa said under his breath as the winner keeled over and fell off his horse before he could enter the holding pen. Sossa slumped into the chair and paid languid attention to the cheers coming from the commoners. As they removed wounded and dead riders, along with their horses, Akonde, who had been watching Sossa's reaction, picked up his stool, crossed over, placed it beside Sossa, and sat next to him. Queen Yiram was livid. Not only was her son going against protocol, but with that singular move, Akonde had jeopardized a well-orchestrated plot.

"What an idiot of a son!" she fumed.

"How do you find the Ouidah people? Akonde asked Sossa as he leaned over to him.

"I'll say they're splendid," Sossa replied.

"And your unveiling? The crowd really took to you. Didn't it?" Akonde asked.

"Yes, so it seemed. It was stirring. All has been remarkable so far," said Sossa.

"All? So far?" asked Akonde.

Sossa didn't reply. After a few moments, Akonde said, "I don't blame you. I've always despised the *Miwui* event. Although, I must add, most of our Ouidah women folk cannot bear to see the sport either."

"Ah, I see," Sossa replied. "I wonder why?" he inquired.

"Oh, you know, women have weak stomachs. Of course, some of our men also do. I consider such men wimpy," Akonde said.

"I suppose there's a fine line between disliking something and being wimpy," Sossa observed.

An astute pupil of palatial history and intrigues, Sossa was good at detecting hidden agendas, at assessing the order of battle of both friends and foes. Akonde's statement had ignited carefully studied courtly subterfuges applicable to all royal kingdoms. The warning signals flickered through his mind.

"How can one dislike something that is core to our beliefs, our customs, our traditions? If you were to ask me, I'd say I despise such people," Akonde said.

"I reckon customs and traditions have their place, don't they?" Sossa demanded, looking at his new half-brother.

"Yes, I suppose so," said Akonde. "If it applies to slaves, it takes on a different meaning," Akonde proffered.

"How so?" Sossa asked.

"If they accept the hegemony of sovereigns such as us, they must be of inferior stock, which means they're incapable of taking care of their own affairs. That means we can use them as we please, for example, in *Miwui*. Don't you agree?" Akonde asked.

"From what you're saying, you must have a deep, well-formed contempt for your slaves. The *Miwui* sport doesn't displease you then, does it?" Sossa asked.

It took Akonde a few seconds to realize that Sossa had unmasked his genuine feelings. A flash of anger and embarrassment spread over his face and disappeared. Sossa noticed and exposed further Akonde's dubious claims.

"So, you believe we're of a superior stock?" Sossa pressed.

"Certainly," Akonde answered.

"And this condition, you think, is permanent?" Sossa asked.

"Yes. Isn't it obvious?" Akonde asked, unable to suppress his incredulity.

"How did we arrive at this condition?" Sossa asked.

"The gods, Sossa. The gods. Aren't there any in Dahomey? Don't your people have any cosmology? Your kings. Don't they represent the gods and may decide who lives and who dies?" Akonde asked.

"Yes, we do. Like you, there is *Nana Buluku, Mawu-Lisa,* and a host of other gods. And we do have a sense of history," Sossa replied.

"I wonder what history has to do with this?" Akonde asked.

"History tells us that the fortunes of kings and kingdoms change. Didn't those of your grandfather change?" Sossa asked.

Akonde was silent. Sossa would be a more formidable foe than he realized.

Another group of contestants entered the arena. Instead of ten combatants, twelve horse riders arrived in the ring. The crowd was euphoric. Two of them wore masks. As the *Ojakari* drums thundered, the masked riders rode around the circular arena, motioning to the audience and urging it to cheer even louder. In front of the king's dais, they brought their horses to a halt and did maneuvers with them. The riders released two doves from side pouches. As they soared into the sky, the masked riders removed arrows from their quivers and shot them. The crowd's applause became contagious. These were, by far, the best archers they had ever seen. The drums roared once again, signaling the onset of the next context. With a hardly noticeable nod from Queen Yiram, the masked riders rode their horses around the arena at full gallop.

Everything happened fast. Two arrows from the two riders found their target. In an instant, King Dozan lay sprawled on the royal dais. He was lifeless. Still leaning into the gifted prince, the clueless Akonde put a wrinkle in their plan to eliminate Sossa as well. It was too risky to take down Sossa. That sempiternal adage couldn't have been truer: *It's difficult to throw a stone at a lizard that's clinging to a pot.* By the time the king's guards and the crowd could react to what had happened, the two masked riders had already disappeared through the entrance to the holding pen.

Chapter 22

The *N'Nonmiton* leader put her hands through the beads around Queen Ena Sunu's waist, pulled her to her powerful body, and murmured in her ear.

"Appears you've accomplished most of the goals you set out for yourself. Haven't you?" Her breath, which smelled like the mild-scented *marula* fruit she had just eaten, was hot in Queen Ena Sunu's ear and on her neck. As Sintana Fansinnou's lips trembled on the three gold-studded silver-necklace around the queen's neck, Queen Ena Sunu's hands sketched the contours of Sintana Fansinnou's powerful shoulders and inched their way towards her buttocks.

"How do you know I've reached most of my goals?" Queen Ena Sunu asked as she pulled the *N'Nonmiton* leader even closer, wedging her thigh into her crotch. Sintana Fansinnou moaned and said, "For starters, you've cut down the number of slaves passing from Dahomey and Allada to *Forte São João Baptista de Ajudá*."

"Yes? Continue," Queen Ena Sunu urged, reciprocating Sintana Fansinnou's moaning that came from a deep place inside of the *N'Nonmiton* warrior.

"Despite being a *kluvi nɔví*, you're the most powerful queen in the kingdom," Sintana Fansinnou said as she lifted one of Queen Ena Sunu's hands over her head. She was wearing a blouse that exposed her magnificent shoulders and high rounded, firm, full breasts. Sintana Fansinnou ran the other hand from one side of the queen's stomach, working her way slowly up until she came to an exposed breast and cupped it.

"You've yet to tell me how you accomplished all of that," Sintana Fansinnou said as she caressed the already swelling nipple. Queen Ena Sunu gasped and said, "I'm not interested in the how, but in what's still to be done."

"As a soldier, I always want to know not only the hows but also my losses and gains before confronting the future," Sintana Fansinnou murmured into Queen Ena Sunu's ear, allowing her breath to tickle the earlap.

Queen Ena Sunu didn't reply. She guided Sintana Fansinnou's other hand to the exposed second breast. Her moaning intensified.

"I can tell you about one of my losses if you'd like," said Sintana Fansinnou, whose lips were just but an inch away from the queen's.

"Uh-huh, go on," Queen Ena Sunu whispered.

"Time," said Sintana Fansinnou.

"Time?" Queen Ena Sunu asked.

"Yes, time. Time lost aside from you. Time lost when my heart fluttered to the point of shattering anytime I saw you in public but couldn't touch you or be with you," said Sintana Fansinnou.

"You're with me now," said Queen Ena Sunu.

"Yes. But for how long? How long can we endure this?" Sintana Fansinnou said, running her tongue over the queen's lips as she slipped one of her hands and sought the queen's soft and yielding flesh.

Queen Ena Sunu whimpered. "Soon, I hope," she groaned.

"How soon is soon? That's not good enough for us. Don't you see?" asked the *N'Nonmiton* warrior.

"It will be sooner than you realize. Sossa is now a gifted prince in Ouidah. He's finally with his father, who he'll supplant in no time. Favi will succeed King Gesa before the brainless king knows it," said Queen Ena Sunu.

Sintana Fansinnou stopped and pulled away. In the semi-bright bedroom, the warrior saw her reflection in the queen's brown eyes. Eyes that expressed no emotions in public. Yet in this space, at this moment, they acknowledged arrested desires eager to be unleashed and detonated. They also announced for the first time a secret, a hidden truth.

"Sossa is with his father?" Sintana Fansinnou inquired.

"Yes."

"How's that possible?"

"He came to visit as Ouidah's crown prince eighteen years ago," said the queen.

"Shit!" Sintana Fansinnou blurted out. The revelation was startling in its magnitude; its genesis kept so concealed from her she could only conclude that she didn't know the monarch. Sintana Fansinnou was familiar with the custom and protocol that underpinned royal visits from other kingdoms. She recalled her first meeting with Queen Ena Sunu when she recruited her for her cause. The soldier had been skeptical, but the more she thought of it, the more the queen had made significant strides: now a defense force, the *N'Nonmiton* warriors no longer took part in slave raids; slave trading had dwindled to a trickle, and palm oil production had supplanted it. What Queen Ena Sunu revealed about her two sons and had planned for them extended beyond stifling the slave trade. It was personal. This was a woman with latent strategic designs in her head she had been implementing in plain sight. A woman, who without verbalizing it, was scalping like a skillful butcher and wounding systems and institutions that had abused and continued to violate by wresting from the body of the other.

The *N'Nonmiton* leader walked to Queen Ena Sunu, plucked her, and carried her to the bed in the room. They were in a house at a secret location that Eunuch Hounsa and Mindivi, the queen's servant, had found for their infrequent trysts. Queen Ena Sunu didn't utter a word as she leaned on her elbows and watched Sintana Fansinnou taking off her clothes. The slow and methodical manner in which the warrior discarded her clothes, announcing a familiar tall, black, and sound body that knew how to give and to receive pleasure, bewitched the queen. Queen Ena Sunu was breathing hard in anticipation by the time her clothes came off. The dim light in the room mirrored the slight sweat bursting out on her brow. She discarded her blouse and flung her wrap before Sintana Fansinnou got into the bed.

They didn't have time for preambles. Queen Ena Sunu's mouth

found Sintana Fansinnou's as their tongues wiggled and interlaced. The warrior caressed the queen's soft flesh. Her hips followed and responded to the *N'Nonmiton* leader's hand with rhythmic motion. Both women moaned as they felt themselves carried into a space where desire and pure sensuality coalesced into a consummate conflagration that burned their bodies and souls. Just as the thickening vortex of sensation pulled them further and further into crevasses eager to explode and rouse involuntary indecipherable spasms and groans, a frenetic knock hammered the door, followed by Hounsa's distressed voice.

"Her Royal Highness, bad news, bad news," cried the faithful servant. Both women got up and dressed hurriedly. Several thoughts tore through Queen Ena Sunu's mind as she walked towards the door. Had someone found out about their hideaway? Were King Gesa's guards outside ready to arrest them? Sure, she had defanged Queen Kin-Ha and had disgraced her and Migan Nagoba at the abortive trial. She was the last person to assume that one could take things for granted in the Dahomeyan court. If her suppositions were true, this was going to be their ultimate revenge. Such was her turmoil when the monarch opened the door to the living room.

"Sossa!" exclaimed Hounsa.

"What's wrong with Sossa?" Queen Ena Sunu demanded in consternation. Hounsa was silent.

"Can you answer me? Has something happened to Sossa?" the queen inquired again.

"They assassinated King Dozan at the gifting, but Sossa's whereabouts are unknown."

"Sossa is dead?"

"Nobody knows. In the confusion and panic, the prince disappeared. Nobody has seen him."

"And Azonton?"

"No report of him either," announced Hounsa.

Queen Ena drew a deep breath. If nobody had seen Sossa and his *Ylon* Azonton, it meant one thing: they were at the safe house. Etiquette prescribed that the Ouidah king hosted the Dahomey entourage in his palace. Steeped in matters of safety and security,

Azonton found a location outside of the monarch's court for the young prince.

Azonton relieved Queen Ena Sunu when he stepped forward to go to Ouidah with Sossa. He was escorting, yet again, another gifted royal family member to a different kingdom. In his characteristic dry humor, he expressed to his cousin he had turned into a professional itinerant for gifted princesses and princes. Azonton dedicated his entire life to her and to her sons. And for that, Queen Ena Sunu was indebted to her cousin. He was Sossa's and Favi's counselor and personal aide in matters dealing with courtly decorum and political intrigues. He remained unmarried to consecrate his life to help the queen bring up her sons. They must become kings who wouldn't hawk their own or gamble on the inevitability of their positions because that was what the gods willed. With King Dozan's death, Queen Ena Sunu reckoned that her long-term plans for Ouidah were now in tatters. It would be worse, she realized, if Sossa wound up dead. Even if he were alive, what was the likelihood of replacing King Dozan? She shifted around to glance at Sintana Fansinnou, who stood beside her with an unsettled expression.

*****

Assassinations were nothing unusual in Ouidah's long history. None of them had been, however, as flagrant and as brazen as the one that had unfolded before thousands of its citizens during Sossa's gifting. Ouidah tradition called for a successor within seven days after the king's death and before his burial. It was the sole window available to transfer the dead king's spirit into the new monarch. The king's death created a legal crisis because they had always declared a successor to the throne before the king's death. The kingmakers had to designate a successor from among the princes, including one whose pedigree, although respected, they didn't know well. Selected based on their expertise of Ouidah history and cultural norms, the twenty kingmakers assembled in a cloistered space next to the throne room, a day after the monarch's death. Amamu, head of the brokers, spoke first.

"My dear brothers, these are gloomy hours for our kingdom, and we confront an unprecedented situation. I hope we can deliberate with absolute care, as we always do," he paused and continued." We have a choice to make between Akonde and Sossa."

"Isn't the pick obvious?" asked Atakora, the youngest kingmaker. "Akonde is King Dozan's son. He was born in Ouidah and appreciates its practices and its people. Sossa is an outsider, a stranger to these lands," he added.

"Kingmaker Atakora, although your views are correct, you may not have considered other factors," Amamu said.

"I concur," said Ajohan, the second oldest kingmaker. "Sossa may not be King Dozan's direct offspring, but he has a lawful right to claim the king's scepter. Isn't our history rife with gifted princes becoming kings?" he inquired.

"Why don't we use the benchmarks we use in our selection?" asked another kingmaker.

"We could, but that will be unfair to Sossa," Amamu responded.

"Well, we can't do anything about that," said yet another kingmaker.

After considerable debate, a consensus emerged: a *Kayaso*—the kingmakers, would hold an open parley on the seventh day of the king's death. The two contenders would appear before the council, make statements, and answer questions, after which they would decide. Because Sossa had, by far, fewer proponents at the Ouidah court, they proposed to send a message to Dahomey for another contingent to supplement the one that escorted him for the gifting. They called for individuals in the second delegation to have intimate knowledge of Sossa's temperament and fitness to be king. This stipulation was crucial: the kingmakers could order anybody from either side to answer specific queries about the candidates.

Queen Yiram was furious when she received the kingmakers' verdict. Her well-orchestrated scheme was coming apart. She didn't foresee these hiccups when she set her plan into motion. Had they eliminated Sossa with King Dozan, she wouldn't have had to fret so much. The prospect of a *Kayaso* terrified her. An open parley could expose Akonde's many deficiencies. It was time to activate and deploy the backup plan.

*****

Queen Yiram had never entered *Forte São João Baptista de Ajudá*. She didn't have to. But desperate times called for desperate measures. She left the palace with her cortege shortly after midday, the same day the kingmakers decided on the open parley. Among her retinue was Hanto Tona, a twenty-eight-year-old man with a lean wrestler's body, black hair slicked down with shea butter oil, a pretty face with full lips, and inquisitive eyes. He was one of the agents that Queen Ena Sunu, with King Gesa's blessing, had planted in the Ouidah court and in some of its most sensitive institutions long before Sossa's gifting. With similar cultural practices and shared common languages such as Fon, Gen, and Fulfulde, these moles infiltrated the Ouidah court without difficulty.

Pedro de Barbosa, along with Kosi Aholuvi and five of the viceroy's escorts, welcomed Queen Yiram and her retinue at the entrance to the fort. Something in Kosi Aholuvi flittered when he noticed Hanto Tona. It had been a long while since he found such a pretty man. The first time he had felt that way several years ago was in Edo, the capital city of the Kingdom of Benin, where he was born and served as an attendant in Emperor Orire's court. Kosi Aholuvi had moved up through the ranks at the palace. Besides the four languages that included Edo, Yoruba, Fon, and Fulfulde that he spoke, he picked up Portuguese from the Brazilian and Portuguese slave merchants who traded with the monarch. Kosi Aholuvi became a vital employee at court. Many sought his services, including those of the opposite sex who couldn't resist his charm and comeliness. He rebuffed blatant sexual overtures, choosing to stick to his role as a lowly palace attendant. Matters changed when Odion, the Emperor's son, cornered him in one of the palace's many halls spread around the court. Odion's brazen move surprised Kosi Aholuvi, who had admired him as a young, outgoing prince. Like him, the prince harbored similar proclivities. Things escalated between them. Dark corners and uninhabited rooms turned into planned and unplanned trysts. Everything came to a head when Esivi, Odion's fiancé, found Kosi Aholuvi and Odion in a compromised position. That night, Kosi Aholuvi left the mansion and the Kingdom of Benin for Ouidah. His linguistic abilities found him working for Federico Soares de Souza, the Portuguese Governor to Dahomey.

"Welcome to *Forte São João Baptista de Ajudá*," Pedro de Barbosa said, bowing.

"Thank you, Viceroy Pedro de Barbosa," said Queen Yiram.

Bypassing the entrance to the fort's dungeons, Pedro de Barbosa introduced his visitors to the large dining room on the third floor, where they had provided a sumptuous lunch on a long mahogany table. Queen Yiram wasn't in the mood to eat.

"Events haven't turned out as we planned," she declared.

"Yes, so it seems," Pedro de Barbosa responded.

A moment of silence followed.

"I don't mean to be disrespectful, but if the queen had presented me with the details of her plans when we met a few days earlier, we might have warded off the present mess. Doesn't she think?" Pedro de Barbosa asked, searching into Queen Yiram's eyes.

"Only fools think arrows always adhere to a straight path. I don't think you could have managed any better. But that's not why I am here."

"What's on her majesty's mind?"

"The kingmakers will hold a *Kayaso*, a parley, in six days. I'm not confident of the outcome. In fact, I am doubtful Akonde will come out ahead."

"So?"

"So, I have arranged for you to meet with General Togodo, Minister of War and Defense, tonight. He's willing to mobilize soldiers that your men helped train. Along with your small group of guards, you shouldn't have any problem invading the royal palace should they adopt Sossa as Ouidah's next king."

"And what is the queen requesting?"

"You're a smart man, Viceroy Pedro de Barbosa. Apply your imagination. I'm confident with General Togodo, you could come up with a plan suited to meet our goal."

It turned out hunger pangs waylaid Queen Yiram once she

carried out her mission. As she sat to eat with Pedro de Barbosa, her five accompanying maids in attendance, including Hanto Tona, evacuated the chamber. He had overheard what he desired to gather. He strolled towards one terrace on the third floor. On this mid-afternoon, the blue Atlantic Ocean flouted its vastness from the shore to a distant horizon that molded itself into a speck.

"Beautiful sight, isn't it?"

Hanto Tona spun around to discover Kosi Aholuvi settling next to him.

"Yes. And terrifying," said Hanto Tona.

"How so?" asked Kosi Aholuvi.

"To be thrown into that huge ocean if one doesn't know how to swim. Traversing that mass to foreign lands with no certainty of ever returning. Wouldn't that be terrifying for anyone, especially those captives you have in the dungeons?" asked Hanto Tona.

Kosi Aholuvi was quiet for a moment. His heart kept quivering as he stayed next to Hanto Tona. It had been ages since he felt that way. He wasn't sure what to do with his feelings. He'd been acting as a mediator between the Dahomey, Ouidah, and Allada kings and the *yovos*. First came Federico Soares de Souza, then Governor Belarmino, and now Pedro de Barbosa. As he drew in the subtle smell of shea butter cream fused with the fragrance of twisted jasmine that Hanto Tona exuded, Kosi Aholuvi understood why he thrust himself so into the role of broker for the *yovos*. It wasn't because of the clout that the position presented him as he thought: he wished to forget Odion and suppress any latent urges that could have deleterious consequences. As he cast a cursory glance at Hanto Tona, he realized how mistaken he was to put those feelings and desires under wraps. But was it his fault? Where could he have expressed them? And how? He wondered if he hadn't turned into a prisoner like those slaves he helped oversee. Kosi Aholuvi didn't have time to answer any of these questions before Hanto Tona interrupted him.

"This is an impregnable fort in which you live with the viceroy. Isn't it?"

"Yes. Built to repel any external attacks. Yet, like all things in life, there's always a weak link," Kosi Aholuvi said as he lay his hand on Hanto Tona's shoulder.

"You don't mean it," Hanto Tona said.

"Oh, yes, and I can show you if you came back tonight," Kosi Aholuvi said, rubbing Hanto Tona in the back.

Hanto Tona understood Kosi Aholuvi's intentions. He was a spy, and he would do whatever was necessary, except that Kosi Aholuvi didn't recognize that he was a eunuch who, over time, had lost his libido and sexual desire for both men and women.

*****

If anyone could string people along, it was Hanto Tona. He had agreed to meet with Kosi Aholuvi the same night Pedro de Barbosa and his henchmen planned a visit to General Togodo. Hanto Tona alerted Azonton to the Queen's and the Viceroy's plans before his rendezvous with Kosi Aholuvi. Azonto instructed him to find the fort's munition storage room, its secret entrances, and the number of sentinels they posted at night.

"You came," Kosi Aholuvi said when Hanto Tona showed up at the east end of the fort that overlooked the ocean. It was a full moon, and twinkling stars, along with their dying brethren that crisscrossed the sky, bejeweled the firmament. The furious waves that crashed the rocks on the beach and Fort Ajuda's walls weren't sufficient to detract from the splendor of a warm tropical moonlight that penetrated every inch of the landscape surrounding the fort and beyond.

"Why wouldn't I come?"

"I don't know. This is the first time that I'm encountering someone like you since I turned up in Ouidah several years ago."

"Someone like me?"

"Yes. Someone with whom I'm comfortable. A person who understands what it means to have tucked away things about himself for so many years."

"Oh, I see," Hanto Tona said, paused for a minute, and asked, "Don't you think you're making assumptions? You met me only a few hours ago. What things do you suppose I've kept buried?"

"Profound thoughts? Deep feelings?" said Kosi Aholuvi.

"Do you have any dreams and deep sentiments that need unearthing?" Hanto Tona asked.

Kosi Aholuvi wasn't sure how to respond. Didn't Hanto Tona understand the meaning behind his invitation? He hadn't recoiled when he touched him earlier that day. He felt an urge to touch him again, to caress the firm square shoulders that sat straight on his powerful body, to breathe in that strong smell of shea butter cream and twisted jasmine that had lingered in his mind the full day as he wondered if Hanto Tona would come. Now that he was with him, and with that familiar smell permeating the air, he didn't know how to activate the fantasies that had plagued him the whole time as he anticipated this moment. He was feeling a most extraordinary intoxication of lust for Hanto Tona, and he wasn't certain if Hanto Tona's queries were a prelude to something dramatic about to happen between them, as he had hoped. But these questions! Was Hanto Tona the kind who required time to know someone first by asking him to spell everything out before he plunged into something that he had interred as he himself had done? Better not rush things. Let them evolve. Kosi Aholuvi counseled himself. Hadn't he told Hanto Tona that, as with any impregnable fort, *Forte São João Baptista de Ajudá*, which had been his home for so many years, had its secrets, its weak links? He should start there. Perhaps Hanto Tona also had his weak links. What could be more exciting than unearthing these nexuses? Yes, show him the secrets of the fort. Take him to the wine cellar and share a bottle of wine with him. Yes, what an excellent idea! He needed to be classy, as he had seen Governor Soares do. Pedro de Barbosa drank little. Sure, he entertained, but he lacked the same finesse and class as his former governor. Yes, that was what he should do. He ought to be deliberate.

"Would you like to enter the fort?" Kosi Aholuvi asked.

It surprised Hanto Tona that rather than answering his question, his host opted to introduce him to a space Azonton had instructed him to spy.

"Are we entering through the main gate? You must have sentries guarding the fort. Don't you?" Hanto Tona asked.

"The guards are on the ground floor, where the dungeons are situated. A few also attend to the terraces on the third floor, looking out on the sea. They remain by the cannons and are ready to use them should any armada be heading this way," said Kosi Aholuvi.

Hanto Tona was silent.

"To tell you the truth, the patrols should be asleep at their posts, as they often are at this time of the night. Besides, Pedro de Barbosa hasn't equipped them with any of the many Flintlock guns that he's tucked away in the armory," said Kosi Aholuvi.

"Doesn't it trouble your viceroy that his sentinels sleep instead of guarding the fort?" asked Hanto Tona.

"Not really. Who'd wish to attack this fort? How would they enter even if they did? We have a good relationship with the kingdoms with which we trade. An assault is inconceivable," said a confident Kosi Aholuvi.

Hanto Tona made a mental note to himself. "So, we're using the entrance?" he inquired.

"No. Follow me," said Kosi Aholuvi.

Both men stepped around the fort to the north edge of the building, where a small, iron grated gate, five feet high and four-and-a-half feet wide, sat at the base of the thirty-foot wall. This was the exit the slaves passed through as they loaded them onto boats that took them to the slave ships. It was the door of no return. Ten feet away from the gate was a nondescript, rotten boat that leaned against the fort's embankment, along with a rusted cannon pointing straight up as though ready to fire into the sky. Kosi Aholuvi stomped on the space between the dinghy and the cannon, producing a thud, thud sound. The guide knelt and, with his bare hands, scraped off the sand and leaves until he felt the handle of a heavy trapdoor. With Hanto Tona's help, they opened it.

"There! I've not come through this door in a while," said Kosi Aholuvi, who lit an oil lamp that revealed a long, narrow shaft. Bending at the waist, the men made their way through the dank, hot, and musty tunnel that invited little air. Sounds from the sea were muted midway through the shaft. After what seemed a long time, they came to a door on the floor of a room that served as a wine cellar. It relieved both men to stand up and to mollify their strained backs. Kosi Aholuvi placed the lamp on a wooden table in the middle of the room. Shelves of wine bottles lined the four walls. The choices were abundant, and Kosi Aholuvi had his preferences. He sauntered over to the rack that housed French wines and selected one. He opened it, took a swig, and passed the bottle to Hanto Tona. So much for finesse and elegance! He thought to himself.

Hanto Tona hadn't forgotten his mission. By dawn, he had extracted from Kosi Aholuvi the information he needed. The munition room was next to the cellar, and the large iron key to it rested on a peg next to the entrance to the cellar. Hanto Tona knew that he had to give Kosi Aholuvi something in return.

"How did you come to work for Pedro de Barbosa" he asked Kosi Aholuvi after they had returned to the basement. A second wine bottle stood between both men, who sat on the stone floor.

"Oh, it's a long story. It's the feelings I had for someone long ago in the Kingdom of Benin, where I was born. Those sentiments came at a high price. But I hope they don't hurt me again, as I open up my cloistered self."

"The man I see sitting here doesn't strike me as opening any cloistered self. Are you?" asked Hanto Tona.

"I'm afraid I have the same strong feelings towards you, Hanto Tona," Kosi Aholuvi said as he inched towards his guest.

"I have similar feelings as well. However, I will feel them better when my head is clear. Not after drinking. Shall we meet again tomorrow at the same time?" Hanto Tona said as he stood up.

"Yes, of course. Tomorrow," Kosi Aholuvi said as he led the way out of the cellar and through the tunnel that took them next to the door of no return.

*****

Queen Ena Sunu received details about Queen Yiram's visit to *Forte São João Baptista de Ajudá*, as she prepared for the trip to Ouidah for the *Kayaso*. Like Queen Yiram, events of the past few days had shattered her plans. She hadn't been sure about how to proceed until they briefed her about Queen Yiram's conversation with Pedro de Barbosa. The intelligence they had gathered pointed to a Queen Yiram who was a ruthless campaigner for her son. What perturbed Queen Ena Sunu more than anything was the extent to which the Ouidah queen would go to achieve her goal. She summoned Sintana Fansinnou and updated her on the latest intelligence.

"You said Hanto Tona went to *Forte São João Baptista de Ajudá*?" asked Sintana Fansinnou.

"Yes, and he has invaluable information about the place," said the queen.

"Is the fort vulnerable?" asked the *N'Nonmiton* leader.

"So it appears," said Queen Ena Sunu.

"Is Pedro de Barbosa still buying slaves?" asked Sintana Fansinnou.

"Yes. What does that have to do with our plans?" Queen Ena Sunu asked, exasperated.

"It has everything to do with it. Based on the intelligence, we can engage the *N'Nonmiton*."

"Only the *N'Nonmiton*? Shouldn't we call upon the entire Dahomey army? This is Sossa we're talking about, Sintana Fansinnou," said the agitated queen.

"A full column of armed Dahomey soldiers marching to Ouidah will set up a needless alarm. It might indicate an invasion, having just lost its king. That's not our objective. Remember, they have their spies among us," responded the *N'Nonmiton* leader.

"A regiment of your warriors raises similar concerns," countered Queen Ena Sunu.

"Not if two hundred *N'Nonmiton* fighters accompanied you dressed up as dancers and musicians to support Sossa during the *Kayaso*, and another fifty approached *Forte São João Baptista de Ajudá* as slaves for sale. How could such women present a threat?" Sintana Fansinnou asked, a slight smile crossing over her face.

Chapter 23

The vast, oval-shaped throne room overflowed with Ouidah's ministers, royal family members, and luminaries, including Queen Yiram, General Togodo, and Viceroy Pedro de Barbosa. Across from them, the Dahomeyan dignitaries occupied the front seats. Pedro de Barbosa was seeing, for the first time, Queen Ena Sunu. *So, this is the queen who, rumors had it, had set into motion the systematic assault on a trade that had enriched him and should continue to do so if the status quo remained the same,* he mused. The colorful batik fabric, along with the life-size statues of gods and goddesses flanking both sides of the chamber, added to the solemn event that would have to unfold.

The twenty kingmakers rested on the raised platform on which the king's throne used to stand. They would re-introduce it after the election. Sossa and Akonde sat on two high stools facing the kingmakers. Backers of both contestants sat behind them. The lucky, ordinary Ouidah citizens who snatched up the hundred seats reserved for them, sat behind Sossa's and Akonde's patrons. A throng of well-wishers and supporters waited on the open patio next to the courtyard. The atmosphere was subdued, jubilation mixed with mourning. They had lost a monarch, but naming his replacement was always an eventful affair. Sounds of muted drumming hovered in the air from many dancing and singing groups. One such group was the *N'Nonmiton* warriors, turned musicians. The *Kayaso* began with the pouring of libation, accompanied by a solemn rhythm of only a single *Ojakari* drum. Kingmaker Amamu spoke.

"People of Ouidah and Dahomey, this is an extraordinary occasion. Never in Ouidah's history have we had a *Kayaso* to choose between two fine princes, one of whom would replace our beloved king," he paused and went on. "As you'll see, the *Kayaso* is an open process. The princes make brief statements, after which the kingmakers ask them questions. We could also call on any of their patrons to tell the kingmakers why they consider their candidate would make a better king for the great Ouidah Kingdom. The princes aren't at liberty to ask one another, the kingmakers, or anyone questions. The twenty kingmakers will adjourn and return with their verdict. This, my fellow Ouidians, is how we plan to conduct the *Kayaso*."

Kingmaker Amamu had barely ended before Akonde shot up, spun around, and waved to his followers. He was six feet tall with jet black hair, wide brown eyes, low cheekbones, and semi-thick lips on a round face. The smile that splattered that face this morning exuded confidence. Sitting not too far from him and Viceroy Pedro de Barbosa, Queen Yiram had an anguished expression on her face. A future king was required to show restraint and courtliness, attributes that her son lacked and wasn't circumspect enough to conceal at this most crucial moment. Didn't he know the *Kayaso* was multifaceted, designed to discover the future king's temperament and worthiness? She had asked Kalesea Adibo, one of Akonde's counselors, to have him do mock *Kayaso*s to prepare for the real thing, but her son brushed them aside, as he had often done throughout his young adult life. If Queen Yiram had been an honest broker, she would have been the first person to recognize her son's many foibles. Here was a young prince who disregarded with total abandonment normal palatial protocol and pranced around the palace bare-chested, taking pride in his robust torso, his wide shoulders, and chest, which he flaunted with fervor before women who were young or old, married or unmarried, fertile or barren, celibate or prurient, willing or unwilling, who crossed his path, an improbable proposition since he had the unique gift of appearing nowhere and everywhere that women assembled. These encounters would have been harmless, except that Akonde had an uncanny instinct, an intuitive genius, to ferret out those women who showed the remotest interest in him. Swift to the core, such women, irrespective of their stations at court and beyond, soon found themselves among the trophies that lined his mental cabinet. It was an impressive one at seventeen, and Queen Yiram knew it. So did she know of her son's visits to *Casa da Silva*. Kingmaker Amamu's voice punctuated the queen's thoughts.

"With Prince Akonde already on his feet, why doesn't he open with a statement?"

The hall became silent as Akonde cleared his throat and turned to observe the audience with his back to the kingmakers.

"Of all the kingdoms, Ouidah is the greatest and the most powerful. It only makes sense that whoever succeeds the late king, my beloved father, is the leader who comes from Ouidah, knows its history, its customs, and its people's way of being. It must be a person who doesn't critique our norms and traditions, such as the *Miwui*. We require an Ouidian on the throne and not a foreigner."

There was applause as Akonde sat down.

"Could Prince Sossa make his statement now?" Kingmaker Amamu asked.

"Yes, indeed, Kingmaker Amamu," Sossa began as he stood up and walked down the aisle that separated the supporting groups. It was hard to ignore the extraordinary resemblance between Akonde and Sossa. However, whereas Akonde had a round face, Sossa's was oblong.

"People of Ouidah, thank you for welcoming me to your magnificent kingdom, which I'm proud to state, is now mine. Prince Akonde was correct when he characterized Ouidah as a great and powerful kingdom. We know from our history that it was the famous King Haffon who helped to make Ouidah an important trading nation with the Europeans and with our neighbors. Other kings, except for King Tezifon, have built on King Haffon's legacy. Our late King Dozan played his part until just a few days ago," Sossa paused, allowing what he said to sink in.

"Should I be fortunate enough to be chosen as your monarch, the first thing I'll do is to find who was behind King Dozan's assassination. I promise you, we will identify his killers and bring them to justice. As your king, I pledge to offer you a dynamic leadership. Rather than a stagnant present, we require a future that, although values our customs and traditions, embraces fresh ideas and alternative ways of doing things. Together we, as a people, can build a kingdom in which we invest in our own communities to form a more powerful and stable Ouidah," Sossa concluded and sat down.

Deafening applause broke from both sides of the aisle. A livid Pedro de Barbosa sat stone faced. If anyone could detect nuances, Pedro de Barbosa was. Sossa's subtle statement left no doubt what his priorities would be if he became king. He would lift a page out of his mother's script if what the rumors said were true. Slave trading would be a thing of the past as well in Ouidah. Queen Yiram's expression, when he spun around to look at her, told him she understood what Sossa, along with his mother, stood for. Sossa didn't have to spell out the fact that he despised slaving as much as his mother did. Queen Ena Sunu, together with *Ylon* Azonton had done enough to etch into Sossa's and Favi's minds that they couldn't and shouldn't countenance slave trading in Dahomey and Ouidah. The two princes knew Allada's history and their grandfather's ignominious end. Their role in the systematic thwarting of the trade was certain, except that for Sossa, it was happening earlier than all had expected.

As Queen Yiram listened to the continuing applause, she realized her fears were being confirmed: Akonde was no match for Sossa. As the kingmakers' questions and the contestants' responses proceeded that morning, no one had any doubts about which of the two princes would make a better king. Although arrogant, Akonde wasn't stupid. Like his mother, he saw the coveted crown slipping away from him. Royal glamor had fascinated him as a young boy. His father's regalia during durbars, festivals, and royal visitations from other kingdoms enthralled and intrigued him. The gilded palanquin King Dozan rode on the shoulders of courtiers, along with the golden crown that bedecked the king's head, captivated him. The king's power and that office's perks might go to Sossa, a stranger. A fit of irrepressible anger engulfed him. Here was a man who, he thought, didn't bear the sight of slave horse riders dying during the *Miwui* event. Neither did he appreciate arrows dangling from the torsos of the slave fighters.

If Sossa was so gutless, it remained to reason that he wouldn't be much of a wrestler. Courtesy of Azonton, who had spread the rumor, Sossa was as effeminate as they came, despite his imposing physique. It wasn't as though he, Akonde, was a great wrestler either. He had been flippant and lackadaisical in his approach to learning the sport, a requirement for the kingdom's princes and males. Still, he wagered defeating Sossa in a wrestling contest. An idea ran through his head. The kingmakers shouldn't reveal their decision based on the *Kayaso*. A wrestling match would provide another dimension to the selection process. Akonde's impulsive nature sometimes prevented him from weighing his ideas before acting. It looked as yet this was going to be one of those moments because, with no explanation, he rose and addressed the kingmakers as they prepared to signal the end of the public parley.

"Kingmaker Amamu, may I approach you?" Akonde asked, much to the audience's consternation. The prince was breaking the rules the kingmakers spelled out at the *Kayaso*'s beginning. Eyes fixed on him, Amamu paused for a while before responding.

"I don't know who the council will select as our next king. It's possible it might be you. In that yet unknown future capacity, and out of respect for the throne, I'll allow you to ask whatever questions you may have, only if they serve us in our deliberations."

"Yes, very much so," responded Akonde with a generous smile. "There's a good reason our customs demand that whoever is Ouidah's king possess physical attributes that befit the throne," Akonde said and paused for a few moments.

A puzzled look settled on many faces. Did Prince Sossa have any physical debilities that weren't apparent? None that anyone could see. He looked as fit as Akonde himself. Why bring up physical attributes? Many pondered.

"To make certain we have a strong and fit king, I propose a wrestling contest between Prince Sossa and me," Akonde said.

Gasps erupted from the gallery.

"The kingmakers shouldn't base their choice entirely on the

contest's outcome. The challenge will only present a further scope to the election," Akonde added.

"What an ass," Kalesea Adibo, Akonde's chief counselor, murmured as he stood up and made his way to the prince. He whispered in his ear. "My lord, you size up before you cut. You've not accomplished that yet. This is not the time nor the place to do so. Please retract the challenge," said the courtier.

It was too late. After a brief consultation, the kingmakers agreed. The wrestling contest would take place that evening on the palace's massive open patio. Azonton had a wry smile on his face.

*****

Spectators jammed the large compound and courtyard. Those who couldn't access the palace grounds stood outside the gates. A high expectation characterized the atmosphere since wrestling in Dahomey and Ouidah was a sport the people followed in towns and villages to celebrate the end of the harvest season. In Dahomey, the celebration culminated in a championship match between the top wrestlers from the kingdom. The fact that the spectators were about to experience this pugilistic art form at the royal level added excitement. The stakes were higher because the ultimate winner of the contest could emerge as their future king.

As with all wrestling contests, two events preceded Sossa's and Akonde's match. Before the contestants appeared at the scene, praise singers recited poems and sang songs that featured the pedigree of both princes, rousing the crowd's excitement and the wrestler's spirit. Clowns performed a parody of the sport and other activities in the square and entertained the public. The three referees arrived, followed by Sossa and Akonde. They both wore tight briefs with amulets around their waists, knees, and elbows. These talismans conferred protection, luck, strength, courage, and invincibility. The wrestling arena had a fifteen-foot circular perimeter surrounded by sandbags. The main referee explained the contest rules to the combatants and to the public.

"Both wrestlers will fight with their bare hands. The contest's object is for a wrestler to knock down his challenger. When the wrestler's head, back, or buttocks touches the ground, fall out of the circle, or he goes down on all fours—two hands and two knees, we declare him the loser. The goal isn't to hurt the opponent, but to throw him to the ground."

The crowd held its breath when the central referee signaled for the match to begin. Sossa wasn't a stranger to wrestling. A proviso for his training as a Dahomey prince, Sossa and Favi started wrestling when they were five. Azonton, who was their trainer, soon gave way to some of the kingdom's champion wrestlers to instruct the princes. In his bid to instill in Sossa and Favi the idea that they weren't any different from other Dahomeyans, Azonton made sure that he invited boys the ages of the princes who had excelled as young wrestlers in their respective towns or villages to compete with the princes at the palace. The result was that, by the time the twins turned fifteen, they were formidable wrestlers.

Sossa and Akonde assayed each other as they circled the ring. Akonde feigned picking something from the sand, expecting Sossa to lunge at his midriff, but Sossa was much too skillful to fall for that ruse. The circling continued. No one moved, aside from the disruptive motions that both wrestlers made with their arms to disconcert the other. A defensive posture underpinned their respective tactics as the two princes continued the circling act and scowled at each other. After four minutes, the referee rattled the wooden bell and challenged the contestants to engage. Yet nothing happened. Sossa put his fists on his waist, stuck his tongue out, and intensified his stare at Akonde. It was a gesture that went beyond taunt and provocation. It was pure psyching, and Akonde fell for it. In an instant, he lunged.

Sossa, who had expected the charge, caught Akonde's torso from below and stood him up. Both wrestlers engaged each other in a tight grip for several minutes. They were equally matched. The spectators thought the fight would be one of those that could last for ten minutes and beyond. But Sossa maneuvered Akonde back to the sideline. This was a classic move on Sossa's part. The unexpected shift caught Akonde by surprise, driving him to expose his left knee within Sossa's reach. Forcing Akonde's head up, Sossa seized his leg. They tumbled, and within seconds, Akonde was sprawling on his back. The contest was over. Sossa had prevailed!

The kingmakers' decision was quick. They had already decided who to appoint as Ouidah's future king. The outcome of the wrestling match wouldn't have altered much their verdict. Sossa's victory made their ruling even smoother. With a signal from Amamu, they brought the throne to the courtyard in the center of the sandbagged arena.

"Citizens of Ouidah, after a thorough deliberation based on what ensued at the *Kayaso* and at the wrestling match, it is my great duty to announce Ouidah's next king," Amamu said and paused. It charged the atmosphere. Those who couldn't enter the palace's grounds listened with their ears glued to the wall enveloping the palace.

"King Sossa, could you please approach the throne?" Amamu asked.

Jubilant cries and ululations echoed throughout the wide courtyard and beyond. The *Ojakari* drums resounded. Ouidah had a new king! The first part of the crowning happened fast. The kingmakers surrounded their new leader and settled the gilded crown on his head. Voodoo Chief Priest Ikurisiare knelt before the crowned king and performed the ritual of transferring the dead king's spirit into the new monarch. He took King Sossa's right hand and slipped on the ivory wrist bangle that King Dozan and other kings had held before him. An amulet from his predecessor found itself around Sossa's waist. They had soaked it in the water in which they washed King Dozan after he died. They performed the ritual within the designated one week following King Dozan's death.

Having delivered his spirit to the young king, they may now lay to rest King Dozan. King Sossa's formal crowning and presentation to the Ouidah people would occur a fortnight after the late monarch's burial. Prior to that, the new king had to remain unseen by the public and his voice unheard until his formal crowning. The Chief Priest removed the gilded crown and gave it to the royal crown bearer and keeper. They placed a leopard's skin mask on Sossa's face along with a wide-brimmed raffia hat with strands all around it. Together, the mask and hat would make it impossible to see the king's face. The symbolic ritual over, the *N'Nonmiton* warriors, who until a few moments earlier were musicians, quickly formed a thick human wall around King Sossa. No one saw what transpired in the closed circle.

*****

As the people of Ouidah jubilated Sossa's crowning, Queen Yiram, Pedro de Barbosa, and Togodo, the Minister of War and Defense, left the open courtyard quietly. Azonton, Queen Ena Sunu, and Sintana Fansinnou exchanged looks. A couple of days earlier, Pedro de Barbosa received fifty female slaves along with a message that supposedly came from King Gesa: Dahomey's internal political and social problems had mitigated against providing the slave trader as many slaves as he would have wanted. However, things were about to change. The fifty female slaves that were being delivered, at half the cost, were to reaffirm the king's trading partnership with the slave trader. Payment, the message suggested, didn't have to be made immediately.

The presumed overture took Pedro de Barbosa by surprise. What did it mean within the context of the rumors that King Gesa's third wife was orchestrating a complete end to the slave trade? What about the plot to assassinate Sossa if he became the next king? How could he reconcile Sossa's murder with his father's proposition? What if he reneged on his commitments to Queen Yiram and hitched his fortunes on Sossa? Should the Dahomeyan prince become Ouidah's next king, the renewed business relationship with the new king's father might ease slave trading in both kingdoms. But could he thwart the power of Queen Yiram's and General Togodo's joint forces if he, Pedro de Barbosa, jumped ship? The viceroy reckoned the most favorable position for him was an Akonde succession. He could manipulate him and Queen Yiram while preserving a minted alliance with King Gesa. Yet from what Queen Yiram had told him, it appeared as though that possibility was distant. These were the thoughts that assailed Pedro de Barbosa's mind when he responded to King Gesa's gesture. He sent Kosi Aholuvi, along with several of his men, to Dahomey with gifts for the king the same day the slaves appeared.

Pedro de Barbosa hadn't determined what course of action to take before the *Kayaso*. He would decide as the parley progressed, he told himself. But once the contest began, he realized Akonde's candidacy was a lost cause. Yet it became clear to the viceroy that he couldn't abandon ship. How could he? Sossa had broached the possibility of dissolving the slave trade. Wasn't it ample reason to hitch his fortunes to the Ouidian prince? He had put all his chips down on a bad hand, and he had no option but to play it. It made sense he followed Queen Yiram and General Togodo as they slipped out of the open courtyard just when Sossa's crowning was taking place.

Although the three conspirators left Sossa's coronation at the same time, they went their separate ways: Pedro de Barbosa rode *Arion* back to *Forte São João Baptista de Ajudá*, Queen Yiram darted to her quarters, and General Togodo hurried to the army barracks within the lavish palace. They didn't have to exchange any remarks. They had met the preceding night.

As Pedro de Barbosa left the fort for their rendezvous that night in the company of four of his guards, Sintana Fansinnou, together with Hanto Tona and ten *N'Nonmiton* fighters, made their way to the fort and crept through the tunnel. Kosi Aholuvi was still in Dahomey bearing gifts for King Gesa to recognize his putative overtures towards the Brazilian slaver. Most of the sentinels, as Kosi Aholuvi had shown, were not at their posts or were fast asleep. The stealth and the speed with which the *N'Nonmiton* fighters carried out their mission impressed Hanto Tona. Their primary target was *Forte São João Baptista de Ajudá*'s armory.

The castle's munition storage room was well-stocked. Two-hundred Flintlocks guns leaned on the depot's interior wall. Wooden crates packed with mixed lead shots stood along the opposite wall. The *N'Nonmiton* fighters were no strangers to a Flintlock's operation: it employed an ignition system that produced flint-on-steel sparks to ignite a pan of priming powder to fire its main powder charge. Intended for priming on the outside with black powder, it was worthless in the rain if the pan for priming the gunpowder became wet. The *N'Nonmiton* fighters' original plan was to fill the priming pans and the locks on the guns with small amounts of seawater. Hang fires and misfires, they knew from experience, kept good company with wet locks. While this idea appeared tantalizing, its infeasibility soon became apparent. To immobilize the guns, they clogged the touch holes in the guns' rear with mud. This was a breach since the combustion of the powder charge went through the touchhole. The plug would hinder the spark from hitting the primary charge.

All the guns in the armory suffered this fate except for the twenty they set aside. If Pedro de Barbosa hadn't been so preoccupied with the plot he had been hatching with Queen Yiram or hadn't been just so obsessed with buying more slaves, he would've looked closer at the fifty female slaves who had shown up as a semi gifted chattel and noted that they weren't ordinary slaves. It was these slaves Sintana Fansinnou sought in one of the female dungeons. Her goal wasn't to free these *N'Nonmiton* fighters. They would form either the invading force from within the fort or the unwelcome rearguard of General Togodo's troops. They provided each of the fifty warriors with the *N'Nonmiton*'s most deadly choice of weapon: machete-like swords used in hand-to-hand combat. Their mission accomplished and, bearing twenty Flintlock guns, Hanto Tona led the *N'Nonmiton* warriors out of the fort. In the distance, they saw the torch that guided Pedro de Barbosa and his men coming back from his secret meeting with the Minister of War and Defense and the queen.

*****

The Ouidian army was on high alert following King Dozan's assassination. So, it was not unexpected when the Minister of War and Defense recruited one hundred and fifty soldiers for his and the queen's mission.

"I've handpicked you because I know you're the best men in my army. I will reveal the nature of your assignment when it's about to take place. The kingdom will reward you if you prevail in the mission," he told the men who assembled in one hall in the compound that housed Ouidah's elite soldiers.

The soldiers asked no questions. They had trained them to follow commands and, if the order came from the Minister of War who enlisted them, it was their duty to obey. General Togodo ensured the soldiers assembled in one of the largest houses in the compound before he went to the wrestling match. It was towards this building he headed when he left Sossa's crowning.

Pedro de Barbosa's part in the plot included delivering one hundred and fifty Flintlock guns and ammunition. General Togodo's men would assemble at the fort before assaulting the palace. The Viceroy's twenty guards who fulfilled different roles in the fort would likewise take part in the invasion. Pedro de Barbosa recruited the four Portuguese ex-veterans. He paid them well over the years for sticking with him after Governor Belarmino left Dahomey. They were no longer in his service, but he sought their expertise when he needed them. Now permanent guests in *Casa da Silvio*, they had become incorrigible drunkards, gamblers, and lechers. Yet Pedro de Barbosa knew they were still damn good ex-fighters.

*****

Queen Ena Sunu, Azonton, and Sintana Fansinnou decided that if Sossa emerged as the new king, he wouldn't spend his first night at the palace. Neither he nor the Dahomey entourage knew the place well enough to ensure the new king's safety. They made that decision before they discovered Queen Yiram's and the Brazilian slaver's assassination plot if Sossa emerged the victor. In anticipation that the Ouidian courtiers and counselors insisted that the new king occupied the royal chambers, the Dahomeyan entourage arrived with a look-alike of the same height and build as Sossa. She was among the *N'Nonmiton* warriors who formed the human wall around the new king after the Voodoo Chief Priest performed his last inaugural act. Twenty *N'Nonmiton* warriors whisked away King Sossa to a secret location after switching his mask and hat for his look-alike. Another twenty lifted his double on their shoulders and made their way towards the palace's second courtyard where the king's quarters were situated. The drumming, singing, and ululations continued. They would keep at it until a courtier informed them that the new king was ready to retire.

Having ensured that King Sossa arrived and was fully protected by ten *N'Nonmiton* fighters outside of the many buildings stretched around a one-mile radius, Sintana Fansinnou conferred with Queen Ena Sunu and Azonton to review their strategies.

"Queen Ena Sunu, you'll remain at the safe house with King Sossa. Azonton and I will proceed to the palace and take up the positions we discussed earlier," the *N'Nonmiton* leader instructed.

"You must be jesting. You expect me to stay back?" asked the queen.

"Yes," said Sintana Fansinnou. "With due respect, you're a powerful woman, but you aren't a warrior. You've never been in battle. Besides, we want you alive. We have a lot to accomplish now and, in the future," the fighter added.

"I am inclined to concur with Sintana Fansinnou," Azonton stated.

"Nobody. I repeat, nobody tells me what I can or cannot do. I embarked on this campaign because, for my entire life, men have dictated and controlled my every movement. You don't suppose I should expect that from you. Do you?"

An uneasy moment ensued. King Sossa, who had been silent, chimed in. "We're witnesses to this day because of the remarkable work all of you have done. What we don't require are dissensions among ourselves. Sintana Fansinnou, the Queen has decided. Don't expect her to change her mind. You need to understand that about her for your future close relationship," said King Sossa.

Sintana Fansinnou and Queen Ena Sunu looked at each other. So Sossa knew about them?

"I will agree to the queen putting herself in harm's way only if she remains next to me during the exercise," declared the *N'Nonmiton* leader.

"Yes, my General. Nothing can be more appropriate," Queen Ena Sunu responded, with a grin on her face.

Chapter 24

The assault on the king's palace began when the intelligence they had gathered said it would. General Togodo and his men left *Forte São João Baptista de Ajudá* at midnight and steered their way to the city. A ten-foot mud wall with a circumference of five miles interspersed by ten gates surrounded the capital. A treacherous ten-foot-deep ditch filled with a dense growth of prickly acacia made it difficult to reach the city wall. Yet another ten-foot wall encircled the king's palace in the city center. The soldiers encountered no resistance entering the capital through a gate the Ouidian royal army guarded.

General Togodo had assured Queen Yiram and Pedro de Barbosa the assault would be swift. It had appeared so until they arrived at the palace's main entrance. It was closed. Their palace agents should have left them open. They could scale the compound's ten-foot walls with their Flintlock guns in tow, but that would disrupt the coordinated nature of the planned attack. Besides, it was unclear if the soldiers could climb the fence at the same rate and enter the grounds at the same moment without the palace's guards spotting them.

"Let's go to the south exit. It's smaller and further away from the central courtyard," General Togodo ordered his soldiers, who scurried around the palace wall to the south end of the dwelling, where they found the gate wide open.

"Dumb fools," General Togodo muttered. His operatives had cleared this passage instead of the main one on the north side, he thought.

The General and his men hardly made it through the gate when gunshots erupted from both sides. Several soldiers fell. As the discharge continued, General Togodo realized the open gate was a trap. And an ambush it was because the *N'Nonmiton* soldiers had positioned themselves in the six buildings close to the entry and in the lush gardens with high bush trees and shrubs next to the entry. A retreat for the insurgent soldiers wasn't an option when they realized, much to their dismay, that a column of the fifty *N'Nonmiton* warriors who had been hiding in plain sight in the *Forte São João Baptista de Ajudá* had infiltrated their rearguard. Soon after General Togodo's soldiers and Pedro de Barbosa's men left the fort, the women fighters followed at a distance.

The renegade soldiers' only choice was to return fire. They had loaded their weapons before leaving *Forte São João Baptista de Ajudá* without testing them. They didn't need to. These guns had been used repeatedly in the past, and on every occasion, they had worked like a charm. Yet, at this critical juncture when the rebel soldiers needed them, the guns failed to fire. Panic-stricken, the soldiers examined their weapons and reloaded them with more gunpowder and bullets. The outcome was no different. Meanwhile, with the twenty guns in their possession, the *N'Nonmiton* warriors kept taking down one soldier after another. The restricted number of guns in their hands could only hold at bay for so long the one-hundred and fifty insurgent soldiers and their commander. In a burst, General Togodo and his men rushed into the palace compound.

"Use your guns to bludgeon these sons-of-bitches to death," General Togodo ordered.

As the soldiers made their way towards the inner courtyard, over one hundred *N'Nonmiton* warriors emerged from adjoining houses and compounds. The north gates to the palace opened, and more of the female warriors entered the main courtyard. Sintana Fansinnou and her fighters met the incoming soldiers head-on with the lethal machete-like daggers they had hidden in their clothes when they arrived in Ouidah. The battle became hand-to-hand combat. While General Togodo and his men used their guns as cudgels, the *N'Nonmiton* warriors responded with their machete-like swords.

Pandemonium reigned, and carnage embodied a bloody battlefield.

The gunshots, the *N'nonmiton* warriors' war cries that sent shivers down the spines of friends and foes alike, and the renegade soldiers' response in kind shattered the quiet of the night and woke up the kingdom's elite who lived in the expansive palace grounds. No one understood what was unfolding, let alone how to respond. The king's palace was the embodiment, the center of gravity of the kingdom's political, economic, and social life. It was the epitome, the nerve center of Ouidah's security, the ultimate bastion of the king's defense. To attack the palace was to assault the kingdom's very soul, its people. In no time, Ouidah citizens learned of the attack on the new king's palace. They remembered the not-too-distant invasion of the palace that overthrew King Tezifon. The current onslaught unleashed a cargo of memories of an atrocious king that everyone despised. The ongoing military operation, they assumed, involved the king's army, some of the same battalion that brought down tyrant King Tezifon. They trusted the troop, and they believed it would do the right thing again by protecting their new king if the ongoing raid was foreign. But most of the king's soldiers that the Ouidians relied on remained in their barracks. The Minister of War and Defense had recruited their fellow officers for a special mission. Those still in the garrisons understood the gunshots and the war cries as part of the general's operation.

General Togodo had taken part in several wars and had excelled as a ruthless commander. His courage was legendary, and he was notorious for his fierce disposition in battle. A veteran in combats, he knew when the odds were against him and his men. The surrounding carnage and the dexterity with which the *N'Nonmiton* fighters wielded their weapons overwhelmed him. The only way to salvage the operation, he reckoned, was to capture the new king rather than assassinating him. Once seized, the yet unknown forces protecting him should lay down their arms. Nobody in his right mind would do anything to jeopardize a captured king's life.

"Follow me to the west end of the palace," General Togodo shouted at Pedro de Barbosa above the din. Blood coated them.

"Cover us," the general ordered four soldiers as he and Pedro de Barbosa broke into a run.

"There goes their commander," Sintana Fansinnou yelled at Queen Ena Sunu, who was mopping sweat from her brow. "Let's go after him."

As they sprinted, Sintana Fansinnou ordered Azonton to take over command. More than half of the recruited soldiers lay dead or wounded. Azonton, didn't have to do much. When the soldiers saw their commander take to his heels, followed by the viceroy, they lost all incentive to continue fighting. They surrendered.

A five-hundred-yard-long courtyard separated the battlefield and the king's living quarters, which was comprised of six detached two-story buildings, one behind the other. Red earth courtyards divided these, along the sides of which were residences of the king's servants, eunuchs, and attendants. The farthest building beyond the sixth was the massive throne room in which the king gave audience. For security reasons, the king rotated his nights between the six buildings. On this night, Sossa's double and the five *N'nonmiton* warriors who guarded her were in the sixth building. It contained a huge verandah that covered the entire ground floor of the structure. Two doors, ten feet apart from the verandah, opened to a rectangular living room, from which four doors led to the enormous bedrooms. Two other side doors, locked, also led to the living room, but from the east and west sides of the building. Stairs to the first floor took flight from the middle of the living room to an open space with large windows overseeing the red courtyard, the throne room building. Tucked in one corner was a large bed surrounded by different statues of deities. In another corner was a shrine dedicated to Nana *Buluku.* The six buildings had a similar configuration.

General Togodo knew the palace like the back of his hand. It wasn't long before they found where King Sossa spent the night. The telltale signs, only known to a few, was all there: the fourth and sixth detached buildings were all illuminated except for the fifth. General Togodo and Pedro de Barbosa crept towards the east end of the fifth structure.

In the meantime, the four ex-Portuguese soldiers that Pedro de Barbosa had recruited were becoming a little anxious despite their inebriated state. Following General Togodo's cue that the operation would be a breeze, Pedro de Barbosa had asked the ex-soldiers to come to the Ouidah palace in case he hadn't returned by the hour after midnight. They had been skeptical when Pedro de Barbosa laid out his plans with General Togodo. No military operation, they reckoned, could be foolproof. There were always surprises. At half-past midnight, the four veterans found their way to the king's palace, carrying with them French double barrel flintlock pistols tucked behind their backs and hidden by long cotton shirts. The soldiers at the gate to the city made way for them. They had arrived to offer the new king whatever help he might need, the Portuguese lied. Gigla, one soldier who guarded the entry, knew the four ex-Portuguese soldiers. He had trained with them and had been part of the mutinous soldiers that overthrew King Tezifon. He took them to the new king's palace. Like his fellow soldiers, who General Togodo didn't recruit for the assault, Gigla was heedless of the motives behind the attack.

The scene that presented itself before the erstwhile-Portuguese soldiers needed no explanation. The cries and moans of the wounded and dying soldiers, along with their brothers in arms who had surrendered and were now sitting on their haunches and surrounded by the *N'Nonmiton* warriors, expressed it all. Azonton had left the battle scene in search of Sintana Fansinnou and Queen Ena Sunu, who were in pursuit of Pedro de Barbosa and the general. He reckoned that they might need his help, even though he was sure Sintana could handle both of them by herself. He wanted to tell them of the capitulation. The clueless Gigla, who believed what the ex-Portuguese officers told him, regurgitated their story and convinced the *N'Nonmiton* warriors guarding the surrendered soldiers that the four *yovos* had come to help the new king. The five men headed towards the palace's central courtyard. No one stopped them.

General Togodo and Pedro de Barbosa crept towards the north side gate to the fifth two-storied building. Locked, Pedro de Barbosa forced it open with the butt of his Flintlock gun. The living room was pitch dark and quiet. Thanks to his knowledge of security protocol, the general understood Ouidah kings never spent a night in any of the four rooms on the first floor. There was no guarantee, however, that King Sossa would occupy the same room and the same bed on the second floor. But if they adhered to tradition and practice, the new king wouldn't do anything differently. His courtiers would ensure that, he thought. With Pedro de Barbosa behind, General Togodo moved to the second floor. It surprised him that there weren't any courtiers, let alone guards. How careless to leave the king so vulnerable! The general mused.

Unfamiliar with the palace's inner configuration, Sintana Fansinnou and Queen Ena Sunu lost Pedro de Barbosa and the general in their pursuit. They contemplated six two-storied buildings of similar size and look. They recognized the throne room at the far end of the long courtyard. One of the six buildings must be the king's chambers. But to which did the *N'Nonmiton* warriors take King Sossa's double? The fourth and sixth houses had dim lights originating from them.

"Let's go to the sixth building," Sintana Fansinnou whispered to Queen Ena Sunu.

"Are you sure they went there?" asked the queen.

"Who?" Sintana Fansinnou inquired.

"The general and Pedro de Barbosa," responded Queen Ena Sunu.

"We're not pursuing them," the *N'Nonmiton* warrior replied.

"If not them, who? Didn't you say a short while ago to pursue General Togodo?"

"Yes. I did. Circumstances have changed," said Sintana Fansinnou.

"What do you mean? How can you change your mind in just a matter of seconds?" asked the monarch.

"That's what you do in battle," said the warrior.

"So, who are we after? Who are we looking for?" asked the queen.

"Can you keep quiet and follow me?" Sintana Fansinnou snapped.

They saw familiar, well-rehearsed movements in front of the sixth building. Sintana Fansinnou whistled, and four sentinels on the verandah came running towards them. The *N'Nonmiton* warriors bowed.

"Where's our king?" Sintana Fansinnou asked, unable to contain a giggle. The others did the same.

"She's in a chamber. She's taken off the atrocious mask and the itchy hat," said a warrior.

"Let her put them back on. We will retreat into one room. Pedro de Barbosa and the General should be here soon," said the *N'Nonmiton* leader.

Queen Ena Sunu now understood.

A breathless Azonton appeared, as if from nowhere, just as they were ascending the stairs to the verandah.

"They've surrendered. It's over," he announced, panting.

"Not quite," said Fansinnou Sintana. "Pedro de Barbosa and the General are yet to pay us a visit. They're looking for the new king. We know why. Let's take our positions and wait for
them."

General Togodo and Pedro de Barbosa got used to the darkness in the fifth building. As they crept up the stairs to the second floor, the room's emptiness became clear.

"No one is here," the minister said to Pedro de Barbosa.

"So much for your telltale sign," said Pedro de Barbosa, who was becoming incensed. That they had lost the battle was clear. If General Togodo was correct, their only choice was to capture the new king alive. But was it possible? The resistance they met right when the assault commenced could have only come from a well-trained force. The *N'Nonmiton*! Of course! How hadn't he and the General realized that? With this epiphany, Pedro de Barbosa wondered whether he and General Togodo could seize the new king. Heck! their Flintlock guns were useless, and their opponents must know it. "*Merda! Estou fodido!*"—Shit! I'm fucked!—he muttered to himself as the impossible reality in which he found himself became clear.

"Let's go," General Togodo said, pulling Pedro de Barbosa out of his thoughts.

They made their way to the sixth house and climbed up the vacant verandah. One door was ajar. General Togodo pushed it open, revealing an empty living room. They both stopped and listened. Silence. General Togodo reckoned that this wasn't the time to go by any damned protocol. He had followed it, and they had gone to the wrong house. They weren't going to the second floor. They'll begin their search in the first-floor rooms. He walked to a suite with a door open. He kicked it with his leg and entered with his Flintlock raised. On the bed sat the person they thought was King Sossa. Two guards stood on both sides of the bed with raised machetes.

"Put down your weapons before I shoot you both," General Togodo hollered at the guards.

"Viceroy! The king's here," he called out to Pedro de Barbosa.

The two *N'Nonmiton* women threw their weapons and fell on their knees, a sign of surrender. General Togodo and Pedro de Barbosa rushed to the bed and grabbed King Sossa's double, who didn't put up any resistance or utter a sound, playing by the book what they required of the king before his formal coronation.

"Now what?" Pedro de Barbosa asked.

"Let's take him to the gate where the fighting is still going on. His defenders will surrender once they see their captured bloody king," said the General.

"No, you won't," said a voice, as Sintana Fansinnou, followed by Azonton, and Queen Ena Sunu, burst into the room.

"It's all over. Your soldiers have surrendered. Besides, King Sossa isn't here," Sintana Fansinnou said as she walked over to Sossa's double and removed the mask and raffia hat.

General Togodo and Pedro de Barbosa gasped, and, as they did, four *N'Nonmiton* warriors surrounded them and pulled their hands behind them.

Just then, the four ex-Portuguese soldiers staggered in with their pistols drawn. Disdain painted Pedro de Barbosa's face. If these intoxicated ex-soldiers had arrived earlier, perhaps the outcome of the assault could have been different, he thought. Yet the more he contemplated it, the more he realized he must have been wishing for an impossible outcome. The *N'Nonmiton* warriors had outmaneuvered, outgunned, and outsmarted them. The four Portuguese ex-soldiers wouldn't have made any difference. They could very well have been part of the carnage, that human detritus strewn over the courtyard. Was this the end of the road? Could he get out of his predicament? He racked his brain, doing his best under the circumstances to devise a way out.

"Put away those guns," Pedro de Barbosa ordered the ex-soldiers.

Queen Ena Sunu and Sintana Fansinnou looked at each other. The Portuguese still had their guns pointed at the two *N'Nonmiton* warriors holding Pedro de Barbosa. General Togodo didn't feature in whatever rescue mission the ex-soldiers fancied carrying out.

"I said put your bloody guns away," Pedro de Barbosa ordered again. "Before us is her Majesty the Queen of Dahomey. We don't want any harm to befall her. Do we?" he added.

A puzzled look flashed across Queen Ena's face. The man who had plotted to assassinate her son if they installed him as the Ouidian King, was asking these armed *yovos* to stand down. She wondered what this meant and what was behind it.

"What the fuck are you talking about?" One of the Portuguese ex-soldiers asked as he looked at Pedro de Barbosa with bleary eyes. "Didn't you instruct us to . . .?"

"Can you shut the fuck up? Pedro de Barbosa yelled at the Portuguese.

"I'll shut the fuck up if you tell us what's going on here. You asked us to assist you in your plot to overthrow the new king and kill him. You're in the grips of an enemy force because you've failed in your plans and you're asking me to shut the fuck up?" asked the ex-soldier.

"None of what you've said is news to us," Sintana Fansinnou said as she took a step towards the Portuguese men. As she did so, one soldier fired a shot into the air. Queen Ena recoiled. None of the *N'Nonmiton* fighters, including Azonton did. Sintana Fansinnou maintained her calm and said, "Pedro de Barbosa, General Togodo, and Queen Yiram have failed in their attempt to kill King Sossa and to install Akonde in his stead. They, along with their conspirators, including the four of you, have all committed treason and will face the full rigors of both Ouidah and Dahomey laws."

"Over our dead body," said one soldier and, as he did so, he aimed his gun at Sintana Fansinnou, who ducked just before the soldier pulled the trigger. Azonton and the other *N'Nonmiton* fighters leaped on the *yovos* who fired. Pedro de Barbosa slumped to the ground after being struck. Sintana Fansinnou wasn't lucky the second time. A bullet tore through her chest. Azonton fell after he was hit in the thigh. Within fewer than three minutes after they fired the first shot, General Togodo and the four Portuguese ex-soldiers were dead. It took Queen Ena Sunu a few seconds to recover from her shock. An earsplitting wail assailed the room as she jumped up, got to Sintana Fansinnou, and placed her head on her lap. The *N'Nonmiton* leader was still breathing. She looked at Queen Ena Sunu and smiled as the queen's tears bathed her delicate face.

"You did it," she whispered.

"No, you did, my love," said the queen, as she smothered the warrior with kisses.

"You remember the first time you summoned me to your living quarters?" Sintana Fansinnou asked.

"How could I forget? It was one of the most important days of my life. You, my love, came into my life and changed everything. Finding you was more important than the plans I had been devising," said Queen Ena Sunu.

"I know. It took little to recruit me to your cause, didn't it?" Sintana Fansinnou asked.

"Yes," said the queen.

"You're an extraordinarily brave woman, you know that don't you?" the warrior whispered.

"No, you're the brave and extraordinary one. You saved me, Sossa, and our cause," said Queen Ena Sunu.

"Yes, but we still have a long way to go. Could you tell me again what you said the day we found each other? I should very much want to hear it before the sun sets for me," Sintana Fansinnou said, breathing with difficulty.

"I told you they must never say that we, the women of Allada,

Ouidah, and Dahomey, never raised our voices in objection to this abominable slave trade," Queen Ena began.

"Yes, I remember. Please go on," said Sintana Fansinnou.

"That although some women have benefited from the largess that has flowed to their powerful husbands who're engaged in the trade, there were others who have defied the traffic because it was their sons, daughters, and husbands who were being hauled away. I said no one could hear the voices of these women as they cried and shed visceral tears."

"I bet because of you, one can now hear their cries," said the N'Nonmiton leader.

"No, my love. It's because of you and your warriors who lost their lives today," said Queen Ena Sunu.

"I remember you said if you died doing your brief part to stop this madness, you'd go in peace. I feel the same way too," said Sintana Fansinnou.

"Yes, I said that. Yet look at what cruel destiny and the wicked gods have carved up for us. It's you whom I'm losing," the queen declared, her soft wails still hovering over everything else.

Sintana Fansinnou's breathing slowed. A few minutes later, she died. Queen Ena felt as though her heart had just shattered. She lifted Sintana Fansinnou's head into her bosom and whispered into her lover's ear.

"When they write the history of this trade, it will remember the lone voice of a brave and beautiful woman, and those of many others who wailed in the darkness, in the fields, in the forests, and on the oceans because they excised a part of them viciously and violently. That same history will tell of those voices that rebelled and cut deep into a system that seeks to extract from the other. Posterity will not be cruel to us, my love. It will be kind to us, the women whose wombs bore those who they carried away."

*****

Pedro de Barbosa whimpered on the floor beside one dead Portuguese ex-soldier. He felt a stinging pain in his left shoulder. He covered his wound with his right hand. It came back sticky. He was losing blood. He felt faint-headed. The room spun. His mind filled with jumbled images and memories. He thought his head was going to explode. Yet a strange lucidity invaded a place in his mind he hadn't visited in a long time. The song the slaves sang at the *Fazenda Barbosa* assailed him as he recalled that thing, the Devil in a red shirt that the slaves determined to slay. He found himself transformed into the image of the Devil with two horns on his head. He shook himself and opened his eyes. The room continued to spin. The terrifying vision of the Devil disappeared. He breathed a sigh of relief. He didn't want to close his eyes, but drowsiness overcame him once more and he slid back again into that space. Flashes of Salvador da Bahia galloped through his mind. He saw *Senhora* Fidelia de Barbosa and the Pious Thread in the San Bento mansion. They pointed accusing fingers at him. He willed himself and escaped from the room. Now he found himself among the Cabula gang members. Cutpurse and Thinker stared at him; their eyes filled with condemnation. He wondered why. He had had nothing to do with their deaths. Why the animadversion? *Refugio Pacífico* entered. He shivered. It was here he resolved that no infraction against him would go unpunished. He smiled, summoning the retributions he had meted out to those he believed had wronged him. The smile faded as Jacinto Cardoso came along with a mischievous grin on his face. It appeared as though he had just seen him a short while ago when he advised him to go to Dahomey to become a slave merchant. The internal dialogue he had with himself came back to him. He had wondered why Jacinto Cardoso wanted him to pull such a stunt. He remembered his rationale for following through with Jacinto's suggestion, acknowledging that it was the brutality of the human spirit along with barbaric and depraved forces which colonized the soul of each slaver and benefiter that had compelled him to make that decision. His mind became jumbled once more with images, memories, and names that teemed forth: Josefina Ferreira, Lucinda, Virgilio Da Cunha, Salvador Viegas, Paulo Álvares de Andrade, José Nuno da Silva Mendes, Trunk, Cutpurse, Brute, Thinker, Alfonso, Governor Belarmino, Kosi Aholuvi, Yaw Agawu-Kakraba. Ah! yes, that jerk of an author who claimed he had invented him. He was glad to have slammed the door behind him when he left him bewildered in his study. He wished he could visit him again. Would he have anything substantive to tell him? He wasn't sure, but at least he could imagine. He constructed an imaginary interview.

"I see you've resolved to come back. I wonder why?" the author asked.

"I may come and go as I please. Can't I?"

"Not if I don't allow you to do so."

"Oh please, shall we not go back to that tiresome author inventor thing again?"

"I'm afraid that's the order of things. I cannot change it."

"Suit yourself."

"As you wish."

"I'm dying, am I not?"

"Are you?"

"For crying out loud, you know I am."

Quiet.

"Oh! I see. I'm not dying of my accord. You plan to kill me. Don't you?"

"You are disillusioned you cannot return to Salvador."

"To become a *senhor*, you mean?"

"Yes."

"And what's that to you?"

"A lot."

"How?"

"Because you staked your entire life on that single goal. It consumed you, and you lost sight of who you might have been."

"And who, pray your lordship, was I supposed to be?"

"I don't know. I admired your periodic self-reflections despite their limited scope. You wanted somebody else to challenge and expose the shallowness behind the *raison d'être* of your stated goals. It disappointed you when Cardoso didn't do so. Yet when Lucinda came close to unveiling your spurious rationale, you switched the subject to avoid confronting the truth."

"What truth?"

"The truth."

Pedro de Barbosa didn't fancy the direction in which his imaginary dialogue with the author was going. He shut it down. He opened his eyes. Now everything was bleary. The room spun.

"Noble savages," he whispered. He closed his eyes. He wasn't sure if he could open them again.

GLOSSARY

Abolição do comércio de escravos: abolition of slave trade

Acarajé: stuffed fritter consisting of a blend of black-eyed peas, salt, pepper, and onions and fried in red palm oil

Agoo do fi: calling for everyone's attention

Ake: patron god of hunters, the forest, and the animals within it

Amee: you have our attention; response to calling for everyone's attention

Armazém: warehouse, grocery store

Arroz de marisco: seafood rice

Arroz doce: rice pudding

Avô: grandmother

Axé: each one of the sacred objects of the *orisha* in West African/Brazilian religions

Babaca: asshole

Bacalhau com broa: cod with corn bread

Balança: balance, a *capoeira* move

Bananeira: banana tree, a *capoeira* move

Berimbau: a single-string percussion instrument, a musical bow, originally from Africa

Bem-vindo: *welcome*

Bicha: faggot

Broa: *cornbread seasoned with fennel*

Cachaça: distilled spirit made from fermented sugarcane juice

Caldo verde: green soup

Candomblé: African diasporic religious system that emerged in Brazil during the 19th century

Capoeira: Brazilian martial art that combines elements of dance, acrobatics, and music

Carne-de-sol: heavily salted beef exposed to the sun for one or two days to cure

Cataplana de lagosta: Portuguese fish and seafood

Cebolada de bacalhau: cod and onion dish

Charqui: jerked beef

Chouriço: spicy sausage

Circo: circus

Cisne Vermelho: red swan

City of Saints: another name for Salvador da Bahia

Cocada: sweet candy made with fresh grated coconut

Cocorinha: coconut, a *capoeira* move

Compatriota: *countryman*

Convento da Anunciada: Convent of the heralded one

Correio da Bahia: Bahia Post (newspaper)

Coxinha: snack made of chopped or shredded chicken covered in dough, molded into the shape of a teardrop, battered and fried

Cravinho: alcoholic drink infused with cloves and cinnamon

Efor: black plum

Engenho: farming facility with a mill for milling cane and refining sugar from sugarcane

Entrudo popular: celebration/carnival held on the Tuesday before Lent begins

Escravo: *slave*

Esfiha: *small meat pie* served either open-faced or folded in triangles

Esquival de baixa: low dodge, a *capoeira* move

Esquival lateral: lateral dodge, a *capoeira* move

Fazenda: Brazilian plantation in the northeastern region during the colonial period

Filho de uma puta: *son of a bitch, motherfucker*

Forró: musical genre popular in northeastern region of Brazil

Forte São João Baptista de Ajudá: *Fort St. John the Baptist of Ajudá*

Fraternidade Cristã: Christian brotherhood

Homem jovem: young man

Igreja: church

Igreja de Nossa Senhora da Glória e Saúde: Church of Our Lady of Glory and Health

Igreja de Nossa Senhora do Rosário dos Pretos: Church of Our Lady of Rosary for Blacks

Jabuticaba fruit: Brazilian grapetree fruit

Kayaso: open parley, arbitration

Kluvi: slave

Kluvi nɔvíwo: relatives of a slave

Ladeira: slope

Miwui: let's kill him

Nana Buluku: goddess in the image of an old woman, considered the creator of the world and the cosmos. She took the back seat after birthing her twin children, the sun, and the moon

Negros de ganho: slaves who work outside of their owner's home, earn wages, and give an agreed upon amount to their owners and keep the rest for themselves

Nocauteá-lo: knock him out

N'Nonmiton: Dahomey's all-female warriors

Merda: shit

Ogun: god of iron and warfare in Yoruba religion

Ojakari: pepper

Lundum: Afro-Brazilian music and dance with origins in the African Bantu and Portuguese people

Malagueta: type of chili pepper heavily used in the Bahia State of Brazil

Mawu-Lisa: creator goddess associated with the sun and moon in Dahomey mythology. In some myths, she is the wife of the male god Lisa. Mawu and Lisa are the children of Nana Buluku

Mestiços: historically referred to any mixture of Portuguese and local populations in Portuguese colonies

Meu amor: my love

Miguel de Unamuno: author of *Niebla* (Mist), Spanish essayist, novelist, poet, playwright, and philosopher

Moqueca aos avos: spicy egg stew

Moqueca: Brazilian seafood stew

Negativa: negative, a *capoeira* move

Oludumaré: Supreme God or Supreme Being in the Yoruba religion

Orixa: any of the minor gods or spirits who mediate between Olodumaré and humanity

Pai: dad

Palácio: *palace*

Pamonha: paste made from boiled sweet corn in coconut milk, typically served wrapped in corn husks

Pataxó: indigenous people in Bahia, Brazil

Pé-de-moleque: candy made from peanuts and unrefined cane sugar

Pelourinho: pillory, a stone column placed in a public place where rebellious slaves were punished publicly; slave market

Peixe-boi: *manatee*

Praça: *plaza*

Preto: *black*

Puta merda: holy shit

Quiejo-de-minas curado: type of cheese from Brazilian state of Minas Gerais

Rasteira: trip, a *capoeira* move

Refugio: refuge

Rei: *king*

Réis: currency of Portuguese empire

Rua: *road*

Salgado: snack of chopped or shredded chicken, meat, and/or cheese, covered in dough, battered and fried

Saudade: longing

Seminário: seminary

Senhora: married Portuguese or Brazilian woman—used as a title equivalent to *Mrs.*

Senhor: Portuguese or Brazilian man—used as a title equivalent to *Mr.*

Senzala: slave quarters on Brazilian plantations during the colonial period

Sóror: sister (religion)

Tranquillo: calm down
Vá se foder: go fuck yourself
Vai tomar no cu: fuck off
Viado: fag
Voodoo priest: man who summons voodoo gods in order to divi
ne the future or to heal
Vovô: grandfather
Xote: Brazilian music genre and dance with a binary or quater-
nary rhythm, local equivalent of the German schottische
Ylon: uncle
Yovo: white man

ACKNOWLEDGMENTS

I should first, and loudly acknowledge my friend, colleague, and former university mate, Arthur Hughes, for his steadfast belief in this novel, championing it, and bringing perspectives I wouldn't have considered. Arturo, your unfaltering optimism, insights, and willingness to chat at odd hours is a wonder to behold and am so lucky to have you on my team.

I am incredibly grateful to Margaret Benson, first reader, for her encouragement, her meticulous reading of different iterations of this novel, and her unwavering support.

Enormous thanks to Tony Guerrero, Meredith Aronson, Patricia Burgevin, Dayle Callender-Aggor, and Bill Dreschel, who will recognize how valuable their astute observations were when they read these pages.

I'm grateful to my dear friend, Roselyn Costantino, for her generosity and brilliance in reading the manuscript.

Joan Landes was kind with her profound and invaluable historical and literary insights.

I must likewise express my gratitude to Paula Gândara, whose work on Francisco Félix de Souza inspired this novel. She was kind in rendering several expressions from English to Portuguese. The same extends to Nonkoudje Remi, who translated words and phrases from English into the Fon language.

I have had the extraordinarily good fortune of Nadhir Ibn Muntaka's friendship. The consummate modest individual, he can perform magic with designs, as he did with this novel's cover, and much more.

Chris Oliver's practical knowledge of guns, and especially how flintlock firearms work, ensured that I got it right.

My infinite gratitude and in loving memory of my mom, Agnes Quansah Akosua, the master storyteller from whom I learned from an early age that stories are a gateway to explore imaginary worlds that circle back to our own.

Many thanks to Penny Smith Eifrig, my publisher, who has been magnanimous and generous with her time and counsel.

I'm grateful to the Pennsylvania State University's Senior Research Grant that enabled me to travel to Salvador da Bahia to do research for this novel.

MEET THE AUTHOR

A Professor of Spanish and African Studies at the Pennsylvania State University, Yaw Agawu-Kakraba is an author, scholar, and educator. Born in Ghana, he received his BA in Spanish and Linguistics from the University of Ghana, an MA in Spanish from University of Alberta, Canada, and a PhD in Hispanic Studies from Cornell University. His fiction includes *The Restless Crucible* and two forthcoming titles, *The Executioner's Stepdaughter*, and *Queens of the Goldmines*. His many research interests and publications include 20th/21st Century Spanish fiction and culture, Latin American literature, Afro-Hispanic literature and cultures, and African literature. His academic publications include *Postmodernity in Spanish Fiction and Culture* and *Demythification in the Fiction of Miguel Delibes*. Co-editor of *Diasporic Identities with Afro-Hispanic and African Contexts* and *African, Lusophone, and Afro-Hispanic Cultural Dialogue*, his essays have appeared in major academic journals around the globe. You can find him online at yawakakraba.com/home/ or on twitter @ AgawuYaw.

The Restless Crucible Recipes

If reading about some of the dishes has you hungry, don't despair. Here a few recipes that will have you eating the same foods as those featured in the novel!

Acarajé

Acarajé is a stuffed fritter common in the Brazilian State of Bahia. A product of a mixture between Brazilian and African cooking, the recipe for the dish originated during Brazil's colonial period from Nigerian slaves who first started selling it on the streets of Brazil.

Ingredients
Dough
  - 1 pound black-eyed peas
  - 8 cups water
  - 4 cups palm oil for frying
  - 1 onion large, cut in 4 pieces
  - salt to taste

Vatapa
Caruru
  - ¼ cup peanuts
  - 1 cup okra
  - ¼ cup cashew nuts
  - ¼ cup dried shrimp
  - ½ cup dried shrimp
  - 3 tbsp vegetable broth
  - ½ cup black-eyed peas
  - ¼ cup coconut milk
  - ½ cup palm oil
  - 1 tbsp palm oil
  - ½ cup bread shelled

1 tbsp cashews crushed
¼ cup tomato chopped
1 tbs[peanuts crushed
½ cup coconut milk
4 garlic cloves minced
¼ cup vegetable broth
Salt and pepper to taste
2 cloves garlic minced
1 teaspoon lemon juice
1 teaspoon coriander chopped
Salt and pepper to taste

Cooking Instructions

Dough

Place the beans in a container and soak them with 8 cups of water the day before for about 12 hours. Put your hands in the water with the beans and rub the beans well with both hands to remove the shell. Continue rubbing and rinsing as often as necessary to remove all the shell with black flecks. Drain using a strainer and set aside. Put the beans, onion and salt in a food processor or blender and blend well until a soft dough with even consistency is formed. Add a little water if the dough is too thick. Place the dough in a bowl in the refrigerator for an hour. Add to a deep skillet the palm oil and set at medium high heat. Mold the dough into large dumpling sized balls and fry them until they are well browned. Cut in half and fill with the *vatapa* and *caruru*, and some hot sauce if you want a spicy kick. Serve while hot.

Vatapa

In a bowl place the sliced bread, add milk until it absorbs the milk. Place in a saucepan and bring to the boil and simmer for 5 minutes. Combine the rest of the ingredients in a blender and blend with vegetable broth. Add to the mix that is already in the saucepan and cook on medium high for 10 minutes or until done. Set aside in a bowl.

Caruru

In a saucepan place the palm oil, add onion and garlic, and cook until brown. Add the okra, the vegetable broth and simmer until the okra is tender. Add the remaining ingredients and cook a little more. Transfer everything to blender until the mixture is even and consistent. Set aside in a bowl.

Fejoada

Feijoada is a stew loaded with black beans and meats of every description: smoked pork loin, bacon, and sausage such as chorizo. The dish was created by African slaves. After feasts given by the owners of the plantations, the slaves would pick up the leftovers and mix them with black beans, making a new stew. It is served with farofa (fried cassava flour with bacon) and orange slices.

Ingredients
1/2 lb. pork ribs
1/2 lb. pork loin
1/2 lb. carne-do-sol
1/2 lb. beef brisket
1/2 lb. Linguiça sausage, or other smoked sausage
1/2 lb. Linguiça sausage, spiced, or pepperoni
1/2 lb. Kielbasa sausage, or other garlic sausage
1 lb.   pork lard
1/2   thick sliced smoked bacon, cubed
1 1/2 cups dried black beans
1 bunch cilantro
1 bunch green onions
5 bay leaves
1 unpeeled orange, scrubbed and quartered
4 cloves garlic, chopped
1 medium onion, chopped

Cooking Instructions

The day before cooking the feijoada, place the dried beans in a large bowl and cover with cold water; soak the beans overnight in the refrigerator. In a separate bowl, soak the cured beef in cool water to cover to tenderize the meat, do this overnight also but change the water a couple of times. Drain thoroughly. In a very large heavy pot, place the beans, the meats and sausages, the cilantro and green onions tied together, the bay leaves, serrano pepper, and the orange. Cover with cold water, bring to a boil over medium-low heat, cover, and simmer for 2 hours, stirring now and again. Remove from the pot when each meat is fully cooked and tender. Let cool, cut into bite-size pieces, and reserve. After 2 hours, the black beans should be fully cooked and soft. Remove 1 cup of beans and cooking liquid, and blend until smooth in a blender. Return 1/2 cup of this mixture to the beans in the pot to thicken the cooking liquid. In a large frying pan heat the lard and cook the bacon in it until browned and crispy. Remove the bacon cubes, and in the same lard, fry the garlic and onion until soft and transparent, but not browned. Remove from heat, then stir in the reserved 1/2 cup of the blended beans. Stir entire contents of frying pan plus the reserved meats and bacon, into the beans in the kettle. Let cook over low heat for 20 minutes for flavors to blend.

Your feijoada is ready! Serve it on a bed of white rice, vinaigrette, *farofa* and orange slices.

Moqueca (Bahian)

Ingredients
Whitefish such as halibut, swordfish, or cod
Large or medium shrimp, peeled and deveined
Garlic cloves, minced
Lime or lemon juice
Salt and freshly ground black pepper
Large onions, chopped or sliced

Malagueta pepper seeded, de-stemmed, chopped or sliced
Large bell peppers
Large tomatoes chopped or sliced
Large bunch of cilantros, chopped with extra for garnish
Coconut milk
Palm oil

Cooking Instructions

In a large, covered pan, layer half of the fish and add half of the chopped onion, tomatoes, bell, and malagueta peppers. Make a second layer with the remaining fish and shrimp topped with the rest of the chopped onion, tomatoes, bell peppers, and malagueta peppers. Pour coconut milk and palm oil. Cover and cook slowly until fish is perfectly done but still maintaining its form. Serve with white rice.

Prologue

The first rule to surviving in Jamestown, a fishing neighborhood in Accra: Learn how to slumber through the perennial dawn racket. Second. If the first fails, locate the nearest culprit plundering your night's rest, holler at the top of your voice and ask whoever it is to knock it off. Third. Should nothing happen, wait for five minutes. Obscure allies from houses next to yours should come to your aid, hurling invectives at the source through their open windows. Fourth rule. Remember, rule number three will not work. But take heart. At least, you and your allies always have the means to unleash your indignation. Rule five. Revert to the first rule.

A sound sleeper, Nii Narh had mastered the first rule. It took extraordinary ruckus to wake him once he fell asleep. The thud, skip, and relentless grinding of steps from the upstairs apartment directly above his second-floor flat in Marlow House, a three-story building on Pratt Street, near Camden Square in North London, was one such racket. Nii Narh had devoted every single day of the last six months since he arrived in London to the laboratories of the Department of Infectious Disease Epidemiology at the London School of Hygiene and Tropical Medicine (LSHTM). Up early, he returned late at night and went to bed without supper. The weekends were no different. The good company fatigue kept with his propensity to sleep through raucous noises, prevented Nii Narh from picking up the footsteps and the emphatic thump on the creaky wooden floor that had become standard affair at odd hours of the night for the past few weeks. But it was different this morning. On this cold London dusk, Nii Narh's cultivated flair to defy sounds once he had fallen asleep abandoned him.

As he turned and tossed on his bed, Nii Narh contemplated deploying rule number two. But this was London, an unfamiliar terrain, a strange landscape. He had considered climbing up the stairs to hammer on the flat's door. But a black man banging on the portal of a white resident at that hour was out of the question.

Nii Narh often grew into an enthusiastic messenger of surliness without a decent night's sleep. But not today. The Autumn term was over, and he was on Christmas recess. He had no lab work that morning. A welcome reprieve from battling the ghastly winter cold that devised a scheme to cling on to him as he made his way to the LSHTM campus on Keppel Street. Nii Narh reckoned he could take an afternoon nap before stepping out that evening to a Christmas party in Africa House. It explained why the loud noises didn't agitate him as much.

Obey Olakunle, a Nigerian medical student at St. George's University of London, and Elliott Carmichael, a Trinidadian political science scholar at Middlesex University, whom he had met at the Camden Market earlier in the fall, had invited him to the celebration. He had declined their earlier invitations. The evening's event in Africa House was going to be his first social outing since he arrived in London.

The tramping of feet upstairs persisted. Nii Narh dragged himself out of bed and ambled to the cramped gallery across the small living room. The teakettle on, he lit up the reading lamp that sat on top of a miniature desk tucked in a corner in the living space. He pulled a drawer from the table where he kept correspondence from Ghana. Despite his hectic schedule, Nii Narh found time to write to Ameley, his mom, and his sisters. Patience had replied none of his letters, but he continued writing her. Of the replies he received, Nii Narh enjoyed his younger sister's the most. Ayele wrote their mom's letters and regularly commented on them in her own mail. Her letters kept Nii Narh abreast with news from the Jamestown neighborhood.

One of such letters had arrived a week earlier. Nii Narh had been busy preparing for his

end-of-term exams and hadn't had occasion to digest the contents of his mom's latest installment. The teakettle hissed, and he hastened to the kitchenette to make himself a cup of tea. He sorted through the pile of replies and found the most recent one. The sight of a stamp flaunting the image of the Akosombo Dam, along with another that celebrated Ghana Republic Day in July 1960 with Dr. Kwame Nkrumah's portrait engraved in the middle, aroused in Nii Narh a nostalgic sentiment. The desk lamp illuminated Ayele's elegant handwriting.

Mrs. Ameley Okine   *2nd November 1960*
C/o Jamestown Methodist Church
P.O. Box 37
Jamestown, Accra
Ghana

My Dear Son,
It was nice to hear from you. When Ayele read your letter to me, I practically wept. As she read, it was as though hearing your voice. I thank God that you are working hard and taking seriously your studies. She said you're experiencing the white man's cold weather and that it's difficult to stay warm even when you slip on several singlets and shirts. Have you got for yourself one of those heavy coats the women wear to ward off the cold? Maybe you should consider that.

After many years, I went to the UTC store in Accra Central last week. I hadn't stepped foot in that bloody blofonyo *store since your father worked there. The place has changed. They featured on the first floor, radios, electric stoves, televisions, and other things I had never seen before. On full display was as well a couple hoping to buy, I don't know, maybe a television? It was a black man and a* blofonyo *woman. Can you imagine that? The white woman held on to the fellow's arm as if to prevent him from fleeing. But run to where even if he wanted? I am certain the man's parents and family want nothing to do with him. And who could blame them? I thought of conveying this message to the* blofonyo *woman but I said to myself, Ameley, why don't you let her stew in her fear of her husband's imminent escape? And they were holding hands too! Did I mention that? And in public, too! Just imagine that! And, as if that wasn't bad, before they departed, the woman kissed the man on the lips. And in public, too! Just imagine that! They were speaking English, and I could tell that the* blofonyo *woman was an English woman!*

Do you remember Charity, the oldest daughter of the headteacher of Jamestown middle school? She's been betrothed to a young man in America. I don't know the man's family, but I hear they're happy he's agreed to the arrangement. Although we haven't settled anything formal between you and Patience, I'm glad we have an understanding with her parents. You should also know that with news of you studying abroad and returning as a doctor, a few mothers, unaware of my plans for you, have approached me with offers. Your uncle Joe says I should leave you alone to concentrate on your studies and not to bother you with such matters. But what does he know?

Your sisters are doing well. Ayele has become a woman now, even yet she said I shouldn't tell you. But you know I'm not like other Ga women. I share it all with my children. That's why I want you to disclose everything that goes on with you in London. Do you understand? Everything.

I will end now.

Your loving mother,

Ameley

The mention of Patience sent Nii Narh's mind back to her. He had asked for a photograph in several letters. In each, he declared his love. Nii Narh had to summon her image whenever he thought of her. At seventeen, she kept the early annals of a remarkable, diamond-shaped face groaning with elegance. Despite Patience's apathy, this attribute, and others yet undefined spurred Nii Narh.

*****

Many African, Black-American, and Caribbean students and their guests milled around the spacious lounge in Africa House. It was December 1960, a week and a half before Christmas and the air was festive with the season's cheer. The large windows in the lobby vaunted red ribbons interlaced with fragrant pine boughs and holly. On the windowsills sat candles that emitted a yellowish glow.

Like the 1930s through to the recent 1960s, Africa House was a historical landmark of significant importance for West African scholars studying in England. Opened in 1938, it served as a hostel for students of the West African Student's Union (WASU) founded in 1925. Although WASU became moribund by the earlier 1960s, Africa House yet was a magnet for African scholars and populations of African descent in London. On 1 Villas Street, not too distant from Camden Square, it was in this building during the war years in 1942 that Africans organized their first demands for self-government and independence from Britain. Illustrious Africans such as Dr. Kwame Nkrumah, Nnamdi Azikiwe, and Joseph Appiah were among many who had graced the halls of Africa House. It hadn't lost its historical and social allure in 1960. They still featured African cuisine and music.

The smell of an array of foods such as fried fish, *waakye*, *kenkey*, jollof rice, *moi moi*, fried plantains, *afang*, groundnut, and pepper soup filled the air. The dishes were an ode to the culinary excellence of African food, a canticle that aroused as it satisfied dietetic yearnings in a foreign land. Nii Narh wondered why he hadn't accepted earlier on invitations from Obey and Elliott to Africa House. Having survived for the past six months on nothing but bread and tea, baked beans, and sausage, Nii Narh salivated at the sight of the smorgasbord of traditional foods. He couldn't wait to dive into them. But dinner wasn't until after cocktails. Conversation with his hosts was inevitable.

"I can't believe you met Dr. Kwame Nkrumah, the president of Ghana. When and how did you meet him? Tell me, tell me. He's my father's hero. He often said he wished Trinidad had politicians and nationalists such as Dr. Kwame Nkrumah with the balls to boot the bloody British out of our country," Elliott said as he nursed the glass of wine in his hands.

Nii Narh didn't respond. Elliot's question inevitably led to his father. Dr. Kwame Nkrumah was among the dignitaries who had hugged him at the end of his father's memorial service. He remembered his words, "I'm sorry for our loss, my son. Your father's death will not be in vain." Dr. Kwame Nkrumah's use of the possessive adjective in "*our* loss" to describe his father's death had touched the young boy very much. His dad's loss, no longer personal but collective, lightened his weight and consoled him. He hadn't mentioned Sergeant Obo Okine to anybody since his arrival in London. He didn't talk about his dad, not even when he was at Accra Academy, where his schoolmates understood what had happened to him and the role he had played in Ghana's march towards independence. Nii Narh had been glad his classmates treated him like any other student and spared him the agony of talking about his father. In London, he had introduced himself as Nii Narh, making it a point to omit his last name. Sure, Okine was a common name among the Ga ethnic group, and it wasn't as though one could associate his last name to his dad's. His and his father's last names didn't embarrass Nii Narh. For the young man, the thought of his dad and reference to him sent his mind tumbling a memory lane that was intimate and public. He had had to cope with his father's passing and his visceral anger towards those liable for his death in his individual space. It was a space in which he had internalized his mom's unyielding disposition towards the *blofonyo*, white people, until he renounced its speciousness. But it had come at a cost: he suffered a sense of betrayal of his mother. The unsettling thought he was on a scholarship in one of England's finest institutions and feeding out of the hand that had caused him and his family so extreme anguish didn't help either. The public sphere remained for Nii Narh, a space that undertook to celebrate the mythic place that his dad had gained. But that eminence led to his private arena, setting into motion a cyclical loop in which the two intertwined with no escape. Two young white women, who strolled towards them, interrupted Nii Narh's thoughts.

"Hello, love," Obey said, as he kissed one of them on the lips.

Nii Narh stood wide-eyed.

"Meet Diana Hawkins, my fiancé." Obey said, focusing his attention on Nii Narh, who didn't have time to answer before Obey added, "Nii Narh is one of those fellows who have peddled their souls to the white man's devil by agreeing to gain his knowledge. He's studying tropical diseases at LSHTM."

"Pleased to meet you. I've heard of you," said Diana. "Oh, here's Charlotte Milburn. We both dance with the Windmill Theatre Dance Company."

Nii Narh turned towards Charlotte. He hadn't paid close attention to her when they entered. The exchange that had just taken place between Obey and Diana still stunned him. As he fixed his gaze on Charlotte, he realized it was the first occasion he was meeting a woman with such flaming hair that rested on a head with cheekbones defining an angular face with hazel eyes. She was slim but solid-built with shaped shoulders along with a rounded hip, the kind that would compel men to spin around to take another glance after passing her on the street. She wore a close-fitting blue velvet dress, and she had affixed her hair at the nape with a bright comb. A pair of plain silver earrings matched the oval white necklace caressing Charlotte's long neck.

"Say something, man," Obey whispered, tapping Nii Narh on the shoulder.

"Delighted to meet you," Nii Narh muttered, extending his hand to Diana and Charlotte. He thought Charlotte's handshake was firm, showing confidence and directness that Nii Narh hadn't noticed in a woman.

"Quite glad to meet you too," Charlotte replied.

Nii Narh's eyes remained glued on Charlotte for several seconds.

"You ladies might recognize my presence if only I brought you a drink. What can I serve your majesties?" Elliott asked.

"Oh, I'm sorry, Elliott. You look lovely in your outfit," Diana replied, reaching out to touch Elliott on the elbow. He sported a *shirt jac*, a belted jacket he slipped on with a scarf and no shirt.

"Flattery will get you nowhere with me, Diana. But it's Yuletide season. It might work this time," said Elliott.

"Such a magnificent gentleman, isn't he?" Diana asked, glancing at Obey.

"A magnificent gentleman? I'm doubtful," Obey said, eliciting laughter from the group.

"Shouldn't you be the one offering us a drink?" Diana demanded.

"My very thought," responded Elliott.

"A man shouldn't wander far from where he roasts his corn. Do you think I'll leave Diana and Charlotte alone with you, Elliott? With Nii Narh, perhaps. There's no way in hell I'll do so with you," said Obey.

"I'm certain Diana wouldn't mind drifting away. You have burnt, roasted corn. Besides, I see more impressive corn roasters," Elliott said, looking at Nii Narh with a grin pasted on his face.

"Ouch! That's a brilliant one, Elliott," declared Diana.

Nii Narh took in the bantering between Obey and Elliott. Charlotte did the same as she watched the witty contestants. She had a smile on her face, and when she laughed at Diana's remark, Nii Narh noticed tiny dimples on both cheeks.

"Alright, Elliott, you've won. I'll fetch the drinks," Obey said, as he directed his gaze at Diana and Charlotte.

"No, you stay put. I'll get the drinks," Elliott insisted. "The usual for you, my lady?" Elliott asked, setting his gaze on Diana.

"Yes," said Diana. "And . . ."

"And I'll get Charlotte's if she knew what she'd like," Nii Narh interrupted, shifting to Charlotte.

"Oh, thank you. I'll have whatever you're taking."

"Gin and tonic."

"Gin and tonic," Charlotte announced, cognizant that this was her stepfather's favorite drink, for which she didn't care. Yet here she was, asking this young African man whom she had just met to bring her a gin and tonic. She recognized something calm about Nii Narh and he gave off inner confidence even though shy.

Elliott and Nii Narh had to navigate through the throng that was swelling with guests and residents of Africa House, many of whom, like Nii Narh, turned out in their traditional African clothes. With his black and gold embroidered long-sleeved shirt that revealed his muscled chest and arm, along with the matching trousers trimmed in gold at the cuffs, Nii Narh stood out. As they waited in line at the open bar, Elliott said, "A surprise Charlotte decided on gin and tonic. White wine is her refreshment of choice."

"Maybe she felt having a fresh drink."

"Or, because she fancies you."

"I beg your pardon?" Nii Narh asked, cocking his head.

"Charlotte. She likes you. I could tell from the way she kept staring at you. She goes out with a chap, Dorian Smith, a stuck-up fellow dancer who thinks the world revolves around him."

Nii Narh stepped back. "That's ridiculous. How can you draw such a hasty conclusion?" Charlotte's presence had struck him, nothing more than that, he confessed to himself.

"Man, I don't suppose there's anything wrong with Charlotte liking you. Is there?"

"How long have they been dating?"

"Who?"

"Obey and Diana."

"A year."

"Do his parents in Nigeria know?"

"No idea."

"And Diana?"

"What of Diana?"

"Does her family know of Obey?"

"I don't know."

"What do you know then?"

"That it's our turn to request our drinks," Elliott responded, indicating the bartender waiting for their order.

"Ah, here you're. I thought you'd gone tapping the palm wine and distilling the gin for the ladies," Obey said when they snaked through the crowd to their little group.

Elliott ignored Obey and handed Diana her white wine. Nii Narh did the same with Charlotte's gin and tonic.

"Cheers to the Holidays," Elliott stated, raising his glass. The others followed suit.

"Let's step to a less crowded and quieter part of the lounge," Obey suggested.

Just then, they announced dinner. Buffet-style, guests served themselves and settled on couches and chairs arranged along the lobby walls and in the great oval dining room next to the lounge. Nii Narh sat next to Charlotte while Obey, Diana, and Elliott sat across from them. Diana's and Charlotte's familiarity with the foods surprised Nii Narh. Surprised still was when both dined with their fingers. He determined Diana and Charlotte had eaten these West African foods frequently to recall protocol demanded using one's fingers and not the white man's artificial ones.

"You're an adventurous diner," Nii Narh said, as he arranged himself to burrow into his well-heaped plate that paraded *kenkey* and fish, jollof rice, fried ripe plantains, and piles of *moi moi.*

"How couldn't one be an adventurous eater in Obey's company?"

"How so?"

"He ensures you eat African dishes in the proper manner—with your fingers."

"You have learned well. I haven't met many Britons. But I can imagine most of them may be reluctant to discard their forks and knives for fingers."

"As a dancer and student of modern dance, one gets exposed to the music and cultures of other people. That helps."

"Aren't you two going to eat? You've done nothing but to talk. You know, there's a saying that wine, women, and food gladden the man's heart. Look at my glowing face." Obey said.

"Isn't your face glowing because of the spicy pepper soup that you've been slurping?"

"Ah! Yes! Elliott. But you neglected to include an essential piece."

"What's that?"

"Diana."

"What a flatterer you're! His highness would have shocked me if he hadn't added me to the items that boosted his glowing essence. Does this saying of yours describe something which gladdens women's hearts?" Diana asked as nearby silverware clinked on plates.

"Absolutely. Except that I've forgotten how it goes," Obey responded, smirking.

"You're such a clod. I wonder why I'm wasting my time on you," Diana declared.

"It's called love," said Obey.

"Sure," Elliot said, rolling his eyes.

...to be continued

www.ingramcontent.com/pod-product-compliance
Lightning Source LLC
Chambersburg PA
CBHW060619100726

47907CB00006B/1681